A Conjuring of Valor

BOOK TWO

J.C. WADE

For Bryce, my greatest love.
You are all I've ever wanted and all I'll ever need.

Chapter One

Ruthven Keep

Caitriona Ruthven frowned down at her appearance in the rain barrel, her distorted and rippling features screwed up in anger.

"...bootless, crook-pated, puttock," she muttered under her breath before plunging the hand pail into the icy water. Her brother, Ewan, was all that and more, but she could only say such things out of all hearing, for she was a *lady*, and shouldn't know such indecent and debase words.

She scoffed softly as she pulled the hand pail from the black water, her mouth twisting mockingly. If her mother had wished to raise Cait as a lady, she ought not to have had any sons. From where did the woman think she'd learned such words in the first place? No, Ewan deserved her sharp tongue. What was she to do? Step aside and meekly let him plan her life with no consideration to her feelings?

Yes. Exactly that, she thought sourly, her mouth pressing tightly with a fresh wave of indignation. That's precisely what her mother and brother expected of her. She'd told her brother—that droning, flap-mouthed clot—just what he could do with his plans. Granted, she ought not to have said it within her mother's hearing, but she stood by what she'd said. He *was* meddling.

She sighed forlornly as another cold stream of water trickled into her shoe. Still, in all her seventeen years of life, she should have learned by now to hold her tongue in front of her mother.

For her impudence, she'd been punished, as always, with menial chores. You'd think her mam, a canny and otherwise astute woman, would have noticed by now that no amount of scrubbing, digging, washing, or carrying would motivate Cait into meekness.

By the Saints, she'd tried to please her mother. She really had. But one can only be submissive and gentle for so many hours in a day before nature took hold and her true character could be suppressed no longer.

Today's task was to keep the kitchen pots full of water and the fire constantly stoked. It would be hours of work that would hurt her hands and back, but it could have been much worse. She shuddered, thinking of the time she'd been tasked with scrubbing chamber pots clean.

Water continued to slosh over the rim of the pail with each step she took on the way to the kitchen; the side of her skirt was damp and her shoe squelched with each step. *Damnation!* She trudged around the corner of the kitchen, careful to step squarely on the wet stone step at the door, and into the blazing hot room.

The kitchen boasted two hearths and a baking oven for bread, which was all fine and well if you weren't tasked with keeping them hot all the day long. Cait moved to the second hearth, on the far side of the room, and dumped the pail of water into the simmering pot the household used for daily tasks.

"Done," announced Cait, turning expectantly to the cook. Alban was a spindly, sullen man, who'd had the run of the kitchen since her other brother, Iain, had been born. For the twenty years Alban had served the Ruthven family, she doubted he'd ever cracked a smile, which is probably why her mother tasked her to work under him so often. Cait could not charm him, no matter how hard she tried.

"Mmmph," he grunted not even sparing her a glance. The cleaver in his hand fell upon a sheep's leg joint with a wet *twhack*, spraying his apron with tiny speckles of blood. "Dinnae ye doddle, lassie. Tae the woodbox, and quick. When ye're done there, I'll need more water. The lassies are scrubbing the tiles today."

"Aye," sighed Cait, curiously eyeing the grotesque sheep's head that laid upon the table as she passed. She swung the large linen sacks used to cart wood into the kitchens over her shoulder and set off, looking to the sky in hopes that the sun was further along in its journey toward the horizon than when she'd last checked. She grumbled slightly, seeing it wasn't even past noon yet. At this rate, her blisters would have blisters.

There was space dedicated to chopping wood for the kitchens not a far way off, clustered amongst spindly alder trees. Someone was already industriously chopping blocks from the sound of it.

Making her way down the dusty path, she felt the weight in her chest lighten marginally when she saw Ewan's squire there, splitting logs with powerful strokes. He was partially turned away from her, so he did not notice her at first; his sweat-soaked liene outlined the broadened expanse of shoulders and muscle that was usually hidden to her. What luck that her friend was here to lift her spirits on such a sullen day. When he turned as he tossed the split logs into another pile, his hazel eyes found her with a look of happy surprise.

"'Lo, mistress."

Alec was fun and loved to tease, which she thoroughly enjoyed. The only thing she didn't care for was his rather worshipful obedience to her overbearing brother. She supposed she couldn't be too judgmental of him; being a squire had a way of forcing such blind adoration. She supposed her brother wasn't all that bad. He was no villain, but still, she could think of no woman who would welcome a man planning her life for her.

Alec's sweaty face was open and friendly, and not a little hopeful. She felt her cheeks warm at the look on his face. She'd kissed Alec last winter at the Yuletide celebration. He'd been rather dashing in his green surcoat and dark hair and she, overcome with the cheer of the day and the wine, had pulled him into a darkened corner and pressed her mouth to his. It had been quick and chaste, but it had been her doing, which she supposed she should be ashamed of. She was a maiden. A lady. And ladies were not to kiss their brother's squires, no matter how winsome or witty. Or anyone, for that matter. She could never quite conjure the remorse she should have felt for her actions, however. It was a good thing her mother hadn't learned of it.

Ever since that kiss, they'd been engaged in a strange dance, where flirtation existed, with hope of more, though they both knew it was forbidden. Still, this dance was diverting, and she could use some entertainment at present. Haps she would kiss him again. It would lift her spirits in no time.

"Good e'en," she replied, unable to hide a coy smile. Alec was tall and sinewy, dark haired and long-limbed. He had the awkward grace of a boy who'd woken to discover he'd grown into a creature he'd never before considered. Like a caterpillar changed to a moth. He would soon be knighted, she thought, and wondered if Ewan would grant him a parcel of their lands to work, not that she would be there to watch him care for it. No. She would be married off to some stranger and only return home when allowed. Sourness returned to her belly at the thought.

Sometimes she hated being a woman of station. How lovely it would be to have the freedom of choice! Instead, she must marry a groom who presented the best advantage for their family. Her sullen mood settled over her once again, making her shoulders droop slightly.

"What'd ye do this time?" Alec asked, leaning against the handle of the ax as it rested on the chopping block. His winsome smile did not mock, but still she could not help bristling.

"What makes ye think I've done aught tae be punished?" *What a stupid question.* She felt her face blush despite herself.

He scoffed and bent to the pile behind him for another log. It *thunked* dully as it hit the block. Nodding toward the sacks that hung limply just below her hips, he said, "Then I'll have tae assume ye enjoy carting loads o' kindling for Alban or is that ye're just looking fer any excuse tae find me alone." He wagged his thick eyebrows at her flirtatiously, making her blush deepen.

Effecting a visage of superiority, Cait mocked him. "Ha! If I wanted ye alone, I wouldnae come here, where the very stink of yer labors mists my eyes."

Without warning, he exploded forward, his ax falling to the ground unheeded, and caught her around her middle before she could even take two steps. She squirmed and screeched against him as he rubbed his sweat-drenched cheek against her own.

"Och! *Gu leòr!*"

He let her go quickly and, laughing, said, "So I was right. Were ye late tae Matins again?"

"Ew!" she panted, wiping the wet patch of his sweat from her face with her sleeve, but she smiled grudgingly. He retrieved his ax, not apologetic in the least, and looked at her expectantly. She sighed and sat down on an upturned log. "I told Ewan I wouldnae do as he bid."

Alec gifted her with a look that communicated his lack of surprise. "And why should this time be any different. Ye've made it a sport tae disobey him all yer life, so far as I can tell."

She tossed her dark braid over her shoulder and said, "Aye, weel. I...may have cursed at him. Within Mam's hearing."

"Ah." His smile widened as he swung the ax up over his head, then forcefully down and into the oak log. It split easily, splintering satisfyingly into three pieces. "What does he bid ye do that ye find so distasteful?"

Cait frowned mightily. "He wishes tae set my betrothal."

Alec faltered only slightly in tossing the split pieces into the pile. His smile had gone, replacing his levity with the proper amount of gravity she felt the news deserved. "Aye, I heard him speak o' it tae Iain last week in the lists. Has it been decided?" He looked at her then, and she thought maybe he understood her anger. And fear.

"He's received some letters. Inquiries as tae what's tae be done with me." She forced herself to move, to stand and remove the bags from her shoulders and start to fill them with the split pieces littered between them. "As if I'm a problem tae be solved...a bundle o' goods tae be sold and delivered. If the idea hadnae been put into his mind by my uncle, I doubt he'd given my future much thought, which is how I wished it."

Alec frowned. "Did ye think he would forget the future of his beloved sister?"

Cait scoffed lightly but felt herself deflate slightly. "Nay. I just...I wanted tae wait a wee bit longer, aye? My Uncle Niael, the Caimbel—that's me mam's brother—says he's got someone in mind for me, but I forbade Ewan from even considering the prospect. And then, suddenly, he recalls a letter from the Stewarts he received months ago. They're keen tae match me tae their middle son. Robert, I think his name is. Can you believe that he's nearly thirty? And they want Ewan tae agree tae it! Ouch!" Cait dropped the kindling she was holding to find a splinter in her palm.

She plucked it out neatly and sucked on the wound briefly.

"So ye told him ye wouldnae do it."

"Aye," said Cait, standing up. The bags were full and so she carefully slung them over her shoulders and across her chest so that a bag hung on each side. She looked at Alec, sweating, with sympathetic eyes in the summer sun, and she knew she could not fight what was to come. His face said it all: she was doomed. She had no choice, despite her words to the contrary. Her own powerlessness threatened to overwhelm her so she turned to flee before Alec could see her weakened spirit.

She turned to go and was almost out of the small clearing before Alec spoke again. She paused just long enough to hear his conciliatory, yet empty words. "My laird has a soft heart for ye. Perhaps he will delay yer betrothal if ye ask it o' him."

Delay it, perhaps. But for how long? And what did it really matter if she was a free maiden for another six months or for only another six weeks? Nothing would change the fact that she had no real power to choose her path. She cleared her throat and shrugged the weight upon her shoulders into a better position, keeping her eyes turned away from her friend. "Aye. Perhaps he might at that."

The walk to the keep's kitchens seemed over long in the summer heat and she wondered what it had been like for her sister, or her mam, when they'd been betrothed. She'd never bothered to ask.

***

Cait's hands were slippery with sweat, even in the cool late afternoon. She gripped the dulled short sword in her hand tighter, her forearm muscles quivering, and blocked the attack from her good sister, Edyth.

Ewan's English wife had turned out to be quite the ally; Cait had loved her quickly and fiercely. Both cut from the same cloth, they enjoyed spending their free time out of doors, and far away from needle and thread or comb and shuttle.

Edyth smiled brightly, her red hair glinting in the dappled sunlight of the orchard. They'd chosen the upper orchard as their practice yard, as it was out of sight and would require less explanation. No questions would arise from the ladies of the manor taking air in the leafy canopy in the north parcel, for instance, but they would quickly notice them sneaking into the lists.

"I thought I had you that time," breathed Edyth. She thrust her sword into a grassy lump of sod and sat on the ground, her back against an apple tree. The dappled light painted her with gold, making her hair shine bronze and copper.

"Aye, I thought so too," agreed Cait. She'd grown stronger since Edyth had shown her how to stand, how to find her balance with a sword in hand, and parry a thrust these last few weeks, but she didn't pretend she was talented.

Cait deposited her own sword in its hiding spot—amongst the branches of one of the larger trees—and picked up the basket she'd brought on the pretense of gathering flowers or mushrooms, or whatever else they could find in a hurry to excuse their absence. "What shall it be today, Edie?"

Edyth shrugged and stood, pulling apart the knot she'd tied in her brown skirts to keep her feet unencumbered. "Acorns for the pigs, perhaps? Or flowers. The meadowsweet is in full bloom."

"Aye, but I picked meadowsweet the last time we met." Cait pursed her lips in thought. "Haps we should go tae the village and seek the spun wool Mam requested. She's wanting tae make a new tapestry for the hall." Cait pulled a face, knowing that her role in this endeavor would be paramount.

Edyth smiled pityingly. "Yes, I heard her tell of it yesterday."

After washing their hands and faces in the brook, they made their way down the hillside and onto the road, passing through the stone fences that separated the land parcels. People dotted the landscape, industriously tending to their animals and fields, all of whom, when they passed, waved in their direction then summarily ignored them.

"Did Ewan tell ye that the King of England has laid siege tae Edinburgh Castle?"

Edyth nodded and filled her lungs, the preoccupied look Cait had noticed earlier returning in full force. She chewed her bottom lip, her eyes far away. "He did, though I confess he did not go into detail. He fears that soon Perth will be met with such a fate, should he resist."

Cait nodded, feeling the weight of her brother's concern, for she felt it too. Having a great talent for listening at doors, she had overheard the private conversation between her brothers and his captain, Rory, that morning. "King Edward bombards the castle with Greek fire with his trebuchets. If he should succeed, he will be the first ever to take it."

"What of Iain?" asked Edyth. "What is his opinion?"

Iain was the second son, just three years her elder. While he was far less serious than Ewan as a rule, he took his responsibility as older brother far too seriously for her taste. "Iain doubts the King will win such a prize, but Ewan, who has seen more of war, kens no keep is without its weaknesses."

"What do you think will happen?" asked Edyth, her large, green eyes betraying her worry.

"I am but a lass," said Cait on an exhale, "who has n'er seen war. I can only guess."

"A woman, yes, but not a stupid one. I would hear your speculation."

The compliment made Cait's mouth twitch upward, but she shrugged humbly. "I dinnae wish tae injure ye with my thoughts on yer English King."

With a scoff, Edyth said, "You know I do not love him, nor claim him as my sovereign. I am a Scotswoman now, thanks to your brother. Speak your mind."

Cait swooped to pick up a rock from a rut in the road. "I dinnae ken what tae think. I hope he doesnae take Edinburgh, for it would rally the Scots who oppose him tae unite." Cocking her hand back, Cait threw the stone down the road and watched as it bounced twice then ricocheted into the tall grass lining the path. "If he takes it," she added, "I think Ewan has the right o' it. Edward will have none tae stop him, then. The clans will submit."

She looked to her sister-in-law for any telling sign that she might know more. Edyth was *bana-bhuidseach geal*. A white witch. A seer, more specifically. She'd *seen* her brother Ewan's death at the battle of Dunbar only a few months previously and had moved heaven and earth to prevent it with some help from herself.

"Mmmph," agreed Edyth, her eyes far distant. "King Edward is a greedy man, who would devour his mother's soul if he thought it would sustain his own."

They walked in silence for a time, listening to the birds and the grass shuffle in the breeze. Cait hesitated briefly, then asked, "Have ye seen such visions, then? Is my speculation true?"

Edyth shook her head, her pretty mouth turned down into a frown. "I'm not sure. I've had a few dreams, but I can't make sense of them. Just shapes and shadows, but always with a feeling of disquiet. I cannot say as yet. It could be nothing."

"Or it could be something," said Cait. They walked in silence for several minutes, each lost in their own thoughts before Cait had the nerve to ask the question foremost in her mind. "Has Ewan telt ye of his plans tae arrange my future?"

Edyth's eyes, distant and clouded with thoughts Cait could not see, darted ashamedly toward Cait then away, an apology written on her face. "Yes, he's told me a very little." She took Cait's hand then and gave it a squeeze. "I don't envy you. I was blessed to find your brother and to have found happiness here, but I know well what you feel. It's a frightening prospect, to be bound to a stranger."

"Aye," Cait agreed. "I think I trust Ewan tae find me a good match, but.... How can he be sure? He cannae know with any certainty what kind o' man he chooses for me."

Edyth sighed and nodded. "Yes. Yes, I know."

Cait slipped her arm through Edyth's and asked, "Do ye think that yer dreams may have sommat tae to do with my future husband?"

The look of surprise on Edyth's face gave her some relief, though it was small. "No. I...we can't be certain my dreams mean anything at all."

"Mmph," Cait muttered noncommittedly. "Ye'll tell me though, if ye think they might."

"Of course I would," Edyth said as they crossed the stone bridge over the river and entered into the sprawling village of Perthshire. It didn't take long for Cait to realize that something was amiss. Shouts were heard from the square and a milling crowd of people were gathered there, hiding whatever spectacle was taking place.

Cait hurried forward and, coming to the edge of the crowd, stood on her toes to see what was happening. Through a gap between two women, she saw that a wheel had come off a wagon, spilling its contents all over the ground, and—somehow—entrapping a child. It was a lad, his legs visible from under the axel, still and lifeless.

"Hurry, *Piuthar*. A child is hurt!" Her hand fumbled for Edyth's forearm, her heart seeming to quit altogether, but the woman was already pushing through the crowd, her skirts billowing out around her as she fell to the ground to assess the damage.

Cait watched, breathless, as Edyth's hands traversed up the boy's body, disappearing into shadow. A woman, the boy's mother, Cait presumed, was weeping volubly, frantically removing the remaining vegetables from the cart along with several other people. Cabbages rolled around their feet, ignored, as men came running, carrying farming tools long enough for prying.

"Hurry!" shouted Edyth from her place, "He lives still!"

The men thrust their long handles under the wagon and pushed against them, their faces screwed up with the effort. Hands, Cait could not tell to whom they belonged, pulled on the boy's legs, slipping him from the undercarriage of the cart smoothly.

The ground shook her feet when the men let their burden go and Cait's worry increased. It had been very heavy indeed. Blood and bone blossomed forth from the boy's upper arm, where he'd been pinned. His face was wan and lifeless. Cait would have thought him dead, had Edyth not said he still breathed. She could only watch with the quieted crowd—collectively holding their breath—as Edyth took command. She tied something around the boy's arm and shouted orders to a man, who cradled the boy and whisked him away as quickly as possible without jostling him, his mother rushing after them. Her cries made Cait's skin pebble to life and her chest tighten in grief.

Edyth found Cait with her eyes, her mouth moving. She couldn't hear what Edyth said over frantic cries of the boy's mother, so she hurried forward.

"I will need Alban's saw," said Edyth calmly, quietly, though Cait saw that her hands were shaking. "I will need my herbal tome and my box of herbs. Go, Cait. Run as fast as you can and return to me at once."

Cait did as she was bid, running so fast that she lost a shoe as she crossed the bridge, but she did not stop to retrieve it, nor did she stop when she thought her ribs might split open from the pain in her side.

Chapter Two

Edyth entered the dimly lit building and found that the boy had been laid upon a table in the tavern. He was awake now, evidenced by his tormented screams. Mugs of ale had been hastily pushed onto the floor, perfuming the air with the sweetly sour scent of spoiled drink and broth.

The boy's mother was sobbing, her tears falling into the boy's hair as she ran her hands over his head and showered him with indiscernible words and desperate kisses. The room was filling with people. Edyth saw people praying but could not hear them over the noise. She had to concentrate.

She pulled her knife from her belt and cut the shirt off the boy as quickly as possible while the man who had carried him in held him still. She had to split the shirtsleeve and peel it away in stages, so great was the boy's pain. When she untied the handkerchief from his bicep, he screamed so loudly her ears rang, but then he fell silent once more as he lost consciousness.

Edyth pulled away the ruined shirt and tied the handkerchief tightly around his arm once more with shaking fingers. The blood loss slowed significantly. The boy's mother was too distraught to respond to her queries about the boy's name or age, so she looked to the man who had carried him in.

"Eachann," replied the man. "He is Beathan's son and this is his mam, Deòiridh." Edyth vaguely remembered the name. She'd met all her husband's clan members after they'd been wed, but clan Ruthven was sizable and she could not remember all of the names, faces, duties, occupations, and families.

"Go, then and fetch his father."

He nodded and hastened toward the door but as he passed, Edyth stopped him with a touch of his elbow. "And the priest," she whispered, hoping the boy's mother would not hear. "It will bring peace to her, should things not go well."

He nodded once more and left. Edyth took a deep breath and racked her brain. What was she to do? Never before had she cut off an appendage. *Mother*, she urged silently, looking for the same assistance she'd been given from some unseen force not so long ago. *I don't know what to do.*

The last time she'd been tasked with saving another's life, and hadn't known what to do, help had come, though she could never put into words how it had happened. Thoughts that were not her own had blossomed in her mind and she'd acted, knowing that she was being guided.

Yet now, she did not feel the unseen assistance return. *Please*, she pleaded. *I cannot do it alone.*

"Why does he not wake?" sobbed his mother, yanking Edyth from her thoughts.

Edyth swallowed heavily and took a shaking breath "He...he is in a lot of pain and has bled much," she replied. "It is good that he sleeps."

"Eachann," the woman moaned desperately. "*Thig air Ais thugam.*" The woman's pain was too much to bear. Edyth, surprised by the wetness on her cheeks, wiped her face with the back of her hand and busied herself, else she lose her own head. She turned blindly to a woman who stood nearby, who was quietly crying into her apron. "You, go and fetch some linens. I will also need hot water, and...and..." She looked about her and pointed to two stripling lads. "I will have need of you here, at the table."

They came forward, their faces nearly as white as the injured boy. "I will need you to hold him down once I begin. He cannot be allowed to fight against me as I work."

They nodded uncertainly with worry-filled eyes. Edyth eyed the boy's mother, hesitant. Not wishing to distress the woman further, she considered not telling her of what must be done to save her son. Not telling her, however, could very well make the situation worse.

She cleared her throat, her own hands feeling numb, and approached the woman, but the words stuck in her throat. What could she say? Edyth touched one of the woman's hands, which was fisted in the boy's shirt at his neck. It trembled, the knuckles starkly white against bronzed skin.

Sobbing, the small woman leaned into Edyth, her bony shoulder pushing into her ribs as she clung to her son. The white kertch atop her head had slipped to her nape; Edyth stroked the dark plait and bent to her ear. "I promise you this: I will do all I can to save him."

Too overcome, the woman did not reply. The only hope Edyth could offer was that it *was* possible for him to live. "He will be changed," she said to the woman, her own tears dripping like raindrops from summer leaves, to fall into her inky strands of hair. "But he can have a life."

She, herself, was living proof of it, after all; but she could not say such a thing here, where the woman could not hear her or understand. What's more, Edyth's wounds were not visible to the human eye, though she thought she might understand what the boy would face, should he live.

Living without such a constant and integral part of oneself would at first seem impossible. The pain would be excruciating, but it would change and lessen over time if he allowed himself to heal. That was the important part: a willingness to accept the change and a desire to fight against the bitter poison of disappointment.

Not long ago, Edyth's parents had been murdered and she, left alone and in considerable danger from their enemies, had sought out the only family she had left to her in the world. Of course nothing comes easily, and her escape from those who had hurt her parents had left her with miles of difficult terrain and unthinkable danger as she'd fled England. Fate or God or whatever one might like to call it, had smiled upon her, however. She'd been found—saved—by Ewan. And she had saved him.

Edyth pulled herself from her thoughts and held the woman tightly. What was she to do? She'd never removed a limb, nor ever seen it done, and she feared for the boy as much as she feared for herself.

It felt like it took an age before the woman returned with linens. The owner of the establishment had produced a hot kettle within good time, but Edyth could not start without the butchery tool Alban used. In an effort to not think about what was to come, she busied herself with ripping the chemise and old sark the woman had brought her into long strips.

Edyth had a good pile of useable linen strips cut and ready by the time she heard the thundering of horse hooves. The door burst open and her heart stuttered in grateful relief at seeing her husband there, holding her box of medicinals under one arm, his face full of earnest concern.

"Command me," he said and she found his hand, strong and steady to her own cold and shaking one. "And I will aid ye as I might."

"I...I will need you to take charge of her, I think," she said, motioning with her eyes, to the boy's mother, who was clinging to her son.

"Aye," he said, glancing at the woman before handing her the box she'd requested. "Dinnae open it til I 'ave her safe away," he murmured. "Alban is come behind. He cannae ride as quickly. Aye, Alban" he said in a rueful way, at her raised brows, "If ye need help with a saw, he is the man ye want."

Ewan pulled the woman kindly but firmly from the boy, wrapping his arms around her shaking shoulders and whispering unheard comforts to her. She wept all the harder, her hoarse cries piercing Edyth's heart.

She heard her husband say something about going to pray and so she nodded to the boys and motioned them forward. "He sleeps now, but once I begin, he will wake; do not let him pull from your grip. I will work as fast as I can."

She directed one of the lads to the feet and one to the head of the table as the door was closed behind Ewan and the boy's mother.

Edyth closed her eyes, a light hand pressed to the boy's shoulder. She wished for her own talented mother but wishing would gain her nothing; she could only pray and hope that inspiration would come. Alban entered then, his rolling gait easily recognizable through the gathered crowd, with another unexpected surprise trailing behind him. Cait had come back, clearly unsure and frightened, but there all the same. Edyth estimation of her sister-in-law increased tenfold.

Alban was grumbling, eyeing the boy's shoulder in an expert fashion when Cait embraced her.

"What shall I do?" she asked. "Mam has gone tae the kirk with Ewan and Deòiridh. I...I wish tae be o' help, where I might."

"I'm grateful you're here," said Edyth as she opened the box Ewan had brought her. There, partially hidden under a sinister-looking saw, was the herbal tome her mother had so diligently penned; it listed all of the valuable uses for herbs, complete with sketches and how to prepare them. Edyth flipped through the pages quickly. "I will need these herbs," she said, pointing to different pages. "I have them here, in my stores. Pound them and boil them with red nettle until the color is dark...like blood."

Cait nodded, clutching the book to her chest, her face stark white. Edyth pulled Alban's saw knife, used for the butchery of sheep, hogs, and goats, from the box. She held the edge up to the light from the window—little hairs stuck to dried blood were illuminated from a previous victim—and swallowed hard. Her hand shook as she moved to the table, to where Alban was instructing the lads in tying the boy's arms and legs to the table.

She hadn't thought to do that and her esteem for the grumbling old man increased. The boy was stirring from Alban's ministrations, his face screwed up in pain. He whimpered quietly at first, then, as consciousness bloomed within him, he cried out in earnest. His wide, terrified, brown eyes roved from face to face.

She bent over him and caught his eye. She could not smile or reassure him. She could do nothing but smooth the fine hairs from his sweating brow and direct him to bite down on a wooden spoon she'd found on a nearby table. She kissed his brow and whispered to him, though she doubted he could hear her over his cries.

Alban had tied another handkerchief on his injured arm, slightly below where she had tied her own. "Here," he grunted, pointing to the space between the two handkerchiefs. He held out his hand for the saw and she gave it to him, grateful to give the responsibility to a stronger, more experienced hand. "Hold him here," instructed Alban, pushing his hand down on the boy's shoulder above the injury. "Press hard, tae keep him from twisting or pulling away from the saw."

Edyth did as she was told; the boy cried out all the harder. His screams of agony lifted the hairs on her nape and caused her eyes to sting with tears. Her breath came short as Alban lifted the saw. "Bite down, lad," barked the cook, and then he began.

He worked quickly; the ruined flesh gave way with each powerful, swift stroke, but the intact bone resisted the butcher's efforts. Screams, unlike any Edyth had ever heard, ripped from the boy's throat and she cried with him. Speckles of blood dotted her hands and forearms. She could feel the wetness even on her cheeks, chin and lips as Alban sawed. Her arms ached with the effort it took to keep the boy's shoulder still, but she did not relent.

Alban grunted with the effort, his stringy hair falling from the queue at the nape of his neck as he cut through the bone and then, suddenly, the room fell silent. The boy lay motionless, his eyes rolled back into his head. It was with breathless terror that Edyth looked to his chest, to his neck where his pulse might be, to his mouth and nose, to see if he lived still. She felt his faint exhale against her cheek and let out the breath she had been holding. "He lives," she said.

"For now," grunted Alban, his hooded eyes inspecting his work. It was difficult for Edyth to look upon the severed limb, so she stared at Alban instead, wondering at how he could be so stoically unaffected. He took his bloodied saw, nodding to the helpers gathered around the table and said, "It's up tae ye, now lass. Sew him up and pray God that the ague doesnae take 'im."

She stared after the cook, at the door as it bounced loudly against the jamb at his exit, and then at the people who had lingered. There wasn't a dry eye in the room; someone had been sick. She could smell the pungent evidence wafting toward the table. At some point in the proceedings, the priest had entered and had taken this opportunity to make the sign of the cross upon Eachann's forehead. He mumbled a prayer as Edyth tried to slow her racing heart.

She exhaled slowly and forced herself to survey the damage. The gore of what was left of his arm was as startling as it was gruesome. The neatly-cut bone was surrounded by layers of bruised muscle and the silky threads of sinew and tendon. A layer of yellowish fat clung to jagged flesh, which hung in limp pieces.

How was she to stitch this sort of wound closed? Edyth's hands shook as she looked to the priest, to the eyes focused on her, waiting for her to take action. Her mind raced, thinking of every injury her mother had ever tended. There had been scrapes aplenty, even a few toes lost to an ax…a finger to a sickle, but never an entire limb. Never this.

Knowing she needed to do *something*, but not knowing what, she filled the space with words. "What of his arm? Surely it should be buried in the kirkyard?"

The priest's mouth turned slightly downward as he considered for a heart-beat, but he nodded solemnly and, picking up a cloth from the table, wrapped the severed appendage carefully within. He carried it, much like a new babe in his arms, through the door. This seemed to be some sort of silent symbol that the people should follow, for nearly all of the people in the room filed out after him, many making the sign of the cross as they passed by Eachann.

She needed Cait's tincture and her needle and thread. The door to the back room was open, where she knew Cait must be. A large hearth was placed expertly along the back wall, which was made entirely of stone. There was no quicklime and sand plaster here, to hide the mason's work.

Stacked gray and brown stones absorbed the light from the window and from the fire, so that the room appeared very dim indeed. Cait's dark hair looked black and her skin wan in the low light; her red gown looking as dried blood. Her hair, just like her mother's and her brother's, was curling around her face where it had escaped the loose plait she usually wore.

"I think I've done it right," said Cait, looking up from the black kettle, which was suspended over the fire on an iron hook. She lifted the pot from the hook using a wad of cloth and placed it upon the wooden table a short distance away.

She wrung her hands and jutted her chin toward a jug on the table. "I found some vinegar. When my skin is broken open, Mam puts vinegar on my wound, but I ken Eachann's wound is far worse than any scrape I've ever…." Cait trailed off and bit her lip. "Does he live?"

Edyth pulled Cait into a fierce hug, feeling overcome. "Thank you, Cait. Thank you for coming. Yes. Yes, he lives. Now we…now we try and apply healing."

Cait squeezed her back briefly and when they broke apart, Edyth showed Cait how to strain the potion through a cloth. She felt strange, as though she were at once within and without herself, so that her head felt detached and oddly afloat. She shook her head to erase the feeling and redoubled her effort to focus her thoughts. They carried the herbal box, which held Edyth's needles and cat-gut thread, the potion, and the vinegar through the door and to the table that held Eachann.

The boy was still asleep—from pain or shock, or both—and Edyth knew she must work fast for his own comfort. She stared at the wound in a detached sort of way, diagraming in her mind how she might stitch the blood pathways, or how she might pull and stretch the skin in a way that would keep his wound best covered.

While she did not know if her plans were correct, she had to act and hope that answers came in the execution. Motioning for Cait, she asked her to hold Eachann once more before dousing the stump of his arm with the vinegar. Eachann awoke instantly, bucking and howling; his hoarse cries pierced Edyth's heart. "I'm sorry," she said, again and again, all while applying the tincture Cait had made. "I'm sorry."

While Cait held down his shoulder, Edyth pulled the skin of Eachann's arm together with needle and thread, stitch by stitch, cutting off pieces of excess with her best knife as quickly as possible, and hoped that what she did was correct. She could not feel or sense any unseen help, as she had once before. She did not see an image in her mind, nor hear a voice. She just moved forward, hoping that she was right.

Eachann sobbed and vomited, but before long, the work was done, his wound was wrapped tightly in linens, and he was untied from the table. Edyth's hand was cramping from holding the needle so tightly between her fingers for such a length of time. As she rubbed life back into her fingers, she looked to Cait, who had stoically stayed by her side. Tearstained and white-faced, Cait ran a shaky hand across her forehead, her eyes locked on the exhausted, now unconscious boy.

"Will he live, do ye think?" she whispered.

Edyth's intake of breath was shaky as she raised one shoulder in response. "I don't know," she said, her voice quiet. "Someone, go and fetch his parents, if you please," Edyth asked no one in particular. She did not even notice who left, she only registered that the door opened and then shut again. "I will have to tend to him daily...change the bandages and reapply the tincture."

She felt wholly undone. Her legs would no longer hold her, and she fell heavily into a chair to rest her head in her shaking, bloodied hands. She hardly noticed when Cait sat next to her, nor did she hear the words her friend was saying. Her mouth was moving, but her voice was very far off.

She felt Cait's hand on her shoulder at one point, and saw her worried face, but she could not focus on any one thing. She wanted to remark on how strange she felt, but the next thing she knew, she'd somehow gotten atop a horse. Ewan was holding her in his lap, one arm across her middle, holding her tightly to his chest, and the other hand loosely holding the reins.

"He must live," she slurred, feeling heavy of body. "He must."

Ewan gave her a brief, one-armed squeeze. "With you standing in the way of Death, I've no doubt that he will. Sleep, now, Edie. I'll see ye safe home."

Chapter Three

The pitch in the torches around the dining hall sputtered in the otherwise silent room. Ewan stood, as he always did, at the center of the table, where he would address his household, his favored knights, and his family. But tonight, Cait could see that there was no contentment in him. There was a deep furrow in his brow and a solemnity enveloping him that stayed people's chatter.

"Edinburgh has fallen," announced Ewan. He could not hide his disappointment from Cait. She knew his heart. She could read his discontent as plainly as she could read the sky.

"King Edward keeps three hundred and fifty of his knights there to defend what he has taken," he continued solemnly. "Let us pray that his campaign tae invade the whole o' the lowlands will keep him far from us fer a time, though I doubt it will be fer long. We must prepare ourselves, and hastily, though I cannae know which course tae take as yet. Our safety and freedom is ever in my mind."

The room was silent. Some mouths hung open, aghast, while others looked fearful, angry, or merely grim. Ewan looked around the table, meeting the eye of each person, family and clan member. "I heard tell just today this news. Scotland's treasured Stone of Scone has been robbed from us as well, amongst other treasures. It's tae be taken back tae London, no doubt, so that we may no' place our own king upon it hastily, in a bid tae rule ourselves." He could not quite keep the bitterness from his voice.

Cait's mother, Roslyn, placed her hand into her own. It was cold but strong, and she took comfort from the touch.

"It is my hope," said Ewan with a notable effort at calm, lifting his cup of cider, "that we will be unified together, whichever path we need take. To Scotland."

"To Scotland," repeated the gathered friends and clan members solemnly, lifting their cups in salute.

Cait forced herself to drink, but she had no taste for it. Dinner was served and passed from hand to hand, but she could not seem to find her appetite, her mind clouded with terrible possibilities. What would happen now? Her eyes roved over the table's occupants. No one seemed willing to discuss the loss of the mighty fortress that was Edinburgh Castle, though it was clear to her that it was at the forefront of every mind.

Iain and Rory—her brother's captain—were seated across from her, and her mother to her right. Edyth sat to her left, her hands folded in her lap, ever the image of grace, though Cait thought she sat rather stiffly. Ewan was quiet and stony faced on the other side of Edyth, not that she blamed him.

"I thought that Edinburgh's defenses were sure," said Cait, her voice sounding over-loud in the subdued room. She felt the weight of every eye and her cheeks pinkened brightly. Sitting straighter, she said, "Is it no' said tae be impossible tae breach?"

"There is no defense so great that it can withstand Edward's war machines," responded Iain, his steel-gray eyes fierce with suppressed feeling.

"Nor any man or woman who can defend themselves against such cruelty," grated Rory. He sneered and huffed through his long nose in derision. "And the English call us savages." She felt Edyth stiffen at Rory's words, saw her eyes falling to her lap.

"Does the King not hold to the laws and conduct of chivalry?" asked Cait, meeting the eyes of the men at the table. They seemed slightly amused, and she wondered if they were laughing at her.

"There is little that is chivalrous in making war, Sister," said Ewan gently. He paused, seeming to think on his words, then said, "Of course there are virtuous qualities one would hope for in a King. Bravery, courtesy, and honor...and haps King Edward embodies these virtues. Some would argue that he does. There is one law of virtue, however, that I have yet tae see him uphold."

"He does not stay the hands of his fighting men," explained Iain at seeing the question in Cait's eyes. "So that women nor children are spared. And those that live are despoiled and left to starve with English seed planted in their bellies."

"That's quite enough," commanded Roslyn stiffly. "Let us not sully this hall with such talk. I will hear no more." She reached for her cup hastily and drank, her face ashen.

Cait recalled overhearing Rory report to Ewan one evening some months prior that King Edward and ordered the slaughtering of seven thousand inhabitants of Berwick—women, children and bairns amongst the garrison's fighting men—for he wished to have the mills be turned by their blood. She felt the color leave her face at the memory.

Cait's stomach turned sour as her fear grew. "But if Edinburgh's great castle upon the rock can be breeched, then what of Perth?" she asked her mother. "We have little chance against such hostilities. What must be done? How do we prepare ourselves?"

Roslyn's jaw tightened in anger, her eyes dark and forbidding. "There will be no war machines here, Catronia. Now, let us speak of something pleasing." She looked to Iain across the table and said, "I heard tell that the wool we harvested is of a fine quality. When do ye leave for the monestary tae sell?"

Wool? She wanted to speak of *wool*? Cait could not help her sputtering response. She looked to Iain, then Ewan, pleading silently for their aid before turning her attention back to her mother. "Do ye think yer wishing will make it so? We have no great position here, high upon a rock, nor a sea wall tae protect us as in Edinburgh. Nor can we boast the same strength of their garrison. How can we hope for freedom, Mother, if Edinburgh has been taken so quickly?"

Eyes of her clansmen fell to their plates as her gaze rested on them, challenging them to answer her. She understood their reluctance, for they loved her mother and out of respect, would obey her with their silence. And while Cait loved her mother just as well, meekness had never loved or served her well.

Agitated and disheartened, Cait wondered if she would be forever learning of the world by listening at doors. She was educated by the priests, tutors and best bards, and yet she was to be ignorant of such important happenings?

"I would speak of it, Mother. If we do not prepare, we have no hope of security."

"No," barked her mother furiously. Cait's face hardened, preparing for a fight. "No!" Roslyn punctuated her remark with a forceful shove against the table, which scraped her chair loudly on the wooden planks.

She stood and looked down at her daughter, her blue eyes ablaze. "Yer father knew well enough what kind o' man King Edward is. I'll remind ye that yer father's mother was Welsh. I've no need tae speak o' the King's cruelty in his campaigns against her people. We watched as our neighbors were slaughtered...their homes destroyed, and their lands taken. Wales is lost!" she cried, her voice breaking, with one arm outstretched toward the wall in the apparent direction of the country, "And we were only glad it was not us!"

Her quick breaths seemed to shake her small frame. Cait moved to stand, so astonished was she at her mother's show of emotion. She did not know what she would say, but she felt concern for her, so incongruous was her outburst.

With a quick gesture, her mother bade her remain, and added, in a small voice. "I will not fill what days remain tae us, with talk of fortification or war making. I cannae lose my sons. I...." Roslyn's chin wobbled with feeling but she cut herself off. "I grow weary," she said in a small, controlled voice. "Excuse me." Ewan immediately stood and took his mother's arm, looking as shocked as Cait felt. As he helped her from the room, Cait felt the acute sting of shame.

She could only stare at her hands in her lap, her fingers mimicking the knot that was in her stomach. It was not often that her mother mentioned her father since his death last year. To hear her speak of him now, as though all happiness and hope that had lived in her breast was now buried with him...it tore at the tender places in Cait's heart.

What was worse, Cait understood now that her mother had already conceded. They were defeated, even now, before it had begun. There would be no stand against the King of England. And while it was Ewan who was chief, and not their mother, she could not see Ewan going against her wishes. Not in this case.

Edyth's hand touched her forearm, a question in her eyes, but Cait's mind was full of her own questions. Questions that had no answers. "I...I have no appetite," she said, her voice small. "Excuse me. Forgive me." Cait could feel every eye on her as she quit the hall, but did not hasten her steps.

Later that evening, when sitting in the solar embroidering thistles on what was meant to bless her future marriage bed—and much later her winding sheet—she could not seem to concentrate. She'd tangled the threads, undone knots only to make them again, and stabbed the needle into the finely woven linen as though it were King Edward, too many times to count.

She held the framed sheet away from her to better be seen in the torchlight and sighed. It was no use. She was too distracted in her mind to work on such a task, but just when she was about to get up to leave, the door opened. It was her mother, covered in her mourning habit. Cait stood and curtseyed in respect, ready for the scathing reprimand, but no words came.

She was shocked to look up into her mother's tear-streaked face. She'd seen her mother cry before here and there...and much more often of late, since her father's passing, but never had she cried after Cait had vexed her. She had expected angry words, not tears. She found she had no defense against them.

But, to her astonishment, her mother had no angry words; she merely opened her arms to her, her breath hitching, and Cait went to her. Even though Cait was taller than her mother, she still felt as a child. "I'm sorry, Mam," said Cait to the top of her head. Her mother squeezed her tightly in response. She felt her mother shake her head against her shoulder in dismissal of the apology, her breath leaving her in a stutter.

"I am no' angry with you," said her mother, letting her go. She motioned for Cait to sit and then chose a seat adjacent. Roslyn wiped her eyes with a handkerchief, her thin mouth turned down. "I was never frightened when your father lived, but now that he is gone, I can find no comfort. Ye are so verra like him, my Cait."

Roslyn wiped away a trailing tear. "For ye're fierce and loyal, and fearless. Ye've got his quick mind but, I think, even a quicker tongue." She sighed very quietly. It felt like a surrender, though Cait could not say for what.

"I miss him so," Roslyn said. Her face crumpled, a soft mewl of anguish escaping her. Cait lept from her seat and sat on the arm of her mother's chair as she cried into her hands. Cait removed the pins holding the dark veil in place from atop her mother's head and stroked her mother's fine, silver-streaked hair.

"Sometimes," she said through her tears, "I wake with the thought that I must tell him some little thing, some small thing, and remember that he is no' there. Other times, when I come upon one o' yer brothers, I'm startled at how closely they resemble him. Just little things...in the way Iain moves his hands or in the way Ewan furrows his brow. And other times, when I hear him in yer words, it's like a knife tae my heart. He is taken from me again suddenly. It wearies me, this mourning."

Cait did not know what to say, so she only cried with her. It was some time later, as Cait walked back to her room in the dark of the corridors that she wondered what was the better choice: a marriage of affection or one with apathy? She could not decide, for both seemed mightily cruel.

Chapter Four

"He is come!" panted Alec. He'd burst through Ewan's study door, his chest heaving as though he'd run a league.

"Who has come?" asked Ewan, already exiting his seat in alarm. The bells in the kirkyard tolled loudly, signaling visitors.

"Him!" panted Alec, his face stricken. "The King! Of England!"

Ewan stopped in his tracks and stared, open-mouthed at his squire. "Surely ye're mistaken." But even as he said the words, he doubted himself. He'd been hearing whispers of the English King's strategic maneuverings throughout the lowlands. He'd laid siege to important castles further south. Only a week previously he had won Stirling. Ewan had heard that the castle was all but empty except for the porter, who'd stayed behind to offer the King the keys to the keep.

Ewan ran to the nearest window. Though it was narrow, he could see a portion of the curtain wall where men scurried about, shouting orders. "Ye're certain tis King Edward at my gate?" asked Ewan, still feeling as though he were in a dream.

Alec could only nod, his eyes wide. "And with at least fifty men."

Ewan wondered at the number but wasted no more time, sprinting to the yard where there was a fury of activity. Fighting men ran from place to place, donning their padded gambesons, gathering pikes, crossbows, and swords. Servants carting wheelbarrows and wagons full of straw, muck, and assortments of vegetables were hastily moved out of the middle of the yard for the fighting men to take their places, ready to be commanded.

Ewan ran to the gatehouse stairs and took them two and three at a time, his chest feeling as though it might burst. There, from the top of the wall, Ewan saw the column of men riding toward his home, identified by the English's red dragon ensign.

He swore softly under his breath, his stomach dropping to somewhere near his knees. It was a great effort that Ewan stopped the whirring in his mind and ordered his thoughts. They were, indeed, English, but Ewan doubted it was the King. Not with only a contingent of fifty men.

Ewan looked about him, searching for Iain or Rory, and found his steward commanding men in the yard, his shouts swallowed up in the noise of so much chaos. There, running from the direction of the armory was Iain, buckling his sword belt even as he ran. He fumbled with the buckle momentarily and then he disappeared from view as he entered the gatehouse.

Ewan grasped onto Alec's shoulder tightly. "You will gather my mother, wife and sister and command them they stay in the solar. You will stay with them, Alec."

"On my life, Laird, I will see them safe."

Ewan's breath caught in his throat at the words. Though it was unlikely they would be harmed, the boy's conviction was heartfelt. He clapped his squire on the shoulder and nodded grimly to him once. "Aye. Go now and see them safe." The women in his life were not meek or defenseless, but he still felt better knowing that Alec would be there.

The young man left in all haste, and almost ran into Iain as he exited the stairs. "Who comes?" asked Iain, sparing a glance at Alec's retreat. "There are some saying it is King Edward."

Ewan nodded needlessly in the direction of the riding party now cresting the last hill. "I dinnae ken if it's him, but they are English, whomever they are."

Iain frowned. "Tis too small of a contingent for a king, I would think. What do ye mean tae do?"

The chains rattled and the planks under their feet trembled as the portcullis was lowered into place. "I will hear them, I suppose. I doubt I have much of a choice," said Ewan. "Aye. It is no' the King. Go tell Rory," he commanded. Iain left him immediately, leaving Ewan alone atop the gatehouse wall with a handful of archers, to watch as the great cloud of dust billowed about the approaching contingent of men.

Iain was back before they arrived at the gate, grim faced and agitated. The contingent reigned in their horses at the closed gate. One of the men removed his helm, revealing the sweat-drenched, sharp features of a man in a curtain of brown, stringy hair. "I would speak to the lord of this estate!" shouted a firm voice from the front of the crowd. He sat atop a decorated warhorse, surrounded by flag bearers displaying the sigils and symbols of their power. English power.

It wasn't King Edward who had come, but his Justiciar, a man who could act as regent when the king was absorbed elsewhere. Ewan exchanged a dark look with his brother before addressing the man.

"I am Laird Ruthven. What business do ye have here, upon my lands?"

There was only the briefest of pauses where the snapping of the flags in the fierce wind filled the silence, then, "I am John de Warenne, warden of the kingdom and land of this God-forsaken place." The man glowered and wiped the grimy sweat from his brow before adding, "These lands are held forfeit in the name of God and King Edward! You will open your gate should you wish to keep these walls intact."

Iain placed a hand on Ewan's stiff shoulder, stalling his words. "Uncurl your lip, brother," advised Iain. "Keep yer head if he dinnae wish tae have the King at our very gates."

Iain was right, of course, though it took all his willpower to keep his voice calm when he responded. "Pray tell me by what means my family's lands are now lost to me."

"Have you been living under a rock or are you only simple minded?" barked the man absurdly. "Even so far from civilization, you must have heard by now that Scotland is under the governance of King Edward. Open your gates, that I may deliver this message, or your resistance will be met with slaughter and ruin."

"My ears hear all his tongue wags, yet he wishes my gates opened to him," Ewan muttered to his brother. He ached to draw his sword from where he stood on the wall, declaring his feelings on the matter, but he closed his fists tightly instead, and said to Iain, "It is folly to let him in."

"It is folly to deny him," advised his brother. Ewan might have been bemused at how odd it was to have their roles reversed, if the situation were not so grave. It was he, Ewan, that was usually staying his brother's hand and hot temper. And now, here, Ewan felt that his skin was the only thing keeping him from shattering into countless, violent pieces. His skin prickled as it always did before a fight and his hands hungered for his sword, but he could not give in to the craving. Not here. Not now.

"How can I bend my will to such a man...to such a king?" He thought of his mother and sister, of their love for this, their home. Not only for the family it housed but for the safety it promised them. And he thought of Edyth. What kind of husband would let such malice into their home, and she having only just having left the cruelty of England mere months ago?

"If you do not," said Iain, moving to stand in front of him to fill his vision, "the violation against us will be ill indeed. Forget your feelings and think of the household."

Ewan swallowed and nodded, clearing his throat to ensure it did not sound as reedy as it felt. "Your men at arms will remain without the walls," Ewan commanded. "You alone will be permitted to enter. Leave your arms without. Ye have my assurance no harm will befall you while you remain here peaceably."

Iain signaled for the gate to be opened and Ewan waited atop for a breath, collecting himself. The planks shuddered underfoot once more as the gate began its noisy ascent. Iain was right. He must do this carefully. He must play the part, lest he bring destruction on any of his people.

He took the steps down to the yard more slowly than he had come up them, wondering how he would keep his temper concealed. It was customary to bring a man of station into his home and show him rich courtesy, which he must do now, though it soured his stomach. Rory had already dispersed the fighting men, and a page was sent to the kitchens with orders for drink and food to be brought to Ewan's room within the garrison.

The gate having been opened, the justiciar sauntered in, removing first his sword and dirk; he entrusted them to an awaiting squire, who would not meet his eye. The Justiciar was followed by a rather short, stout man, who reminded Ewan of a bull. His shoulders were overlarge and rounded with muscle discernible even under chainmail. His large, pooching waist was set atop narrow hips. His legs appeared to be perpetually set far apart in a bow, as though he were born on a horse, and rarely walked on his own power.

The gate closed noisily again as de Warenne removed his gauntlets; he looked around the yard, taking stock of all the hidden spaces between the outbuildings within the yard where potential violence might lie in wait.

"Laird," said de Warenne with a slight nod. "This is Baldwin de Biggar, newly appointed sheriff of Midlothian, who will be assisting myself as a governing officer of these lands."

Ewan's lips tightened into a line. He resisted the urge to frown as his eyes met the shorter man. He'd heard about the office of the newly appointed sheriffs throughout Scotland, whose position it was to enforce Edward's rule. Swallowing discourteous words, Ewan said, "Come, let us retire, where ye might deliver yer message. I'm sure ye dinnae wish tae tarry here in the yard."

Ewan led the way into the anteroom of the garrison, where they could remove their armor and clean the dust from their faces. He waited as they did such, giving orders quietly to a page to see to their horses. When they were ready, he took them to a private room on the second floor of the garrison which was void of beds and comfortable enough for such a discussion. Iain followed, grim faced yet cordial.

It wasn't long before some lads from the kitchen brought in refreshment, which was summarily ignored. De Warenne lounged in his chair across a wide table, filled with rolled maps, a few samples of barley and oats that his crofters had brought him, and a stack of ledgers, leveling Ewan with a look he could not decipher. Iain did not sit, but stood behind Ewan, his long dark hair framing his serious face.

Likewise, the sheriff did not sit; instead, he openly roamed about the room with an air of ownership, taking in the decorated walls, the rush-strewn floor, and the narrow, shuttered window with a slight sneer. While it wasn't as grand as his great hall, nor was it as spacious, it was as far as Ewan would bring them within the walls.

"How many men do you house in this garrison?" asked de Biggar, moving to the desk. Audaciously, the man sifted through the contents on Ewan's desk with a blunt finger, eventually picking up his ledger, which held an inventory of weapons, names of his fighting men, and their dates of service.

Ewan's knuckles were white with strain as his hands gripped the arms of his chair. While he would like nothing more than to put this man in his place, he forced calm. He could almost feel Iain silently urging him to be cautious. Ruthven was but a smallish holding, comparatively, and with some luck, they would deem it not worth their time and move on quickly.

Ewan inhaled slowly through his nose and forced his fingers loose from the arms of his chair. "Our clan is no' so great as others, though we are able to defend ourselves should the need arise."

Baldwin ran a blunt finger down the list of names, all of which consisted of nearly one hundred and fifty men. He raised a skeptical brow and turned the book toward Ewan, as though to show him the evidence that he, himself, had written therein. "Mmph. Tis seemingly a sizeable stronghold. Tell me, how many men have pledged their fealty to you. False modesty is no better than lies, in my mind, so tell me true."

Ewan swallowed and leaned back in his chair, his face a mask. "Do ye make it a goal tae be rude, sir, or is it incivility borne from ignorance?"

Baldwin de Biggar sneered and tossed the open ledger onto the desk, scattering the items upon the polished surface in a markedly rude manner. He leaned heavily onto the table so that he drew his face close to Ewan; he could smell that stale sweat and feel the hot breath of the sheriff on his face. Ewan felt his jaw tick in annoyance and anger at the man's disrespect.

"If ye think yer impertinance is a mark of honor, ye're mistaken," the man hissed. Spittle bespattered Ewan's face.

Ewan looked away from the sheriff at de Warenne, who viewed the entire interaction with detached consideration from his seat across the table. "Surely the King does not wish tae incite the displeasure of Scotland's noblemen," said Ewan, hoping de Warenne would step in and control the sheriff, but de

Warenne only considered Ewan for a moment, his mouth turned down in thought.

"T'would be best for all, I think, if you answer the question," said de Warenne succinctly.

The tightly coiled rage in Ewan's belly unfurled and clawed at his throat. "I will *not*." Ewan stood then, his chair scraping loudly on the wooden planks. He felt Iain press close to him, either in commiseration or as a warning. His heart hammered relentlessly against his ribs, so swiftly had his suppressed anger burst forth from its bonds. His fingers tingled as the spark of his ire caught flame.

Ewan flexed empty hands, wishing for a weapon. "Ye come 'ere, intae me walls, claiming ye wish tae impart a message of a most serious nature, yet I have heard no such message. Ye ask answers tae questions ye have no right tae ask. Ye've dishonored my house and disgraced the name of the King ye claim tae serve. Ye will state yer business, noo, or ye'll leave. Aye?"

Ewan did not spare a glance for de Biggar. He would not give the man the satisfaction of addressing him as a man in a position of authority. Instead, he met de Warenne's shrew eyes squarely and waited, one brow raised expectantly.

De Warenne cleared his throat and gestured with an impatient hand to the sheriff, who stood at the ready at the end of the table, a cruel rictus tugging one corner of his mouth. Ewan spared him a glance, only because he pulled a folded bit of parchment from a black leather wallet and tossed it on the table. It landed with a small, neat *thwack*, on top of the ledger he'd thumbed through only moments ago.

"Here is your message, Chieftain," replied de Warenne. He stood then, and pulled on his gloves with exaggerated care, his dark eyes conveying just how tedious he thought the entire interaction had been. "You will present yourself in Berwick in one month's time to pledge yer fealty to King Edward. If you do not, know this: you will not even have a pot in which to piss." He moved toward the door and seeing Iain's movement to open it for him, drawled, "Don't bother. I know the way to my horse."

His heavy boots striking the floorboards were as drum that reverberated in Ewan's breast. The sheriff followed closely behind and, pausing long enough to glance over a thick shoulder, said menacingly, "Ye think ye can withhold information, Chieftain? I am the King's eyes, his ears, and mouth in this part of the world. Step warily."

Ewan barely noticed Iain following them out, no doubt to ensure they made their exit as they should. He felt hollow and numb, as if the world were holding its breath. With shaking fingers, he ran his hands through his curling hair, his mind a whirl. So his lands were forfeit. He had failed in his goal to be viewed as unremarkable and felt the shame his father must surely feel at his lack of control.

He should have kept his temper. Ewan smoothed a hand over his new beard and inhaled sharply, thinking of the sheriff's demand. No, he did right. He would not tell the man anything he wanted to know, especially when it came to the families that he was responsible for.

Picking up the missive from the King's court, Ewan read it to himself, a feeling of dread overtaking him. Not for the first time, he wished his father lived still. He would know what course to take.

Chapter Five

There was a great cloud hovering, bruised and roiling purple, black and gray. Streaks of lightning flashed in its depths, dimly lighting the landscape around her. With the brief flash, she saw a wide river, snaking through an indeterminable landscape.

An unadorned wooden bridge spanned the looping river at her feet, void of life. So much she saw before the cloud moved, settling over it—and her—swallowing them whole. Oppressive and clinging, the veil clung to her, filling her lungs with warm, wet air.

There was no breeze, however small; her hair clung to her sweaty face and neck, making her itch. Fear that did not belong to her lanced through her body with such force as to make bile rise in her throat.

To her horror, she suddenly felt movement within the fog, wisps of tangible nothings that were at once present and gone in the same breath. They brushed against her legs, her back, as soft as a whisper but with all the malice of a many-toothed beast.

Edyth trembled as the thundering of a thousand horses shook the ground—shook her very bones—and the scream of beasts and men alike filled the air. She was rooted to the spot. A battle? But she could not see for the dark cloud enveloping her. It curled its smoky tendrils around her, as heavy and as tangible as a shroud. A streak of lightening crackled to life once more, illuminating the shapes she had felt and had only guessed at.

Clashing swords. Shadows of men danced with death, blades swinging, men falling, some prevailing, and then the light quit and she was blind once more. The metallic smell of spilt blood filled her nostrils. She was going to be sick. A man screamed in pain and she covered her ears ineffectually.

Be swift! Make haste!

The thought was not her own, separate but distinct and keenly felt. But to where was she meant to run?

"Wheesht, *mo ghradh.*"

Edyth jerked awake, feeling Ewan's warm, heavy hand upon her shoulder. Gulping air, it took several moments before the terror dissipated enough for her to recognize her surroundings. While Edyth had had dreams all her life—portents of little inconsequential things that she'd often ignored—visions of death and war were rare. Rare they may be, but much harder to forget.

Indeed, only a few months ago, she'd seen her husband's death at the hands of the English at the Battle of Dunbar. Had she not intervened, he would have been impaled on a lonely field and left to the corbies. She shuddered and rolled over to face Ewan, whose sleepy eyes were marked with concern. "Did I cry out?" she asked, her hands tunneling through quilts to find his own. She found one and grasped onto it.

Ewan yawned, not bothering to cover his mouth. "Aye, and with a fair bit o' thrashing about. Bad dream?"

Edyth sighed. She'd hoped preventing Ewan's death would have been the end of such gore, yet still the visions continued. She didn't know what this dream might mean or how she played into it—if at all—but it seemed fate or God, or whatever power that had thrust such a burden upon her, would give her no peace.

She sat up, feeling cold and hot in the same instant, and closed her eyes to better replay the scene. "It was..." she paused, at a loss. "There was a battle and a great sense of urgency to *go*, though I don't understand if I was meant to run away with all haste or to rush to their aid. I don't...." Edyth scoffed softly, shaking her head at the futility of it. "It's senseless to try and dissect it, really. I don't know what any of it means." She sighed and wiped hair from her eyes. "I'm sorry for waking you."

Ewan left the bed and poured her a cup of water from the ewer, the soft dawn light winking from the shutters highlighting the curve of muscled shoulder, back and buttock. His lithe body was no longer a secret to her, but still her eyes lingered upon him, appreciating his beauty. He returned, offering her the cup.

"Who were the players?" he asked, as she gulped down the water.

"I don't know." She shook her head and closed her eyes, searching her memory for any telling features but could find none. "Just shadows," she murmured. "Everything was in a dark cloud. I...I could only discern shapes, but there was blood and—" she suppressed a shudder, recalling the screams. "I needn't tell you what battle is like."

Ewan pursed his lips thoughtfully as he replaced/ the cup before settling himself back into bed. Edyth could not help but notice the dark circumspection that shadowed his eyes. "It's too soon," she said determinedly. "It could simply be a bad dream. Let us not borrow trouble."

She paused, her thoughts a jumble, before saying, "All my previous visions of war had been to save you at the Battle of Dunbar. I saw you plainly in those dreams, but in this one, there were no faces. No telling circumstances...just shadows and fear. It was probably just a nightmare." The quiet between them stretched on, heavy and oppressive. She could feel Ewan's doubt marry her own.

She stared at the dark canopy over their marriage bed before Ewan pulled her to him, cradling her back against his chest. She sighed at the touch and the instant comfort his nearness provided. After a long moment Ewan spoke again, his breath tickling her ear. "If it was merely a dream, then why are ye shaking so?"

She shrugged, unsure. "I wish only that I did not wake you." Ewan kissed Edyth behind her ear in response. She felt one shoulder lift in a shrug.

After a long pause, Ewan said, "I've been sleeping ill as it is. I cannae decide what course I should take. It is the same question that I have so far avoided, come at last. I must choose England or choose death, but either choice gives me no pleasure."

The tension returned to Edyth in full force. Turning in his arms, she searched his shadowed face and saw there the stoic determination he wore when preparing for a fight. "Why only those two choices? Is there no life to be had separated from England?"

He shook his head slightly, the shushing movement of his head on the pillow overloud in her ears. "With sae many captured at Dunbar, who is left tae resist the King? The great men who did not come to Dunbar's aid will not change their minds, especially now that Edinburgh has ceded. My lands are forfeit. If I do not bend the knee, I choose death."

Edyth fingered the lace on her shift. "Surely there are those who would follow you?" she asked, her voice the barest whisper.

Ewan exhaled slowly through his nose, his lips pressed into a thin line. "Edyth, if I refuse, I'll be in the tower and Perthshire will be granted tae another. You and the rest o' the family will be disgraced and homeless."

Edyth nodded, frowning in thought. She didn't want Ewan to have to swear fealty to an invading monarch, especially one so ruthless as Edward, but she did not want him to lose his birthright either. "What would your father have done?" she asked, curious. She'd heard him speak of his father from time to time, and always with an air of reverence.

Ewan laughed, breathy and humorless. "That's the problem, aye? I dinnae ken." Ewan's father, Malcolm Ruthven had been a political master, expertly balancing upon the double-edged sword that was England and Scotland. He had paid Longshanks in gold while he'd paid King Phillipe in blood. Sent to France to fight against the English, Ewan had done his duty by his father, but Ewan was not his sire. He shook his head briefly, his mind elsewhere. "There are some who have sworn no fealty."

"And where are they? Where are their wives and families?"

Ewan's eyes rested heavily upon her in the dark of the room. "They have fled their homes and are hiding amongst friends or family in secret, hoping, haps, that someone else will stand against Edward."

Their time had run out, then. Their escape from Castle Dunbar four months previously had bought them very little time. Four glorious months of loving her husband and his family, his people. Four months of sharing his bed, his home, without Edward disrupting their lives. But the knowledge that a choice must be made had hung over them like an executioner's axe, ready to fall. And fall it had.

"You...you shouldn't go. Don't pledge your fealty."

Ewan stared, his eyes searching her face. "What of my people? What of my birthright—of our future son's birthright? If the loyalist Scots are on the losing side, we lose all."

Edyth licked the dryness from her lips and pressed Ewan's hands which rested between them. "I know you well, husband," she whispered. "I know your conscience will not allow you to betray the King once you've given your word. And I know your heart demands you stand with freedom."

Ewan nodded. "Tis a choice once made, that cannae be undone."

"Yes. Yes, you're right," she whispered.

She felt him hold his breath; knew his inward battle. After several heartbeats, he stroked her hair and kissed her forehead. "But what of you? Of Cait and my mother? If I make this choice, it would mean change for you as well."

Edyth felt breathless as she imagined what cost this choice, once made, would mean. "As for your mother, I know not, but Cait...she is old enough to marry. Can you find her a husband outside of Edward's reach?"

"Mmph." Ewan's frown was one of thought rather than displeasure. "There is a man my uncle would like us to consider. He's in Nairn and could be a good match for her. Perhaps he will also take you and my mother if the dowry is large enough."

A desperate sound caught in the back of Edyth's throat. "You would...I do not think it wise to separate us."

Immediately his demeanor changed. "Edyth," he warned. Where he had just been at ease, she now felt a tension grow taught between them. "If I choose this course, there will be war. I cannae fight with any hope of victory when I'm worried over your comforts and safety. Yer heart is in the right place, but I willnae allow such. If I am to go against England, I will be in considerable danger."

She shook her head, stubbornly refusing his words. "I need no comforts aside from you, Ewan," she protested. "I will not be parted from you."

She could feel his reluctance in the pull of his body but she could not hold her tongue. "Do you not recall how it was when you left for your death at Dunbar against my better judgement? How well did I bend to your will then?"

She had said the wrong thing. Ewan scoffed and flopped onto his back. Edyth followed, pressing her pliant body against his unyielding one. "Do not separate us," she pleaded. "Our own history is example enough."

Ewan ran a hand over his weary face. He shook his head. "It's unheard of. A man bringing his lady wife to battle. It's.... No. It's too dangerous, Edyth." He sat up then, forcing Edyth to let go of him. "I dinnae wish tae be parted from you, but I also cannae allow ye tae accompany me. A distracted mind will bring death on swift wings."

Edyth worried a corner of the bedclothes. "What shall I do if my visions spell out disaster? I would be a guide for you and your men. How am I to share such knowledge if I am days—weeks—away? You would die, and hundreds more, if I could not get you word in time."

Ewan shrugged. He'd turned his back to her. She wanted to reach out and touch the hills and valleys of his shoulders but restrained herself. "I dinnae ken," he said, his frustration evident. "Are ye so confident that ye'll receive such instruction?"

"You know I cannot say what will come, if at all, but I am unwilling to risk it.

They fell silent. Edyth held her breath. Ewan seemed fixed upon the growing light leaking in from the shutters for a long moment and, after drawing a deep breath, he threw back the coverlet. "I dinnae wish to argue. Tis late, indeed." Edyth watched, feeling helpless, as he pulled on his discarded hose. "I ha' much tae get done today."

Edyth remained silent and unmoving. She worried at what schemes were now taking root in his mind. She imagined she would wake one morning to find he and his brother, and all their fighting men gone. She would find herself carted off against her will to an isle or to the northern-most recluses of Scotland with no word of his welfare as he fought against England.

"You will not keep your own counsel in this, husband." She'd meant it as a statement, but the words fell like a question between them.

He did look at her then, his face limned in the weak morning light. She could not see his eyes well enough to read them, could only see the wave of his hair, a long nose, and the slight curve of lip as he frowned. "Ye think I would steal awa' without word? Do ye think me too great a coward, then, tae speak truth to you?"

She fumbled out of bed with the intent to touch him, to soothe this confusing hurt she had somehow caused, but she found she could not bring herself to touch him, so great was his irritation. "Not out of cowardice, no," she said, "but in the name of keeping me safe."

Ewan eyed her coolly before pulling his liene over his head. "Aye, I've tried that once afore." He spoke the words in the barest of whispers. "Ye didnae obey me then. Would ye honor my wishes now that there is a vow between us?"

He was, of course, referring to her escape from Perth in April. She'd followed him to Dunbar against his wishes. Everything had hinged on that choice. She'd saved him and countless others. They'd married then, in haste, to save her from conspiring men. They had saved *each other* and yet, now.... Something twisted inside of Edyth's belly. An anger that reared up and clutched at her throat.

Ewan's fierce gaze bored into Edyth. "There 'as been truth between us, always. At least from me. I'm no' the one who hides their intent."

Deserved or not, Edyth felt as though she'd been struck. She reeled back, sputtering. "If I...you hold resentment in your heart for this still? I would remind you that if I had obeyed, you and all your men would be dead."

"Aye," said Ewan. He was nodding, his brow wrinkled. "And I'm grateful. Always. I willnae have ye think otherwise. But I am laird, brother, son...and now husband." He pinned her with a look that made her somehow ashamed.

He softened his voice slightly, his eyes losing some of their sharpness. "I will always seek your counsel, Edyth, but I am laird here. Your laird and husband. If I am tae choose this path—the path against Edward—then ye must also play yer part, aye? Ye must honor my desire for ye tae stay well hid and safe. I willnae bring ye tae the battlefield, nor risk your life by leaving ye here where I am no' present. And I will no' have ye plot against me as ye did in Dunbar."

His severe look might have made her shrink in contrition, but she could not. She felt herself bristle instead. "You would have me counsel you in all things, would you not? Where shall I go, Ewan? Of what may I do this day, Husband? If I were more biddable, I might ask you, but I am not a dog, Ewan. I am your *wife*."

He rolled his eyes, clearly annoyed. "Aye, ye are at that." He pointed a long finger at her. "And I'll remind ye that ye promised tae honor and obey me. I would hear the words again, that ye'll keep yer vow."

Edyth crossed her arms to hide her trembling hands. They did not tremble from fear, but from anger. Her face was hot and she knew her cheeks were most likely as red as her hair.

Swallowing her choler, she said: "From where does this venom come, Ewan? Do you say that you wish you had died at Dunbar? That I had left you in the hands of fate?" How had their conversation taken such a volatile turn?

He ran a hand through his hair. She saw his desperate attempt at collecting his unsteady emotions in the shift in his body, in the softening of his brow.

"Ye do ken my mind well, Edyth. Taking up the English yolk would be difficult, indeed, but it's no' just me I'm thinking of. Where I would risk my life tae avoid it, I cannae so easily risk my people, my mother and sister, nor my wife. I need ye tae be...I need tae ken that my wife is with me in all things. I cannot navigate this choice otherwise. And if it be that I do choose England, I would have ye honor that choice."

He grabbed his plaid on his way out the door, flinging the garment over his shoulder, and shut the door heavily behind him, leaving her alone with a riot of emotions.

Edyth sat heavily onto the mattress. What had just happened?

She didn't have long to dwell on these matters, however, for her maid entered then to make her ready for the day. She made a promise to speak to him later, but first she had to see to her own duties.

***

Edyth met Alban, as per their usual, to discuss the coming week's menu. The earthy aroma of dried barley and oats filled her senses as she entered the dry storage room. Alban was using a large barrel as a tabletop, whereon a register was laid.

"How fares the lad?" grumbled Alban in his usual gruff manner, not bothering to look up from his work.

"He lives, but the ague has caught hold of him. I...I mixed some herbs to help but I cannot say...."

"Mmph," replied Alban knowingly. "Aye, twas only a matter o' time."

Edyth pressed her lips together to keep her sharp rebuke from escaping. What he said was true, but in her current state of mind, she didn't want to hear of her failings. "How is inventory coming along?"

She'd insisted that Alban take stock of all their stored goods, as the kitchen hadn't been keeping a strict record. Wanting to contribute as the keep's chatelain, she'd found the kitchen to be the only rusty gear in the otherwise well-oiled machine that was Ruthven Castle, and while Alban admitted the dowager's previous command that he keep stock, he'd not done so with any great detail. Alban had given her a verbal, loose count of food stuffs, drink, and preserved meats, but no receipt.

"Elwick desires payment for the flour he milled Saturday last."

Edyth raised her eyebrow at his dismissal of her question but answered all the same. "As I've stated before, you have my permission to make payments as they are needed, Alban. I only ask that you write all transactions down in the ledger I provided you. I have supplied you with the necessary coin for such matters; you needn't ask for permission for every little purchase."

Alban's bottom teeth, mottled and crowded, bit into his top lip. He sucked his teeth briefly and eyed her in a way that spoke of his displeasure. "Beggin' yer pardon, but I dinnae feel it right to dip my hand intae the master's coffers as I please, no matter as his wife tells me to."

Edyth repressed a sigh and pinched the bridge of her nose. "You have my complete faith, Alban, to handle such matters. Your laird has given me full authority here and I would see it done."

Alban sniffed, his bushy brows contracting over a hooked nose. "As ye've said, Mistress."

"Now, I would like to hear how your inventorying of our stores comes."

Alban opened his mouth to reply but his answer was cut short when a rather dirty kitchen boy rushed into the room, his large eyes filled with panic. "Come quickly, Master Alban! The pigs have broken through their pen and are amongst the neeps!"

Alban uttered a curse and brushed past Edyth with nary a glance.

Still feeling scattered from her argument with Ewan, and her mind distracted by the fate of the injured boy, it was a difficult task, indeed, to focus on the job in front of her. She moved to the back of the room where large barrels were stacked with no outward sign of what was in them. She'd need some help unstacking the casks and labeling each for easy identification.

While Alban probably knew what was in them, she did not, nor when the contents had been harvested. Each item should be rotated by date to ensure nothing spoiled. She sighed, pushing the resident mouser out of her way with her foot. "I suppose you'll be of little help." The cat merely twitched its ears briefly before slinking away.

There was nothing for it. She made her way out of the dry storage room and into the kitchen proper to gather some helpers. "You there," she said, nodding to a boy stacking more firewood into a large basket by the hearth. "And you," to a rather stout girl carrying half a sheep across her shoulders. "Come and help me move some barrels, if you please."

Chapter Six

It was several hours later that Edyth emerged from the storerooms, dusty and tired. The boy nor the girl could read or write, so that job had been left to Edyth, but she made a mental note to start schooling the servants in such pursuits.

She supposed she should ask Ewan first, though, remembering suddenly the conversation they'd had that morning. She frowned slightly as she made her way up the dusty trail toward the orchard. Until their argument, she wouldn't have thought twice about taking charge of such a thing, but now she worried that she'd somehow overstepped an invisible boundary.

Cait was waiting for her in their usual spot. No one, so far as Edyth was aware, knew of their unladylike pursuit. Ewan's words that morning burned brightly in the forefront her mind as she climbed the hill to their secret. *I'm no' the one who hides intent.* Guilt suffused her; each step she took closer to her good sister filled her with more shame.

Cait had begged Edyth to teach her what she knew about swordplay, who had been tutored in the sport by her father. Sonless, Edyth's father had tutored her in all the subjects he prized. He had, that is, until her mother had put a stop to it two years ago. While Ewan thought it humorous that his wife had been trained in such a manly sport, she doubted if he would find much humor in his sister learning such things. Especially so that it was done in secret.

Edyth crested the hill and wound her way through the apple trees, looking over her shoulder once to confirm she was unwatched. She heard Cait before she saw her, could hear the huffing pants of her effort and the shuffling of grasses at her footfalls. The clearing they'd chosen was near the center of the parcel, where the tallest of the trees had grown in a way that would allow for their ease of movement.

Cait had her skirts tied up to keep her legs unencumbered, a dull short sword in her hand. She was practicing the oberhau: the strike from above, with her legs split apart, her hips square to her imaginary opponent. Her left leg was scandalously exposed to the view of any who might happen upon them. Pride and remorse battled within her breast as she entered the sanctuary the boughs provided.

"Yer late," said Cait, eyes still trained on her invisible adversary. Her shift forward onto her leading leg and the execution of her swing had improved greatly.

"The pas-d'ane is in want of a finger," replied Edyth.

Cait, flushed with her movements, corrected her grip, and swung the sword in a great arch, eliciting the pleasing whistle as it cut the air. "What's kept you?"

When Edyth did not answer, Cait lowered her sword and finally set eyes upon her. "What has happened?" she asked.

Were her emotions so easy to read? Edyth shrugged and simply said, "Your brother and I have quarreled."

Cait's soft smile and knowing glance did not lighten Edyth's heart. "Speak peace to me, Cait. I'm in want of a friend."

Cait let her sword arm drop to her side. "It was bound to happen. He's got the brains o' a mule. Is that comfort enough, sister?"

Edyth could only respond with a breathy laugh before taking up her own sword, which was set amongst the branches of a nearby tree. She moved to stand apart from Cait and took up her stance opposite. Cait, ever eager, regained her footing and thrust forward, her sword cutting toward the vulnerable joining of neck and shoulder. It was easily blocked.

Edyth felt some of her balance return as she moved into a moulinet, causing Cait to retreat. She pushed again, again, Cait avoiding each blow with only a little effort. She was getting better. Edyth could now use more force in her advances and still be checked by Cait's parries.

"Good," said Edyth, dropping the point of her sword. She moved back to the center of the small clearing. "Again."

Cait took her place and readied her feet. "Of what did ye quarrel?"

Edyth swung first, aiming for Cait's midline, but her opponent had been ready. Cait blocked the strike, readjusted her footing, and drove Edyth back with a blow aimed to remove her head from her shoulders.

"Balance," chided Edyth, as the weight of the sword pulled Cait's feet forward. "Again."

Cait complied, shaking her head in an effort to dislodge errant strands of hair from her lashes.

"I'm having dreams again."

Cait's sword tip faltered. "Are you?" It was the look of concern upon her pretty face that brought the tears to the backs of her eyes. Edyth cleared her throat and swallowed them away. It was silly to cry over such a confession.

"What have you seen?"

Readjusting her grip on the hilt of her weapon, Edyth held the sword as she would a bird, gentle yet firmly steady. "I cannot see who is doing battle, but blood is being spilt." She shrugged, feeling over-tired and emotional. She swallowed them away and motioned for Cait to raise her sword.

Cait drove forward, this time holding her balance as she attacked. Edyth pivoted away and hit Cait on the arm with the flat of her blade.

Grumbling, Cait moved back to the center of the clearing. "Your lines are good," said Edyth, "but you must be mindful of your footing. Be ready for my counterattack, always. Do not root yourself to the spot.

Cait nodded but did not raise her sword. "Why should a dream result in a quarrel? Does Ewan not believe them to be of import?"

Edyth shook her head, the desperate feelings she'd been trying to ignore all day clawing their way to the surface. "He does not doubt my sight. It's something else. I do not understand why we quarreled." At Cait's insistence, she told her of their conversation that morning.

"He must choose his course," finished Edyth, feeling miserable. She wondered what he was doing at that moment. Mayhap if she found him in his study, she could remove the invisible wedge she'd driven between them.

Cait smiled slightly. "He will choose Scotland."

"This a battle between his heart and his mind and not easily won. It is rational to choose England," said Edyth simply. "But if his heart wins this battle and he chooses Scotland, he would hide me away when I would stay by his side."

Cait's eyebrows rose in surprise. "As he should. We are ladies, Edyth, no matter how well we might play at being men." She gestured with her sword hand to encompass the clearing.

Cait was the very embodiment of Woman. Where Edyth was lanky, Cait was lush. Where Edyth was spotted with sunshine, Cait's skin was cream. Too tall for a woman, too broad in shoulder, Edyth felt always set apart as a spectacle.

Cait, on the other hand, was curves and softness. Elegance and beauty. Edyth thought herself pretty to a point, and Ewan's worshipful whispers in the dark strengthened these feelings within herself, but standing here, next to Cait, Edyth felt wanting.

"He would be unhappy with our game," admitted Edyth, scattering her unwelcome thoughts. It was a pointless confession because Cait knew her brother just as well as she did herself, which is why they were holed away in the orchard.

And why, until this moment, they had not spoken it aloud. Edyth eyed her sword sadly. "Perhaps my father is to blame, with his tutelage and his doting, but I cannot seem to find room within me to play the meek wife."

Cait's laugh bubbled from her. "No. I daresay ye cannae, but Ewan could no' love a passive wife."

Edyth's mouth tugged into an almost smile. While she did not wish to upset him, nor did she desire to sit and wait for an indeterminable amount of time to get the news of her husband's victory or of his death. Especially if she could prevent it in some way.

"Why must women have the hardest of tasks, always?"

Cait put an arm around Edyth's shoulders and turned toward the keep, her sword dangling toward the ground. "Because we are the sturdier of the sexes, Sister. We are made tae bend under our loads, where men, if they were taxed in the same way, they would break."

"Mmph." Edyth lifted her dull sword in front of them, the sun glinting off the edge. "I fear we must put our weapons away, Cait. I shouldn't have agreed to tutor you without your brother's consent."

Cait frowned. "I hate asking permission for things that should, by rights, be mine. Why is it I cannae be trained with a sword? Yer faither taught ye."

"Only in secret for the first two years. When my mother learned of what he was teaching me, she put a stop to it."

"I'm no' quite ready tae let our secret lessons come tae an end just yet. If we cannae continue swordplay, then let me play master and you student. Let me teach ye tae swim." Edyth grimaced at the thought of conquering that fear but said nothing.

When they made it to the baily with their swords in hand, they drew some strange looks from the guards, but Cait—always a quick thinker—handed their "found swords" off to the first page they spotted near the stables, commanding the weapons be returned to the armorer for sharpening and oiling.

Edyth squeezed Cait's hand as they parted and made her way to her garden. Her heart wasn't in it, however, so after only a short time pulling weeds from between leafy herbs and pulling off seed pods, she stood and, as though compelled, searched out Ewan.

She found him the lists with Iain, practicing at war. It made her heart swell to aching as she watched his graceful, powerful sword strokes from where she stood under the covered walkway, which was littered with padded tunics, leather armor, and neatly stacked weapons. Their skill made hers and Cait's attempts at swordplay look childish in comparison.

Ewan was beautifully made, with long legs and arms corded with muscle. His curling, russet hair was darkened with sweat, his blue eyes fierce as he fought against his brother. Dust billowed around their legs as they advanced and retreated, dodging and thrusting with expert precision.

"Ye cannae do it, Ewan," panted Iain as he reset his feet. Ewan charged so quickly Iain barely had time to block the blow. They grunted and pushed against each other until Ewan shifted his balance and spun on his heel, effectively putting distance between them but keeping his sword between them.

Ewan grunted a reply Edyth could not hear, dropping his sword and returning to his spot across from his brother. He ran his forearm across his brow, pushing aside sweat-drenched locks of hair, his breast heaving from exertion.

Iain was looking at his brother as though he'd sprouted wings. "This is our land. You gamble with more than your life, Brother. Do this, and you put those in your keeping in peril."

Edyth's unease intensified. Gone was the usual teasing banter that pervaded every conversation between brothers. She'd never seen them quarrel before.

"It's them I'm thinking of," retorted Ewan. Edyth could not see his face, turned away from her as he was, but she didn't need to see him to know he was very angry indeed.

Iain scoffed. "What of yer people, *Laird*? Can ye so easily forsake Perthshire to that damnable king?" Edyth's mouth fell open in surprise and quiet indignation. Could it be that Iain wanted Ewan to choose England?

Ewan's shoulders tensed as he brought his sword up and threw it across the yard with a shout that raised the fine hairs on Edyth's arms; the woosh of the sword as it cut the air and the dull clang as it struck the earth punctuated his unspoken fury.

"What would you have me do?" cried Ewan. Edyth braced to run, to intervene, to keep the peace between brothers, but stopped herself. Ewan would not thank her for interrupting. Besides, what could she say?

"If I pledge fealty to England," continued Ewan, his voice a rasp, "we will keep Perthshire. Aye, it will be ours. The keep, the lands...it will all remain in Ruthven hands. But what will we gain, Brother? Edward's sheriffs will take up residence here. Do ye ken what his sheriffs have done in Haddington? They despoil newly married maidens...plant their English seed in their bellies right before their husband's eyes. They say it's their right tae do so. Would ye have me invite them into Perth? Would ye have me bow to the English king to keep our scraps?"

Iain's face drained of color. "What do ye think will happen tae our Cait...or Edyth, once you've snubbed such a king, Ewan? I dinane want tae be an English subject no more than you, but if that's how he treats his vassals, imagine what he'll do tae his enemies!" Iain took steps forward and planted a hand on his brother's unyielding shoulder. "If ye dinnae swear fealty, then Perthshire is abandoned tae Edward's man, a new lord...and the sheriffs will still come."

Ewan brushed off his brother's hand and turned toward the walkway where Edyth was hidden. "If I fight for Scotia, then we can have all," he said over his shoulder.

"Only if you win!"

Edyth did not wait for Ewan to discover her eavesdropping, but slipped away in the lengthening shadows to the keep.

***

Ewan's father, Malcolm, was entombed under the kirk alongside his sire and grandsire. Dozens of other family members were interred there, keeping silent company. Their white linen wrappings glowed like moons in the low light.

The torchlight sputtered on the iron ring overhead, casting the stonework with dancing shadows. Ewan ran a hand along the cool edge of the stone, wishing he could speak to his father in truth. Edyth had spoken to her father in a dream when she'd needed him most just a few months prior. How he wished to have that ability himself.

If nothing else, the solitude in the cold under the earth had at least cooled his temper, if not provided him with the answers he sought. The truth was that Ewan didn't know which choice to make. While he did not want to pledge fealty to Edward, it might be the best course of action for his people.

Iain was right: Edward was a formidable enemy. It would be best to have him as an ally or be dead. But the thought of pledging his life—and all his men's lives—to such a man was like a thorn in his heart.

"What would you have me do, Father?" The whispered question hung in the thick, musty air. "I would hear yer counsel." Ewan sighed and ran a hand through his hair. He'd missed the evening meal. He hadn't been hungry at the time, being too agitated, nor had he been fit for company. And if he were completely honest with himself, he'd taken the coward's way out and had come down here to avoid Edyth.

He'd been too harsh with her this morning, perhaps. While he wasn't sorry that she'd taken matters into her own hands and followed him into Dunbar, he didn't know if he could trust her to do as she was bid, even if her own life depended on it. She was a damn stubborn, willful woman, but she was also smart and canny, and he'd be a fool to discount her advice—or her intermittent visions.

Ewan looked around him, at the lairds that had come before him, now at rest. They'd had difficult choices to make in their own times. They'd somehow navigated the rough waters that they'd found themselves upon and had survived.

He would, too, he supposed. The thought was comforting in a way. But would they wish him to keep their lands and titles at the cost of their people's freedoms and way of life? When he thought of his people surrounded by Edward's sheriffs, their laws forced upon them—and his hands tied—it made his blood boil.

"Speak peace to me," he whispered to the still air.

He turned abruptly to a sound on the stairs. It was Edyth, come to make reparations, no doubt. His heart filled with love and pride at the sight of her, despite his earlier frustration with her.

She paused on the last step, looking small and unsure.

"Come," he said, and then she was rushing into his arms.

"I'm sorry," she said against his chest. He kissed her sunny hair and stroked the lines of her shoulders and back.

"I'm sorry, too," he said. How simple it was. He'd tortured himself all the day with what he might say to her and held his anger tightly to him like a talisman. But he could not hold it any longer.

Indeed, he realized now that it wasn't Edyth he was angry with. It was the weight of the choice laid before him and the danger encompassing them, regardless of which road he led them down.

"You didn't come to supper and I worried."

"Aye." He laid his cheek against the softness of her hair, feeling foolish now for avoiding her. "I was too harried tae eat. I came down tae talk a spell with my betters."

Edyth pulled away and looked around them, her hands on his waist. When her eyes rested on the stone holding his father, understanding lighted in her sad eyes. "What counsel does he offer?"

Ewan shrugged and smiled regrettably. "I dinnae possess the talent tae speak tae the departed as ye do, lass. If he has given me counsel, I am deaf tae it.

Edyth moved to the carved stone coffin with a likeness of his father. "He was handsome," she said, running a light finger along a cold cheek. "I see him in you."

He said nothing as her eyes took in the details of his father's stone likeness. "I think you're wrong," she said after what felt like a long time. Her voice was a whisper in the dead air. She turned to him then, her eyes shining. "I have not met him, but I know he has counseled you, just as my own father has counseled me. They do not leave us, Ewan. Death does not sever their influence upon us."

She took his hand and placed it upon the stone sarcophagus and bid him to close his eyes. "Imagine him here. Hold him in your mind's eye; say nothing. Only see him."

Ewan bit his lip with uncertainty, feeling only foolish, but after a time his nerves settled and his mind quieted enough to conjure an image of his father. Deep chested and wide in shoulder, his rich, brown hair had been kept long, touching his shoulders. It was swept with lines of gray at his temples, as it had been the last time Ewan had seen him.

His hazel eyes were direct and sharp, his jaw strong as he gazed upon his eldest son. Something in Ewan's chest tightened. There was no disappointment or censure in the lines of his face. Only pride. Something like relief softened the joints of his bones and, at the same instant, tightened his throat. He cleared the obstruction away and opened his eyes to find his wife smiling knowingly up at him.

"Of what does he communicate?"

Ewan could not speak right away. The dust in the air was irritating his eyes and throat. "I think he...I felt only his pride for me."

Edyth's smile widened and she squeezed his hand. "Yes, he has much to be proud of. Come, I've saved you some food."

Chapter Seven

Cait was a reasonable woman, despite her brother's insistence to the contrary. Just because she didn't want to marry some obscure nobleman in the far north of Scotland—far removed from family—didn't excuse their name calling.

"William Cawdor is a good match for ye," sighed Ewan, the eldest of her brothers. His curly hair was mussed up from all the times he'd run his hands through it in frustration. "He's to be the second Thane of Cawdor...and Nairn isnae so far away as all that. Ye act like we'd be sending ye tae yer death."

"Oh, aye? Tell me Ewan, how well did ye like him last ye met? Ye must have, tae say he'd make a good match for yer baby sister."

Ewan growled. Actually growled. She felt a spike of pleasure at his frustration. "Ye ken well enough I've no' met the man, so quit yer bleating, woman."

"Nairn *is* far, Ewan" she countered, her chin thrust out defiantly. "And I've ne'r heard of him."

"Oh, aye, if *ye* havenae heard o' him then I suppose he must be unacceptable." The roll of his eyes made Cait want to slap him but she curled her fingers instead, feeling the bite of her nails in the sensitive skin of her palms.

"Da said that I'd have a say, and I say '*no*.'"

Iain, her older brother by three years, snorted loudly. "Regardless o' yer feelings, and what Da might have said, it's not yer place to choose, Cait. It will be up tae Ewan. Uncle Niael has been kind—"

"More like he's been a meddling scut, to my mind," spat Cait, arms crossed over her chest. She glared at her brothers in turn.

"Da spoilt ye, Cait," said Iain, shaking his head mournfully.

"Is there some man ye have in mind, then? Someone ye're doe-eyed over?" asked Ewan, a suspicious look in his eyes.

"No," spat Cait, trying not to sulk. There was no man she felt met her—perhaps unrealistic—expectations. Ludan Lindsay had shown interest, but her Da had turned him away at her behest. In fact, several families had shown an interest in aligning with their clan through a marriage contract, but her doting father had said she was too young, or the terms not to his liking, or he'd simply never answered their proposals.

She was the baby, after all, and though it was never vocalized, everyone knew she had been his favorite. There was Alec, but while she enjoyed his company, he was not marrying material.

But now her father was gone and she wasn't so young as she had once been. Her brothers—and even her Uncle Niael—were involved now. Apparently seventeen was past time to find her a husband.

"Can we no' wait?" she pleaded, trying a different tactic. "Edyth is older than I am and you two married only these past few months. Can I no' wait until I'm a bit older? Please?"

Ewan moved in front of her chair, half sitting on the table so that he was very close. His eyes softened slightly as he looked down upon her, a good indication he could see the fear she was desperately trying to hide.

He put a light hand on her shoulder. "While I dinnae ken what it's like tae be a lass, I do ken something about shouldering the burden of the unknown. We would no' bind ye tae a man who would mistreat ye, Cait, but nor will we leave yer future unplanned and insecure."

Cait bit the inside of her lip, feeling awash in anger and defeat. "But...but I dinnae wish tae—"

"Aye, we ken well enough ye dinnae wish tae marry him," interrupted Iain, exasperated. "Or anyone else for that matter. Ye've told us already. Several times."

"He's accepted our terms, Cait. It's done."

Cait felt like crying, which annoyed her. Huffing, she stood and, giving her brothers her most caustic glare, said, "Then *you* marry him if ye like him so well. I'll not!"

"You will," promised Ewan, his voice reaching the low, dangerous tones that warned her he'd finally run out of patience. "And sooner than ye think."

Cait swallowed the scream of frustration that clawed at her throat and inhaled through her nose. When she felt she could speak, she said, "I seem tae remember ye being none too chuffed about the match they wanted tae make between you and the Stewart lass. If I recall aright, ye told Mother ye werenae ready and tae hold off her scheming. And look what waiting did for ye, brother: ye marrit an English lass of all people. For love!"

Ewan pinched the bridge of his nose, his eyes screwed shut. "Caitriona, ye may no' wish tae be wed yet, but there is good reason tae have ye wed tae the man, and well away from Perth. We have no lands, sister. They are forfeit. Gone. Unless I pledge fealty to the English King, we have nothing." He looked at her then with his steely eyes challenging her. "Ye'll marry the man fer yer safety and for my own peace of mind."

The air caught in Cait's throat and she looked at her brother's grave, stubborn face. Was that fear she saw behind his eyes? Her brother, whom she had never seen balk at a challenge? Ewan, who had stoically gone to his death despite what his witch of a wife had told him was sure to happen.

She bit her lip, fear threatening to overtake her anger. "For *yer* peace of mind," she muttered, looking at a dark knot in the floorboard. She could *feel* Ewan's roll of eyes at her pouting. She tried a different tactic: "What of mother and Edyth then? They will still be here, in harm's way. What is one more soul to anguish over, Brother? Grant me your leave tae stay here with my family."

"Are ye no' listenin' tae the man?" complained Iain. "Forget about yer wishes and think for one damned minute. Mam isnae staying here either. After ye're wed tae the Thane, Mam will stay with Uncle Niael, where his lands and protections are greater than what we can provide."

At this Cait's mouth fell open unbecomingly and she could only take it in turns to stare at her brothers.

"He's right," said Ewan, pushing off from where he was still perched atop his desk. He moved behind it and shuffled through papers until he found what he was looking for. He barely glanced at it and handed it to her. While she wasn't as talented as he was with letters, she knew enough to recognize her uncle's name with a glance.

"Wh—what does it say?" she asked on a swallow.

"It says that all the arrangements have been made. All that remains is my agreement, which I will give him in a return letter. William has accepted the terms and we are tae travel there next month, where ye'll be wed. Mam will stay on, under her brother's charge, until things settle politically."

Everything had been taken care of, wrapped up nicely; not even her hardened heart could deter what was to come. Her eyes stung with suppressed emotion.

"What happened to the lass unafraid of a challenge, eh?" chided Iain, clearly uncomfortable with seeing her misted eyes. It was a rare thing, indeed, for Cait to cry. "Who was it that was first to jump off the high cliff into the loch?"

"Me," mumbled Cait, digging her toe into the uneven floorboards.

"And who was it that climbed the tall beech near the dovecote to the very top?"

Cait scoffed. "Ye ken it was me, ye daft fool, but marriage demands more bravery than I have. I cannae marry a man I dinnae ken." She was proud her voice did not waiver.

"Ye'll ken him soon enough," said Ewan. Cait pressed her lips together. She'd never done well with defeat. It went against her better nature. "By this time next month, we'll be heading west."

"To a new life," supplied Iain with forced cheer. "Surrounded by the inexperienced...think of all you can do to vex your new husband and his household. Your tricks are poorly spent on us, experts that we are after all these years."

Ewan smirked at his brother, then leveled his gaze on Cait. "Och, aye. The poor sod will ne'r know what hit him."

"And here he's thinking he's getting a meek, biddable bride!" laughed Iain good naturedly, though he sobered when Cait did not smile. "Take heart, Sister," he added, his smile turning rueful. He stood and put a comforting arm around her shoulders. "I very much doubt there's room for either of us to choose our lot in life. We, unlike Ewan, must take on the role of respectable progeny."

Cait sniffed irritably. "How nice that ye can laugh and make sport of my discomfort. I grow weary," she added with a sigh, wishing heartily to be alone. She brushed hair from her brow and said, too tearfully for her liking, "If you will not take pity on my plight and hear my pleas, then I have nothing more to say."

She turned on her heel and left her brothers, not willing to look them in the eye lest she lose all composure. She went straight to her rooms, too morose to play games in the solar or pretend interest in any sort of intercourse.

Chapter Eight

The walk down to the village was not long enough, thought Edyth, as she crossed over the bridge into the town square. The simple fact of the matter was that she could walk from here to York and still find herself wishing for more miles. Each time that she made the trip—herbs and freshly rent linens for bandaging in her basket—she found her feet slowing as her heart grew heavier in her breast.

While Eachann's bleeding had slowed near to nothing, and the skin puckering at the end of his arm was healing, the boy's fever had increased. She was, quite simply, scared to walk into his home to find that he had died in the night. Even at the thought, her breath hitched in her throat.

Would his parents blame her? Would they call her a meddling witch? She could not know. All she could do was pray and continue applying the healing herbs her mother had taught her. And then there was the difficult truth that even if he lived, his life would be forever changed. What kind of life could he have with only one arm?

She ignored the pedestrian who hurriedly passed her on the road, but was so distracted in her thoughts that she didn't feel the usual pang of dejection as they crossed themselves. She'd dreamed again last night. Not the same dream, but a nightmare all the same. *It's because you're worried about Eachann*, she told herself. Haps the new poultice she'd made would help, then she would sleep more soundly.

At least she hadn't awoken Ewan with the nightmare this time, but she'd awoken with a sudden jerk, her heart pounding. She could not explain the feeling that had overcome her, but it had been as though the shadow that had formed around her, had settled within her breast, heavy and oppressive.

Edyth closed her eyes briefly, lifting her face to the sun as she tried to recall all she'd seen. There had been a cloud, as she'd dreamed before, but this had been different. There was a disembodied sobbing, muffled at first, but growing in intensity until the weeping reverberated in her brain. She'd looked at her hands, which were slicked red with blood, the metalic tang sharp in her nose. And with the realization that her hands were covered in gore, came a cutting grief so sharp that made it difficult to breathe.

Edyth opened her eyes in an effort to remove the image from her mind—to take in the dappled sunlight through the trees. The mottled rays painted the hard-packed earth with a dozen different hues of gold.

It was a beautiful day, and welcome, but she only felt cold. Edyth took a deep breath as though doing so would break the invisible vice around her heart. No amount of sunshine or birdsong could lift the heaviness in heart, it seemed, adding to the hopeless feeling that had settled like a stone in the pit of her belly. *Did the blood on her hands in her dream belong to Eachann?*

"Do not give up hope," she muttered to herself as her feet found the bridge into the village square. Eachann hadn't yet succumbed to his injury and she would hold out hope for as long as he breathed.

The village square was densely packed, with carts surrounding the communal well at its center. Animals, driven by their tenders, bleated and squawked as they moved around the bustling activity of the day. Buildings were close here, at the center, leaning into each other as though sharing gossip. Edyth nodded politely at people as she passed them, some of which actually nodded in greeting. Haps her frequent visits in the village were having a positive effect after all.

Edyth's heart felt a little lighter as she arrived at her destination. The carpenter's home —sizeable and in good repair—was advertised with a sign of an hammer and a chisel above the door. Before she could knock, the door opened, revealing the priest, Father Thale, who appeared to have been just leaving.

The priest's eyes registered no surprise at seeing her; she could detect no malice in his gaze, but still, she could feel herself shrink from him. Having been defamed and unlawfully accused of heresy and witchcraft by her childhood priest back in England, she was now leery of all church men. Despite having been tried in Yorkshire for the crimes and being found innocent, Edyth knew people still questioned her innocence. Bowing her head, she stepped away from the stoop to make way for his exit, but he did not move.

"Mistress," Father Thale said in greeting, his bronzed face unreadable in the shadow of the doorframe. "I'd hoped that I might see ye this morning. How fortuitous that we should meet just now. Please come in."

Edyth swallowed nervously and stepped into the dim light of the house. Edyth loved the cozy space, full of the wood shavings and the spicy aroma that they generated. The vice around her heart loosened slightly at seeing no mourners present, no anguished cries that might befit the boy's death. The sight of the priest at the house had worried her.

A woman bustled in from a back room, her arms full of laundered linens. Edyth smiled shyly at the woman, nodding her head in greeting, but the woman did not return the smile. In fact, upon seeing her there, the woman turned on her heel and retreated back to where she'd come from.

Villagers had taken it in turns to fill the wood box, scour dishes, prepare meals, care for Eachann's siblings, and generally tidy up for the family. Edyth had loved seeing the outpouring of support from the clan members, but there only seemed to be so much to go around, as no good will seemed left for her.

Eachann and his mother, Deòridh, would no doubt be in the back bedroom, where she tended to him day and night. Thus it had been each time Edyth had come calling. A neighbor in the kitchen, the other children seeing to their chores, and Deòridh holed away in the back room with her ailing son.

The priest was as tall as she was, so it was quite an easy thing to see the slight pinch of his brows, the thinning of his lips, as he motioned them to a quiet corner less encumbered with lumber and half completed projects. She set her basket atop a rough-hewn table and looked at the priest expectantly.

"I fear that the child's fever grows. I have prayed for his soul, but..." he paused here, his sunken cheeks pinkening slightly. "I fear the end is soon at hand."

Edyth's shoulders slumped on an exhale. It wasn't unexpected news, but still, her heart had hoped. "Thank you for telling me," she muttered. "I will do my best to keep him comfortable until...until the time comes."

"There's a small matter," whispered the priest, looking uncomfortable. He leaned closer to her, so as to keep his voice from traveling beyond their private corner. "His parents—they've asked for me to tell ye that they no longer.... That is, they wish for me tae say that yer services are no longer required."

"Why?" asked Edyth, dreading the answer. "I've done nothing wrong."

"No, no, my dear. No one has accused you, but there is the matter of your, erm, *unusual* potions. They fear for his soul and wish it to remain pure until he passes from this mortal realm."

Edyth's confusion turned to anger in an instant. "Unusual potions?" she hissed. "What is so unusual about tincture and vinegar?"

The priest straightened, his resolve growing, and said: "It is not a question of the tincture, but of the application. Surely you can see their hesitance. It is well known who you are—" At Edyth's raised brow, the priest hastily added, "These are superstitious people, Mistress. If they hear whispers of your *past*, no matter how embellished, their fear will control their better sensibilities. You mustn't take offense."

Well, she did take offense. Hurt and angry, she dug through her basket until her hands found the crock of medicine she'd freshly brewed last night. Thrusting it into the priest's hands, she swept around him, and stalked to the door. Quickly stepping out, she turned just long enough to spy the discomfited priest over her shoulder. "Haps if you're the one to smear it on, his soul won't be tainted. Good day to you!"

Chapter Nine

Two weeks later Ewan found himself at Berwick-Upon-Tweed, overlooking the seaport city. It did not look as though it had been ravaged—that more than ten thousand souls had perished within its walls—from this distance, but with the passage of time, all things are changed. It had happened only six months ago, which was enough time to rid themselves of the dead, at least.

He did not want to be here. Every step of the nearly one-hundred-mile journey that took him here had been anguished. The glen that spread before him was a sea of tents and milling English soldiers outside of the city walls. The meeting would take place in the garrison, but the Scots who'd come to give their lives to the King of England would tarry here, in their tents without the walls.

Ewan's eyes scanned the tents. Among them were the brightly colored ensigns of the noble sons of Scotland, heralding their stations as they waited their turn to die. Perhaps not their physical death, no, but it was a death all the same. How fitting that the clans would be withheld from the city, while the King and his army enjoyed its comforts.

Ever since the Scots had conceded Castle Dunbar a few months prior, the English king had been parading through his newly won land, his retainers unchecked. Villages had been sacked, the men cut down, animals slaughtered or stolen, and the women violated. Left to fend for themselves, with no food or men to protect them, the villagers would no doubt starve or succumb to the elements.

And here were Scotland's free nobles, come to lick the boots of the bastard responsible. Longshanks had seized their lands, on account of their rebellion, and demanded that they assemble together to pledge their fealty to him. Only then would the lands that belonged to them, lands they had fostered and nurtured for generations, be theirs once more.

Sitting atop his destrier, Ewan squinted against the slanting rays of sunlight. The summer sun was still high and hot on his back, aggravating his already sour mood. Wiping sweat from his eyes, he bit back a curse and gritted his teeth. He couldn't hate his peers, though he wished he could. They were simply doing what they thought best, just as he was. But with each step that led them closer to the English king, his self-loathing increased.

Furthermore, it was impossible to tell whom among his peers was with Edward in heart from those who, like him, belonged only to Scotia. And none else. His wame curdled at the thought of what he was about to do, all in the name of keeping his family safe.

Iain, Ewan's brother, squinted at the sea of tents against the garrison wall. "Perhaps it won't be so bad now that Edward has had his fill of the spoils. Once the ragman roll is signed, perhaps he'll just...go home."

Ewan glanced at his brother briefly and shook his head. "He's already replaced the sheriffs with his own men and his soldiers linger in the larger towns. There will be new laws forced upon us and his men left behind to ensure they are followed."

Iain's mouth twisted into one of distaste as he looked over the milling crowd below, like so many ants scurrying to grasp whatever spoils were left to them, content with their meager ration. His hazel eyes darted to Ewan, uncertain. "Has, er...has Edyth *seen* anything?"

Ewan inhaled through his nose, considering how much he should divulge. While his wife saw much, she hadn't seen this. She hadn't seen the cost of living. He cleared his throat and shook his head ever so slightly. "She's been dreaming of battles, but...she has no' seen faces she kens."

Iain's face hardened. "Battle with whom?"

Ewan shrugged. "There is no way to know."

"As yet," said Iain. "Perhaps more will be made clear to her in future."

Ewan nudged his horse down the grassy hill. "Come. We dinnae wish to miss anything." He wanted to get this over with as quickly as possible and return home to Perthshire.

As though Iain had read his thoughts, his brother said, "Do you think Edward will assign a sheriff to Perth?"

Ewan urged his horse into a canter, his eyes set upon his kinsmen up ahead. He could see the Ruthven ensign flapping weakly in the breeze, the curly horned ram winking in and out of view. Deid Schaw it read. *Deeds show*. He felt sick at the very thought of what deed he would soon commit by pledging his fealty to England's king. His Norse ancestors would surely turn in their graves if they knew.

"Aye," clipped Ewan. "Aye, I think the bastard will do that and more." With a final thrust of his heel, he urged his horse into a gallop with Iain close behind.

***

"Yes, just outside of Edinburgh. Kincardine O'Neil it's called," said John Comyn. He had come, along with Sir Gilbert Hay and Robert Dundas—Ewan's southern neighbors—to the Ruthven camp. Rob Bruce had come as well, but seeing his rival, John Comyn there, he'd made his excuses and left. Both men having strong claims for the throne of Scotland, and both with large followings from the clans, they had nearly started a civil war.

Ewan scoffed to himself, disgusted. The Scots, it seemed, were hungry for a fight, whether it was with their own, or with the English, it didn't seem to matter which.

"Thomas de Morham's wife said that they burned all the fighting men alive in a croft, then slaughtered their kine and sheep." The Black Comyn ran a hand through his beard, his face burning with righteous anger. He looked as heartsick as Ewan felt. "You can imagine what they did next, with no men left to protect the woman folk."

Iain spat on the ground, muttering a curse. "With her husband locked away after Dunbar, his holdings will be easy pickings for King Edward. I've heard that much the same has transpired in other villages."

The men's eyes roved around the circle, dismayed. "And we've come to pledge our lives and clans to this beast," said Ewan.

"Aye, he is no' a man," agreed Fingal in a voice like gravel. "What's tae do, then? What's the plan?"

"Plan?" asked the Black Comyn, his brows knit together in consternation. "There is no 'plan', man. We go back home and take what's coming with a smile and when the king asks us tae slaughter more o' the Welsh or the French, then we do it and be damned. If we dinnae, then it's our own that will suffer."

Sir Gilbert, who closely resembled death himself, raised a long-boned finger, his skin looking stark white in the firelight. "I fear that our pledge will not stay the hand of the king."

"But," sputtered Fingal indignantly, "if ye cannae gain relief from the slaughter for yer people, what purpose do ye have here?"

"It is my hope," interjected the Black Comyn, "that with my fealty, the English sheriff appointed to my lands will not feel the need to exercise his authority in such a violent way."

The man's acquiescence did not surprise Ewan. The Black Comyn's son had been pierced with English arrows whilst scouting the night before the battle at Dunbar was to take place. And, if rumor proved true, the new sheriff appointed to Comyn lands—Lanark, he thought his name was—was just as vicious as Old Nick himself.

Sir Gilbert's sad eyes seemed to hold some secret knowledge. "Your heart is in the right place, Comyn, but I have known men very much like this English King. Suffering of the innocent will not trouble his sleep."

"We share feelings," said Ewan, staring into the flames. "I dinnae ken if I can follow Edward and appease my conscience."

"Hst." Robert Dundas made a plaintive movement with his hands, craning his neck to look behind and around himself. "Hst. Be canny, lads. And you, just come to kneel before him and kiss his ring." He shot a dark look at Ewan. "This is no' the place to discuss such opinions."

Ewan poked a stick into the fire, sending flaming ash into the air.

"We have little choice left to us now," said Sir Gilbert gravely. "He has taken Haddington, Lauder and Roxburgh, among others."

"Aye, even Edinburgh dinnae last but the three days against the bastart's siege," said the Black Comyn. How are we, with our villages and hamlets tae hold against such a man?"

Ewan shook his head. It was impossible, and yet there were some who would not yield. "We must band together."

Sir Gilbert scoffed at Ewan's suggestion. "With all of the larger holdings' Lords imprisoned after Dunbar and our lands stripped from us, we are as beggars. Tomorrow we will be pardoned and welcomed back into the fold with a mere wave of the hand." Here he motioned with his skeletal hand as though signing his name. "Even if we, here, were united," he added, "there are just as many, if not more, who are eager to kiss the English ring. No," he said, shaking his head solemnly. "We have no one to lead us nor a vast army to command."

"There are some who would lead," hissed the Comyn.

"You mean yourself?" intoned Sir Gilbert softly, his thin brows raised mockingly. "We have been down this road before." Indeed, it had been the Comyns and the Bruces fight for the crown that had divided Scotland in the first place. When Edward of England was asked to impartially choose, he instead chose John Balliol. Edward easily manipulated Balliol and forced his hand. Before long, Edward had taken Scottish lives, property, and the crown for himself.

No one spoke then, each lost in their own thoughts. Ewan couldn't sit still a moment longer, his wame in knots. He removed himself from the party and took to pacing in the woods round about the camps. He knew he would get no sleep this night, so resigned himself to a long, tired ride back to Perthshire on the morrow.

***

"The amount of shite a king carts around astounds me," grumbled Fingal. Ewan's best archer, Fingal was small and lithe, with a rather long, twitchy nose poking out between curtains of stringy gray hair. "Look at all the tents the fobbing pumpion has."

He gestured to the nearest offending pavilion, rich with ornate chairs, laden with furs, and several large trunks, hiding unseen treasures. There was a costly suit of armor on display there as well, all polished to a lustrous shine. "I counted five in all. Five! What kind o' man needs such comforts?" He scoffed disapprovingly and none too quietly. Several people had taken notice. Ewan could feel their eyes heavy upon them.

Ewan pressed Fingal onward down the aisle between the tents, his hand on the man's sinewy bicep.

"He's a king," grunted Ewan. "No doubt he needs them to keep all the riches he's been lifting off us Scots. There," said Ewan, indicating the hogshead of ale just opened in a crossways up ahead. Men had already started to gather, eager for a drink in the hot summer sun. "Let's drink and find our bearings."

"Mmph." Fingal's frank disapproval deepened in the stark lines on his face. "Did ye hear he's taken the Stone of Destiny from Scone, the mewling fat-kidneyed maggot. Taking it back tae London with him." He narrowed his eyes at the tent they were passing as though it contained Elgin's historic treasure. "As if he owns it!"

Ewan bit back a sigh. "Aye. I heard. There's naught we can do about it, Fingal, and still come away with our heads attached to our necks. Come, let's get some drink before it's gone."

The sun was high and unhindered by clouds. The ale was cool and welcome, but Ewan could not enjoy it. "I dinnae like you having to make yer mark upon the roll, Laird. I dinnae like it a bit," Fingal muttered, his nose in his cup.

Ewan bit back an angry retort and rolled his bad shoulder, which was always tight and aching lately. "Aye, Fingal. I dinnae like it either, but I've little choice left to me now."

A herald's powerful shout broke through his thoughts, his ale barely touched. "Good Sirs of Scotia. It is the King's desire that ye presently assemble together at the gate, where he will deliver his conditions."

"Find Iain and Graham," commanded Ewan quietly, his eyes searching the crowd for familiar faces. "I would have them gather our neighbors together so we can speak afterward. Quietly."

The tent was dark and musty, reeking of sweating bodies. It took a minute for his eyes to adjust to the dim, but once he could see, he had full view of the vacant throne some poor sop had the misfortune of carting around.

There were dozens of landowners there, all summoned to swear allegiance and affix their seals upon the roll. Ewan recognized Robert Bruce, the Lord of Annondale, and his son, by the same name. They were both looking rather surly, speaking to each other quietly.

There was also the Earl of Carrick there, and several of the Comyns, many of whom Ewan had recently drawn swords with in defense of Dunbar Castle. Or he would have done, if it hadn't been for Edyth. Next to the earl was his uncle, Niael Caimbel, whom he hadn't seen since he was nigh on twelve years of age.

Making his way toward them, Ewan had to squeeze carefully between two dour-faced noblemen who seemed intent on ignoring him.

A sudden hush fell over the cramped quarters of the tent as armed guards escorted the English king into the tent at the flap near the back. Edward was tall and straight and still held himself like the warrior he was in days gone by. His auburn hair was streamed with gray, which framed his long face like a curtain.

Fingers adorned with jewels, Edward waved his guards away impatiently as they adjusted the ermine robe about his shoulders.

"My lords," barked King Edward. All whispered conversations ceased; the air was so thick that Ewan found it hard to draw breath. "I am pleased with your choice to attend me."

As if he'd given us any choice.

King Edward's eyes seemed to pierce through armor, bone and sinew to the very heart of each man, so great was his dominance. Ewan held his breath as the king's eyes glanced past him and could only feel relief that the light of recognition did not flare to life at the brief contact.

Edward stood then and motioned to the cleric to his right. A long length of parchment lay upon the little desk where he sat, an elegant feather and ink pot awaiting signatures. The cleric was surrounded by church leaders, each colorful vestments signaling their strength and power. With the church backing the English, it would be folly, indeed, to withstand him.

Edward's booming voice seemed to drill into Ewan's brain. "You have been invited here to pledge your faithfulness as subjects to a united people, under one king and one law. With your homage, you will receive the symbolic titles that acknowledge you as noblemen. Your lands, now forfeit, will be granted back to you once you've sworn your fealty."

Ewan rolled his shoulder, uncomfortable. He could not force his feet forward. His uncle gave him a questioning glance but Ewan did not acknowledge him.

God help him, but he backed his way through the crowd of men and, before he knew it, he was outside the tent. A guard eyed him none too kindly but Ewan ignored him, stumbling away as though he were drunk on ale and not sick with disgust. He couldn't do it. He could not choose England.

"Ewan!" barked his uncle, his long legs eating up the distance between them. He grabbed his bicep and, pulling him close, growled in his ear. "Dinnae play the fool, lad."

Anger surged up in Ewan like a striking snake, but before he could spew his venomous words, his uncle put an arm around his shoulders and walked him a little way away—not far—just to the shade of a nearby tree, far enough to not be overheard. "I ken yer mind, for I feel the same shame, but ye must play this out, *mo mhac*. Ye must sign yer name, or God help ye, ye'll have consigned yerself tae death."

Ewan closed his hands into fists. "Ye ask me tae align myself tae that murdering, greedy...."

"Aye!" spat his uncle, one of his large, warm hands grasping the back of his neck. He was very close. Ewan could see every vein in his blood-shot eyes. Was it from drink or from tears? "I ask ye to live and care fer yer people, as ye might. I ask ye tae bide yer time, Ewan, until we can be a united people."

At that Ewan scoffed; his uncle shook him slightly. "Aye," he spat. "Aye, we can unite, but not this day. There is none who can defend themselves now, with what lords are left signing their lives away and the church choosing Edward. Think, Ewan! All the great men who would take a stand are now imprisoned. Dunbar failed. They are captured. Will ye stand alone against such a man—such an army? There are not enough sons in Perth tae withstand an hour's time against him."

"Then join me, Uncle. The Caimbels are powerful, indeed. Dinnae sign yer name. Come awa' with me and we can plan our defense. There are others. There are more clans who do no' wish tae pledge this day."

His uncle shook his head and let his hand fall from Ewan's body. "And yet they are here, signing even now. They ken, lad. They ken as well as I do. Today is no' the day tae take a stand."

Ewan felt impotent. Powerless. He could not concede! He could not bow to the man who had stolen his country from him. And yet...and yet he knew his uncle was right. His uncle, who had fostered him for so many years, who loved him as a son.

"Do no' put yer neck in a noose, Ewan. Come. Come with me quickly afore it's too late." When Ewan did not immediately obey, he added, "Think, man. Perthshire is no' so small as to be ignored, and no' so far away that he cannae send troops tae take it from ye tomorrow or the next day."

Ewan knew he was right. The English could easily harm his family quickly should he disobey, and he unable to stop it. He took a deep breath and thought of his father. Is this what his father would have done as well? Is this what he would wish Ewan to do? He couldn't know, no matter how desperately he wanted to.

"Now, Ewan," commanded his uncle.

Ewan felt like he could weep if he allowed himself the weakness, but he forced himself forward, back toward the pledging ceremony. "God help me," he whispered.

"Aye," agreed his uncle, taking the lead. "God help us all."

Chapter Ten

The slow moving water of the river was vast and, to her view, perilous. Edyth imagined all the slimy water weeds, sunken boats and logs that hid toothy creatures, and faltered. Some unknown beastie could drag her down into the murky depths of the water and she would be powerless to stop it. "Iain told me a story about kelpies. This river isn't home to such a creature, is it?"

Cait scoffed. "Gotten to ye, has he, the great gomrel? No. If there's kelpies here, they've ne'r shown themselves tae me, and I should have had occasion tae meet one, as often as I've swam and fished here."

Skeptical, Edyth eyed the shoreline with distaste. "He said they're water spirits. Can they not travel from place to place?"

Cait pursed her lips and looked out to the expanse of water. "They might at that," she mused, considering, then shook her head. "They're just stories, Edyth, and besides, if ye happen tae see a water horse, avoiding one is simple enough: dinnae mount it. Ye'll be quite safe. I promise."

Cait stripped down to her chemise and tied the length between her legs just above her knees with a sigh of contentment. It was August and quite hot, despite the higher elevation. "Come now," Cait encouraged. "Dinnae ye wish tae take off all those layers? I feel as free as a bird."

Wading in up to her hips, Cait splashed water on her face. Little rivulets of water soaked through the fine linen of her underclothes and plastered them to her pink skin. Edyth gathered her courage, looking about herself once more to assure they were alone, and stepped out of her skirts. Her bodice and sleeves had already been discarded and lay on a fallen tree just behind.

"There's naught in here but lake trout and water snails," announced Cait, plunging in. Edyth watched, envious of her fearlessness. Her long, dark hair was loose and fanned about her under the water. Her skin looked yellow below the surface, as though the sun shone from within her instead of from high above. Little bubbles rose to the surface of the water, popping noiselessly. Edyth bit her lip. Cait's head broke through the rippling surface, a smile on her face. She stood and Edyth was surprised to see that the water was only to her breasts.

"You won't make me go too deep?" reaffirmed Edyth, knotting her chemise just like Cait had done between her legs. "And you'll stay by me?"

"Och, aye. I'm no' me brothers...I willnae toss ye in, if that's yer worry. We'll start small, with floating, then once ye master that, then we'll worry about moving yer arms and legs."

Edyth gathered her courage and waded into the refreshing water to just past her hips. The pebbles and larger, rounded stones were slippery with green algae, and she quickly lost her balance, falling completely into the water. It enveloped her, covered her as though it would like nothing more than to possess her, and she panicked. Kicking and lurching to her feet, she gasped for breath in a huge, arching spray of water.

Cait's strong hand steadied her elbow and she spoke soft words, much like one might speak to a spooked horse. "There now, Edie. Dinnae ye fash." Edyth waited for her heart to slow and shot Cait an apologetic smile. "Naught will happen tae ye, I promise," soothed Cait. "Let's just wade a wee bit further, so that I can more easily hold ye while ye float on yer back." Being of a similar height, it was easier for Cait if they were further in, so that she didn't have to bend over at the waist. Edyth tried her best to hide her fright and obeyed, her hands shaking.

Cait led her to a spot where the water lapped high upon her waist and the ground was free of larger stones. Something slimy flitted along her left ankle and she shrieked in terror. "Something's touched my leg! It's alive!" Edyth frantically fought to walk back toward the shore, but Cait caught her floating chemise, keeping her in place.

Cait, clearly trying to suppress a laugh, did her best to calm Edyth down. "It's just a wee fish. It willnae hurt ye." Edyth grimaced but gathered her resolve, doing her best to see the hidden creeping things beneath the surface.

"Only fish, you say?" asked Edyth, dubious. "Don't fish have teeth?" Edyth turned her head just in time to see Cait force a smile from her face.

"Aye, but they dinnae care for the English any more than most in these parts," she teased. "You're quite safe. Dinnae ye fash. The key is tae relax. Ye cannae float with yer muscles jumped up and tense, like. Let yer arms and legs go wobbly, as if you're in front o' a warm fire. That's good. Very good. Now, fill yer lungs and lay back. Let yer legs float up."

Despite Cait's hands supporting her back, once Edyth began to sink into the water, she panicked and every muscle in her body tensed. She fought hard to place her feet under her, but Cait was patient. They tried again and again, with little success, and Edyth began to apologize. "Let's try something else," suggested Cait, pulling Edyth closer to the water's edge.

Cait lay down in the water, resting her elbows in the sand and pebbles, her legs spread straight behind. Her bottom bobbed up out of the water, her legs only just submerged. Edyth followed suit and found that if she walked her hands a little further out, she could feel the sensation of floating that Cait had been trying to describe. Her body felt weightless, bobbing and moving with the motion of the ripples. She couldn't help but laugh.

"There, see! Ye *can* do it."

After some time, Cait encouraged Edyth to flip over on her back and try floating that way, but it was still too frightening to her and Cait did not push her. Instead they splashed and talked and Edyth was feeling much better about swimming lessons by the time they were done.

"How is Eachann?" asked Cait, as they walked back up toward the keep, their under clothes clinging damply to them beneath their skirts and bodices. Edyth could only sigh, not wishing to chase away the good feelings she'd just conjured in the river. She could not hide what had happened from Cait and told her what the priest had said.

Cait, as ever, was a good listener and Edyth felt better for her good sister's outrage on her behalf. "Why, those lack wits!" she stormed. "If it weren't for you, he'd have died straight off! And they, consigning him to death with your absence." She shook her head angrily and quickened her pace. Edyth, her feet slipping in her soggy shoes, struggled to keep up.

"Wh...where are you going in such a hurry?" she panted.

Cait turned, walking backwards, and said cheerily, "Well, as you say, if it's *you* that's the problem, then they won't mind *me* doing the witching."

Edyth huffed a laugh and shook her head. "I gave the tincture to the Father Thale. And he did seem sorry for it."

"Not sorry enough for my taste," said Cait, and she turned round once more and marched all the way to the keep with Edyth at her side.

***

Ever since Ewan's return to Perthshire, he had been distracted, which Edyth could well understand. He had come home to Edyth, exhausted and sullen, but determined to move forward and prepare. Perpare for what, she wasn't sure. He spent his days exhausting himself in the lists with his men or holed away in the war room with his captain and his brother. Ewan spent the entirety of their evenings together—which had previously been filled with comfortable companionship wherein they were entertained with stories and games in the great hall—to Ewan's preoccupied mind. He was present only in body, his mind withdrawn from her.

Her own mind was burdened, and Ewan's discomfort only compounded her feeling of unease. So it was that, the next time Cait suggested they return to the river for a swim lesson, Edyth agreed. She needed to clear her mind and focus on something other than her worry over Ewan and her own concern over the villager's perception of her.

This lesson went much better and Edyth was feeling quite proud of herself. She'd floated on her back, first with Cait's helpful arms under her, then on her own. She hadn't even screamed when waterweeds touched her foot. She had stayed close to the shore in the shallows, but she could feel that her confidence had grown.

Beaming, they walked side by side, speaking of everything and nothing at once. Their giddy manner was cut short on the low road coming from the river, however, when a villager, spotting them, ran across the field to meet them.

"Whatever is wrong?" asked Edyth, suspecting the worst upon seeing the stricken look the villager wore. *Eachann.* Edyth braced herself for terrible news. She imagined in her mind's eye being blamed for his death. Her breath came short and she grabbed Cait's wrist when she spotted the terror written on the young girl's face.

She was only of about thirteen. She huffed as she came upon them, holding herself up with her hands on her knees. "Men," she said, panting. "Men…have taken the alehouse…." She stood and held a stitch in her side. "They say…they say they are there…by order of the King. They've hurt Donald and Idina…turned the family out of their own beds."

Cait and Edyth looked at each other, gripped with dread. "What men?" asked Cait urgently, looking through the tree line toward the village, as though she might spy the culprits there, lying in wait in the broom.

The girl shook her head, her blonde hair whipping about her shoulders as she gasped for breath. "Are there guards with you?" asked the girl, looking down the grassy path toward the river that they'd just traversed.

"No," said Edyth guiltily. She'd chosen not to tell Ewan about their excursions lest they send guards with them, which she didn't feel was necessary. She was self-conscious enough as it was about her lack of swimming ability. She didn't need a soldier trailing after them and gawking at her in her wet chemise. "The keep doesn't know we're down here."

The girl looked helplessly up the slope to the keep, looking as though she would cry. "They're giving orders to the villagers even now. Anyone who defies them is beaten. Me Da bade me run to get help."

"We'll help you," promised Cait, but instead of turning uphill, she started off toward the village. Edyth caught her elbow and pulled her back. "Are you mad? We need soldiers! We must tell Ewan."

Cait glanced at Edyth but only hurried toward the woodline, where, on the other side, was the bridge into the center of the town. "Aye, we do, but I'll do what I can until ye can get to the keep. Hurry now, Edie, and fetch Ewan. I'll see what's going on."

Edyth made a desperate sound in the back of her throat. "Go," she commanded the girl. "Tell the men at the gate all you know. I must go with Cait."

"But...but that's dangerous," the girl said needlessly, her red-splotched face turning white to the lips.

"Yes," replied Edyth, already walking away from her. "So you must hurry."

Cait was nearly to the woods by the time Edyth caught up to her, her legs tangled in her wet chemise beneath heavy skirts. "What will you do?" she asked to Cait's back.

Cait spared her a glance before stepping over a rotting log. "I dinnae ken," said Cait, her voice tight. Edyth knew her well enough to see she was scared, but also angry. Very angry. She walked as though a pike was fastened to her spine, her shoulders thrown back, a deep frown on her face. She muttered under her breath, pushing aside branches and forgetting to hold them for Edyth. "I willnae sit idly while some cockered, fen-sucked harpies bully us about," she hissed.

"The girl said they were here by order of the King, Cait," reminded Edyth. "These won't be untested men; they'll kill first and ask questions later!" When Cait ignored her, Edyth pulled on her arm, stopping her. "They will not listen to us. We need soldiers. We need Ewan."

Cait looked through the trees. They could hear the faint sound of raised voices carried to them on the wind. "Aye," agreed Cait reluctantly. "And Ewan will come, but I willane be idle, while villagers are being cut down. If I can help, I will."

The bridge was wide and long, spanning the river's slow moving current. Raised voices could be more easily heard from this vantage and Cait picked up speed. Someone was yelling; there was the sound of steel being pulled from a scabbard, and then a grunt of pain. With their hearts in their throats, they ran between the buildings and turned into the square, where the scene unfolded before them.

Three people lay on the cobbled road, maybe dead, with armored men standing over them, who were gathered before the alehouse as though guarding it from the crowd of people. Some villagers were fleeing. Doors and shutters slammed closed, while a handful of others stood their ground.

"Ye've no right tae this!" shouted one man. *Robin*, Edyth thought his name was. He was tall and thin. A farmer, but strong and fueled with righteous anger. He held his hay fork at the ready, his bearded face screwed up in anger.

"It *is* mine, you reeking puddle of cow piss!" shouted a shorter, thick man standing opposite. The door to the alehouse was open but the man was wider than the door, so she could not see in. She saw that he was bald, his hat having fallen to the ground, and in one beefy hand, he held a short sword. Edyth's fear increased when she saw that the blade was stained red with freshly spilled blood. "I'm taking it in the name of the King!"

"This is the property of the Earl of Perthshire!" shouted Robin. There was an echoing agreement from what men that were left, though they had no weapons. As they neared, Edyth saw a beaten woman, her nose bloodied and an eye swollen into a purple welt, a man, who was stirring, though he had no visible injuries that she could see, and another man, a gash in his thigh. His hands shook as he tried to scoot away on his behind, his pantleg rapidly being soaked with blood. Edyth pushed through the agitated crowd and put her hand on his shoulder. He jerked at her touch, but when he saw who it was, he relaxed.

Edyth quickly tore the hem from her chemise, thinking humorlessly that this was the second of her underclothes that she'd ruined in short order. She tied it tightly over the man's wound, ignoring the hiss of pain he emitted when she tightened the knot.

"Who are they?" asked Edyth quietly, sparing a glance through the legs of the clansmen.

"A sheriff, sent by the English King," he mumbled, "and a mean bastart if I ever saw one."

Edyth opened her mouth to reply but forgot her words when she heard Cait's voice raised above the murmuring crowd. Edyth helped the man to stand and pushed her way back to the front of the gathered crowd where she could better see Cait. Her good sister had stopped short of the bald man, her skirts swishing around her ankles, her face full of disdain.

"Hold! By what authority do you come upon these lands and harass these good people?"

The sheriff, or so Edyth presumed, smirked at Cait, his eyes glittering dangerously. "What do we have here?" he asked, lowering his sword. He boldly stepped closer to her, too close, and Cait stiffened. She held her ground as the man appraised her. He sniffed at Cait rudely, a lecherous smile spreading across his face.

"Haps I was wrong, lads," he announced to his men. Edyth saw there were eight of them, all with the same dark tunic bearing a yellow lion in silhouette, well-muscled and scarred. Some wore chainmail, while others only wore leathers. They stood opposite the crowd with their backs to the building. Edyth had no doubt that they would cut these people down if given the word.

The stout, bald man sneered. "We just might find us some entertainment after all." Here he looked Cait up and down and walked around her in a circle, his tongue smoothing over his front teeth as he considered her with a grunt of approval. "And she's fiery too." He faced her once more and fingered the end of her long, dark braid that hung over her shoulder. "I've heard about Scotswomen. What a delight, to tame this one, eh?"

Cait looked as though she wanted to spit in his face. "We cannae be broken, milord," she warned, "and we bite back."

His lewd smile widened at her words. "Oh, I'm counting on it."

"Ye'll no' touch milady!" warned Robin. He moved forward, his hay fork gripped tightly in his hands. One of the sheriff's men was ready for him, though, and intervened in a whirl of arm and blade. He knocked the fork from Robin's hand, which came to pieces, and then rose his sword arm to swing at Robin's head.

Edyth screamed as the hilt of the sword connected with Robin's brow. At least he hadn't cut him, but Robin had crumpled like a marionette whose strings had been severed and lay motionless on the ground.

She rushed forward to help, but someone from the crowd yanked her back, holding a fistful of her skirts. It was Haverl, a cooper. He shook his head at her in warning. "Himself wouldnae allow it, and nor will I," he said, speaking of her husband. No, Ewan would most definitely not want her anywhere near these men or the trouble they caused, but she couldn't help that now.

Edyth forgot to protest being held when the sheriff grabbed the back of Cait's neck and yanked her forward. The villagers, outraged, yelled in protest. They made to intervene, but were impeded by the sheriff's men's menacing swords pointed at their throats. The sheriff crushed his lips against Cait's mouth and held her there as she fought him, kicking, punching and scratching, her shriek of protest muffled.

He let go only after Cait bit him. He threw her to the ground and spat, wiping the lingering, red spittle from his chin. Edyth thought he would be angry, but he merely chuckled, his eyes dark with excitement. Edyth had been frightened of him before, but now, seeing how his lust ignited so powerfully at another's suffering, made her blood run cold in terror. She must never find herself alone with him.

Suddenly there was a sound of thunder that shook the ground. Edyth felt her knees weaken in relief when she saw her husband and a handful of his men enter the square. Even before Ewan's horse stopped, he had jumped to the ground, his sword pulled from its scabbard. He walked with deadly purpose, followed closely by Iain and Rory, stony faced and radiating menace.

The sheriff's men had moved closer to their master, ready to defend him. The clansmen, nervous of a deadly fight, edged backward. Ewan stooped and lifted Cait by her upper arm, his eye flashing dangerously. "Which of these men touched you?" he asked, his voice darkened with deadly promise.

Cait wiped her mouth. She spat on the ground and held her chin high. "*Mac muc seo, a chanas gu bheil e na dhuine.*" Edyth's Gaelic was very limited, but she understood enough to know that Cait had called the sheriff a pig. Ewan put Cait behind him, who was quickly taken away by Iain. She followed without protest, turning back to glare at de Biggar.

Ewan's eyes swiveled to the man, who smiled unashamedly. The crevices of his teeth were colored red with his own blood. A comrade handed de Biggar a roll of parchment, which he handed off to Ewan. In the quiet of the crowd, Edyth could hear the cold snap of the wax seal being broken and the shuffle of parchment as he unrolled it. Edyth followed his eyes as they traversed down the page, his face growing wan the further he read.

"You see," said the sheriff succinctly. "Unless you'd like your people to suffer, *Laird*, with the English calvary at your gates, you will follow that edict. I have the authority to demand lodging for myself and my men. They need not have been harmed, if they had obeyed."

Ewan's mouth thinned to nothing in obvious displeasure. Edyth could see him thinking behind his eyes, behind his mask of anger. Iain moved forward and took the parchment from Ewan. He scoffed as he read, shaking his head. "It says," he announced to the crowd, "this man, this...*sheriff*, has rights given tae 'im by the King o' England, tae take what is needed, punish whom he sees fit, and ensure compliance to His Majesty's laws."

A ripple of unease ran through the crowd that Edyth was not immune to. Ewan spotted her then, amongst the crowd and he lifted his chin ever so slightly. She shrank deeper into the crowd, knowing what he wished, and came out the back, where she circled around to stand behind his fighting men.

"This edict will be honored, de Biggar," growled Ewan, "only when ye show the proper amount of respect. You are few, and we are many. Remember that. Go home," he said to his clan. "Give these men beds and food, but do nothing more. Stay out of their way. If he oversteps his bounds, you will speak to me for justice." Edyth could not see what happened next, but there was a thud as something heavy hit the ground, and then Ewan was there, tossing her upon his horse. Seated there, she saw that Ewan had somehow cut the sheriff's belt from him so that his scabbard fell to the ground. She wished he hadn't, knowing that the sheriff would retaliate.

From atop his horse, Ewan looked down upon the sheriff and his men, all of whom looked like they'd like nothing more than to run him through. "Step canny, for ye gamble with yer very lives. I will no' abide yer cruelty."

Ewan's arm around Edyth was tight, his breathing harsh in her ear. Once they had crossed the bridge, he demanded to know why she'd been without the walls of the keep without an escort. "And I, with no notion that ye were gone." He was angry with her. She'd frightened him, she realized. She was frightened herself, but she'd never before had reason to be afraid in Perthshire. Until now.

"I was at the river. Cait was teaching me to swim. I...I didn't tell you because I knew you'd send men to watch us and I didn't want a guard to see me in my wet shift." Ewan inhaled sharply. Without seeing him, she knew he was gritting his teeth, something he did when trying to control his temper. "No more swimming lessons, Edyth. Ye'll stay within the walls o' the keep," he commanded. "D'ye hear?" he asked, tightening his hold around her middle.

"Yes, I hear."

"Dinnae disobey me, Edie. That man..." He rolled his injured shoulder as he often did when agitated, but he did not finish his sentence. Instead, he said, "Do no' disobey me, Edyth. I dinnae wish tae punish ye."

She could only nod as he spurred his horse faster, running the remainder of the way to the keep. When they arrived, he did not let her down at the edge of the yard, as he usually did. This time he rode them both into the muddy, manure strewn stable yard and pulled her down from the back of his horse at the building entrance. He led her into the quiet dim of the stalls, his stormy gaze hidden in shadow.

There were a few servants working there, forking hay and oiling leathers, but they quit the place at a quick word from Ewan. "Tell me what happened," he commanded, pacing in front of her. "Leave nothing out."

When she finished relating all that she had witnessed, she said, "There are people hurt, Ewan. They need to be cared for."

"And it's you that's got tae do the tending, aye?"

"Who else," she asked, her arms folded across her middle. Cold from her damp clothes and jittery from the events that had just transpired, she wasn't prepared for his surly mood. "And I'll remind you that I'm not the one you're angry with," she said, only just able to keep her voice even. "I will take an escort. Two...as many as you require but go I must. We cannot show fear," she added at seeing his disapproval. "We cannot disrupt our lives for the sake of this tyrant."

Ewan's frown deepened. "Must ye argue with everything I say?" he chastised. "Nay. I dinnae like it. If they need tending to, they may come here, but ye'll no' be venturing into the village while the sheriff is there."

Edyth agreed with a nod, choosing not to press the issue. She shivered and Ewan pulled her to him, running his hands over her arms and her back to warm her. "Why is it that whenever there's trouble, I find ye in the middle o' it?" he asked miserably.

Edyth could only shrug. "I couldn't let Cait go alone."

"No, I suppose ye couldnae." He kissed the top of her head and then, with a sigh, said, "I need tae marry the lass off, and soon."

Chapter Eleven

Donald and Idina, the brewers who had defended their home from the sheriff and his men did, in fact, come to the keep. They arrived late that same evening at Edyth's insistence to meet with her in the great hall. Rather, they came once Edyth had sent one of Ewan's watchmen to fetch them, and it was a good thing, too, for she doubted very much they would have come of their own volition.

Idina, a stout, sturdy sort of woman, grumbled mightily at Edyth's ministrations. With the application of leeches to her swollen eye, the puffiness was greatly reduced so by the time Edyth had finished with her, she could see out of the extremely bloodshot eye, but she didn't seem very cheerful about it. Or grateful.

All Edyth received for her good works was the woman's gimlet eye and muttering in Gaelic, which she suspected wasn't complementary.

Her husband, Donald, was only suffering from a sore abdomen, after being knocked down and summarily kicked there. Edyth tried to be patient with their grumblings and apparent dislike of her. She had held her tongue when Idina had flinched as she moved to touch her. Nor did she respond to Donald's repeated crossing of himself whilst she inspected his middle, muttering prayers under his breath.

It wasn't enough that Ewan and his family accepted her. The other clans members, while mostly polite, treated her...differently. They were never overtly rude to her, but she couldn't help but notice little oddities. Some would go out of their way to skirt well around her—so as to avoid being close enough to jinx, she supposed—while others would pass her while making the sign of the cross, or the sign of the devil's horns, which was supposed to ward off evil. How, she wasn't sure.

She tried not to let it affect her. She was an outsider, an Englishwoman, after all, and not only that, but she happened to have a rather complicated past. Despite her being found innocent of witchcraft and heresy by the Church only mere months ago, unlike her mother had before her, no one seemed to want to believe it. She sighed inwardly, trying not to let the brewer couple's attitude affect her, hoping that by tending to them—helping them—they would change their opinion of her. Even if it took years, she was willing to be patient and understanding. At least to a degree. Even now, she felt her patience slipping.

"Only eat soft foods, like bread soaked in broth or ale until your stomach heals," she suggested to Donald, who only furrowed his brow at her unpleasantly. He grumbled an incoherent reply, picked up his hat, then quickly whisked his wife away without so much as a "thank you" or a "goodbye".

Edyth sighed forlornly and looked at the swollen leeches in the crockery. "Well, *I'm* grateful, at least," she said to them, before replacing the lid.

"Do they talk back, then?" asked one of the kitchen maids curiously who had come to help her.

Edyth looked up, distracted. "Does who talk back?"

The maid pinkened ever so slightly and picked up the tray from the table. "The gellies," she said, motioning to the little pot Edyth held containing the leeches with her chin. Edyth tried to suppress the grimace on her face. *Great.* All she needed was for people to think she talked to the slimy things.

"Ah, no," replied Edyth, replacing the crock on the tray. "Thank you." Edyth hesitated, feeling foolish for forgetting the girl's name. "I'm sorry. I seem to have forgotten your name."

"No need tae trouble yerself o'er it, mistress. I'm Ceana." She bobbed a curtsey, the tray in her hands steady.

"It's lovely to meet you, Ceana," said Edyth carefully, pronouncing the name as she'd heard it. *Kenna.* She was a lovely girl. Small and demure, with large brown eyes that, for once, did not skitter away in fear.

Edyth smiled at her and when Ceana lingered, asked, "Do you need something?"

"I only.... That is...." Ceana looked around the large room and, spotting other servants cleaning, set the tray back on the table and drew closer to Edyth. She tucked her bottom lip between her teeth before whispering, "I wished tae ask ye for a wee charm is all."

Edyth watched as her eyes darted around the room before the maid sat, leaning forward slightly as though she were about to impart a great secret. "One that might turn the head of someone. Haps help a lad tae take notice o' me?" Her face flushed hotly.

Edyth inhaled slowly and pressed her lips together tightly lest she say something she would later regret. Of course Ceana would ask for a love charm. This girl, like everyone else, thought Edyth some sort of conjure woman. A potion making, spell casting witch. Granted, Edyth thought with an inward frown, she wasn't sure she *wasn't* a witch, but she wasn't what they thought of her.

There were the visions, after all, that she could not account for. And there was that incident at the Battle of Dunbar where she'd distinctly felt some unseen hand guiding her, but *witch*, to her, was far too dangerous of a word. Her mother had died for being labeled as such, so it was no wonder that she, herself, was loathe to claim the title. It didn't matter that Cait had told her being a witch was not bad or evil, but something to be praised and honored.

But a witch would certainly know about love charms, hexes, and jinxes, wouldn't they? All Edyth knew was how to apply healing as she'd been taught by her talented mother. She'd never danced in the full moon nor uttered a single spell. Wasn't that what witches were supposed to do?

Edyth folded her hands on the table and met the girl halfway, leaning forward so that their faces were illuminated by the candle on the table. "Have you tried the *usual* charms?" she asked, her brows raised expectantly. At Ceana's blank look she added, "Haps if you *spoke* to him...spent some time in his company?" The girl looked horrified at the suggestion, shaking her head emphatically.

"Nay. I cannae speak tae 'im, mistress!"

Edyth chose not to point out that if she couldn't even speak to him, she could hardly hope for more. "Haps you could linger where he goes. Say, if he entertains himself with some sport out of doors, you might watch and congratulate him on his abilities. Men can be just as vain creatures as women. He could take notice of you then."

She looked terrified of the prospect. "I could never," she vowed. Looking around the room once more. Finding that they were alone, Ceana continued. "There is more," she whispered, implying some great impropriety. "He is above me in station, mistress. Him to be a knight and I only a servant." She bit her lip again, looking as though she were about to be punished.

Edyth frowned. "There is no reason a young man such as he could not court you. Why, your lord married me with naught to my name. It does happen." Truthfully, Edyth was a nobleman's daughter, so she had been equal to Ewan in station, it was only that she'd had no dowry to entice prospective suitors. Ewan falling in love with her had simply been luck. Or fate.

Ceana's eyes sparked with hope. "Aye? Tis so?"

Edyth nodded. "Haps if you brought him his nooning meal and shared it with him under the trees, or by the river?"

The girl's cheeks pinkened brightly. "He doesnae even ken my name, mistress, and ye wish me tae share a meal with him?"

Edyth suppressed the exasperated smile that tugged at her lips. "That's where you must start then. Introduce yourself."

Ceana did not like that idea, from the look on her round face. "Can ye no' just make me a wee tonic?"

"Like a love potion?" Edyth asked knowingly.

"Aye," she said brightening. "That's it!" Sobering quickly, she lowered her voice once more. "Aye, a love potion."

Edyth pursed her lips and chose her words carefully. "I'm not sure what you've heard, Ceana, but I'm not what you think. I don't know any spells or hexes, and I certainly don't know anything about making love potions."

Ceana looked disappointed. "But...forgive me, mistress," she said hesitantly, "then how is ye came tae be married tae Himself? Alban said that he wouldnae have married such a one as you save for witchcraft. Oh!" She covered her mouth hastily, no doubt fearful of Edyth's reaction to her impropriety. "Dinnae be cross with 'im, mistress. If he kens I said such a thing he'll warm my bum for me."

So, Alban had been spreading rumors about her. She wanted to press Ceana and ask what else he'd been telling her—and heaven knows who else—about her supposed abilities and actions, but decided against it. It would do nothing but anger her and she wasn't so simple minded that she could not imagine what he'd been saying. It was evident in the way people treated her what rumors had been spread. She would have to deal with him later.

"If you want to know how I won your lord's heart, I will tell you." Ceana's eager face loomed on the other side of the candle; the flame was reflected in her brown eyes, making them shine with promise. "Listen well," started Edyth, gaining a willing nod from the girl. "There were no charms applied, other than those womanly arts we've employed since the dawn of time. That is to say," she added at seeing the girl's fallen expression, "I simply spent time with him and, in those hours spent together, he happened to notice that I was a woman." She shrugged here and smiled apologetically at the look on Ceana's face. The girl looked positively morose at the simple truth.

"My advice to you," continued Edyth with as kind of a smile she could muster, "is to contrive a way to be introduced. Spend time with him. Become friends, then see if that esteem grows into more."

"That's asking quite a lot, mistress," she said, looking thoroughly depressed.

Edyth tried not to laugh. "You were brave enough to come ask your mistress for a potion. You're a beautiful girl. He would have to be blind not to take notice of you. And I will help you where I can. What is his name?"

"Would you?" she asked, brightening at the complement and, no doubt, the offer. "I would be most grateful!"

"I am happy to try, and we can always utilize Cait. She is bound to know the lad better than I."

"Oh aye? Och, that's most kind of ye, mistress."

"His name?"

Here Ceana blushed. "Alec. His name is Alec."

Edyth considered the girl for a moment. She knew that name. She'd heard her husband speak of him enough. And she recalled Cait speaking of him as well from time to time. "Do you mean your master's squire?"

Ceana nodded, and looked away, her eye catching on another servant as they neared. "Forgive me, mistress, I've tarried too long." The girl jumped up from the table as though she'd been burned and grabbed her tray. Edyth could only blink after the girl's swishing skirts as she left the hall.

***

The week since de Biggar and his men had arrived in Perth had been surprisingly quiet, though that could have been due to the fact that Edyth hadn't been permitted to leave the keep. And while she understood Ewan's concern, she wasn't used to being cooped up. Not only was she restricted to the grounds, but she felt blind to all happenings and could only gauge goings on through what Ewan told her and what Cait overheard whilst unashamedly eavesdropping at doors.

But Ewan had said there had been no further complaints from his people save for losing a few eggs and chickens to feed them, and Cait had not garnered anything different. Ewan's soldiers reported that de Biggar and his men had kept to themselves in the alehouse, only venturing out to make use of the smithy and to care for their horses as needed. Idina and Donald were staying in with neighbors, though she'd learned that Ewan had offered them a place at the keep. They'd refused, however, and Edyth wondered if it was because she was there.

Edyth was starting to feel a bit like a bee in a bottle, with how much time she'd been spending behind the curtain walls. There was only so much idle women's work she could do before she thought she might go mad.

She'd stitched closed the other injured man, whose thigh had been cut during the skirmish but hadn't seen him since. She could only hope that if the injury became inflamed, that he would seek her out, but she wouldn't hold her breath.

Her close confidant, Cait, was busy with her mother working on the dreaded tapestry in the woman's solar, which, she learned, was to be of a unicorn. There was nothing whatsoever that could entice her to such a task save Roslyn asking her to, which she hadn't. Yet. So with nothing else to do, she found herself in the kitchen stores once more, going through the inventory ledger she'd tasked Alban to complete. She could see, however, that he still hadn't taken it upon himself to inventory anything. It infuriated her.

In addition to that fact, she also noticed that since she'd been there last, he'd used portions of the barley and oats and hadn't deducted the amounts from the record. There were also several new barrels of ale now cluttering up the hallway which hadn't been inventoried. Edyth suspected that they'd been brought here from the alehouse to prevent the sheriff's men from using them, but still, they should have been written down, as she'd asked.

Trying to swallow her frustration, she went in search of Alban, clutching the book across her chest as she went, as if it could protect her from his surly attitude and his obvious dislike of her. She hadn't forgotten what Ceana had said, that Alban had accused her of bewitching Ewan into marriage. She scoffed as she wound through the hallways, her temper barely under control. He would be the right sort of person who could easily spread nefarious rumors about her, being in contact with nearly every clan member throughout the week.

She found him in a room off the main body of the kitchen where herbs were hung from racks suspended near the ceiling for drying. There, standing in front of a large vat over the fire, three kitchen maids were busy melting and skimming debris from harvested honeycomb. Alban was instructing a lad in how long to make the wicks using his forearm as a measurement at a long table opposite.

It smelled strongly of her childhood. She might have taken time to savor the smells if it wasn't for the difficult task that lay before her. Alban eyed her unpleasantly from where he worked. She held aloft the ledger and said, "I would speak to you about the dry storage inventory."

Alban grumbled unpleasantly. "As I've telt ye afore, Mistress, I dinnae need such. I've got it all here." He tapped his temple in illustration. "Noo, if ye dinnae mind, I've important work on me hands." He turned his back to her coolly, dismissing her, and continued cutting string. Her anger erupted to life and before she knew it, she was taking great strides across the room.

"I'll speak to you now," she demanded, dropping the ledger down on the table with a pleasing *thwack*. He turned to her then, his heavily lined face pinched in annoyance. They were standing very close. She could smell the dried blood on his apron from his daily butchery. He frowned heavily, chewing the inside of his bottom lip. "I want to know why you refuse to follow my direct order to keep stock of our stores," she demanded.

"I dinnae need yer fussy book," he growled. "I dinnae need yer meddling. I've got the run o' the kitchen—and have—for these last twenty years!"

"*I* am the mistress of this keep," reminded Edyth, her patience gone. She glared at the man, her hands on her hips, "and you *do* need this *fussy* book!" She picked it up and waved it an inch from his face. "You've made gross errors in accounting for our stock! I will not have our people starve come winter because you're too obstinate and proud to allow that someone might do things differently than you!"

Alban turned a very ugly shade of purple all the way to his thinning hair line. He sputtered, indignant. Then, with a finger wagging in the air, shouted, "Our people? *Our*? Dinnae think that just because ye married Himself that ye're one o' us, ye hasty-witted harpy!"

Edyth reeled backward as though she'd been struck, her mouth agape. "What did you call me?"

"Ye heard me," he barked. His bony shoulders were bunched up to his ears as he glared daggers at her. "Ye may have bewitched Himself and his family, but I'm no' so easily taken in. I kent what ye were when I first laid eyes on ye. Yer a craven, common-kissing barnacle!"

Edyth could have laughed at his name calling if she hadn't been so angry. She looked around, as if someone might come to her aid, but she only saw the uneasy gazes of the servants, nervously eyeing herself and Alban. Of course they would not speak for her.

She took a deep breath and opened the ledger to the page she had dogeared earlier. She pointed an accusatory finger at the number of barrels of barley she'd penned there herself. "A month ago, I noted that we had eight barrels of barley. I asked you to keep track of what you used, but such a simple task has been deemed unworthy by the great Alban. *Two* weeks ago, I had to do go through it all myself and recount. Do you know how much we have Alban? Do you know how much you've used since?"

"We've plenty to last through the winter! I've ne'r run out of stores!"

"We're down another hogshead of barley, Alban, but I wouldn't know that because you *won't write it down*!"

"What good is writing it doon, eh? It doesnae change anything!"

Edyth waved the ledger in his face again. "It makes *all* the difference, you surly scut!" She was shouting now. Somewhere in the back of her mind, she heard her mother's voice chastising her as she had so many times in the past for her quick temper and loud mouth, but she easily ignored it. "Having an accounting means we're not all eating barley for two months straight because you've used all else!"

Alban, red faced, looked as though he'd like nothing more than to spit in her face. He didn't, though, largely because Ewan would have his hide for it. Or maybe he was afraid she might curse him.

She gestured jerkily at the wall, her arm thrust out in the direction of the dry storage room. "And I see that there are at least another half dozen hogsheads of ale that have been delivered from the village cluttering up the hallway, yet there's no indication they exist in this book!"

"I'll no' tell ye again," growled Alban, his wrinkled face pinched in animosity. "I dinnae need tae write it down! Leave me and my kitchen alone!"

Edyth was as tightly strung as a bow. She clenched her fists at her sides, striving for control, but she could not seem to find the space for composure. Alban had spread lies about her. It stung. Badly. It was *his* fault that the clan distrusted and disliked her. "If you're so unwilling to do as you're bid, then I relieve you of your duties! Leave here at once!"

Alban was more angry than she'd ever seen him. He stared, wide eyed, his mouth working but no words escaped. After an angry huff, he pushed past her roughly, knocking her into the table, and exited the room as hastily as his bad leg would allow. She watched as he left, her breast heaving for air. She felt as though every hair on her head would be standing on end were it not for the kertch she wore. *That damnable man!*

An uncomfortable silence filled the air as Edyth tried to catch her breath. She looked to the stupefied faces in the room without registering them. A log in the fire popped, making one of the servant girls jump.

Edyth wiped her brow with a shaking hand, feeling lightheaded and heavy hearted. "I'm sorry," she breathed. "I shouldn't have...not in front of you all." With some surprise she realized she was still holding her ledger. She looked at it, feeling as though it were foreign to her.

"He cannae read it, mistress," said a meek voice. Edyth looked up from her book; it was the stout girl who'd helped her make an inventory of the dry storage two weeks ago. Edyth's righteous anger changed shape. It settled as a heavy stone in her belly. She had to try twice to swallow.

"I see," said Edyth to the stillness of the room, feeling spent and unsure. "I see," she repeated, not knowing what to say.

He's the cause of all this distrust, she thought stubbornly. *He's been the one causing all the discord.* But something in the corner of her brain rebelled. *And yet you distrusted his methods*, it scolded wryly. "That's different," she hissed, realizing too late that she'd said it out loud.

Four pairs of frightened eyes stared back at her. She cleared her throat. "That changes things," she rectified, "though I wish he would have just told me."

But those words were hollow and she knew it. It was uncommon enough for a man to know how to read and write, and even less so for women. Why had she asked it of him? She should have known he could not do it. Her mother's kitchen staff had known how, but her mother had taken the time to teach them the methods for keeping inventory.

Her anger melted away, leaving her ashamed. Excusing herself, she steeled herself to find him and...what, exactly? She didn't want to have to put up with his surly looks and dour attitude, no less his disrespect, but she also needed a cook. She knew of no other who could take control and have run of the kitchen with such little notice.

She had done little, save fuel his hatred for her. And now she had no head cook.

***

Edyth found Ewan in his rooms within the garrison talking with Iain and Rory. She hovered outside the door, unsure. She'd sought him out without conscious thought, drawn to him as an apple to the earth when it grows too heavy for its branch. While her mind was preoccupied with conflicting feelings of what had transpired in the kitchen, her feet had taken over and, before she knew it, she'd come to herself outside of the garrison war room.

The reassurance she'd been seeking would have to wait, however, for when she saw how uneasy he was, all thought for herself vanished. His usual, easy manner was gone. He stood, pacing, agitated, his russet curls mussed up, no doubt from how often he'd run his hands through it. He was fidgety, rolling his injured shoulder, and so much unlike himself that she forgot her woes. She hesitated in the hall. The garrison was not a woman's place, and she had a sneaking suspicion that they had moved discussions here to ensure Cait could not so easily eavesdrop.

Running out of floor to pace, Ewan turned on his heel and, upon doing so, caught sight of Edyth standing in the doorway. He stopped short at seeing her, surprise written on his features, but beckoned her to enter. The entire party stared at her, silent and expectant. Perhaps irrationally, she suddenly felt a stranger to them all. Did she have no place here, at Ruthven Keep? Despite knowing this was a man's place, she could not help feeling as though she *should* be accepted here, and because she was not, she was not accepted in any place.

Her throat tightened with sudden feeling and, unwilling to let her true emotions show, she did the only thing she knew to do, she filled the silent space with words: "What news?" she asked lamely.

Iain smiled slightly. It was more like a twitch of his lips but gone so quickly it might have been nothing. Was he laughing at her? Her brother-in-law stood and offered her his vacant seat, but she declined. Already feeling like some unwelcome child, who they must keep indelicate truths from, she feared that if she sat, the feeling within her breast would only grow. Ewan, who could read her much better, frowned, but not in disapproval. He could see something plagued her mind and she felt her heart flutter. Would that they could be alone, so she could pour out her heart. He would judge her fairly, she knew, but not unkindly. She was pulled out of her selfish thoughts when Rory spoke.

"Milady," intoned Rory respectfully, bowing at the waist.

"News could be better," said Ewan. He kissed her cheek in greeting "We've just received word that the sheriff, de Biggar, is demanding a tax in payment for his services."

Edyth frowned. "He calls turning people out of their homes and taking food from their mouths 'service?'"

"She's smart as well as beautiful" said Iain with a wink. "Would that I could be bound tae such a lass." Edyth's spirit's lightened somewhat at Iain's flattery. Mayhap she was welcome here after all.

"The pickpurse wants a portion of our wool earnings," explained Rory.

"Surely you denied him," replied Edyth, looking from face to face. "On what legal grounds can he make such demands?"

Ewan leaned over to his desk and handed her a missive, written in a scrawling hand that she did not recognize. The seal on the bottom of the parchment, however, was easily recognizable: the official seal of John de Warenne, the Guardian of Scotland. "It is by de Warenne's approval that we are taxed," said Ewan distastefully.

"Have we no recourse?" she asked.

Ewan shook his head. "Edward is ever eager tae take our coin and find any reason tae keep his boot heel firmly upon us."

"Twenty percent?" said Edyth, incredulous, as she read over the document. "Surely this is not in addition to the King's yearly taxes on trade."

"I'm afraid it is," replied Ewan with a dark look.

"And if you refuse?" she asked, meeting his soulful eyes over the top of the page.

He took the letter back with two long fingers, as if it was some disgusting article that would soil his hands. "Ye ken well enough what will happen if I refuse."

She did know. The sheriff would then be well within his rights to forcibly take his portion of taxes in any way he saw fit, and with de Warenne backing him, it wouldn't be difficult to make that happen. It would be the start of a war that they would surely lose.

"What good fortune for the sheriff that the shearing has ended so recently so that he may enjoy in its proceeds," intoned Edyth darkly. "So, you will pay it."

"He leaves me little choice."

"He doesnae ken," offered Iain, "how many sheep our shepherds have, with them being up in the high country just now. What do ye think, Brother, of sending word tae them? They are hearty men. They can stay quite comfortably in the pass until the weather turns."

"But there are records," reminded Edyth, ignoring for the moment that the sheep and shepherds would need to come back sooner rather than later. Winter would be upon them in a few short months. "And do not forget that the Cistercian house knows the value of your harvest. Even the lowly fuller knows well enough how many sacks of wool were sent to Flanders."

"Aye. Tis true," replied Ewan with a nod, "though I dinnae think de Biggar will ken the going rate of a bag o' wool, nor take the necessary trip tae inquire at the monastery. Do you?"

Iain shook his head. "He will be content with what we give him and say no more."

Rory agreed. "Mmmph. De Biggar willnae care what he's given, so long as he makes us bleed any way he can. No doubt once we give him what he wants, he willnae stop. How many more o' these well-timed missives from de Warenne will we receive, bleedin' our coffers dry?"

Iain rubbed the back of his neck, a twist of disapproval on his lips. "The harvest festival is no' far awa'. De Biggar will surely dip into our quarterly rents as well."

Ewan shook his head in frustration. "Aye, the scunner will greedily drink from our teat 'til we run dry."

Edyth shook her head. "Surely he will not wish to take a portion of goods from your rents, unless your people are far richer than most. What would he do with a wagon full of hay or a milch goat?"

"Tis true we get little in the way of coin," replied Ewan. He rested his blue eyes on her, thinking.

"Swine, sheep, kine and butter can be sold," supplied Iain. "He could turn it to a profit regardless."

Ewan waved a hand, dismissing his brother's words. "De Biggar willane want tae work such a scheme. It'd be far too much effort for so little a reward."

"That doesn't resolve the issue of the wool tax, though," reminded Edyth. "What will you pay him?"

Ewan pursed his lips in thought. "I must pay him, but I willnae give him such an outrageous cut as twenty percent. I'm willing tae bet he willnae take the time tae learn just how much o' a profit we gain from the shearing. I'll give 'im a bag o' coin and leave it at that. When he comes back with more taxes, we'll pay him in goods."

Edyth nodded, thinking. "Is there a way to gather the rents before the festival? It would best if de Biggar isn't present and can't know what you gain."

"The harvest is no' yet in," said Ewan in a shake of his head. "I cannae ask for a portion o' sommat they dinnae yet have."

Edyth understood, but surely there was a way to keep de Biggar out of their business.

"Haps your usual way of collecting can be amended," she suggested. "Less public."

Ewan scratched his neck, the stubble rasping as he considered. "Aye. I'll think on it."

Chapter Twelve

Once the issue of the tax had been decided, Ewan had asked Edyth what she'd needed, having come out of her way to find him, but with Rory and Iain looking on in apparent interest, she found she could not find the words. She'd dismissed a member of her husband's staff, a clan's member, who had served his family for twenty years. And all because he couldn't read or write. Well, that wasn't the whole of it, but she was afraid that's all they would hear should she tell them.

So instead of confessing all, as her heart bade her, she merely asked for him to kindly send someone into the village to inquire about those that had been hurt, including the boy, Eachann. While she had been forbidden from administering to him directly, she could not so easily dispel him from her thoughts. She'd made more of the tincture, this time modifying the recipe slightly with the use of valerian root, to help with his sleep. Of course, Ewan had agreed to have it delivered and to inquire after their health with a swift kiss to her cheek and then she had left with an uncomfortable weight in her belly. What was she to do?

She should not have let Alban's gossiping and sour demeanor affect her so easily. If she had had a stronger resolve, the household would still have a cook and the servants would have less to whisper about. Even as she wished herself unaffected, she wondered what he was saying now...and what the kitchen staff thought of her. *Stop it. It doesn't matter what they think.* But it did. Somehow, what they thought did matter.

With no other options, she thought she ought to seek out Alban and work out their differences. She looked all around the keep but he was nowhere to be found. With the fall festival soon upon them, she had little time to place a new member of staff, and no matter how much she disliked the man, she could not disagree that he kept the kitchen running smoothly.

When she'd ventured to the kitchens once more, however, she'd found that at least five others had left, all in support of the man who'd had the run of them for longer than Edyth had been alive. With nothing left for her to do, since she could not go to the village to seek out the missing staff, she got to work.

Putting on an apron, she commanded those left to continue with their usual occupations while she finished with Alban's usual task: butchery. Bustling servants moved about, kneading dough for bannocks, peeling and chopping vegetables, filling the wood box, stirring the pot suspended over the fire, while she carefully chose a knife. A partially butchered deer lay in pieces along the long block table, skinned and quartered. Her eyes followed the lines of silky sinew that ran over purple mounds of muscles, not knowing where to cut first. It smelled strongly of blood and something else she could not define, but it was gamey and pungent and made her stomach quiver.

Edyth looked around her, searching for a helpful, friendly face, but everyone was busy with their own tasks. Taking a deep breath, she pulled a hind leg toward herself and made her best guess, thinking that a hearty stew would be easiest. The meal on the menu would be impossible for her: venison pies, filled with savory, thick sauce and root vegetables, neatly formed into flaky pies. While Edyth had been educated to run a household, she, herself, had limited knowledge of how the fare was actually prepared. She'd watched her family's cook from time to time—mostly when she wanted to sneak sweets—and had even done some simple tasks like chop mushrooms or pour honey over biscuits. Cooking an entire meal for the whole of the household plus the garrison men was daunting, to say the least. Stew would be much simpler but far less appetizing.

Grasping the skinny foreleg in one fist, she made the first cut, doing her best to follow the bone with the flat side of her knife. It was hard, dirty work, butchery. By the time she'd clumsily cut all the meat from the leg and shoulder, her back was hurting and her hands were cramped from clutching the knife and grasping the slippery, tender pieces of meat.

Eyeing the remainder of the carcass, she thought maybe she knew why Alban was always in such a bad mood. She did not have the time, nor the energy to do the rest of the deer and, instead, focused on cutting what she did have into more manageable pieces. Her work had been artless, leaving jagged, mangled pieces of meat where she knew a skilled hand would have produced something at least unbruised. Despite that, she wasn't altogether unpleased. She'd done it, hadn't she? Where there had been no meat for supper, now there was some.

She smiled to herself as she cleaned her hands on her apron and began to mentally construct her soup. Thankfully, there were a variety of chopped vegetables ready, thanks to the kitchen aides, an herb room with a variety of dried spices, and a kale yard full of other flavors, all at her disposal.

Why, this might even be fun.

***

Cait stood and stretched her aching back and shoulders, not even trying to stifle a yawn. She ignored the look her mother gave her, which plainly said she wished Cait would act more like a lady, and instead looked out the window. It was late, not that Cait needed the sky to discern the hour. Her stomach rumbled, signaling that it would soon be time to eat.

She flexed her hands. Her fingers were cramped from attaching the warp—hundreds and hundreds of strands of spun wool—to the loom. "I thought it would never end," she sighed, looking over their work. "This is always the worst part," agreed Roslyn. "Things will move faster now. We can take it in turns tae work the pedals from now on."

A soft knock sounded, and mother and daughter turned in time to see a maid poke her head through the door. "Pardon, Mistress, Dowager," she said shyly. Everything about the girl seemed to be an apology. She looked out of place, and no wonder. Cait recognized her as not a household maid, but a kitchen maid. But she carried no tray of refreshment.

Cait looked to her mother, who looked equally surprised to see her there. "Good e'en tae ye, Dolly. Is there something I can help ye with?" asked Roslyn

Cait knew the girl to be rather mousy, but never had she seen her look so much like a dog who was afraid of a beating. "Yes, Mistress," said Dolly quietly. She came forward and curtseyed, her eyes falling onto Cait, as though she could help her by simply reading her mind.

"What is it that I can help ye with?" encouraged Roslyn.

Dolly straightened, clearly gathering her courage, and looked first the Dowager then Cait full in the face. She took a deep breath then said, "I dinnae wish tae go above Mistress Edyth's head. I'm no' one tae be difficult or...or disrespectful, but I dinnae think it proper, like, tae have the lady working as she has all the day in the kitchens. Why, it's nearly supper and she's drenched through with sweat and covered in filth. She nearly caught her skirts on fire, standing too close tae the hearth. Twice."

Cait looked to her mother questioningly. Did her mother know something she did not? But her mother's brow furrowed in confusion. Her mother made a soft sound of inquiry and said, "Dolly, do ye mean that Lady Edyth has been laboring in the kitchens?" At Dolly's nod she asked the obvious question: "Why?"

Dolly then explained that Edyth had dismissed Alban earlier that day, and ever since, the kitchen had been in disarray. The butchering had only been partially completed, the bread started late, and a variety of other jobs left undone. "I fear supper will be a poor affair," she confided, looking apologetic. "Only a weak soup with bannocks, I'm afraid,"

"Why should your lady dismiss Alban?" asked Roslyn. The lines on her mother's brow had deepened, going from what Cait knew to be mild concern to displeasure.

"Och!" exclaimed Dolly, her face going pink. "He called her some awful names, my lady. I dare no' repeat what he said. I suppose ye ken well enough that they dinnae get on. Mistress Edyth and Alban, I mean tae say," she added, lest anyone be confused. "The lady wished him tae keep record o' the stores, which he took as insult."

Dolly rolled her lips inward here, her eyes betraying that there was more she wished to say, but held herself in check. Their patience paid off, though, for Dolly's words tumbled out of her mouth like wine from a carafe after only a moment of stretched silence. "He's been tellin' any who would give 'im ear, which is everyone in the kitchens, mind ye, that she's...well, that she bewitched Himself. He's o' a mind that Lady Edyth is only after his wealth and power and holds his mind in a binding spell or some such with a powerful wickedness."

She took a deep breath, looking from Cait to the Dowager in apparent embarrassment for what she'd just said. "Forgive me," she muttered in a small voice. "All who pass through the stores or kitchens must listen to his mutterings. Any who enter the kitchens hear how well he dislikes the lady."

"Is that so?" asked Roslyn, a gray brow rising sharply. "Is there else Alban has been saying about his mistress? You will not be punished," added Roslyn at the stricken look upon Dolly's face.

"Weel, it's no' just what he says, mind. It's what he does. He'll make the sign of the devil's horns as she walks past, or cross 'imself like he's afraid o' the evil that's in her. That makes others wary o' the lady."

"And so yer mistress dismissed him," said Roslyn with some astonishment, "and then set herself tae the kitchen tasks."

Cait would have given up a month's worth of sweets to have seen Alban put in his place. "What did Lady Edyth say to 'im?" asked Cait eagerly.

Dolly, brown eyes wide, said, "She told 'im that if he couldnae do what she asked, she would find someone who would and...and she told 'im tae leave." She looked to her hands, her fingers intwined in front of her, and said, "She did look sorry after, when I told her that he couldnae read nor write, as she'd asked of him. But then she left and didnae make assignments. There's been an awful strammash in the kitchens e'er since. Some willnae work at all, out of loyalty tae Alban, aye? They refused their tasks and left, though I cannae say to where. The mistress did come back and took charge of those of us that are left, but, as I say, we havenae been able tae keep up with all the work." She trailed off here, looking afraid of a reprimand. None came, of course, but the girl was used to working under the exacting rule of Alban, so it was no wonder she was rather fearful.

"Ye've done right," said Roslyn. "I'll speak tae yer mistress and see if I cannae straighten out the kitchens. Dinnae ye worry, Dolly."

***

Dinner, as Cait expected, was a rather poor affair. The real issue was not that the soup was mostly tasteless and the venison tough, but that there wasn't enough to go around. Edyth had not prepared quite enough food for all of the garrison men and the family together. People grumbled in confusion when the food ran out. To be fair, many of the fighting men ate as though every meal would be their last, so it wasn't entirely Edyth's fault that her preparations hadn't met expectations. The men were not rude, per se, only wondering what had happened. Cait heard people asking after Alban's health, which she knew Edyth had also heard, seated as she was across from her.

Edyth, pink cheeked with embarrassment, had ordered platters of salted meats and cheeses to be served, as well as more ale and cider for all in the hall. Ewan and Iain, who had both been late to the table, were completely confused at the shortage. Being uninformed of what had transpired that day in the kitchens, they did not seem to notice how Edyth's eyes glittered with disappointment. Edyth pushed her bowl toward her husband, claiming she wasn't hungry, to which he refused. "I'm no' so hungry as tae suffer through a second bowl."

Cait opened her mouth to say something, but Edyth, her face flaming, spoke first. "It wasn't my favorite meal either." Iain, seated next to Cait, reached across the table and pulled the bowl to himself, claiming that he'd not waste it, no matter how poor.

Cait watched as Ewan bent his head to Edyth, his eyes searching her face. "Are ye feeling well this e'en, Edie? Ye've been awfully quiet and ye havenae eaten."

Edyth mustered a smile and nodded. "I'm well. Only tired...my stomach isn't up for food."

"Are ye?" he asked, his eyes going soft. Cait couldn't account for his soppy behavior. A long forefinger brushed a fallen strand of hair from her forehead before he leaned in and kissed her brow. Something within Cait thawed at the look her brother held in his eyes for her good sister. She felt joy for her brother and, at the same moment, jealous longing. Would that she could have such a match.

"That was fine meal," said Roslyn as way of announcement. No one was willing to accuse her of being a liar, of course, so nothing more was said. She was seated on the left of Ewan and patted his forearm to signal she was ready to leave. Ewan stood and pulled out his mother's chair for her. "I thank ye, Edyth," said the dowager. "When ye've finished here, would ye kindly come tae me in my rooms?"

Edyth blanched slightly but agreed. Cait reached a comforting hand across the table and gave Edyth's hand a squeeze. "Dinnae ye fash, Edie," she whispered after her mother and her brother had left the dais. "She only wishes tae help."

Chapter Thirteen

Edyth walked carefully into her darkened, shared bedroom. She'd spent the last two hours in Lady Roslyn's chambers, discussing what was to be done about Alban. The Dowager had said that she would speak to the cook herself, and command that he apologize to Edyth for his slander. Edyth felt gratified at Roslyn's defense of her, but also felt as though she, as new mistress of the keep, should be the one to resolve the issue herself.

"Will it not only complicate matters with him, should you come to my defense?" she'd asked. But Roslyn had only patted her hand in a mollifying way and dismissed her concerns. She'd assured Edyth that not only would Alban return to his duties, but that he would apologize to her publicly. Edyth didn't see how that could possibly help—he was a proud man, after all—but she wanted to believe that the nightmare of the kitchens would soon be only a bad memory.

The servants had been dismissed for the night, so she would have to undress herself. Her feet and back ached from slaving on the stone floors, bent over the table for so many hours. She readied for bed as quickly as she could, wiping her face and neck with a moistened towel and brushing her teeth with a birch twig. Her hands fumbled for the ties at her sides that laced up her bodice. She was able to wriggle free from her bodice and sleeves and drop her skirts into a puddle on the floor. All the heat seemed to go with them; she shivered in her shift as she hurried to the bed.

Ewan was asleep, his face relaxed and his mouth slightly agape. He stirred when she slid under the furs and woolen blankets, though, and pulled her toward him. "Yer late," he rasped before kissing her behind her ear. "What did my mother want?"

Edyth suppressed a sigh. She didn't like keeping things from him, but nor did she feel like telling the tale again. She gave his hand a squeeze, which was pressed lightly over her middle, and said, "It can wait til morning. I'm rare tired. I don't think I can keep my eyes open much longer." There was a pause. She could practically hear Ewan thinking. "It's naught to trouble you with, my love," she said. "She only wished to discuss an issue in the kitchens tonight."

"Ah," he said, "I had hoped...." He took a deep breath and flattened his hand over her stomach. "When ye came tae see me earlier today and then ye said ye didn't feel up to eating, I was thinking that ye might have some happy news to share."

Edyth turned in his arms, searching his face in the dark. The only light came from the fire in the brazier, a steady thrumming glow that seemed to pulse with her breathing. Each month she, herself, had been somewhat saddened to find that her courses had not stopped. And while they hadn't openly discussed having a child, it occurred to her suddenly that Ewan had the same hope she had been secretly nurturing. She ran a hand over the stubble on his cheek, breathing in the scent of him. "It takes time."

"We've been wed these past five months," reminded Ewan. "Is that no' time enough?" He pressed his lips together in thought, then after a pause, added, "It always seems to happen quickly with the sheep and kine."

Edyth couldn't help the breathless laugh that left her. "We are not farm animals, Ewan."

He smiled crookedly in response, then sobered. "Aye, I suppose it's best. We cannae know what's in our future now that the English have taken power and a sheriff has been appointed to Perthshire. It might be best if we wait."

"Haps it's me," confided Edyth softly. She'd wondered, each month when she found she was not yet with child, if it was somehow her fault. "Haps I'm barren." She held her breath, waiting for Ewan's response, but he merely shook his head.

"Let's no' borrow trouble," he said softly. He kissed her then and stroked her arm. "If we cannae have children of our own, there are plenty of other ways to get them. Fostering, I mean," added Ewan at Edyth's stretched silence.

"Yes, I suppose," she said finally, though she really did want a child of her very own. "My mother had trouble conceiving," she admitted. "I remember there were pregnancies and losses. My mother mourned for them for years. She'd made tonics and prayed. She'd helped other women to conceive yet it never worked for her. I had always wished for a sister."

Ewan pressed his warm mouth to her forehead. "And now ye do. Ye've got the twa, Cait and Aldythe. Ye havenae met Aldie yet, but I'm sure ye'll like her well enough." Ewan's elder sister was married to Robert Lindsay and living on clan lands in Alberlady. From what she'd gleaned from Ewan and Cait, Aldythe and Robert had a son they called Eadgar. Eadgar Graeme, he'd said.

Ewan held her closely, her mind full of potential hurts and losses of their own. "We will meet trouble if it comes, Edie," he added, stroking her face. "Sleep now, *mo ghàdh*. Dinnae ye fash."

All that night, despite her tiredness, she dreamt of screaming horses and dying men.

***

In the morning, she felt sore in every muscle, but she forced herself out of bed when her maid came to the room and got to work. Before Ewan left, she'd asked him to order a wooden box to be constructed from Beathan, Eachann's father, for Cait upon her marriage. As they were to leave for Caimbel lands in two weeks for the happy occasion, she hoped it would be built for her quickly.

She next sought out Dolly in the kitchens, who she'd tasked with picking plums in the upper orchard with the rest of the kitchen staff who could be spared. Cait, happy to be out of doors, had cheerfully picked up a basket and walked beside Edyth on their way to the upper fields in easy conversation. With so many women together, the cartmen, and the orchard being in the opposite direction of the village, Ewan had agreed to only send two escorts for the lot.

The trees were heavy with the yeasty, purple-blue fruit so that the branches drooped toward the ground, weary with their load. The picking was easy; their baskets filling quickly. Once their baskets were filled, they deposited the fruit into crates in the back of a wagon, careful not to overfill them and squish them into pulp.

By the time the cart was halfway filled they stopped for rest and to eat. The women gathered there, around the foot of the tree closest to the wagon and ate their lunches: cheese, cold ham, and bannocks. Edyth wondered as she ate, who had gathered the fare, since Alban was gone. Could have Roslyn already reappointed the man to the kitchens so early?

Edyth bit into one of the plums. Warmed by the sun, it burst open, golden hued juice running down her chin. One of the kitchen staff laughed too, then sobered quickly, looking as though she'd committed a grievous sin.

"Here," said Edyth, laughing herself. She offered the servant one of the fruit from the crates, chuckling. "Try one. I've never tasted anything so sweet."

The woman hesitated, as though Edyth were trying to trick her in some way, but took it after a moment of hesitation.

"It's a good crop this year," said Cait, choosing a fruit for herself. She assessed the servant who'd laughed, but not unkindly. When the servant took a bite of the plum Edyth had given her, it, too, burst open, juice dripping from her chin and fingers. The servant smiled and met Edyth's eye briefly before offering a bite to the girl next to her. "Eat," commanded Edyth to the group at large, feeling hopeful that these women might view her in a more friendly light. After eating their fill, they got back to work, their fingers and lips stained a dull blue.

Some time later, as the last of the plums were deposited into the wagon crates, Edyth caught a glimpse of Cait, standing near the edge of the field. They were on a rise, above the keep, where they could enjoy the sweeping hillsides that rolled down, green and verdant, toward the wide, snaking river. She stood, with her back to the orchard, its leafy shadows dancing on her person, her eyes filled with a longing Edyth could well understand. "I will miss this," said Cait. Her words were as soft as the breeze.

"It's beautiful," agreed Edyth, watching her friend. "Nairn is sure to be as beautiful, if not more so. Ewan told me it's in the far north, near Inverness."

Cait merely nodded, staring at the landscape that unfolded around them. "I fear that, once I leave, my heart will break in twain. How can I live and leave my home behind?"

"It's been a good home to you," agreed Edyth softly, "and it will feel your absence."

Cait looked at Edyth then and smiled sadly. "And I will miss you just as much, Edyth."

Edyth hugged her, letting her basket fall to the ground. Plums rolled around their feet as they embraced. Edyth held back her tears, thinking they would make Cait, who was not prone to such emotion, uncomfortable. But when they pulled away, Cait's eyes glistened, bright with emotion held in check. Cait looked away and cleared her throat before saying, "Promise me, sister, that ye'll no' let that sheriff harm my village or its people."

Edyth could make no such promise, but she held Cait's hand as she said, "I promise to love your people as you do."

Cait nodded once and then looked away. "I do love them."

Much later, when Edyth entered the kitchens that afternoon to help put up the plums, Alban was there. She stopped in her tracks at the sight of him. A strange sort of emotion gripped her throat that made her falter. He was barking orders at several of the kitchen staff, as per his usual, with a bloodied cleaver in his hand. She did not want to speak to him despite her determination to do so. She was surprised to also feel relief, most likely due to the realization that she would not have to cook another subpar meal, put up the plums, and plan for the fall festival without him.

Nothing seemed to have changed since yesterday, however. Had it only been one day? He was just as grumpy as he had always been, but when he turned and saw her there, in the doorway, he seemed to steel himself for some unpleasant task. His perpetually curved spine straightened, and his jaw worked, searching for the words. "Mistress," he said finally. "I'm bade...that is, I mean tae say...." He cleared his throat and looked about, as though gauging how may ears would hear.

There were several servants in the room, though in Edyth's opinion, not nearly enough. It didn't matter, though. The ears would hear and their owner's tongues would wag. All would eventually know what he would say to her. "I, eh, beg fer yer pardon." Alban shrugged one shoulder jerkily before removing his cap. He looked thoroughly agitated and slightly green. He made an uncomfortable sound in his throat then said, "I shoulnae 'ave said what I did, nor left my duties."

It looked to her as if it had cost him say it, but she pressed for more. "And?" she asked, one brow raising in expectation. "What have you to say about telling everyone that I'm an evil temptress? Half the clan will not trust me thanks to you."

Alban's wrinkled face lost its green color and went purple instead, his mouth pulling into a grimace so pronounced, it could have been comical. He looked about him once more, glaring at those who were in the room, who by this time, had given up the pretense of work and were openly eavesdropping. "Dinnae ye have work tae do?" he barked. Servants jumped and scurried away. He grumbled to himself under his breath. *Cùm do shròin far am buin iad. Keep your noses where they belong.*

"Careful, Alban, I might think you're cursing someone with all that grousing," advised Edyth. Was it wrong of her to relish in his discomfort? She eyed his crooked frame, his obvious discomfort at being forced by Roslyn to apologize to her. That conversation must have been difficult for him. And while she did feel that he was not truly repentant, there was little to nothing she could do about it. He was here and he had been given a set down by whom he considered the true lady of the house. It would have to do.

Edyth did not wish to be petty, but he had injured her more than she cared to admit. She swallowed her own feelings for the sake of the long list of duties she could not accomplish without him. "You are forgiven," she managed, and offering an olive branch, said, "and now it is my turn to apologize for presuming more than I had a right to. You will no longer have need to take inventory of the kitchen stores. That task has been given to Dolly, whom I will train on the task."

Edyth could not read the look on Alban's face at that news, as perpetually sour faced as he was. He bobbed his head and merely said, "What percentage o' the plums do ye wish dried and what amount would ye like turned tae wine?"

So that was it. Back to business as though nothing had happened. She certainly hoped he would stick to business and cease his gossiping.

"I think you know best," answered Edyth evenly. "I would request that, in the future, when you do not agree with me, that instead of defame and slander me, you speak to me. And if you feel you cannot speak to me, then you can speak to the Dowager. She can be our mediator, if you so wish."

Alban nodded wordlessly and replaced his cap, summarily dismissing her. "Boy! That kindling box willnae fill itself. Get ye gone, lad, and see tae yer duties!"

Edyth sighed and, taking another plum for herself, sought out Dolly for her first lesson on inventory.

Chapter Fourteen

It was several days later that Edyth received her ordered box from Beathan, unadorned but well made. News about Eachann was delivered as well. It was not promising, but he'd held out far longer than many had anticipated. Perhaps he would pull through after all. She made a mental note to make more of the tincture to be delivered to his home and set to work on the box.

She was not a woodcarver by any means, but she wanted to turn the box into something beautiful for Cait, something that came from her heart. She picked up a chisel and a small hammer and set to work, gouging the smooth wood. It looked like a mistake, a scar, but she continued her work, thinking of the river that wound through their village, the tall oaks and fir trees that dotted the landscape.

Several hours later, there came a soft knock on the door before it was summarily pushed open. Edyth hid her work quickly with a cloth, thinking it might be Cait, but she needn't have worried. Edyth's heart skipped a beat at seeing her husband.

"I didn't think I'd find you here of all places," said Ewan as he closed the solar door behind him. While it was true that Edyth didn't care to stay indoors when the weather was so fine, she needed to finish her wedding gift to Cait. She was rather proud of it, despite its rudimentary decoration. Her intention was to fill it with parchment, ink and quill, and ask that it, selfishly, be used to communicate with her. Cait had become her dearest friend, and she was loathe to be without her.

"I was startin' tae worry I might have need tae rally a search party. What has ye holed awa' in here on such a fine day?"

Edyth removed the cloth covering her gift, biting her lip.

"Och. Verra bonny," said Ewan with a soft smile, leaning over to inspect her work. He kissed her neck, making her shiver slightly. "I like the wee lamb there on the top."

Edyth's smile turned to a frown. "That's a bird."

Ewan made a choking sound as he tried to hold in his laugh. "Is it?" He gave up and laughed outright when he saw the look on her face. "I'm sorry, Edie. It's verra bonny. Ye've done a braw job o' it."

"You're a terrible liar." She couldn't help but smile. She pushed her tools aside with a sigh. "It's supposed to be for Cait, upon her marriage, but haps it's not fine enough. It's a stationary box so she can write to me, but perhaps it was a silly idea."

Ewan picked up the box and turned it around, inspecting it. A long finger followed the groove of the river that wound around like a ribbon, and the vertical lines meant to be trees. "No, lass. Tis a fine gift. I ken Cait will love it because it comes from you. Ye've become good friends. It gladdens my heart tae see it."

She turned and looked at him; his face still held signs of mirth, but his eyes were serious. "I will miss her," she admitted. Upon retrieving the box, she could only now see the flaws she'd made in the wood. She didn't have time for another box to be constructed, and she could think of no other gift she wished to give. She forced her feelings of inadequacy away. "Did you wish to speak with me?"

"Aye. I do." He produced a knife from his person and handed it to her, hilt first. The blade was short, only three inches, with an antler handle that fit nicely into her palm. It wasn't ornamental in any way aside from the leather sheath which was decorated with thistles. "For your protection," he explained at her questioning look. "I would feel better if you had it on you at all times."

Edyth nodded, thinking of the sheriff and his men. "Do you think I'll have need of it?"

"I hope no', but there's always the chance. And while I ken ye've got some skill with a blade, a dirk is much more practical of a weapon for a woman. It's easily concealed, for one."

"Suitable for a woman, you say?"

Ewan shrugged. "There are some that say a woman's best weapon isnae a blade, but poison."

Edyth raised a coy brow in response. Ewan's mouth twitched into a smile. "Of which, we can agree ye need no training. Now, show me what ye ken of using a dirk."

"I only know which way to point it." She demonstrated by playfully jabbing the pointy end toward him. He laughed lightly then corrected her grip. His hands were light but warm, fluttering over her skin. It felt like an age since they'd had time alone together with how preoccupied he'd been of late, not that she could blame him. Being this close to him, away from any pressing duties, where the heat of his body and the smell of him enveloped her, she felt slightly giddy. She missed his easygoing smile and lighthearted teasing. What with everything happening lately, she felt like she hadn't seen this side of him in ages.

"I see a lesson is at hand. Come, I'll teach you." He led her to the open floor nearest the windows and showed her how to stand. His hands settled on her hips from behind, turning them squarely to face an imaginary opponent. She held her breath, hoping for another kiss to her neck but he moved to face her. His hands were warm, moving to her wrist to adjust the angle of the blade. She searched out his eyes, but he did not meet them. A current raced up her arm as his fingers brushed her pulse point. Every place his hands touched seemed to awaken. She found herself leaning toward him without thought. He was speaking; her eyes lingered on his full lips.

He stared at her expectantly and she realized that he'd asked something of her, though she hadn't paid the slightest bit of attention. Well, at least not to his words. "I'm sorry," she said, clearing her throat. She forced herself to resurface from her lust-filled thoughts. "My mind wandered. What did you say?"

His long mouth twitched slightly. "I said I want ye tae try and stab me." He pulled off his surcoat in a fluid motion, tossing it to some unknown place. Edyth did not see nor care where it landed. Her eyes were fixed upon the opening of his shirtfront, where his bronzed skin peeked through the corded opening. His shirt, though baggy, hinted at his muscular frame and she had to force herself, once again, to attend to his words.

One eyebrow was raised teasingly. He'd noticed her ogling, it would seem. He wet his lips and smiled slightly, making her pinken. "Do try and keep yer mind clear, ye temptress. Now, pay attention. If I try tae strike ye," he said, lifting his right hand as if to slap her face, "like this," he said, demonstrating slowly moving his arm at a downward angle, "the best defense is simply tae no' be hit. Avoid my strike by leaning away. Good. Again."

He adjusted her footing and bade her practice until she was able to avoid his potential strikes from different angles. His hands seemed to linger upon her as he readjusted her body. She could not help her body's response. Standing behind, with his arms guiding hers, he showed her how to strike. She mimicked his movements, but her mind was on his hands, the broad expanse of his chest against her, and the strength of his arm. She breathed in his scent and closed her eyes briefly, thinking of what she'd rather be doing now that she had him alone.

"Ye're a quick learner, if no' a bit distractable." The thrum of his voice in her ear made her shiver. She could feel him smile against the sensitive skin on her neck. She turned, craning to kiss him but he denied her with a soft grunt and pulled away.

"So eager tae end yer lesson. Ye'll make a poor warrior at this rate." He left to face her once more, leaving her wanting. His eyes had darkened; she knew he was not immune to the lustful thoughts she was having, but he did not relent. "This time when I attack, ye're tae avoid my strike, then immediately slice at my forearm. Here," he said, rolling up his sleeve to demonstrate. His sword arm was thick with muscle, his tendons bunching and flexing as he made a fist. "If ye cut here," he said, pointing, "I cannae grip my sword, nor anything else for that matter. Show me."

Edyth practiced, moving slowly and clumsily. Her brain seemed to be in a fog. She dodged his open-handed attacks then pretended to slice at his arm until he was satisfied. He next showed her that, if she failed to cut his arm correctly, where to strike next. He removed his leine, baring the muscled expanse of his upper body. Edyth swallowed, her eyes following the smattering of hairs across his chest and downward, to where the trail ended at his hose.

With his arm extended, as if he'd just tried to strike her, he bade her slice the back of his upper arm, where the hills and valleys of his triceps met his biceps. "If ye cut here," he said, pointing with a long-fingered hand to the correct place, "I willnae be able tae use my elbow."

"Wh...what if they're wearing armor?" she asked, her mouth gone dry.

"Most men willnae wear armor unless on the battlefield, but, if for some reason ye find yerself in such a situation, there are some weaknesses. Here, under the arm, which if done right, can give ye a straight line tae the lungs, and if deep enough, the heart. Ye willnae reach such with this knife. The eyes," he added, pointing to his own, "the neck, here, under the helm, and here," he pointed to his groin."

Edyth nodded, and wet her lips, trying, with great effort, to hear his words. She supposed she should take the lesson more seriously, to focus on the task, but her body did not wish to obey. "Come, take up yer knife, and practice." She obeyed, moving to strike again and again until he relented, and her breath came short. She would have normally mastered the movements rather quickly, most likely due to her knowledge and experience with swordplay, if it weren't for her distracted mind. And even then, though she was talented to a point with a sword, she would be no match for Ewan, who was far heavier, stronger, and vastly more experienced. A hidden knife would be to her advantage if she knew how to use it properly.

"We'll continue this. Ye need more practice."

"Where should it be worn?" she asked rather breathlessly, openly eyeing his exquisite frame. Having him so near, undressed as he was, where she could see the play of his muscles under his tight skin, she felt as though she'd had too much cider. "In...in a pocket?"

"Aye, a pocket," he said with a cocky smile, moving to stand very close. He looked to the neckline of her dress and ran a finger from her belly to the valley between her breasts. "Or here," he said, tugging slightly on the fabric. Her blood began to race all the more; heat pooled in her belly. His hand traced the long column of her neck and then he took her in a kiss that made her moan with longing.

Without effort, he lifted her, kissing her passionately. She tried to wrap her legs around his hips, but her skirt would not allow it; she grunted in displeasure, which only made Ewan laugh. He pulled away from her, his curling hair falling in his eyes. "Eager are ye?" he whispered.

Her response was to fist her hands into his hair and pull his mouth to hers once more, eliciting a grunt of pleasure from him. There were no words, only hands and soft gasps as he kissed her. A hand at her ankle moved upward, soft and deliberate, pulling the fabric of her skirts with it. He found in the inside of her knee, touching her garter. "Or ye can hide yer knife here." She no longer cared and mumbled something incoherent, running her hands down his neck to his rounded shoulders

She continued her descent, running light fingers over his pecs and the taught muscles of his abdomen to land at the tie holding his hose in place. His skin was warm and smooth, corded with muscle. The muscles jumped as she touched him. He was beautiful in all the ways a man could be and she wanted him very badly. He pulled away slightly as she tugged on the string she held. "Wouldn't ye rather go—"

"Here, now," she panted, uncaring that they were in a public room and could be discovered at any turn. And Ewan, ever the gentleman, obliged her.

***

Edyth found Cait in the women's solar the next day to fulfill her promise to Ceana before they left in a few days. Roslyn and Cait were industriously employed at a horizontal loom, which was set up by the windows closest to the fire, where the light would be best. The warp now complete, was composed of hundreds upon hundreds of threads stretched across the frame. Roslyn smiled at Edyth as she approached, her hands deftly moving the shuttle through the warp.

"Edyth, dear, have ye come tae help? Cait could use some assistance filling the pirns."

"Of course," said Edyth, sitting next to her friend and selecting one of the long, thin rods in the basket on the floor. She selected a deep green ball of spun wool and began the process of winding it around and around the pirn. Meeting Cait's eyes, she tried not to laugh as her friend pulled a face. The room was filled with the clunky sounds of the shafts rising and falling as Roslyn worked the foot pedals on the loom.

Cait leaned forward, her eyes darting to the loom. "Whatever brings ye tae this hell?" she whispered so that her mother would not hear. "Ye were clear and free, yet here ye are."

Edyth smiled, her eyes on winding the strands around the long wooden dowel. "I came to speak to you about Ceana."

Cait's eyebrows rose slightly. "Aye? And what about?"

Edyth told her friend all that had transpired in the hall after tending to Idina and Donald.

"Alec," said Cait with a slight frown. "Ye mean Ewan's squire, Alec?"

"Yes, the very one. Is there a problem with their potential union?"

"No," said Cait, her hands stilling and settling on her lap. "It's only that Alec is soon to be knighted. He will likely seek an advantageous alliance through marriage to increase his income."

Edyth nodded, her lips pursed. "Does Ewan have someone in mind for him? I did not think to ask."

Cait did not answer immediately, picking up her pirn and resuming winding the spun wool onto its length. "I wouldn't know," she said in an offhand way, shrugging. "It is only what is usually done."

Edyth continued her work, looking up at Cait from time to time, who seemed deep in thought. "Perhaps if they meet," she suggested, "and they like each other, I can speak to Ewan. If he is planning on giving Alec a parcel of land upon his knighthood, then it would be a happy outcome for Ceana, don't you agree?"

Cait glanced at her mother at the loom then away. "Aye," she said, "it would at that."

"Then let us contrive a way for such a joyful union to take place," insisted Edyth. "Do you have any ideas on how we might put them together? Are you feeling well?" added Edyth. "You do not seem yourself."

Cait smiled but it did not reach her eyes. "Aye. Quite well, Edie. I'm just ready tae be out of doors is all and done with...this." Here she gestured with her pirn, which Edyth took to mean the long process of weaving. "I...I know Alec," she said after a pause. "I will speak to him, if ye'd like."

Edyth nodded and smiled. "That would be wonderful. Thank you. It would please me to see Ceana well cared for, and for Alec to be settled with a wife so soon after his oath. It would be best, don't you think, to have him choose a wife from the village?"

Cait responded with a sound that could have meant her agreement but said no more. They worked in silence for several minutes before Roslyn ceased the foot petals, asking for more thread for her shuttle. Edyth offered to take her the basket of filled pirns and watched as her mother-in-law threaded the shuttle with a rich green color. Roslyn explained to her about the women in the village who dye and set the wool, but Edyth only listened with half an ear. She knew about fulling and waulking the wool. She was more concerned with Cait's strange behavior.

She wondered if she were preoccupied with what had transpired with the sheriff and his men when Roslyn asked her about the plans for the gathering to happen in a month's time. "Alban will ken what tae prepare, dinnae ye worry. It's more important that ye be present at the games, tae award the victors."

"Games?" asked Edyth. She'd never been to a gathering. "What sort of games?"

"Mostly the kind o' game where men throw things," said Roslyn with a shrug, indicating to Edyth that she didn't quite understand the thrill. "The men will line up tae throw stones o'er ropes, across a field, or even toss a caber o' all things."

"Truly? A caber?"

"There's also archery," supplied Cait, brightening slightly. "But my favorite thing tae watch is the war o'er the rope. That's where a number o' men, usually from the same village, will line up on one side o' the rope, and their opponents on the other, facing each other. They pull mightily and try and pull the other team across the center line. I've won...I mean, *some* people win a good deal o' coin betting on the teams." She pinkened at her mother's look of disapproval but then shrugged. "Och, what do ye expect, Mam, with me hanging around Iain and Ewan all my life? They were bound tae teach me things of which ye disapprove."

Roslyn gave her daughter an exasperated look. "Ye'll no' be betting this year, Caitriona. Do ye hear me, lass? I mean it."

"Oh, will you be here for the gathering?" asked Edyth with some surprise. She had understood that she was to be married in a short two weeks, and the gathering wasn't to take place for another moon.

"We'll be coming back here after we wed," said Cait, "to gather my things, afore going north."

This was very good news as far as Edyth was concerned and she said so. "It will be good, too, I think, for your husband to see you amongst your family."

Cait, looking sullen again, asked her mother if they could continue with the tapestry task tomorrow. "I need some fresh air." Edyth watched Cait go, her brow furrowed in concern.

"She'll only be worrit about her upcoming marriage," supplied Roslyn, looking at the closed door that Cait had just exited. "And it's no wonder. She's far past the age o' when a young girl thinks that just wishing things away can bring miracles."

"How old were you when you were betrothed?" asked Edyth, busying herself with more yarn.

"I was ten, and had no idea what tae expect. I only knew it was my duty tae wed Malcolm. O' course we didnae marry until I was of a better age. Fourteen," she supplied with a rather wry expression on her face. "I didnae wish that for my girls." She sighed, looking out the window, a frown on her face. "Though I suppose it might be harder now. Cait's set in her ways and as stubborn as a rock."

"Much like her brother, then," said Edyth with a smile.

"Aye. And whose fault is that, do ye suppose? I'll tell ye, they dinnae get it from me."

Edyth only smiled and wound the spun wool around another pirn. She was growing to like her rather stern mother-in-law more and more.

Chapter Fifteen

Cait found Alec in the armory, sharpening, cleaning and polishing Ewan's favored weapons. An array of knives and swords were laid atop the table which was set between them. The room smelled of leather, sweat and the sharp bite of metal. Cait picked up the smallest of knives at the end of the table, a short sock knife with which Ewan was particularly skilled. She'd seen him effectively stick a red grouse that had just taken flight with a mere flick of his wrist. She'd never been able to throw the knife well enough to hit a target with any real accuracy, despite how long or often she practiced.

Alec raised a brow at Cait, his eyes darting to the door she'd closed behind her when she'd entered. She could tell he was feeling uncomfortable, but she couldn't very well come here and do what she planned with the door open, could she?

"Erm," muttered Alec as he scratched the back of his neck. "Haps yer choosing which knife would best dispatch yer brother?"

Cait wanted to smile at the jest but she couldn't. She would be married in a fortnight. They were leaving in a few short days to make the long trip to her uncle's estate. She thought she ought to feel something more akin to excitement rather than trepidation, but she could not muster the feeling.

She looked at her friend through her lashes. She hadn't planned on coming. She didn't know what to say or how to begin, but only that she must, once Edyth had confessed her intentions of uniting Alec and Ceana. She didn't know what it was that had bothered her, after hearing of her good sister's plan. It wasn't as though she, herself, could marry Alec. Yes, she'd kissed him last Yuletide. Yes, they'd flirted and teased and skirted around each other with blushes and winks, but he was not hers. They had no claim on each other. They simply couldn't, nor did she want one. Or did she?

"Haps ye're shopping fer yer intended's murder weapon?" Alec asked, the teasing smile falling from his face at the sharp look Cait gave him. She did not want to talk about William Cawdor, her upcoming wedding, or her thickheaded brother.

Cait looked at the sharp edge of the blade as she ordered her thoughts. "I came tae ask ye something." She waited a breath, then two. How could she ask it of him now, with her wedding so close and they, such good friends? Their previous kiss had happened, in large part, because of the copious amount of wine she'd drunk as well as the joyous atmosphere that had permeated the hall. Even less so, it had been because she wanted Alec. She had seen him, dashing and flushed with excitement and she'd acted on instinct. She'd wanted to taste his lips, to see what it was to kiss a boy. But had she really wanted Alec? Did she love him?

When Edyth had mentioned Alec's name and her plans for his future, Cait had felt her heart twist slightly. She'd felt a surge of...what? Jealousy? Anger? Love? She couldn't know until she spoke to him and kissed him once more.

Cait looked at her friend, at his questioning look, at the broad set of his shoulders, at the way his hair fell into his eyes when he bent to retrieve a weapon from the table. "Will ye let me kiss you, Alec?"

He plainly hadn't expected that. His eyes darted to the closed door once more before swallowing noticeably. He let down the dagger he'd been holding with careful precision. "Why?" he asked, careful concern written on his face. He was brave, she'd give him that. It was all she could do to keep from looking away. Instead, she took a steadying breath and set the sock knife down. She squared her shoulders.

"Because I'm tae be wed tae a stranger and...and because I'd like tae ken my own mind afore I'm bound tae him."

Alec ran a hand through his hair, his eyes narrowing in thought, looking uncomfortable. "It's no' that I dinnae find ye bonny," he hedged, "but it's as ye say...." He licked his lips and glanced at the closed door once more. She could tell he was uneasy with being cloistered with her alone. Indeed, her mother would take the tawse to her should she find out what she was up to. And Ewan, should he find out Alec had laid a finger—or his mouth—on her, it would be far worse than a warmed bum for him. He cleared his throat. "As ye say, ye're pledged tae another. How would kissing me ease yer mind?"

Cait shrugged, feeling like in any other circumstance, she might take offense at his hesitancy, but she knew Alec and knew he was an honorable man, which is why she felt that she could ask this of him. She was in no danger from him. But what could she say? That she wanted to know if she loved him? And what if she did find that she loved him? What then? There was nothing she could do to stop her wedding and if she did find that she loved Alec, wouldn't the pain of it be worse?

But not knowing seemed impossible. Absurd. It would seem such a waste, would it not, to marry a stranger never knowing if you loved another? "Do you love me?" she asked pointedly. She felt her cheeks warm at her boldness, but kept her gaze fixed on Alec's pinkened face.

"Weel," he said carefully, "I...I cannae say."

"Nor can I," confessed Cait, tipping her head to the side in thought. "I wonder, though, if my fears in marrying another are because my heart is elsewhere. I think if we kissed, I would know."

Alec leaned his back against the stone pilar that supported the ceiling behind him, crossing his arms across his chest. "T'would be dishonorable for me tae do such a thing, and ye being promised tae another. Aye?"

Cait waved her hand as though she could dismiss the idea from reality. "I'll no' be the one tae tell him and I suggest ye dinnae either, should ye have chance tae meet."

Alec made a sound in the back of his throat denoting skepticism. "No' tae mention what yer brothers would do tae me should someone come through yon door suddenly, and my person far too close for excuses."

Cait looked over her shoulder at the door. "Then we'd best hurry." She rounded the edge of the table slowly, making Alec straighten, his eyes betraying his alarm. A gurgle of unease rumbled in his chest and he licked his lips, eyes darting to her mouth, then away. "Dinnae be afeard 'o me, Alec. Tis only a wee kiss."

Alec shot her a disparaging look and said, "Och, aye? That's right easy fer ye tae say, and ye no' being at the receiving end o' Himself's wrath.

Cait shook her head, dismissing his concern and stopped in front of him. Awkwardly, Cait pulled one of his hands to her waist. The warmth of his body seeped through the fabric of her bodice even as her face flushed. She was being far too bold, but Alec's principled character would never allow him such liberties. It was she who must do it. And it was now or never.

Cait stretched onto her toes, brushing her lips against Alec's closed mouth. She tried it again, more firmly than the last, feeling nothing save foolish. Her heart was beating faster than usual, but was that due to the kiss or to the danger of being caught? "Hmm," she thought, pulling away with a slight frown.

She was about to suggest that this time, he actually kiss her back when he suddenly pulled her closer, his arms wrapping around her possessively so that her body was flush against his own. His mouth found hers in a rush, their teeth colliding. "Sorry," he muttered as he pulled away slightly. "That wasnae a good one. Let me try again."

He did. It was much better this time and she tried to follow him. His lips were soft and careful, tentatively curious. She felt his tongue touch her bottom lip and she pulled away, shocked. He shrugged slightly at her look. "Too much?"

She touched her bottom lip with a finger and shook her head in thought. "I didnae think of using tongues." She waved him closer and, this time, Alec met her mouth softly, but with more assurance. And this time, when he deepened their kiss tentatively, asking permission, she let him, opening her mouth slightly. When the tip of his tongue touched her own, she wasn't wholly disgusted, but she wasn't sure if she liked it. She pulled away, opening her eyes, and looked up into Alec's.

"Well? What'd ye think o' that?" he asked. Cait rather thought any criticism might ruin him for life, so anxious was his expression.

But before she could answer, there was the sound of voices coming down the hall. Cait and Alec sprang apart. He waved her away, mouthing commands for her to hide as he busied himself with the whetstone. She stood against the wall near the door so that should it open, she would be hidden behind it. She held her breath for several heartbeats. The voices grew louder as the owners neared the closed door. Cait held back a giggle at the casual, unaffected look Alec had tried to adopt. He was staring so hard at the stone in his hands, that he looked as though he were trying to divine the future from it.

He shot her a warning look as she snorted behind her hand. She shrugged, then sobered as the voices came right to the door. She held her breath, waiting. It seemed like forever before the voices moved passed the room. Finally, when she thought they weren't coming back, she allowed herself to relax. Letting out her breath, she met Alec's gaze. He hurried toward her and, giving her another warning look, opened the door a crack to peer out.

He let out his own breath and waved her closer. "It's clear," he whispered. "Be careful, though, tae look up the stairs before ye run up them. Hey," he added as she slinked through the opening. He pulled on her skirts, his eyes alive with adventure. "Did that help?"

She nodded. It *had* helped. She'd felt nothing but curiosity aside from the thrill of being caught, which she had felt countless times before. "You're a good friend," she said. "Terrible kisser, but a good friend." She swallowed a shriek of alarm as Alec's booted foot swung toward her backside. He was smiling as well, knowing she was teasing him, and shooed her away, looking in the opposite direction down the hall.

When she made it to the bottom of the stairs, she looked back to Alec, who was looking at her with such longing that it made her heart stutter.

***

The news that Eachann had died in the night was like a knife to Edyth's heart. More than that, though, her sorrow was interlaced with anger. Anger and guilt. Anger at his parents for refusing her aid and guilt for her interference. It was like a double-edge sword, twisting in her heart. With every breath she took, she felt the keen sting. Guilt. Anger. Remorse. Fury.

Would it have been better for him had she done nothing? If she had left him alone, he would not have had to endure the pain of the blade and the long days of fever. If his parents had let her minister to him as she'd wished, would she have been able to save him? But even if she could go back in time, she knew that she would do it all again. She would not have been able to stand by and do nothing, despite the end result.

"My heart aches," she cried into Ewan's chest as he cradled her in their bed chamber. "Would that I could have ministered to him." He'd come to tell her the news as she prepared for bed. He'd found out that morning but had kept it from her until now. "Why did you not tell me?" she demanded, but did not give him time to answer. She knew why. He hadn't wanted to ruin her day. "Why would they not let me help him?"

"Yer no' to blame, Edie," said Ewan firmly as he held her. His liene was soaked with her tears. "Ye cannae take it tae heart, *mo chridhe*. Ye did what ye could."

"They would not let me even try. Why do your people hate me so?"

Ewan's arms tightened around her. "These are superstitious people. They fear what they dinnae understand."

She pulled away, her anger growing. "What's not to understand?" she demanded. "Eachann needed help and I was willing." She wiped at her tears with the back of her hand. "It is because I am English. It is the same with them all, Ewan! Eachann's parents, Alban, the servants...they hate me without knowing me."

"They will grow to love you—to accept you," Ewan replied, his eyes fierce, as though he could command their respect through sheer will of force. "Give them time. They will ken yer heart as I do."

Edyth tugged roughly on the laces holding her skirts, letting them fall to the ground. It was cold in the room. The fire hadn't yet warmed the large space to be comfortable enough without wearing many layers, but she welcomed the chill. Her legs erupted into gooseflesh, pebbling to life. Her skin stung slightly. It felt like a penance for her sins, though she could not name her offence. "Father Thale said that his parents wished for his soul to remain pure. They believed my potions were tainting his soul! Not because of what was in the tincture, but because it was *I* who had made them." Her face screwed up into an angry scowl.

"Father Thale said they'd heard rumors of my past. Even now, I am not free of Father Brewer's lies."

Father Brewer, the priest from her childhood village in England, had spread nefarious lies about her mother, calling her a heretic and a bride of the devil, all in an effort to cover up his own sins. These lies had resulted in her parent's murders, and because Edyth knew of Brewer's sins as well, she had been his next target. Father Brewer had spread the same rumors about her, as he had her mother. A heretic. A witch. A worker of evil deeds in the dark places of the world.

But despite the church absolving her of the priest's allegations, people believed the worst. They *wanted* to believe the rumors. So here she was—in what felt like a world away—and still Father Brewer's lies dogged her heels.

"Ye ken as well as I do how difficult it is tae keep such a secret from spreading," said Ewan darkly. "Ye said so yerself: it's like trying to catch smoke with yer hands. Ye must show them what ye are, Edyth. Ye must prove them wrong by doing good."

"Have I not been trying?" she railed. She was not angry with Ewan, but it felt good to shout, and he was strong enough to let her. She bent to the ground and gathered her skirts, balling them up and tossing them onto the chair near the hearth.

"Aye. Ye have," he admitted, "but it's no' been long since ye arrived here, and ye with yer visions o' my death. Ye cannae forget what ye did tae poor Rory tae bring yer schemes to fruition as well. That gave a strong impression of ye, Edie. People are afeared o' ye, so ye must be patient."

Edyth deflated slightly, remembering how she'd schemed against Ewan to save his life. Had that only been five months ago? It felt like a lifetime had spanned between then and now. She'd poisoned his captain, Rory, by steeping some broom into his tea, so she could get away from him on the road to Dunbar. She'd lied and caused him discomfort. She'd disobeyed their laird and, as far as they saw, bewitched him into marriage.

"Ye see," he said softly, tucking a strand of hair behind her ear. "Ye've shown them what ye are, a *fìosaiche*—a seer—which is no small thing. What's more," he added with a wry look, his fingers holding her chin, "ye've brought with ye a reputation, which has only spread through your own deeds."

She frowned, not liking how his words tugged at her heart. He was right, of course. He was always, infuriatingly right. "How is it you could look past these faults but they cannot?"

Ewan scoffed, his smile broadening. "I am ever the benevolent lord, am I no'?" he teased. When she rolled her eyes, his fingers tightened on her chin slightly, telling her he was ready to be serious. His thumb brushed the line of her jaw, his fingers stroking the column of her neck. It made her shiver, and not from the cold. "I knew I wanted ye the moment I saw ye fight so fiercely in the forest glade." His voice grew soft, his eyes darkening as he gazed at her, "but I knew I loved ye when ye told me I would die at Dunbar and then cursed me for it."

Edyth remembered well that night in his office. She'd bared her soul to him, told him what she, herself, had not wanted to believe. She was a witch. A seer. She'd foreseen his death, but it hadn't swayed him. "You said your duty and honor was worth death."

"Aye," he whispered, "I did." She'd called him names. Railed at him. Told him he was fool. "I like the way ye stand yer ground, Edie. I love yer conviction. Yer heart."

She'd followed him onto the battlefield. Had risked all to save him. Her hand found his, pulling it from her shoulder. She kissed his rough knuckles, bruised from swordplay in the lists. "And I would do it all again."

"Dinnae let the clan's fears trouble ye o'er much, *mo ghràdh*. Their esteem will change, once they see how fierce yer heart can be, for ye are *gaisgeach*. A warrior."

He kissed her then, pulling her close. She melted into him, letting him erase her anger and her guilt with his hands and his worshipful mouth. It was enough, for now, that he loved her, that he would stand by her. She felt loved, cherished even, when he touched her. She was enough, despite what the clan might believe of her.

Chapter Sixteen

The carriage swayed as it took the curve in the road, slowing to a near crawl as they navigated the rough ruts cut in the poorly constructed road. They'd been travelling for days, stopping to eat and sleep under the stars, only to climb back into their carriage to watch the scenery creep by. Having their fill of trees, hillocks, and sky, from their view through the small window, it was a welcome distraction when they happened to pass a small village or crofter's hut. They did not stop, but Cait could not help envying the people they saw.

They would live the whole of their lives in their communities. These people would not wed strangers, nor be forced from their homes in pursuit of some advantage. No, that was a burden left to such as herself.

"I think we'd get there faster if we walked," remarked Edyth. She was looking out the window, the soft grimace on her face lifting as she spotted something to her liking. Her brother, Ewan, no doubt, thought Cait, bemused. As happy as she was for her brother, she could not help the sting of envy that she felt whenever she caught the two together.

She, herself, would meet her husband mere days before the ceremony and, whether she liked him or not, she would be his. She would have to give herself over to him for that was the duty of a maiden. She'd known all her life that she would be matched in such a way, but it had always been as far away as the stars. Now that it was upon her, she felt as though the very ground beneath her had shaken free, leaving her scrambling for any sort of handhold. It could have been far worse, she told herself. She was seventeen, after all, and much older than many other ladies who found themselves bound to a stranger.

Cait blew an errant strand of hair out of her face and grunted her agreement. "But as I'm in no hurry tae reach my uncle's holding, I'm of a mind tae stay right where I am, aye?" She stretched and yawned hugely, only remembering to cover her mouth at her mother's sharp look who had chosen the seat across from her. No doubt to better view and list her faults. She'd slept ill last night. She hadn't slept well ever since Ewan had announced her betrothal to William, but now that they were on their way, the ever-present hum of panic she'd held in check was becoming harder and harder to repress.

"Do ye think that ye can at least pretend tae be the lady ye've been brought up to be while we're there?" asked her mother. "At least for as long as it takes for the man tae say his vows?"

"Sorry, Mam." Cait tried not to fidget. She felt full of nervous energy from which she could find no reprieve. "I'm sore tired of being cooped up in this box." She looked out her own window, careful to fold her legs at the ankles as she'd been taught. The tall pines dotted along the road offered little shade in the late summer heat and her damp handkerchief was doing little to rid her face of perspiration.

"I understand your reticence," said the dowager countess kindly. Or was it pity that shone in her dark blue eyes? "I remember being none too eager myself when I was in your shoes. I'd remind ye that your faither was a good man, and once a stranger tae me." The countess smoothed her gown, her eyes focused on some distant memory. "Malcolm was no' what I expected, but he grew on me with time." She smiled to herself, biting her bottom lip softly. "He had a bonny laugh," she confessed. "When he was no' burdened of mind o'er his duties, he was...canty."

"How did you grow together?" asked Edyth.

Roslyn's smile turned inward and somewhat sad. The creaking of the wheels over the packed road filled the cabin. After several heartbeats, she spoke, her voice soft. "He would leave me wee gifts...a flower one day, a sweet from the kitchens on another...a ribbon for my hair. Little things. I'd find 'em in my clothes chest, at my seat in the solar, or with my hair combs."

Her hand went to her wrist, where a yellow ribbon was tied. It was frayed on the ends and blotched with ink or some other blemish. The fingers of her right hand stroked the length of it, smooth against her wrist. "They werenae jewels, nor expensive scented oils, but they might as well have been. They were just as precious to me. It told me that I was in his mind, e'en when we were apart, ye see, and that was enough tae turn my heart."

The coach lurched over a rather large rut in the road, nearly unseating them. The spell broken, Roslyn *tsked* lightly as she straightened her mourning habit, which had fallen forward to cover her eyes. Once resettled, she settled her gaze on Cait. "Your uncle and brother have gone through great lengths tae ensure a good match for ye. They wouldnae tie ye tae a man who would mistreat ye."

The words felt only hollow to Cait. "I ken they wouldnae wish tae bind me tae a cruel man, but how could they know? They cannae truly ken the man, can they?" She felt better for sharing her fear, though it changed nothing.

"Both of our mothers were matched in such a way," said Edyth, pulling her eyes away from the window. And both of our fathers excellent men. So it will be with you."

Repressing a retort, she instead said, "Do you think we could stop soon? I might feel better if I could stretch my legs."

"I think the horses might appreciate a lightened load at least," agreed Edyth.

"Rest while ye can," urged Roslyn, "for once we arrive and the festivities begin, ye'll give yer eyeteeth for a minute alone."

***

Caimbel Keep
  Argyle, Scotland

"Bloody, jobby castle!" Cait hissed, restraining herself from kicking the door. She couldn't hear a single word of what was being discussed through the thick barrier—and she knew of what they were discussing: her marriage contract to William Cawdor, the Thane.

She'd learned rather belatedly that her intended had arrived to the keep and she'd missed his arrival, being rather caught up in watching a heated contest in the yard of her uncle's home. Six different fighting men were competing against each other by attempting to throw a rock the size of her head over a gibbet holding a target for arrows. Now, as it was, she found herself unsuccessfully attempting to glean whatever she might through the thick door of her uncle's office.

"Damn," she muttered, giving it up. It wouldn't do to have them suddenly appear before her, caught and embarrassed. If she was to marry this man, she didn't want him to know that she would eavesdrop at his doors, because she had no intention of stopping.

Cait wandered toward the great hall, taking her time, stopping here and there to take in the expansive tapestries. She was quite engrossed in a graphic image of the beheading of John the Baptist when she heard footsteps and male voices around the corner.

"She will be biddable enough, I daresay, once she is broken." Cait did not know the voice.

"Och, aye," said another speaker. One she knew as well as her own. "As it is with all willful females," said Ewan. She could well hear the smile in his voice and could easily conjure the image of his easy, commiserating smile.

The other man agreed, chuckling, and then the voices moved too far away for her to understand their speech.

Cait felt her eyebrows knit together as she imagined Ewan speaking to her betrothed—a spotty, fat monster, she imagined him to be—comparing her to a stubborn horse in need of the strap. Her belly soured at the thought and she ground her teeth. Moving as quickly as she could, she lifted her skirts and all but ran to catch up. Her slippers were silent on the rush-free corridor floors, hiding her presence.

She could hear them better now. They had paused at the door to the great hall. She dared a peek around the corner and saw Ewan exchange coin with someone who must work for her uncle. He was dressed as a servant and some of the bile left her throat. He hadn't been speaking to her intended after all.

The servant tipped his bonnet cordially and pocketed the coins with a smile. "I thank ye," he said, and then he was through the door. Ewan did not follow him, though. Instead, he turned on his heel and stared right into her wide eyes as she peered around the corner.

"Ye can stop skulking about, Cait," he said, good humor coloring his voice.

Cait straightened to her full height, ignoring the blush on her cheeks and strode to meet him. "What business did ye have with that man?"

Ewan considered her for a moment. "T'was the stablemaster, Cait. I just bought ye a wedding gift."

"Oh," was all she could deign to say. "I thank ye," she added, remembering herself. She cleared her throat and put her hands behind her back so as to keep from twisting her fingers together in full view. She looked behind her to confirm they were still alone then stepped closer to her brother.

"Well," hissed Cait. "I ken ye were in meeting with Uncle and my betrothed. Tell me about him. What do ye think of him?"

Ewan rubbed a finger under his nose thoughtfully. "Of Uncle or of William?"

Cait scoffed softly and restrained herself from rolling her eyes. "Dinnae be a dolt, Ewan. What of Willam?"

She could see him control his smile, urge it away until only an indifferent, cool visage took its place. He took a breath and said, quite solemnly, "Weel, I suppose he'll do for ye, Cait. There could be worse men."

"Mmmph. And what of his temperament? His looks?"

"Ye'd like tae ken if he's handsome then? I'm sure his mam thinks so."

Cait waited, her brows raised. "His mam?"

"Aye. Dinnae all mother's think their children braw and bonnie?"

Cait did roll her eyes then. "Tell me, Brother. Is he fair or dark? How tall is he?

Ewan pursed his lips in thought and raised a hand to about her height. "He's about...eh..." he said, bouncing his hand up and down to show an approximate height. "Aye, I'd guess he's about yer height. Mayhap a bit shorter. But what he lacks in height, he makes up for in girth."

Cait felt her eyebrows raise. So he was rather short for man. And fat. While she'd always been drawn to taller men, like her father and brothers, she supposed it didn't matter much. At least Ewan was giving her information. "Mmph. What else. Is he fair or dark? What color are his eyes?"

Ewan seemed to consider for a moment, his eyes squinted as though searching his memory. "Och, Aye! I remember the eyes in particular seeing as how they were twa colors." He held up two fingers unnecessarily.

"T...two colored eyes? Oh, do ye mean a bit o' green and brown together, like?"

"No, no," he replied. "I mean he's got one brown eye on the one side and gray eye on the other."

Cait frowned. She'd never seen such a thing. "Hmm...weel...tell me about his hair. What color is it?"

"He hasnae any," Ewan replied with a shrug. "Least on his head. He's got bonny, full eyebrows, though. Shall we go to dinner? I'm famished."

Cait's hand grasped onto Ewan's forearm like a striking snake, the hollow feeling spreading from her stomach to her throat. She swallowed and asked, "Wh-what of his temperament, Ewan? Do ye think he will be...is he kind at least?"

Ewan, pausing, seemed to take pity on her at last. His large hand covered hers, a warm comfort she'd never grown out of enjoying. "Sister," he said, his blue eyes full of understanding. "Do ye think I would bind ye tae a cruel man? And if he were unkind, I would have ye tell me sae I can cut the manhood from him." He smiled and turned abruptly to the door, leaving her there, feeling a sort of empty bellied terror she had been fighting since the business of her betrothal had begun.

Her stomach sour, Cait could only follow Ewan through the door into the great hall, speechless. How old was this man? She knew quite well that a maiden had little to no choice in who she married, and on a list of important qualities, physical appearance ranked low. A bride would want, for instance, a kind man of means, who could secure her way of life and safety. She should wish for a husband who valued her abilities and education. She should hope for a man who gave her independence and respect. Cait wished for all those things. But she also wished for a man who she might find...well, attractive.

Was it too much to ask for? Was she being greedy, to want comforts, esteem, as well as attraction? Aye, she supposed her mam would say she was greedy and spoilt and that she should make the best of the situation.

The great hall was high ceilinged and vast, full of people and the noise they produced. Her uncle had many retainers filling the tables. She followed Ewan's trail through the tables to join the rest of the family at the high table, where many of her uncle's family sat.

"Well?" asked Edyth expectantly, when she plopped down in a very unlady-like fashion.

Cait shrugged. "I didnae see him, though Ewan told me some of what I can expect." She pulled a face, letting Edyth know it was not good news. "He's probably got more hair comin' oot 'is ears than on his head." She felt like weeping and she *hated* crying.

She watched forlornly as a group of men entered, all in high spirits. They were tall and youthful and everything she had hoped might be in her future. She looked away quickly, dismissing her hopes. "Look for a short, bald man, for that is to by my husband."

"Oh, Cait," said Edyth, looking and sounding very sorry, indeed.

The vacant chair to Cait's left was pulled from the table with a rude sound. Cait glanced that way and saw it was being occupied by a rather large man with thick, dark blonde hair, worn long. She glanced at him, then away, looking out toward the crowd.

"Haps that's him?" suggested Edyth. Cait followed her gaze to a pudgy man drinking greedily from a horn cup two tables away. He was dressed well, she noted mournfully. Did Thanes dress well? She supposed they would.

Cait could only make a helpless gesture, her brow furrowed. "Aside from having...sizable girth, look for bushy eyebrows." Her voice, even to her own ears, sounded pained.

"What are we looking for?" asked the man at her elbow in a commiserating way. She glanced at him quickly, showing her displeasure. He was probably well into his cups.

"Nothing of concern," said Cait miserably, returning her gaze to the sea of faces. There was another balding man toward the back of the room in deep discussion with a woman, but when he turned her way, she saw that it couldn't be him, for his eyebrows were ordinary.

"Or haps it's that man, there," suggested Edyth, this time pointing to a man who had just entered. Cait groaned at the thought. "He's nearly dead!" said Cait. "Or he should be. He's older than my uncle!"

The man next to her cleared his throat, gaining her attention. He had smiling blue eyes and a groomed beard a few shades darker than his dark blonde hair, which could not hide his grin. "Do ye fancy auld men, then?"

Cait turned fully toward the stranger and summoned her most caustic glare. "If ye must know, ye nosey nelly, I'm looking for my betrothed."

The stranger's light brows rose in interest. "And who is it ye're tae be marrit to? Surely not any of these auld men?" He looked at Cait as though she was putting him on.

She huffed, her cheeks pink. "Aye, for that's who my fobbing, fat kidneyed brother and uncle have bound me to. I'll be the wife of...of a rotund troll."

"Weel," said the stranger, "haps it's no' all bad. If he's as old as ye say, he may die soon."

Struck by the thought, Cait's sprit rose slightly. "I hadn't considered that." But Ewan hadn't said he was old. Rather, it was that all the balding men they could spot in the room appeared that way. Most everyone's heads were covered, though, so it would impossible to discern.

"What's this troll's name, then?" asked the handsome stranger. He *was* handsome. Cait couldn't help but notice his striking blue eyes that seemed to spark with good humor. His jaw was wide and firm, his cheekbones high and prominent.

"His name is William Cawdor. Do ye mind him?"

He seemed to consider her question for a heartbeat before he nodded once with a slight grimace. "Aye, I ken the man."

Cait's stomach tied in a knot. The pitying look the stranger was giving her could mean nothing good. She steeled herself for the bad news, gathering her courage. "Pray tell, sir, what sort of man is he?"

The man's brow furrowed slightly as he looked over the crowd, then his gaze settled once more on her, making her feel like squirming in her seat. He leaned forward, as though about to impart some great secret. He smelled of leather, outdoors, and something wholly male that she could not name. "I have heard some call him handsome."

"Ye mean aside from his mother?"

The man laughed richly. Cait felt a sort of fierce pleasure at having said something that could elicit such delight from him. His wide shoulders bounced as he did so, drawing her eye to the lines of his body. He had the body of a warrior. Thick with muscle, but lithe and agile. She would wager that he was light on his feet and a great horseman. Most certainly one of her uncle's fighting men, then.

Chuckling, the man reached forward and refilled her cup of cider. "Aye, even if he is a rotund troll. A toast, milady." He handed her the cup he'd just filled and said, "To your union. May it be blessed with much laughter." He touched the rim of his cup to her own, then drank, his sparkling eyes watching her over the rim. Cait, feeling that she must oblige or be rude, took a sip and bowed her head in what she hoped was graciousness. She didn't feel gracious, only ill.

He stood then with his drink in his hand and, winking cheekily, wandered away. Cait was full of questions but he had not stayed to answer. She looked to Edyth, whose eyes followed the man through the crowd of tables to the back of the room, where he was greeted loudly by a raucous group of her uncle's retainers.

"Did ye hear, Edyth? He said he knows the man." She paused, watching him. The unsettled feeling in her middle worsened. She thought she might be sick and clutched her stomach with trembling hands. The stranger had said her betrothed was handsome, but he had said nothing of his temperament. What if he was handsome and kept mistresses? She would not allow the insult.

"Strange that he should come to this table and sit, only to leave," remarked Edyth, interrupting her sour thoughts. Edyth was still staring at the man, her lips pressed into a thoughtful frown.

"He is most likely a retainer of my uncle's," Cait said absently, "and well into his cups already, it would seem." She sat in silence, looking through the crowd, guessing who was to be her husband until her uncle stood and called for silence.

Her Uncle Niaell looked very much like her own mother, dark haired, tall, thin, but forbidding. He commanded many men and it wasn't difficult to see why. As fearsome as her mother was, her uncle could put her to shame.

His voice, deep as it was, carried far through the room, which quieted quickly. Bodies stilled and faces turned to listen as his booming voice welcomed them all to his home. "It is with joy," he said, looking down the table at his sister, Roslyn, with affection, "that I welcome my most beloved sister and her children here." He turned to his left, where Ewan sat, and touched his shoulder. "It is our great pleasure to invite ye to Kilchurn, tae celebrate the union of my niece, Catriona Ruthven, tae her betrothed, William Cawdor, Thane of Nairn."

Edyth nudged Cait with an elbow, a signal for her to stand, which she did, praying her legs would hold her. She plastered on what felt like strained smile and nodded graciously to the polite claps that resounded.

"Come forth, William," commanded her uncle, motioning with his arm to someone in the crowd, "and take your place at this table of honor. Join us in celebration!"

Cait's smile faltered when she realized the trick her brother had played on her. And she'd fallen for it! William was the man who had sat next to her, to whom she had barked answers and summarily ignored. She felt her face redden; heat flushed through her face. She felt an odd, sweeping relief at knowing he was, indeed, handsome, but that feeling was quickly squashed by the hundreds of other worries that plagued her. He'd lied to her! Well, perhaps not, but she felt the affront just the same.

Edyth tugged on her sleeve. Cait sat slowly, staring at her betrothed. "Close your mouth." Edyth's whispered command finally wormed its way into her brain and she snapped her mouth shut, averting her eyes as William made his way through the tables, smiling cheekily. "Smile," she hissed. Cait obeyed as best she could, feeling as though she were about to leave her body altogether.

She'd been staring quite unabashedly at her soon-to-be husband. Ewan had lied about everything. He was, in a word, beautiful. He walked with an assurance that, at least to Cait, screamed arrogance. But his smiles and laughter had come so easily. She could not believe that someone so cheerful could be cruel.

William clasped forearms with her uncle, then with Ewan, congratulating each other on the blessed transaction that was marriage. Cait glared at her brother, who smiled unapologetically at her before seating himself. William caught her eye as he moved toward his vacated seat to her left. She looked away quickly, feeling a riot of emotions. She'd wished him to be handsome and he was, so why did his beauty feel suddenly like a curse?

"My apologies Mistress Caitriona," William said with a slight bow before seating himself.

She glanced at him, then away, then back. "I suppose ye think yer clever."

His smile only broadened, revealing neat, white teeth. "Ye'll no' be cross with me o'er a wee bit o' fun. Yer brother assured me that ye appreciated some humor."

"Aye, but only if it's good humor." She cast him a glance from the side of her eye. "Iain, was it?" She felt her iciness thaw slightly, but not for her brother. "What else did he say?"

A servant appeared with a tray of eel with a white sauce. William offered some to her. She declined, doubting she'd be able to eat anything at all this night. She felt sick with nervousness. William waved the servant away then said, "Ewan spoke of yer beauty. I'm happy tae see he didn't lie to me as he did to you."

Cait raised a haughty brow. "Is beauty so important tae ye, then? What of my character. I might be a shrew."

Another servant appeared, this time bearing a tray of meats ranging from rabbit to mutton. It smelled heavily of rosemary and her stomach growled. Haps she would eat something after all. She nodded to the servant and William took the liberty of serving her, giving her a bit of each. When the servant moved down the table, William said, "Iain did tell me ye were bonny, aye, but he also said that yer as spirited and as stubborn as they come."

Cait felt like frowning, but worked hard to keep her face neutral. "And Ewan? Pray, what did he say?"

William took a bannock and, pulling it apart, offered half to her. She took it, but kept his gaze, waiting for an answer. "Ewan said ye were kind and loyal, and assured me that no better wife could be found."

Cait flushed slightly at the complement and looked down the table to where her brothers sat. They were speaking with her uncle, their faces devoid of levity. Something serious then. Cait wondered at that, but there was nothing she could do about it now. Edyth was listening, it appeared, her face wan. Most likely they spoke of King Edward and his sheriffs.

"What did ye hear of me, then?" asked William, "Aside from that I was an auld man, past my prime?"

Another servant appeared, carrying a dish of roasted pheasant. William took a serving, but Cait declined. "I was told that if ye treated me unkindly, they'd cut the manhood from yer body." Cait punctuated this statement by lifting a leg of rabbit and taking a bite from the bone. She chewed happily and reveled in William's throaty laugh.

He nodded in agreement. "Aye, they warned me o' that, too."

"Why did ye no' introduce yerself?" she asked once she'd swallowed.

William wiped his mouth on a cloth. "I had planned tae do just that. Earlier today, yer brothers pointed ye out tae me, while ye were watching the lads sport in the yard. When I spotted ye here at the table, I thought tae introduce myself. Imagine my surprise tae find ye searching oot all the auld men." He nudged her softly with his elbow, shooting her a crooked smile. "Tell me true, are ye disappointed I'm no' an auld troll?"

Cait smiled sweetly and picked up her goblet. "That remains tae be seen, aye? Ye've yet tae even introduce yerself properly."

William's smile grew, arrogance radiating from his face like the sun. He held his hand out to her, hovering between them. She hesitated only for a breath, then begrudgingly she offered her hand. His own was large and warm. She could feel the callouses under his fingers and the roughness of his thumb as it caressed her knuckles. "It's my pleasure tae make yer acquaintance, my lady," he said in a low rumble. The sound of it made her stomach feel queer. "Allow me tae introduce myself. I'm William Cawdor...yer husband." She watched, rather breathless, as he brought her fingers to his mouth. His beard was surprisingly soft; it tickled her skin, sending a strange shock through her arm. She pulled her hand away as politely as she could.

She felt a strange sort of thrill at hearing him call himself her husband. "I'm pleased to meet ye," she said rather more breathlessly than she liked. She took a breath, gathering her courage that seemed to have flitted away momentarily and forced herself to meet his gaze. "Why did ye agree tae this? Why me?"

William glanced down the table to where her uncle and brothers sat. "I ken yer uncle well. Our families are connected through marriage." He picked up the ewer and refilled her cup. "Yer uncle kens my needs well and suggested I align myself with his sister's family, who, he tells me, raised a wonderous and fearless creature." He was, for the first time since Cait had met him, wholly serious. Gone was the teasing glint in his eyes and the crooked smile. "There are few comforts in Nairn, my lady. I've no need o' a wee lassie. I need a woman, who kens who she is and isnae afraid o' hard work. I've been assured that ye bear these qualities."

Cait flushed slightly. She looked at her plate, wondering what her family had consigned her to. There was a fair bit of pride that swelled within her breast, to hear how highly her uncle had spoken of her. No, she wasn't afraid to lead, nor of hard work, but just what sort of difficulties lay in her path? She could not deny, however, that his words pleased her.

She met his gaze once more. He was waiting for her reaction, she knew, watching her with quiet contemplation. "I am gratified that they would speak so highly of me, but do not let them fool you. I am no' always brave. I'm terrified of this union."

"What part of our marriage has tested yer courage, milady?"

Cait would be honest, no matter how impolite it was to do so. It would not serve her to lie. "My only fear is being controlled. I fear what sort of man I've been bound to. Will ye be a tyrant? Will ye oppress my freedom tae speak? Take awa' my choice? Or will ye give me the same freedoms I've had the whole of my life? I am no' biddable," she warned. "Nor am I prone tae hold my tongue. If you wish for a meek wife, or one that cowers from men, then ye will have made the wrong choice. I dinnae ken how tae be such a person, nor was I raised tae be."

William lifted his goblet, a look in his eyes she could not decipher, so ill did she know him, but she would like to have thought it was one of satisfaction. "Tae a woman grown," he said and took a drink. She followed suit. "Tae freedom."

The rest of dinner was spent in idle chatter, with William telling her about his family, which was large. The only son, and the eldest, he had five younger sisters, two of which were already married. His mother had passed shortly after birthing the youngest girl, who was now ten years old. His parents had also lost three children in their infancy, which wasn't uncommon, but still sad.

His father was still living and in good health, but away on the continent, visiting his sister who was married to a Frenchman. He would not come back home until after the winter season had passed.

"Are any of your sisters here with you? I'd be glad to meet them."

William shook his head. "Only myself and a small company of men. It is a long way to Nairn and while I ken they would have loved to come, it wouldnae have been safe for them."

Cait raised her brow. "Is the road to Argyle so dangerous that a maiden cannae ride, even amongst a contingent o' men?"

William swallowed his bite and shook his head. His gaze scattered across the tops of heads, not meeting her gaze. "It's no' the road that is dangerous, milady, but I would no' risk my sisters. Wee Joanie isnae well enough tae travel sae far. She's...frail. Has been the whole o' her life. Her sisters dote upon her. They wouldnae leave her alone, even to witness their brother's marriage."

"I'm sorry to hear of her poor health."

William gave her a small smile and took a drink before changing the subject. "Ewan tells me of a fine gift he's granting ye. Shall we take her out tomorrow after we break our fast?"

He was speaking, of course, about the unseen beast that she'd overheard her brother paying for when she'd been eavesdropping in the hall.

Her nerves had settled somewhat, but they erupted back to life at his suggestion. To be alone with this stranger, her husband, still felt unreal. There would be an escort, no doubt, and she was grateful. She was not ready to be wholly alone with him, though soon enough there would be no need for bodyguards and escorts. They would be quite alone, and expected to do much more than she was ready for. "A...aye," she muttered, feeling her face flush with her thoughts. "It would be best if we could learn more about each other, afore we're officially wed."

"It's settled then," he said with a smile, offering her a bowl filled with honied figs.

Chapter Seventeen

The weather was still fine despite the onset of fall. Golden hues glittered brightly in the forest where the sun cut through the branches, making them appear as though they were lit from within. Cait was seated astride Ewan's wedding gift, a beautiful chestnut mare who was lovingly called Seòlta, which meant "crazy." They would be a good match, she thought. Even Ewan had been happy to report that the mare had the same fiery disposition as her new owner, but so far Seòlta had been nothing but pleasantly docile.

Spirited women are often maligned, she'd told Seòlta after she'd mounted her, uncaring that her skirts bunched up immodestly. Cait cooed at the horse, whose long ears twitched to better hear her. She could not be expected to put Seòlta through her paces and ride sedately for something as ridiculous as exposed calves. Knowing this, she'd worn her most accommodating dress, without all the layers of heavy petticoats. Her mother would have disapproved, but her mother was not here and Cait really didn't care.

As it was, William was riding alongside her on his horse, a silky black courser with beautiful lines, that moved swiftly and elegantly. He didn't seem at all bothered by her insistence of riding astride. Indeed, William seemed to understand her need for it.

She'd been right about William being a skilled horseman. He moved with his horse so well that they could have been one body. Cait could not keep her eyes from the pair as they made their way down the trail. There was something about a man atop a powerful horse that stirred Cait's blood. They were nearly out of the trees now, followed by an escort, but she could not wait to get to the open field where she could give Seòlta her head and see what she could do. That, and see how well William handled his horse at a full gallop.

"Did ye have yer own horse in Perthshire?" asked William conversationally.

Cait nodded. "Aye, a Galloway pony. He was as fat as a sow and n'er liked tae be too far from home." She laughed lightly thinking of him. "He would bolt for the stables if he thought he could get away with it. Once, when I was younger and no' so experienced, I didnae keep hold o' him, thinking he would be content to eat where I put him. Left behind, I'd followed my brothers up the pass, where they would go for the red deer. I'd stop here and there, tae read their tracks, aye? Weel, he must have had enough, for when I dismounted to make certain I was on their trail, the scunner turned tail and ran. That was a long walk back."

William's rich laugh felt like a boon. "Ye walked the whole way back?"

"Mostly," she replied, returning his smile. "I eventually came upon a drover road and waited for someone tae come along. By then my parents were wondering where I'd got to and sent out a team tae search for me. Da had come across my pony, cantering doon the road some miles from home, and followed his trail backwards. He came upon me in due time, with blisters the size o' silver pennies all o'er my feet. I've seldom seen him sae angry. But before long, with me safe in his arms, he saw the humor in it. He told me it served me right for stealing off without word, and I should be grateful for the blisters on my feet, for they saved me from blisters on my bum."

"He didnae punish ye?"

She shook her head as she negotiated Seòlta around a large boulder. "He never did. He left the punishments for my mam."

"Oh? What did she do?"

Cait smiled ruefully. "Took a tawse tae my bum that time. She was mad with fury! I'd n'er seen her sae angry. Aye, it wasne pleasant," she added at William's commiserating grunt. "I couldnae sit proper for a week, but it didnae stop me from following the boys again."

"Stubborn, are ye?"

"Ye might say that. Iain did warn ye." She gave him a not-quite apologetic smile.

"How old were ye then?" asked William, clearly amused. The dappled light rippled over his face, as if he were under water and not in the forest. The shadows moved over them, highlighting the red in her horse's long mane. She was a beautiful creature. It felt nearly otherworldly in the quiet of the forest. She watched the light play over his hair, making it seem to glow like candlelight.

"Six? Seven, maybe?" she answered with a slight shrug. "I cannae rightly say, though I thought I was plenty old enough tae be on my own."

"Did yer brothers begrudge their little shadow?"

Cait gave him a look that plainly said, *are ye daft?* but she settled for saying, "O' course. Didn't you, the eldest and only sisters for company?"

William shrugged slightly. "Ye seem tae have a good bond, ye and yer brothers. I wondered if they welcomed you."

"I entertained them, more like," she said with snort. "They kent well enough that if they dared me to some manner o' mischief, no matter the risk, I couldnae say no, which would then induce them intae the same behavior. They couldne let a wee lassie show them up, now, could they?"

The canopy of leaves thinned and the field she had been looking forward to riding in opened before them, dotted with thickets of brush in the low places. "Shall we?" she asked before she she nudged Seòlta forward. The horse instantly picked up speed into a gleeful trot. Giddy joy filled her. Seòlta gait was smooth and comfortable. Cait melded easily with each step. It was effortless. Exhilarating. "Care tae see how well she does?" asked Cait, gesturing with her chin to the open canvas before them.

William flashed her a swift smile then nudged his own steed forward without warning, bounding past her into the grassy pitch. She urged Seòlta after him, who leaped forward instantly. Cait gave her her head, holding tightly to the horse with her legs. Much larger than her pony back home, riding Seòlta gave Cait a new sort of thrill. She was in awe of her power and speed. And she was all hers.

The wind tugged on her hair and billowed her skirts, exposing her knees She didn't care, laughing outright. Seòlta's speed was magnificent. There was no other feeling like it. William slowed enough for Cait to catch up, but she had no intention of slowing. She flew past him, her eyes set on the line of trees up ahead that lined a stream cutting through the field. William hurried forward once more. He was pacing them now, his tawny hair streaming behind him. She wished she had her hair down. It would have felt wonderful to have its cool fingers streaking through, tangling it into a wild mane.

Too soon, she had to rein in. Seòlta was still unknown to her and while she had no doubt the horse could take the stream in one great leap, she would not chance it. At least not today. Cait was breathing heavily as though she had been the one carrying them across the wide expanse, her heart thudding wildly against her ribs, and the beautiful beast under her.

"Ye like her," announced William with a knowing smile. "Ye seem suited to each other."

Cait stroked Seòlta's neck fondly. "Aye. I think we'll be great friends."

"What of us? Do ye think we're suited?"

Startled by the question, Cait looked sharply at him. For one brief, shining moment, she'd forgotten about her betrothal, her forced wedding, and the loss of her home. Those thoughts, and all the feelings associated with them came crashing into her once more. It nearly took her breath away. "I cannot say as yet. I dinnae hate ye, which is a pleasant surprise." It was the truth, at least.

William tugged on his reins, bringing his horse around so that they faced each other, their knees nearly touching. "Aye. We'll suit."

The look that William gave her made her squirm. She looked around, wondering where their escort had got to. She saw him, within view, trotting across the field in their direction but not near enough to discourage intimacies. Cait's stomach knotted, but not in an unpleasant way, as William moved closer. The heat from his steed warmed her leg. His gaze was heavy upon her, filled with promise of something that frightened and excited her.

There was a squeak of leather as he leaned forward, his left hand moving to the pommel of her saddle. She swallowed, her eyes darting from where his hand rested so close to her body, to his face, then back again. His lips were turned into a crooked, arrogant smile. Far too close. He was taking too many liberties, yet she did not stop him. She did not admonish him as she ought. Her mouth did not work.

"Do ye ken, milady," he whispered, low and throaty. His eyes moved to her mouth. She swallowed, her nerves jumping. Was he going to kiss her? "That ye've go a wee bit o' food stuck in yer teeth? Just there," he said, pointing with his smallest finger to the offending spot.

Cait gasped, her fingers flying to her teeth and glared at him. She scrubbed her teeth with her finger, her face red. "Why didnae ye tell me sooner, ye scabby smout?"

William pulled reign, laughing as he moved away from her, an arm thrown across his middle as though it hurt to have so much fun at her expense.

"I take it back," she shouted to his back. "I do hate ye!"

***

Ewan rotated his shoulder, the short sword in his hand still clutched in his fist, as he sized up his uncle. The sounds of swordplay rang around them in the practice yard. It had been some time since he'd raised swords with his foster uncle, but Niael was still as strong as he remembered, and just as prone to trickery. He wiped the sand from his face, which his uncle had recently thrown at him in an attempt to get Ewan off of him. He'd been about to strike the winning blow, the auld cheat.

"I see yer time in France did ye no favors," Niael commented, gesturing with his chin to Ewan's injured shoulder.

Ewan spat sand out of his mouth and readjusted his feet. He motioned his uncle forward, who came at him with a burst of speed, his sword coming down in a deadly arch. Ewan blocked it and used the momentum to swing around to slice through Niael's middle. His uncle jumped backward, his back arched away from the tip of the blade and smiled cheerily. "Aye, perhaps I was wrong," he amended. He bowed graciously, his sword held to the side. "Ye're as braw as e'er, Nephew."

"I see auld age as no' yet robbed ye o' yer sword arm," Ewan conceded. "But I can do this all the day. It'll soon be time fer yer nap, aye?"

His uncle laughed lightly, his teeth bared. Sweat coated his face and soaked his liene. He bounced the dirk in his left hand quickly to readjust his grip then charged again. Niael feigned right, but Ewan knew better than to fall for his tricks. Sure enough, the dirk in Niael's left hand thrust upward between them, preparing to sink it into Ewan's wame, but Ewan jumped backward and deflected the sword in one fluid motion.

Ewan did not give his uncle time to set his feet. He drove him back and back again with punishing strokes. His uncle was tiring. Indeed, the bones in Ewan's hands and arms rung with the judder of the clashing blades. It would soon be over, but it would not be himself who conceded.

His uncle lost his dirk to one of Ewan's strikes. Their swords locked as he pushed his uncle up against the railing of the yard. "Do ye yield?" asked Ewan, pushing hard against his uncle's sword. Niael was a strong man for his age, but Ewan had the advantage of height and muscle.

With a burst of effort, his uncle pushed against Ewan, unbalancing him enough that he had to put distance between them, lest he get a sword to his throat. Niael dove for his fallen dirk, but Ewan got there first and kicked it away. His uncle lay in the dusty yard, heaving breaths with a smile. The tip of Ewan's sword went to his uncle's throat. "Ye are overtaken, Uncle. Throwing sand will not work a second time."

"Aye," grumbled his uncle between gasps. "Aye. I yield."

Ewan removed his sword and helped his uncle to stand. He patted his back making dust billow in the crisp, autumn air. "Just like old times."

"Ye learned some things, I think, warring in France."

Ewan shrugged and walked to the shelter which held their belongings and various other types of weapons, his uncle by his side. He found his scabbard, which he'd tossed aside earlier and replaced it upon his person. "As one does in war. It's different when it's real."

"Aye, it is."

Ewan removed his liene and used it to wipe the gritty sweat from his face, grimacing against the sweat in his eyes.

His uncle was looking at the edge of his blade, holding it aloft in the slanting rays of sunshine. "Do ye mind the Moray?" he asked in an offhand way.

Ewan frowned in thought. "Aye. Sir Andrew of Petty, do ye mean? He was captured at Dunbar in April, was he not? He and his son."

His uncle nodded. "The very same."

"What about them?" Ewan looked about warily, as though speaking of them were treason.

"We are free to speak," intoned Niael softly. "There is no danger to us here." His dark blue eyes, so much like his own, glittered with the promise of some secret knowledge. He picked up an oiling rag and ran it down the length of his sword as he spoke. "Sir Andrew, the faither, is in the White Tower. I doubt we shall see his face again. But his son is no' so heavily guarded. He is in Chester."

Ewan nodded. Escaping the Tower of London would be nigh on impossible.

"There have been whispers," hedged Niael, replacing his sword into its scabbard. He sat next to Ewan and pulled off a boot with a soft grunt. He upturned it, emptying it of the sand that he'd collected during their sparring match. "I heard tell that there is a plan to help him escape."

"What then?" asked Ewan with a shrug. "His lands are taken from him; his is a fallen house. Who would willingly hide a fugitive when so many have pledged their fealty to England?"

"Andrew wishes tae take back what is rightfully his, given tae his family by King David. Avoch belongs to him. It's calling tae him."

A spike of nervous excitement shot through Ewan at his uncle's words. Could it be that Andrew, like himself, was not willing to let England have their way? "But...how?" asked Ewan. It would not matter how keenly he or others wished to strike the English canker from their lands, but there was little chance of that happening. His uncle had said as much. "What's changed, then?"

His uncle shrugged and sucked his teeth before answering. "There is someone within Chester Castle who is loyal tae Scotland and willing tae help our cause. They've been getting Andrew's messages out and tae the right people, people who are speaking more in favor of a united Scotland without English rule. Now that they've got a wee taste of what it's like tae live under the thumb of King Edward, they're no' so comfortable."

"How will he fight back? Does he speak of particulars?"

His uncle shook his head. "It is dangerous enough as it is, sending letters out o' the castle. But if the handful of men are willing tae help him escape, as they say they are, I think they would be willing tae fight. Andrew's escape will be seen as a triumph against Edward. And now that the King's sheriffs have been placed amongst us, many nobles' kind feelings—or I might say—willingness tae serve England has soured."

Ewan ran a finger under his bottom lip, unsure. This is what he wanted: a free and united Scotland. He wanted that damnable sheriff off his lands. But would Moray escaping be enough? What good was one man's escape? "Who are these men ye speak of? Who is it that are willing tae help him?"

"The Comyns have expressed interest. They would ultimately wish tae see their faither released from bondage. They are eager tae fight for what is theirs. And the burgesses of Inverness...they have taken a keen interest in Moray's imprisonment as well. If the burgesses unite under Moray, the Comyns will follow suit. If the Comyns fight, so will I."

The burgesses of Inverness, Ewan knew, were made up of the freemen of the northern burghs. They existed from the time of the Saxons. Freemen were above in station over the serfs and tied to their lands. They paid their dues and pledged their oath of support to the land and its officers, but they were free to work and trade without penalty or tax from their lord. There were many in Inverness, he knew, who relished the old ways, and would no more like Edward's coup than he did himself. If they were willing to fight, perhaps others would be encouraged to join in the cause. "What is tae be done?" asked Ewan. "How might I help?"

His uncle placed a hand on Ewan's shoulder, squeezing it slightly with a satisfied smile. "I kent ye would be willing," he said with a nod. "I didnae forget yer mind at the oath taking in Berwick, aye? Did I no' tell ye tae wait? That the time would come? It is still no' here...not yet, but I will send ye word, when the time *does* come, and what part ye can play."

Ewan nodded then faltered. "I'm loath tae leave Perthshire again, Uncle. Ye've seen my letters regarding the sheriff appointed there, de Biggar. I fear he would torment my people should he get the chance. Even now, I worry what is happening tae my people in my absence."

"Mmph." Niael looked thoughtful for a moment. "I will share yer concerns with the others. There may be no need for ye tae leave. Iain could do just as well."

Upon Ewan's agreement, his uncle stood, saying, "Now, let's get a drink. I'm parched," as if they had only been speaking of the weather and not treason.

Chapter Eighteen

B efore she knew it, the day had come. She stood in her auntie's rooms, surrounded by at least a dozen women. There were jewels, pins, brushes and combs, perfumes, paint for her face, mounds of frothy fabrics, and all of it was for her. Or for the spectacle that was to be her wedding.

Cait's mother had chosen red for her wedding clothes, which she'd always said looked best with her coloring. Aside from Cait's height, everything else about her had been inherited from her mother: rich, wavy, dark brown hair and skin so fair you could see the veins just under the skin. Her blue eyes were also her mother's, though the shape was more akin to her father's. Large and expressive, she had had to learn from a young age to mask her feelings. When your eyes so easily betrayed your feelings, brothers took advantage.

Cait had never fussed over her appearance, nor cared what she wore, but as the maids finished dressing her, she could not deny that she felt beautiful. The heavy fabric, embellished with vines and flowers in rich blues and greens, fell in wide, elegant pleats from under her bustline. Her fingers traced the silky ribbons that decorated the bust, crisscrossing in a beatific pattern. Her shift, which was finer than anything she'd ever had previously, caressed her skin under the gown and peeked through at her shoulders, elbows and wrists. Her soft hose, the color of fresh cream, were tied fast above her knee with a ribbon, made new for the occasion.

Soon to no longer be a maiden, it was inappropriate for her to wear her hair free. The maids braided her long hair and curled it upon her head in an intricate design. When they were finished, she felt her nervousness redouble. There was nothing left for her to do to prepare. It was time. Her hands shook with nerves. She barely heard the ladies' compliments and good wishes, but then her mother was there, pinching her cheeks, looking proud and a little breathless herself.

"Aye. A bonny bride if I e'er saw one," said her mother. "And I'm no' just saying that because I'm yer mam. Ye *are* beautiful, Cait, inside and out." She placed the cream-colored veil over her head, topping it with a golden circlet, and stepped back to admire their efforts.

The ladies' maids were bustling about, picking up after themselves. Cait grasped her mother's hands tightly. "I'm scared," she admitted in a whisper. "It's come so quickly. My wame is curdled." She placed a hand over her middle, grimacing. How terrible it would be to be sick now!

"O' course ye are," said her mother in her usual, no-nonsense tone." Ye'd be a daft fool no' tae be. He'll be just as nervous, though he'll likely no' admit such a thing. Dinnae ye fash. Be brave. It will all be o'er soon."

She wanted to argue with that statement. The ceremony wasn't what was making her so nervous. It was what came after than had her stomach wound tighter than a fisher's knot. Instead, she simply said, "I wish Da were here."

Her mother's eyes softened slightly, but she only nodded before fishing about in her pocket. "I've sommat for ye," she explained, pulling out a long, silver chain. "Yer Da gave it tae me afore we were wed. It was his mother's. I wish ye tae have it...a bit o' him tae carry with ye."

The links of the chains were very small. It would have been tedious to make, but it was very fine and elegant, with a shining cross at the end, beset with sapphires. Her mother placed it over her head and settled it neatly between her breasts. "There. It's time, lassie. Best we dinnae doddle."

"Wait," said Edyth, coming forward with mint leaves. "You might be wishing for this." She did. Cait chose a few leaves with a thankful look. She'd told Edyth all about her embarrassment with William the day before. Taking a few leaves, she popped them into her mouth and gathered her skirts in her hands. All the blood seemed to rush from Cait's head, making her feel quite giddy. Cait followed her mother down the hall, the maids and Edyth trailing behind, to where her escorts awaited her.

Her brothers, dressed in their best clothes, kissed her cheeks and pressed her hands in greeting where they met at the bottom of the stairs. "Bonny lass," said Ewan, as he appraised her. "Where's my sister and what have ye done with her?" teased Iain, looking about as though the real Cait were in hiding. But soon his teasing fell away when he realized Cait could not be cajoled out of her nervous condition. All too soon, she was swept out of the keep and placed into a carriage with her mother and Edyth. They were all very quiet. What were they to say? There was nothing anyone could say to smooth the wrinkles from Cait's brow, nor to stop the tremor in her hands.

The kirk was probably beautiful, but Cait did not see it. She followed her brothers into the darkened entrance, where her uncle took her hand. Her eyes traveled over a blur of faces, none of whom she really saw as Niael escorted her down the aisle. They might have been mere specters rather than honored guests for all she took notice of them. She gritted her teeth against the cowardice she felt, settling her eyes on the long rug that ran down the center aisle. It was brightly colored with reds, blues and golds. Flowers were expertly woven into an intricate design running its length. How easy it would be to falter, to stand and stare at the false garden at her feet. Her uncle urged her forward softly with the smallest of pulls from where her hand was gripped around his forearm.

Never before had Cait thought of herself as a coward but she did now. It felt like a very long way to the altar and she was grateful for her uncle's arm holding her, keeping her steady. Her legs felt as unsure as a new foal and her stomach was not faring much better. She hadn't been sick yet, but she didn't fully trust herself not to be. Somewhere, someone was singing, though she did not even try to locate them.

She dared a look at the end of the aisle, where the priest stood with William, surrounded by brightly burning tapers in grand candelabras. The groom was richly dressed, of course, in a dark blue surcoat embellished with gold embroidery with matching golden hued hose, calling attention to his well-formed calves. William was broad in shoulder and deep chested, with narrow hips and long legs. His hair was gathered neatly in a queue at the nape of his neck, held together with a simple black ribbon.

He had shaved for the occasion. To her mind, he did not appear as ruggedly handsome as he had before but at least now she had a better view of his strong jaw, high cheekbones, and full lips. He looked younger than she'd first thought and she wondered at his age. She hadn't bothered to ask.

William looked as amiable as he always did since she'd met him and completely at ease. It settled her nerves slightly, seeing his relaxed state. But before she was quite ready, her uncle stopped them before the priest. Niael kissed her cheek softly and squeezed her elbow briefly in goodbye, and then he was gone, leaving her alone. Well, not completely alone. William took her right hand into his own, large left hand, giving her trembling fingers a squeeze. She could not bring herself to look in his eyes. She felt like a withered weed, hollow and brittle. Surely she would crumble and blow away in the wind with the slightest provocation.

The priest started speaking. Cait tried to listen. This was a life-changing event, after all, but she could only think of how small she felt next to the stranger who was her husband. She thought of how little she knew of him, of what she was giving up. She wondered about his life, of Nairn, and when she would see her family again. It wouldn't do, to mourn what she was losing, she knew that.

Yes, she felt as though she were losing her family, but William had a large family. She hoped to love them as well as she loved her own family.

Not only did he have a large family, but Nairn was on the northern coast, where Ewan had told her waves washed onto league upon league of white sand-kissed oat grasses, which give way to the rolling hills of the shire. She imagined that it was beautiful there and was looking forward to finding seashells and discovering all the wonders that lived in the salty ocean. Cait had never seen the ocean; she hoped she could love it as well as she loved her mountains.

William squeezed her hand, pulling her from her thoughts. He raised his brows, darting his eyes toward the priest in a marked manner that told her she'd missed something important.

Panicked she could only shoot him a stricken look. William graced her with a slow smile before leaning closer to her and whispering, "He asks are ye willing."

What a question to ask! The papers had already been signed; the banns had been read. The choice had long been made. "Aye," she said hoarsely. Lovely, she sounded like a frog. "Aye," she said again, this time more strongly.

The priest nodded, not looking even the slightest bit amused and put the same question to William, who, of course replied in the affirmative confidently. He did have a rather nice voice, she conceded. She could at least give him that. And he *was* handsome, even if he was an arrogant tease.

Next the priest went into a rather long soliloquy about Adam and Eve and the purpose of marriage, which Cait did her best not to yawn through. The priest then bade them face each other and clasp each other's wrists so he could bless their union. Her uncle came forward then and bound their wrists together with a strip of linen. Willam's hand was warm upon the skin of her forearm; she could the feel the calloues of his labors. Far too soon, the priest announced them united in marriage and William moved to kiss her. She held her breath as he bent his head to hers. His lips touched her softly, tenderly, and then it was over. She was a wife, and he, her husband.

The fact did nothing for her stomach.

William, still holding her hand, walked her back down the aisle, flanked by her family. They stopped to hear felicitations, well wishes, and blessings wherever people sought them out and engaged them in conversation. She nodded mutely through it all, only thinking of her pinching shoes, her rumbling stomach, and their shared room somewhere in her uncle's keep. Dread filled her. Her hands grew clammy. A shared room, where they were expected to consummate their marriage. And far sooner than she was prepared for.

Oh, dear God, she was going to be sick.

***

The banquet was lively enough. Musicians played, ale, cider, and even expensive wine was poured into cups held by known and unknown guests. Gifts were offered, which were littered amongst the platters of food. Cait sat at the table, an untouched plate of food set before her. William was silent, seated on her right. He'd given up trying to make idle small talk, for which she was grateful. She could not seem to find her mettle. It had gone its way with her appetite.

She watched as people danced and laughed. Would that she could feel such merriment during her wedding feast. She spotted Edyth then, pushing through the throng of people, clutching something to her bosom. Seeing her friend sparked some relief within her breast. At least she would not be left alone with William now that Edyth had come, for she had long since run out of things to say to him.

Edyth smiled somewhat shyly at William, curtsying in a rather wobbly fashion. "I'm Edyth," she said. "I'm Ewan's wife." She placed a dainty hand on her chest and repressed a burp. Cait smiled. She'd never seen Edyth in such a state before and it was lifting her sprits magnificently. "I, erm, have no gift for the pair of you. Only for Cait. Sorry." Here she handed off her gift, which was wrapped in a linen cloth. "That's a sparrow," instructed Edyth with brightly pinkened cheeks after Cait pulled the fabric away. She pointed toward the top of the box, her eyes glassy. "Ewan says it looks like a sheep." She snorted here making Cait's smile grow. It did look rather like a sheep.

Cait opened the lid to find parchment, quill, penknife, and a stoppered bottle of ink tucked neatly away inside. There was even a little portion sectioned off to keep the ink bottle from moving around inside the box.

"My gift is borne of selfishness," Edyth confessed, her flushed giddiness giving way to something else. Her eyes suddenly glittered with suppressed emotion, but she blinked as if shooing the sudden rush of feeling away. "Write to me," she said, "and I will do the same. I...I will miss you, Cait." More blinking. Cait felt her nose start to sting with emotion. Edyth, as if she could sense it, turned away from her, settling her wide, green eyes on William. "You will treat her well," she said, "or you'll have me to contend with. It will be most unpleasant, I can assure you." She nodded resolutely then hiccoughed again, not looking dangerous in the slightest.

William raised a humorous brow at Edyth, glancing sideways at his new wife, as though hoping for a story.

"I love it," said Cait, stroking the lid with her hand. "I will write to you as often as I can."

Edyth's gaze swung back to Cait, her face softening. "And I will await them eagerly."

Her uncle's voice rang out over the merriment, signaling that the priest was ready to bless William's and Cait's consummation. Edyth giggled, then, seeing the stricken look on Cait's face, sobered. "Don't worry," she whispered loudly. "I was scared too, when it came time for your brother to take my maidenhead, but it turns out I quite liked it in the end." In any other circumstance, Cait might have laughed, but here, now, her humor had abandoned her.

Edyth swayed slightly on her feet, blinking owlishly, then suppressed another burp. Cait's maid appeared at her side, waiting silently. She felt all the blood drain from her face. Even her fingers felt numb, but she stood on shaky legs and walked toward the stairs that would lead to her doom—of the forced intimacy that was about to take place. She thrust out her chin as cheers sounded, loud enough to shake dust from the rafters.

William followed behind the priest and her mother, who she was grateful for. Surely nothing could happen between them so long as their escorts tarried. Or were they to stay the entire time? She faltered, catching herself against the stairwell wall at the thought. She made it the rest of the way, thank the heavens, without tripping over herself to the appointed room, evidenced by the garland of flowers that outlined the frame and the guard who stood without. She groaned inwardly. A guard as well? What a barbaric custom!

She stopped outside the door while the priest made the sign of the cross over it, muttering something she didn't have the capacity to attend to. He entered then, beckoning them all inside, save for the guard. Thankfully *he* wasn't invited. Someone shut the door. It felt like it might have been prison bars for how she felt. She gulped air and looked beseechingly to her mother, who lowered her lashes in semblance of the meekness Cait supposed she wanted her daughter to embody.

The lady's maid and her mother carefully removed her gown, leaving her in her shift and hose. William was not immune either. He was instructed to remove his outer garments as well. Cait was gratified to see that the action caused him some distress as well. His cheeks had turned a ruddy color, at least. Haps the heat in his face had nothing to do with embarrassment and everything to do with anticipation, however.

She sat on the end of the bed with William, as the priest instructed, and waited in silence as he blessed both them and the bed on which they were supposed to...sleep. Saints above, she thought she might faint. Or vomit. Which would be worse? She fisted her hands in the coverlet, staring at the floor.

Once the blessing was completed, and the room emptied, neither of them moved. A candle sputtered. A log in the grate fell with a rush of sparks. What was she supposed to do? Well, she knew what she was *supposed* to do, but did not know how to start. She opened her mouth but no words came out. No thoughts would form. This was, by far, the most torturous night of her life. This was worse than scrubbing out the chamber pots, worse than mucking stables. William cleared his throat, making her jump slightly. "Weel, that was...painful." Cait glanced nervously at him. He smiled crookedly down at her. "I was worried they'd wish tae stay all the night."

Cait could only laugh nervously in response. She supposed it was best that they hadn't stayed, but now, utterly alone with him for the first time, she realized how very large he was. She swallowed and forced herself to let go of the coverlet. She wiped her sweating palms on her shift and, spying a ewer and cups near the fire, said, "Would...do ye care for a wee nip?"

William followed her gaze and agreed. He was wearing nothing but his hose and his liene, which fell to his knees. She watched him go to the small table near the hearth and pour their drinks. His hair, in the low light took on the color of dark amber honey. Tied in a thong, the candlelight sparked glimmers of gold along his crown. She looked away as he turned back toward the bed, afraid of being caught looking at him.

"Weak ale," he announced regretfully, handing her a cup.

"Better than naught, aye?" She adjusted herself on the bed to seat herself a little farther away from him. He noticed.

"Ye needn't be afeard o' me." His brow was furrowed. He held his cup in his hands, which were rested between his knees. He looked at her, his eyes never straying from her face.

"Shant I?" she asked, finding a thread of her usual boldness and grasping onto it like a lifeline. A minute ago, she hadn't a thought in her head aside from fear, yet now it was filled to the brim, begging to be let free. And what good would it do to hide her thoughts or feelings anyway? "Ye ken well enough as I do what is expected of us this night. While I cannae speak for you, I can tell ye, for myself, that I dinnae relish in the idea that I've got tae bare myself tae a complete stranger and...and more."

William ran a hand through his hair, tugging it loose from the ribbon that held it. He shook his head as though searching for the right words. Or perhaps he was merely shocked that she would be so honest. Maybe people did not speak to him freely because he was cruel and callous, and because of it, they choose instead to flatter such a man of power. Feathery strands of hair fell over his cheeks, hiding his eyes, as he stared at the floor.

He did not speak for what felt like a long time, but finally he said, "Ye think that I wish tae be commanded tae bed a stranger? That I wish for a bride that shrinks from my presence? Ye think this is the way I'd like things tae be?" He looked at her then, his eyes pinning her to the spot. He wasn't angry, she didn't think, only shocked that she might think otherwise. "I can tell ye, that's no wish o' mine."

His words softened the sharp edges of her feelings. Could it be true? Admittedly, she hadn't thought of his feelings at all, so engrossed she'd been in her own inner turmoil. "But yer a man," she said flatly.

For whatever reason, William thought that was funny. He chuckled, but not in a way that communicated that he'd liked what she'd said. His laugh effectively changed the nervous energy coursing through her into annoyance in a flash. "Can ye deny, sir," she demanded in a hard voice, her brow furrowed, "that men are free tae sample in carnal pleasures while women—*ladies*—if found tae act similarly, are ruined? Forever tarnished? Unwanted and unworthy to any man of station? Can ye deny it?"

"No, I cannae deny it. What ye say is true." He stared at her with a hardness that she welcomed. He was probably only disappointed at not finding a meek and tremulous bride.

"And can ye deny," she continued, "that often men of station take advantage of their position and take women as it pleases them?" She didn't give him the chance to answer. "O' course ye cannae deny it!" In a voice laced with distaste, she said, "So it stands tae reason, sir, that the male sex has no qualms whatsoever about how well they might ken a lassie, so long as their baser desires are fulfilled. And now that I am your *wife*, I have no way tae refuse." Rather breathless after her speech, she swallowed, her body jittery with nerves.

"Ye assume, madam," he said, with narrowing eyes, "that I am like other men."

"Aye, I do at that," she challenged, jutting her chin out with false bravery. Indeed, her hands were shaking so badly she had to stand and move away from him, clenching them tightly. "I ken sae little of ye, that I must assume ye're like other men." She hid her hands behind her back, looking down her nose at him, daring him to argue with her.

"Haps ye've been spending too much time around the wrong sort," he answered in a low timber. "Tell me, who has colored yer view of men in this light? Yer faither? Yer brothers? Or, haps, a lost *lover*."

Cait smiled with far too many teeth. "Och, and what if I did have a lover? What will ye do about it? Annul the marriage? Beat me?"

"Do ye make it a rule tae needle and irritate people or am I just a lucky exception?" He cut off her next retort when he stood, towering over her. She could not help the step she took backward. He was at least a whole head taller than she was, and a hell of a lot bigger. "I couldnae care less who is in yer past, madam," he said evenly, "only yer future. It is our marriage that concerns me, as it should you. If ye had a lover, then it's done, but ken this, *wife*, it is only *I* who will fill yer bed from this day on, and ye can expect the same from me."

He knocked back his cup and swallowed his weak ale in one go. He moved to the side of the bed and set down the cup there, where a little table held a pricket and candle. He pulled back the covers roughly before getting in. Cait watched, her heart somewhere in the vicinity of her throat.

A sound not unlike the squeak of a mouse escaped her. "Wh...what are you doing?"

He glanced back at her over his shoulder dismissively. "What does it look like? If yer looking for someone tae insult and argue with, there's plenty o' people downstairs. As for me, I cannae be bothered just now. Good e'en tae ye."

Cait pressed her lips tightly together, looking at the vast expanse of bed. The floor was cold despite the fire. As hard as she tried, she could not seem to hold her anger. It spilled from her, like sand from between her fingers, leaving her feeling quite cold and ashamed at her outburst. She looked around the room for a chair or some other place in which to sleep, but there was nothing save the bed. She couldn't go downstairs. Everyone expected her to be here, in her marriage bed. Her mother would march her straight back up here; she might even insist on a witness.

She cleared her throat softly and rubbed her arms with her hands to warm herself. There was the entire other side of the bed just waiting for her. And William was insulted enough to dismiss and forget her. It would be a stupid person, indeed, who chose misery over comfort. Moving quickly, before she could change her mind, she sidled into the bed, but kept as far from William as possible. He did not stir. She lay on her back, looking up at the canopy above them. Some of the candles were still lit. She should get up and blow them out, but she did not move.

She felt as though she were standing on the edge of knife. Her balance was precarious and, while her available choices would not bring certain death, her choice would determine her future with the man beside her. What was she doing? What had she gained by bristling up like a thistle? Yes, he hadn't touched her, but she'd also caused a divide. That's not the kind of relationship she wanted with her husband, but she also wanted the freedom of choice.

She looked to her right, where the vast expanse of his back was as an impenetrable wall. She had allowed her fears to overcome her and she'd disrespected him. This was a sorry start to their marriage. William had been kind and friendly. He'd teased her and attempted to ease her nerves and she'd barked at him. Accused him. "I'm sorry," she said in a small voice, though it felt loud in the stillness of the room. After a beat, William turned over on his back with a sigh but did not look at her. His hands were folded atop the bed clothes.

"Care tae share what that was that all about?" He sounded resigned, which only made her feel all the more foolish. He was probably thinking what a mistake he'd made in choosing her as a bride.

Cait shook her head, searching for the right words. "I'm...I'm scared. It's easier tae be angry but it wasnae fair o' me." Her words hung in the air above them like a prayer.

"Ye're like a wee badger, backed intae a corner, aye?" He said with a hint at humor. "I thought ye might take my bollocks clean off given the chance." He glanced at Cait, who couldn't help the small smile at his description of her. "I can see ye're a woman o' conviction and yer no' afraid o' an argument," he said seriously, "but I will ask ye, for the sake of our marriage, tae no' speak in riddles. Speak plainly tae me and I will promise ye the same. If ye're frightened, just say so."

Cait swallowed, meeting his gaze briefly. It went against her nature to confess such feelings, but for the sake of their future together, shouldn't she try? His request seemed, if nothing else, *fair*. "I will do my best tae no' let my temper get the better of me," she promised

"I wasnae going tae force myself on ye, Cait." He was looking, as she was, to the dark stretch of canopy over their heads. She heard more than saw him turn to look at her, the soft shushing of his hair on the pillow overloud in the quiet. "Did ye have a lover in Perth, then?"

"No," she admitted. "Nor were the men in my family as ye suggested. None have lovers or take women as they please, but because I was surrounded by men, and I the youngest, they took care tae warn me of how a man can be. But ye're no' like other men. Aye?"

"No, I'm not." He rolled over onto his side to face her. A hand reached across the divide between them, waiting patiently, resting on the quilt. It was an invitation, she knew. An offer to start anew. With a tremulous breath, she met his hand halfway, placing her own hand into his. His hand was broad and warm, his fingers curled softly around her own, warming her cold skin. His hand was hairless, save for a smattering of fine blonde hairs across his long fingers and near his wrist. Broad, square fingernails were cut short, some stained with ink. Her hand felt so very small within his.

"Cait," he muttered, drawing her eyes, "I'd like verra much tae kiss ye. May I?"

She swallowed heavily, her eyes locking onto his own in the dim. She gathered her courage around her like a cloak. "Yes," she whispered, staring at the shadow of his mouth. He moved closer, the heat of his body warming her faster than any fire ever had. He smelled lightly of rose water from his bath mingled with something wholly male she could not identify.

His knees touched her own but she did not pull away. He let go of her hand to run his thumb along the line of her jaw, his fingers wrapping around her slender neck. She wondered if he could feel the rapid beat of her heart there, which was growing steadily faster as his eyes ran over her features. "Ye're a bonny lass, Cait." She felt his breath on her chin, could see the fathomless dark of his eyes touching and retouching upon her mouth, her eyes, her nose, her brow. Again and again.

His lips moved to the corner of her mouth, soft and unhurried. His lips were dry and warm, slightly rough from being in the wind and sun. Slowly, he moved to the other corner of her mouth. She kissed him back that time, feeling breathless and shy.

William's fingers stroked softly along Cait's neck, making her want to stretch like a cat wishing to be petted. His thumb found her collar bone, stroking along its length once before his mouth settled over hers. Her fingers curled into his liene as his warm, soft mouth slanted over her own. He was closer now, somehow, though she had no memory of either of them moving. William's warm hand stroked her arm and settled on her waist. Even that small touch set her heart to racing.

He pulled away then, giving her waist a small squeeze with a large, warm hand. "Good night, Cait," he whispered, before turning onto his other side. Cait, breathless, smiled ever so slightly to his back, her fingers lifting to touch her mouth. Haps she did not hate him after all.

Chapter Nineteen

The hunting dogs were whining, pulling against their leashes as the women were helped onto their horses in the stable yard. Today was the morning of the celebratory hunt, which was a custom of Argyllshire. A social affair, they'd just finished breakfasting and had made their way to the stables where they would enter the forest par force, in quest of the animal.

Today they would hunt a hart, the male red deer, which had been tracked the day before by Niael's master of hunting and his lymer—a scent hound used to track large animals. Cait would only watch today, not expert enough with a spear or with a bow to land a killing blow to such a large animal. Edyth, however, had a bow slung over her shoulder, looking like a fierce goddess in the early morning light.

William had a sword strapped to his back and a short spear in his hand. She watched openly as he mounted his steed, which pranced in place, its mane and tail bouncing as his weight settled into the saddle. Tall and straight, she noted again how well he sat a horse, like he and the beast were one entity. His eyes swept over the heads of the milling hunters and looked away lest she be caught staring at him. She arranged her skirts, reaching down for the proffered reins, feeling her cheeks warm. She could feel his gaze on her, as warm as the spring sun.

All members of the hunt had positions to uphold, though Cait had paid little attention to the instructions, as she was only to follow and stay out of the way. The relay lads, tasked with keeping the dogs under control were leaving ahead of the party, the dog's eager whining waning as they left the fenced enclosure of the mounting yard.

"Let the chase commence!" announced the hunting master atop his gray courser. The master hunter was stocky and red-nosed, as though perpetually drunk, but his dark eyes were clear and severe. His surcoat was crisscrossed with leather straps holding quivers of arrows. Horn-handled knives stuck up from his long boots, easily accessible for the *unmaking*, when the deer would be disemboweled. Someone blew a horn, its discordant bleating piercing Cait's thoughts and then William was at her side, his easy smile and smiling eyes focused solely on her.

He'd been gone when she'd awoken that morning, which had filled her with equal parts relief and disappointment. She wasn't sure of herself, nor of their relationship, and did not like the unbalanced feelings his nearness elicited, so when she'd opened her eyes and found only the empty expanse of their marriage bed, the conflicting feelings coursing through her amplified. Why would she be glad of his absence yet wish him near in the same breath? It made no sense to her, but she did not have the luxury of time to dissect her feelings.

She'd scarcely had time to pull herself from the bed and use the chamber pot before her maid had arrived and started the process of dressing. And now she was mere feet from him, staring up into his face like a brainless fool. "Good morning," said William with a secret sort of smile, his deep baritone seeming to tease her. She felt that with those eyes on her, she could keep nothing from him, as if he could see her imbalance, could read her feelings, so at odds with each other. "Did ye sleep well, my lady?"

The question wasn't indecent, yet she could feel her face warm. She armored herself against him in the only way she knew how. "As well as can be expected, with a snoring boar in my bed."

"Och, aye. I heard it too, but I wouldnae call ye a boar, wife."

The word disarmed her. *Wife*. Yes, she was one now. His. Cait opened her mouth to retort, but the hunting master was speaking now, ushering them out of the yard and onto the road into the forest. The trees were sparse here, thinned and pruned, so that Cait could easily see the procession ahead of them, winding their way through the thick tree trunks to the trail the dogs had indicated.

Iain was with her uncle nearest the front, speaking in an animated way that bespoke of his excitement. Ewan was riding next to Edyth close behind, who laughed at something her brother had said, her laugh like a chime in the wind. The smitten look on Ewan's face embarrassed her, filling her an uncomfortable pressure in her chest. She hoped no one ever caught her with such a look on her face. She glanced at William who seemed completely at ease and redoubled her efforts to swallow her nervousness.

"Did you? Sleep well, I mean?" she asked, glancing at him.

"Mostly. Someone stole all the quilts in the night and I had to keep wresting them awa again."

"I'm sorry...I'm not accustomed tae sharing a bed."

"No, nor am I. I suppose we'll get used to it."

Cait did not answer. She looked straight ahead, between her horse's ears.

"Do I frighten ye, Cait?" he asked quietly, so that no others might hear.

"Yes," she answered, then grimaced. "No." She looked fully at him then. His face was open, curious. They'd promised each other to speak plainly with each other and she would keep her word. "The truth is, I scarcely know how tae feel, let alone act. I..." she shrugged here, unable to find the words. "I feel like a stranger tae myself, bound tae a man I know even less."

William did not answer right away. He merely held his right hand out to her, offering it to her. She took it, feeling a flutter within her middle as her hand slid into his. "Does my touch frighten ye?" he asked.

Cait looked at their hands bound together then at his face. She took a deep breath and made the choice, once more, to be truthful, no matter how silly it might make her sound. "No. I feel—I feel a wee stirring inside, like afore I jump from the high cliff into the deep bend in the river."

He smiled softly. "And last night, when I kissed ye?"

Cait looked away, at the horses ahead of them as she formulated her response. Could she tell him, truly, how his kiss had made her feel weakened and euphoric? How her belly had burned, pooling heat between her legs? How her body had desired to press itself bawdily against him? She could not. Not here, in the open, where so many ears might hear. And perhaps not even alone, could she divulge such thoughts. She drew a steadying breath and met William's blue eyes, intent. "I liked it."

"So did I," said William, giving her hand a squeeze before letting go. "So ye see, there is no reason to fear me. It's no' my nearness that causes yer hesitance. It's something...other. Perhaps ye're afraid that what ye hope for us will no' come to fruition; but we are joined now, forever. We are allies, you and I. We needn't fight what is between us, only let it grow."

She could only nod and take her reins in both hands again, wondering if this is how it started for her sister, her mother, and countless other women bound to strangers. He'd said they were friends, but she hardly knew him. No, not friends. Allies. But perhaps they could be friends. She looked through the trees ahead, past the horses and riders separating herself and Edyth.

Edyth had been a stranger to her mere months ago, yet now, she counted her as a sister. It hadn't been difficult to like Edyth and she was finding it easier to like William the more time she spent in his company. Her mother had said marriage was as difficult as it was joyous, fraught with all of life's troubles. When her father had spoken to her sister, Aldythe, before she'd wed, he'd said marriage was like a battle, but instead of fighting your spouse, you had to constantly fight your own selfishness. Cait frowned inwardly, not sure she wanted to know her flaws, let alone fight to suppress them.

They rode mostly in silence as they left the wide road for the narrow track that led up the slope of the mountain. They could not ride side by side here, but in single file. William took his place directly in front of her, where she could enjoy the view of his wide shoulders and narrow waist where he sat atop his beast. The forest was thicker here at the foot of the hillside, where smaller game could easily hide from their party. Up, up, they climbed. The large thickets of trees gave way to sparser scrub where the fierce wind whipped and shaped them.

The mountainside became rockier the higher they climbed, where the wind and the rain had eroded away the soil. Veiny outcroppings of granite peeked through the earth, like the bones of a great beast, long dead. Before long, the distant baying of the hounds signaled that the hart had been spotted and the party gained speed. William stayed close by Cait's side, though he could have easily outstripped her. She, careful not to push her horse too hard in such an unfamiliar landscape, held back, letting others pass her.

The hunting party crested a bald, rocky ridge and disappeared over the side as they chased the hounds down the other side of the mountain. Cait let Seòlta have more rein, trusting her to pick the best path over fallen logs and clinging boulders as they followed the sound of the dogs and the melancholy horn. They had come to a heavily wooded dell at the bottom of the ridge when a sharp cry of alarm pierced the air.

"Quickly," said William, bidding her to follow. Someone was screaming; voices were raised in alarm. Branches whipped by, catching on her skirts and in her hair but she ignored them. She heard what the trouble was before she saw it. Guttural and nasal all at once, the growl from wild boars could make the stoutest heart stutter. "Boar," she breathed, though she needn't have given the warning, for William was pulling his short spear from his back, guiding his horse with the reins in his left hand.

She could see the colorful clothes of the hunting party ahead between the trees and brush, could hear their overlapping shouts of alarm. "Spears!" shouted Ewan, sliding off his horse. Edyth was sliding off her horse as well, her bow forgotten as she hurried to a spot where several other hunters were gathered, kneeling in the mossy, fern-strewn forest floor around what looked like a body. Someone was most assuredly hurt.

Cait's eyes scanned the thicket quickly, assessing. "There!" she pointed into the swaying ferns twenty or thirty feet in front of them. William urged his horse forward, holding his spear at his shoulder, his knuckles white with the force of his grip. He let go of his reins completely, turning at the waist to better face the hidden target. It was moving faster now, sending the fronds swaying, going right for Ewan, who was knee deep in the leafy cover to their left.

Cait's warning shout wedged in her throat; her breathing arrested as William's horse followed the boar's path. The boar was grunting and growling so loudly Cait doubted she would be heard even had she called out. Ewan took his stance, holding his own spear at the ready, his eyes narrowed at the oncoming threat. The boar was very close now. *Move!* She silently urged. *Run!* But Ewan did not move.

At the very last moment, when the beast's unseen tusks were sure to slice into Ewan's legs, her brother jumped to the side as he struck downward with a powerful stroke. The angry squeal of the boar filled the dell. Boars had tough skin and while Ewan's spear had struck the beast, her brother's aim had not given it a killing blow. Ewan's spear had stuck the beast in its muscular shoulder, which had only seemed to enrage it further.

Cait tracked the boar by the twitching fern fronds, the tops of its shoulders just visible. It turned around to take another pass at Ewan, the spear bouncing with its steps. She saw a flash of yellowish tusks, thrashing from side to side, ripping ferns and tossing debris with righteous anger. The spear fell from its shoulder soundlessly, blood weeping from the wound. Ewan pulled the short sword from his back and his eyes narrowed on the trotting beast, still several yards away.

Iain, who had been ahead of the party with the hunting master, was coming back down the trail, a look of alarm on his face as he quickly took in the situation. Cait could see Iain's determination to reach, to intervene. He pulled his own spear from his back but there was no clear shot from such a distance. She could see the white of Iain's face as he urged his horse forward. The boar, which was picking up speed, would be on Ewan within seconds.

Cait's heart was sure to beat right out of her chest. "William!" she cried, pointing at Ewan, who's stern face, white with determination, braced himself, his sword held at the ready to slice at the furious boar.

Edyth was shouting as well, telling Ewan to move aside, but he either did not hear or ignored her warning. William had already been on his way, however. He reached Ewan a breath after she and Edyth had shouted. His spear was held to his side, the deadly point dangling toward the ground. He leaned in his saddle and jabbed at the pig. With an almighty squeal, it toppled, then tried to rise once more, only to fall, its little hooves beating the earth ineffectually. It shrieked and thrashed about, its movements lessening as its life ebbed away.

Silence filled the space. The forest seemed to ring with it after so much commotion. Cait could hear her heart in her ears. Her hands shook, her fingers cold. Edyth's white face, eyes wide, stared at her husband, who had not gone unscathed after all. His blood-soaked hose was ripped—shredded across his shin—where the boar's tusks had swiped at him.

It had all happened so quickly; Cait hadn't even moved from her spot atop her horse where they'd first entered the bowl of the dell. She dismounted, her legs feeling like water, and made her way over to the gathered hunting party. She saw then, who it was that had first screamed. One of the hunting master's pages had narrowly escaped being hurt when the boar had spooked his horse. The boy had fallen off as his steed had reared and ran away, leaving him with sore ribs and an injured shoulder. His shoulder looked *wrong*, sticking out where it shouldn't, his arm limp.

"I'll deal with Ewan," said Cait, touching Edyth's elbow. "I cannae help the lad." Edyth blinked, looking away from a limping Ewan, who was bloodied, yes, but he was walking, making his way toward them. The hunting master, Iain, and other members of the hunting party were now standing around the boar speaking about what was to be done. Surely the hart—and dogs—were long gone. Cait only listened with half an ear as the hunting master bade one of his pages to ride ahead and tell the relay team what had happened.

Cait met Ewan halfway, stopping him with only a look. He sat on a fallen log nearby, his face white and damp with sweat. "Looks like that smarts a bit," she said as way of greeting. She pulled her knife from her waist and sliced his hose away as carefully as she could. Ewan hissed slightly when she pulled the wool away from his tattered skin.

"He'd have liked tae have gouged me," he murmured, "but the wound is no' deep. I'll bide."

"I can see your bone," murmured Cait, peering at the gouge in his right shin. The blood had slowed, beading up around the rather neat gash.

"Well there isnae much meat on that part of me, thankfully. All he got was a wee bit o' skin. Hurts tae put weight on it just the now, though"

Cait grunted her ascent. "I'm sure Edie will wish tae bind ye with some tincture or other, but I see it's no' so dangerous as first supposed. Ye'll have a bonny wee scar ye can boast o'er fer years tae come."

Ewan squinted at the wound, leaning forward so their heads were very close together. "I'm glad yer husband is quick witted and has a strong arm."

Cait looked over her shoulder, to where William stood by the fallen boar, watching as the hunting master said the appropriate Gaelic prayer over the animal. "As am I."

"Do ye like him so far?" asked Ewan, following her gaze. "Do ye think it a good match?"

"As ye say, it's a good thing he's as clever as he is."

"Aye, he'll learn quickly enough how tae be what ye need."

"I hope I can do the same," admitted Cait. "It's no' so easy for me, as it is for you, *bràthair*, tae bend and shape my will tae another."

Ewan stared at her for a breath. "No," he agreed. "Ye've ne'r welcomed being told what tae do, even it was what was best for ye. That's why marriage is a commandment, aye? It forces us tae think of someone else o'er ourselves."

"Expert are ye?"

Ewan shrugged. "It's only what I've observed. Adversity is a strong teacher."

"Is marriage so difficult then, that ye would label it as misery?"

Ewan's mouth tugged downward slightly at her words, his eyes on his shin. "Adversity need no' be misery, Cait. Only a lesson."

Cait opened her mouth to respond, but her words were forgotten when the injured page boy howled in pain. Both Cait and Ewan turned toward the noise in time to see Edyth pushing the lad's shoulder back into its proper place as two others held him still. The boy's face was white to the lips, but his scream trailed to a whimper as his shoulder joint found its home once again. Edyth was speaking to him softly, pulling sticks and leaves from his dark hair.

The master of the hunt ordered his pages to prepare the boar for transport back to the keep. The hunt over, Cait remounted her horse and waited for the others to do the same. She listened as members of the hunting party praised William's spear work, but he merely shrugged, letting the praise roll off him as easily as summer rain falls from leaves.

***

Much later that night, as the feast came to an end, Cait found herself growing nervous once more. Her fear of being thrust back into the bedroom with William had far less to do with the expectation of force, however, and everything to do with her conflicting feelings. Did she want him to touch her? To kiss her?

She thought of the way his hands felt at her neck and her waist late last night as he drew her in. She recalled the warmth of his lips on hers, could easily conjure the fuzzy, heady feeling they induced. The remembrance of it made her breath hitch, but in the same instant, she felt herself hold her resolve to resist him firmly in place.

What had changed? Mere days ago, she'd daydreamed of running away, or of even marrying Alec so she could stay in Perthsire against her brother's wishes. But Alec had never made her feel so at odds with herself. She'd chased him from time to time, teased him. She'd liked him well enough. They were friends, weren't they? He was handsome and witty and *comfortable*. But with William it was...different.

She could feel herself softening to this stranger. And so quickly, too. What had happened? Some pretty words? A display of skill and courage? Cait looked at him carefully, trying to out her feelings. Was it solely his aspect? His handsome features?

"My lady," intoned William as he met her searching look, his blue eyes as dark as sapphires in the flickering torchlight. Something thrummed in her, a chord vibrating through her core at his look and the sound of his voice. "Is there ought I might offer ye? More drink, perhaps?" Not just his handsome features then; even his eyes resting upon her and the sound of his voice was affecting her.

Cait shook her head. She'd had plenty to drink and had eaten her full. "I only...I only wished to look upon ye."

Humor touched William's features as he said, "The rotund troll. And why would ye wish tae look upon such a creature?"

Cait should have been embarrassed for what she'd said to him two days before—for calling him names—but she could not conjure the feelings. She could only wonder. She lowered her voice so that only he could hear. "Ye said that we were allies today, on the hunt."

"Aye," he replied with a slow nod. "And I meant it."

"Then why do I feel that giving myself tae ye would be relenting tae an enemy?"

The humor on William's face fell away, replaced with one of contemplation. "Ye're a strong-willed lass, Caitriona. Haps tis only that ye made up yer mind tae resist me. Haps yer no' yet ready for such intimacies. We *are* allies, though. I willnae ask ye for more than ye can give."

Something around Cait's heart lessened its hold at his words. There was time. There would be no pressure from William. She looked around her, at the merry making, the drinks being poured and the people who paid them no heed. "I spoke true this morning. I did like it when ye kissed me."

A warm hand touched Cait's under the table, where it rested in her lap. She took it, feeling the same giddy, sweeping feeling she'd felt before when he touched her. Perhaps she wasn't quite ready to give herself to him, but the thought didn't seem so impossible now.

That night, as they went to their room, she wasn't filled with fear or anger at her loss of choice. Instead, she felt the nervous excitement of unknown possibilities. Of a real marriage, where the simple willingness to trust could grow into respect and eventually—hopefully—love.

As William washed his face in the basin and scraped his teeth with a willow twig, seeming completely at ease within his own skin and unaffected by her perusal, she was struck with how strange yet familiar this new life of hers was. Nothing had really changed. Not by much...at least so far. But this stranger that she had been convinced would be so different from her, who she had been determined to dislike, was just a man. William had all the same routines as every other person she knew. He wiped his face on a towel and, noticing her stare, smiled apologetically at her.

"I should 'ave asked ye if ye needed help with yer laces. Or do ye wish for me tae call yer maid for ye?"

Cait shook her head and turned around, pulling her long braid over her shoulder to give William access to the laces that ran up the length of her spine. "Seems a shame tae call the lass out o' her bed just tae pull my ties loose."

Cait's breaths were shallow as William's shadow fell over her. She thought, even blind, she would know his nearness solely from how her insides squirmed. His hands were gentle, but her body swayed slightly as he tugged the laces through the eyelets. Her skin tingled as the bodice loosened its tight hold.

She left the sleeves of her clothing tied to the bodice and let it fall, all apiece, to the sheepskin rug on which they stood. *Turn around*, she commanded herself. *Do it. Be bold.* But she could not force herself and instead busied herself in the ties of her skirts. She held her breath, waiting for a touch, a hand on her shoulder, her waist, but after a moment, she felt William move away from her. She forced herself to breathe as she pulled the last tie with a tug and let her skirts pool at her feet.

The cool air immediately slithered up her legs, erupting her flesh in countless pebbles. She should have undressed closer to the fire, but that's where the ewer and basin were, and that's where William had been standing. She bent to retrieve her heavy, woolen skirts and bodice and placed them neatly over the trunk in the corner, thinking how silly she was being. William was adding another log to the fire, his back to her.

She hurried to the bed and clambered under the covers, pulling them up to her chin. She tried to steady her breathing, which was coming fast, as though she'd just run up the stairs.

William pinched out the candles, bathing the room in the soft, orange glow from the fire. She averted her eyes just in time as he pulled his liene over his head, leaving him bare. "A—aren't you going to be cold?" she asked timidly, still not looking at him. The ropes on the bed strained at his added weight, bringing with him a rush of cool air as he lifted the covers.

She could hear the amusement in his voice when he said, "Is this what lowlanders call cold?"

Her uncle's lands were not really in the lowlands, but compared to Nairn, Caimbel lands were far enough south as to be considered almost sultry. "In Nairn, the winter winds off the sea grow so fierce that my beard grows icicles."

"Is it very cold there much of the year?" asked Cait, pulled from her discomfort by curiosity.

"The summers are bonny enough, but the winters are long and often hard. The fisher folk dinnae venture oot much for all the storms, but we bide well enough. It will be nice tae have ye in my bed tae keep me warm at the very least."

Cait blushed and prepared herself mentally for a diet abundant in smoked or pickled herring for all the long, dark months of winter.

"Ye'll need an extra wool petticoat and some better stockings. I wouldnae hurt tae have new boots made either. I'll have some seal skin boots made as soon as I may. They'll keep ye dry, if no' warm."

Cait tried to imagine her new home but had never been so far north. "Tell me about Nairn."

William took a deep breath and considered silently for moment. "I suppose it's like any other hamlet or village, with people depending on each other tae survive. But Nairn is a rare beauty. The bluffs that o'er look the sea cannae be matched and the land is rich and fertile. I do hope ye'll like it, Cait."

"I'm sure I will grow tae love it," she said diplomatically.

His hand found hers under the coverlet, large and solidly warm. It sent a bolt of awareness through her body, pulling her nervous anticipation to the surface once more. "Are ye tired, lass? Should I let ye sleep, then?"

Cait bit her lip and held tightly to her husband's hand. No, she wasn't tired. She was curious and far less apprehensive than she had been before lying next to him. She was interested in the man beside her but more so in what he roused within her. There was time enough to learn of Nairn and what her life might be like. For now, Cait wanted to know what would happen should she let him kiss her again. "I'm no' so tired as yet. Do ye think—" She swallowed nervously but forced herself to continue, her face warm. "Do ye think ye could kiss me again, William. I did like it when ye kissed me."

William moved closer to her, his body heat permeating through her shift and warming her to her toes. His hand moved up her arm, his fingers tracing the lines of her bones until his hand brushed her neck to cup the side of her face. Every place he touched came alive, his hands both familiar and novelty. He was not smiling now; his eyes were intent upon her. "I'd gladly kiss ye, Cait. I only ask ye tae tell me when I must stop, for I fear that once I start, I'll no' wish tae end it."

Cait could only nod, swallowing her nerves away, before he pressed his lips to hers. It was a good kiss, soft and slow, undemanding, but this time, she knew enough to kiss him back. She moved closer, pressing her body to his experimentally, so that her thighs and breasts met the solid lines of his own body. His hands moved to her waist, pulling her even closer. Her heart was beating a wild tattoo against her ribs and her breath came short.

William deepened the kiss, his tongue lightly touching her own and she gasped aloud. Alec had kissed her in this way, but his hands on her waist had not felt so intimate as William's did now. Nor had Alec's kiss made her heart flutter as if a caged bird lived therein. She had not felt a coiling warmth deep inside her at Alec's touch. But she did now. And she, God help her, she wanted to know more. She wanted to experience what it would be, to give in to the feelings that were coursing through her. Powerful, instinctive feelings that seemed to come alive whenever William was near her.

William pulled away slightly, a question forming on his lips, but Cait did not wish to talk or to give place to doubt. She pulled his mouth down to her own once more and gloried in the grunt of pleasure that she could feel in William's chest.

William was gentle and unhurried. His mouth moved to her neck where he did something that made her eyes roll into the back of her head. This was wonderful. This was easy. Thinking and fretting over what might happen in their marriage bed had been ridiculous, considering how she was feeling now. At how she felt with William's mouth and hands on her too-warm body.

"I am a fool," she admitted, breathless.

William laughed softly, his breath warm on her skin. "Yer no' a fool, *mo luaidh*, but ye make me smile like one."

My darling. Her heart seemed to soar at his words, the soft roll of his timbre stirring her blood. Could it be true? Was she his darling? They hadn't known each other but a short time, and yet.... And yet she wanted it to be true. Cait kissed his palm, filled with the warmth of her own body and returned the gift. "I dinnae mind being a fool, so long as I'm yer fool."

"Ye are mine, *m'eudail*." said William softly, "and I am yers." And then he took her mouth once more and Cait could no longer think.

***

A short week later and they were on their way back to Perth. The way was as slow as ever but with Roslyn staying behind with her brother, Niael, Edyth and Cait were free to discuss the events of Cait's wedding. And while Cait was willing to talk about her wedding night, she felt unaccountably shy suddenly, despite Edyth being her closest friend.

What had happened between herself and William seemed almost too private to talk about. Would doing so be a betrayal somehow? As if she were no different than a bawdy fisher's wife, tossing the best parts of her to idle gossiping tongues. Edyth was no gossip, of course, but even so, Cait had not yet mentioned their joining. Nor had Edyth asked. At least not yet.

So far, they'd only discussed the upcoming festival and games, but Cait could feel the weight of Edyth's unspoken questions between them. They hovered there, like clinging raindrops on an eave, gathering into themselves until the weight would grow too much to hold itself back.

William had joined the men riding horseback and had left the women to the carriage, as expected, but Cait's eyes seemed to find him of their own accord, when they turned a corner and the view afforded her a forward vantage. They would stop and camp tonight, just as they had on the way to Caimbel lands. Cait was wondering what it might be like to sleep with her husband under the stars when her thoughts were interrupted by Edyth clearing her throat.

"William looks quite at home on a horse. I'm impressed at the way he handled his steed on the hunt," she said in an offhand way, nodding to where Cait was currently staring out the window. William was in view as they circled a bay of a large loch. His dark blonde hair shone in the sunlight, blowing softly to lift off his shoulders. Cait had braided it for him early that morning, but it had come undone in the stables, where she'd run her hands through his hair as he'd kissed her soundly. The thought of it made her cheeks pinken.

Edyth smirked knowingly. "So, it's done, then." It wasn't a question and Cait did not answer, but the hot flush of her cheeks was answer enough.

Cait looked away from the window. "I've ne'er seen a man so well seated atop a horse, and me from a family of horsemen. Thankfully for Ewan, he is a quick thinker."

"There is no greater benefactor of his skill than Ewan—and through him, me." Edyth paused, looking at Cait askance. "Is your husband skilled in *other* ways?"

Cait flushed, easily divining Edyth's meaning. What could she say? She shrugged. "I've naught tae compare him to, but I can say that I do enjoy his kisses. Quite a lot, in fact."

Edyth's smile grew wider. "I'm glad to hear it. How did you find the experience *as a whole*?" Her friend's eyes asked the question her tongue did not.

Cait's fingers found the hem of her cloak. "We didane...that is, naught happened the first night."

Edyth raised her brows, silently waiting for Cait to continue. The gravel of the road was loud under the horse's hooves and under the carriage wheels and Cait found some comfort in that fact, thankful no one would hear them. Still, she lowered her voice so that Edyth had to lean in across the aisle to better hear her.

"I didnae ken what happened between a man and a woman. I mean, I *knew*, but I didnae understand what it would be like. How I would feel. I was rare frightened."

Edyth nodded. "Yes, I remember the feeling. It's an awkward circumstance, and more so for you and William, I would imagine. At least Ewan and I had the good fortune to know and love each other. I can't imagine what you must have been feeling."

Cait nodded then shot her good sister a telling look. "But I'm no' scared now."

Edyth sat back, looking satisfied. "I'm glad to hear it. I'd wondered, but I couldn't ask with him around all the time. He seems fond of you."

Cait's eyes darted to the window, but she could not see him now. She only saw the passing pines and spindled alders as the carriage dipped low through a hole in the road. "Aye," she responded, "he does at that."

"And you seem rather fond of him as well."

Cait shrugged slightly and smoothed her skirts. "Aye, we get on. We havenae argued, yet, at least not since the wedding night, so that seems well and good."

"You argued?" asked Edyth, sounding hungry for details.

Cait waved a hand in a dismissive fashion. "Och, just me being a ninny. I didnae much like the idea of being forced intae the marriage, muct less being forced tae give my body tae him."

"And he didn't like that idea?"

"No, no. He agreed with me. Said as he wouldnae force me, nor ask anything of me that I wasnae willing tae give. It made me feel like a shrew for screeching at him. But he did kiss me goodnight, and I liked that enough tae let him do it again. Then a bit more."

Edyth nodded. They were silent for a time, looking out the window. "I wished tae ask ye something," said Cait, her bottom lip caught between her teeth. "I didnae wish tae ask Mam. Is there some wee tonic that will help keep a bairn form coming? Do ye ken o' one I might brew?"

"You don't wish to have children?" asked Edyth, sounding somewhat surprised.

"Aye, *someday*. But no' just now," supplied Cait. "I ken well enough that the Church doesnae approve o' such, but...." She trailed off and shrugged.

Cait watched as Edyth fiddled with the end of her braid, her eyes unseeing. She nodded slowly. "Yes. Yes, I remember my mother told women who didn't wish to have children to take a tea with mugwort and tansy leaves. It's simple enough to make but you must take care to drink it daily, and in the right amount."

Cait nodded and smiled kindly, leaning forward to grasp Edyth's fingers. "Yer a good friend tae me, Edie. I thank ye."

Edyth smiled back and squeezed Cait's fingers before saying she was rather tired and closed her eyes to sleep.

Chapter Twenty

The gates to the bailey were opened. A steady stream of people entered into the busy courtyard under a clear sky, where vendors had set up their wares, hoping to make a good trade. The festival was larger than usual this year because Ewan had invited the Stewart clan to attend. He'd said that since he'd declined their interest in betrothing Cait to their Robert, they were now interested in joining Iain with one of their daughters. Persistent lot, the Stewarts.

Edyth had met the potential bride, Alice, last evening when the Stewarts had arrived. She was a small, mousy looking thing, with large, dark brown eyes set in a round face. She'd carried herself well but spoke so little that Edyth could not make any judgements on her. Iain, for his part, had been cordial, but seemingly unaffected. They'd hardly said two words to each other as they'd supped last night, though her parents had been talkative enough.

Ewan had explained that the Stewarts had been allies with their clan for many generations and that potential union through marriage was only one reason they were present at the games. A wealthy clan, the Stewarts had agreed to help Ewan hide Ruthven assets in an effort to keep de Biggar's hands out of his coffers. Clans members had been instructed to give the majority of their quarterly rents to the Stewarts, who would keep them hidden on their lands for a time.

Rory and a small contingent of Ruthven men had been gone for weeks, where they had helped gather and deliver the larger portion of the rents to their trusted neighbors, the Stewarts. Of course the smaller portion of the rents would be given publicly at the gathering, so as not to cause suspicion. If—or when—de Biggar demanded a portion of the rents, Ewan would have much less available to be stolen.

The larger portion of goods would be delivered slowly, over time, and in secret. Edyth thought her husband very shrewd, but worried that with such a plan, if the Stewarts would expect an agreement for marriage between Iain and Alice. It was no small thing they were doing. What would happen to their friendship and the Ruthven goods, should Iain refuse the union?

"Hot pies!" one stout, toothless woman shouted, pulling Edyth from her thoughts. The woman was holding a platter with her pastries as Edyth and Cait—followed closely by their escort—passed her stall. Edyth's stomach rumbled, her mouth watering the instant the aroma hit her nose, but they could not tarry. They were on their way to the open field without the walls to watch the games that had already started. They passed stall after stall, some with bolts of fabrics, some selling crocks of pottery, another with cuts of meat. Flies buzzed all around and they took a wider berth to avoid the smell.

"I'm surprised Ewan opened the gates with the sheriff and his men milling about," said Cait absently as she wove around and through the crowd.

"He didn't wish to shut the people out." Edyth replied to Cait's back. *Nor does he wish to hide the small portion of the given rents.*

"No," agreed Cait, her voice raised over the noise of the crowd. "I suppose it wouldnae be hospitable tae keep the clan without the walls. And it would not do tae show his fear of the sheriff in the presence of the Stewarts."

"You think Ewan fears him?" asked Edyth. She would have said Ewan disliked the sheriff and his men, and especially their liege lord, but she did not believe her husband feared the man.

Their escort and guard of the day, Alec, was trailing close behind, as always. He was quiet and did not engage them much, but Edyth couldn't help but notice that his eyes were often on Cait. "He does not fear him," he said gruffly. It was the first time he'd spoken outside of necessity that day.

Cait met Alec's eyes then, for what felt like a long moment as they waited for a cart to be cleared from their path. "My brother is flesh and blood, Alec, no matter how well ye wish him tae be otherwise. He has fears."

Alec's eyes hardened and Cait looked away. "Why do you say he fears the sheriff?" asked Edyth, confused at the tension between the friends.

Cait waved a dismissive hand and set them all into motion again as the cart rumbled through the gate. "Ewan's greatest weakness," she informed them, "is his sense of duty. His obligation to his people—to keep them safe—is foremost in his mind. He fears what the sheriff and his men might do to them, and he powerless to stop them."

"He is no' powerless," countered Alec, his brows forming a grim line. "He has a host of fighting men and many allies who would join him with only a word."

Cait shot Alec a look as though he were simple minded. "What would happen, do ye think, if he roused Midlothian against the English King's men? War would come down upon our heads, and such destruction the like o' which we 'ave ne'er seen. Ewan wouldnae call upon his allies and no one would dare tae aid us, even if he did. He will no' fight against de Biggar and the man kens it well. This is what strikes fear intae Ewan."

"When did ye become such an expert on men?" demanded Alec arrogantly. "How is it ye can disparage yer brother—and his allies—sae easily? He is no' weak, nor afraid. Ye forget, what I have witnessed of him."

This was followed by a tense silence for the space of several breaths. They walked through the gatehouse, the toothy portcullis like the open maw of a great beast. Edyth hadn't counted, but there had to be at least a hundred tents pitched outside of the walls from Ruthven and Stewart clan members alike, coming to enjoy the gathering, and for those obligated, to pay their quarterly rents. That's where Ewan was, presently, holed away with the barrister within the garrison, collecting his dues.

Cait shook her head as she finally said, "Ye mistake my meaning, Alec. I ken Ewan's heart is as stout as a dragon's and that he would gladly go tae his death if it meant saving those he loves. Ye told me what he did for ye in France, and I can well believe it. But, can ye no' see? It is his sense of duty that births his fear. He will do all he can to appease the sheriff to save his people hardship."

Edyth privately agreed. She'd seen his discontent, his worry, and his sense of duty all heighten since de Warenne and de Biggar had shown up outside their gates with a missive from King Edward. She hadn't considered his worry as fear, however. They walked down the pathway, which was lined with colorful tents, smoking campfires, discordant music, and with the hum of indistinguishable voices. There was an air of excitement that permeated the scene, which Edyth found catching despite the conversation they'd just had. Even with the worry of the sheriff and his men at the forefront of her mind, she couldn't help how her heart began to speed up with the promise of some unknown delight as the gaming field came into view.

Once they made their way through the village of tents, their view of the games was unencumbered. Different areas on the great field were set apart for different competitions. Today there was a group of men tossing heavy stones on the left-hand side, closer to the line of trees that kissed the feet of the mountain. She watched, fascinated, as men would cradle a chosen stone in their hands, close to their bellies, turn in a tight circle, then lob the weight into the air. The stones were clearly quite heavy, for when they reached the pinnacle of their arc and fell back to the earth, they did not roll atop the grass, but sank down, scarring the surface with black divots and hefty thuds that she could almost feel in her feet.

This game, whatever it was called, was not their intended destination, however. Straight ahead there was a group of spectators already assembled around what Edyth knew was the war over the rope game. Iain was competing, along with several of his closest friends. He had insisted that Cait's husband, William, join him as well against clan Stewart. Victory, she had been told, was paramount, as it showed not only the strength of the clan, but their unity.

It made little sense to Edyth, but many shows of strength did, especially when it came to men. What did it matter, who could pull a rope? She would rather see a competition of real skill, like in swordplay, where strength only played the smallest of parts. "Are you disappointed you are stuck with me and cannot compete, Alec?" asked Edyth as she avoided a large pile of horse dung.

Alec glanced at Edyth, shielding his eyes from the sun. "Nay, mistress. Tis an honor tae stay by yer side and guard ye."

Edyth made a noise that indicated her disbelief. "A young man like you, so soon to be knighted, doesn't wish to tout your skill and strength? Why, I'm sure that there are several young ladies who will be saddened to hear of you having to tend to two old married women instead of participating."

Alec had the good grace to affect a visage of humility, but Edyth thought she saw a pleased gleam enter his eye at her words.

"What say you, Ca—Mistress Cawdor," asked Alec, catching himself. Edyth supposed it would be strange for Alec, who had grown up with Cait, to be so formal with her now, and she with a new name. "Do ye wish tae see me compete?"

Cait's face flushed at the question. She did not quite meet his eye when she said, "I am happy to cheer for all who compete in the name of our clan. Should ye wish tae compete, I would be glad tae applaud."

"Yes, come Alec," said Edyth, looking between the two old friends. "We all know there is little danger to us here, with so many eyes upon us. What sport is it that you favor?"

Alec's eyes were still on Cait's back, who was only a few steps ahead of them. "If it is yer wish that I compete, I would let my lady choose." It could not be clearer to Edyth that she was not the lady of whom he spoke.

Cait's back stiffened slightly at his words and Edyth, who had thought she'd only imagined some unknown constraint between them could no longer doubt her suspicions. Edyth looked to Alec, who wore a look of carefully placed indifference, though the pink of his ears gave him away. Something was affecting him. And not just him. Cait as well.

Edyth cleared her throat in the awkward silence and said, "I know of one young lady who wishes to gain your notice. Haps I will ask her in which sport she'd most like to see you compete, hmm?"

Alec's cheeks pinkened, his hazel eyes finally finding Edyth's. "If that is your wish, mistress.

"I think it's starting," announced Cait, weaving her way around elbows as cheers erupted around them. The names of those competing were being announced. Edyth heard Iain's name just as they broke through the crowd.

The pitch was all green, save for a muddy line where previous pulling competitions had already taken place. Along the length of the muddy line lay a thick rope, marked with three ribbons. There was a red ribbon in the middle, besmirched with wet earth, then two more ribbons spaced a few feet down the line from the red marker—these blue.

"The victory goes tae the clan who pulls the opposite blue ribbon past the middle mark," explained Cait, pointing to a stake pounded into the ground. She had to get very close to Edyth's ear to be heard over all the shouting. William and Iain were talking, heads bent closely, while the rest of the Ruthven team were announced. There were six players on each side of the rope, all doing their best to look fierce and strong. One man on the Stewart side of the rope was pounding his chest, shouting into the crowd as though he were about to enter battle instead of a tugging contest. Edyth felt like laughing. Men were such strange creatures.

"Find yer feet!" shouted the officiator, a stout man Edyth did not know. "Pick 'er up, lads!"

William spotted them then, his smile turning rather smug, as he took his place at the back of the line of men. He lifted the end of heavy rope, slinging it over his left shoulder. He tightened his grip onto the rope just at the base of Iain's back, who was standing just in front of him. Iain stomped his feet into the muck to set his feet just so, all mirth now gone from his face.

Edyth, incredulous, looked to Cait. Did people really take such a silly game so seriously? But Cait was shouting at one of the Stewart men who had taken off his shirt in a display of pale muscle. "Yer as fit as me ol' granny," she shouted, her hand cupped to her mouth. "Put yer clothes on, Willie, ye daft arse!"

Edyth did laugh then. She watched as the men set themselves to their task, stomping their feet into the turf. The crowd quieted as the officiator raised both of his hands high above his head.

"Take yer slack!" commanded the officiator. The rope immediately tightened into a straight line, hovering over the ground. The officiator waved the fingers of his left hand to indicate that the rope needed adjusting. When the red ribbon tied in the middle of the rope was placed exactly over the marker in the ground, his hands dropped and he shouted "Pull! Pull ye glaikit bastarts!"

The line of men braced and pulled, leaning back as one, shifting the rope slowly. Feet slid through the churned muck, scrabbling for purchase. Grunts filled the air as muscles strained, faces pulled in a rictus of pain. The red ribbon traveled left of the marker, then back right, then left again. "Steady lads," one man yelled near Edyth. "Lean!"

The player's faces were screwed up as though in anguish, their faces ruddy. Their feet were slipping. One of the Stewart men slipped in the mud and fully lost his footing. The rope moved swiftly to the Ruthven side, causing them all to fall over in a heap. Cheers erupted as the Ruthven men were declared the victors. Covered in mud and happy to be so, the men congratulated themselves with swift pats on the back and nods of acknowledgement.

Never had Edyth seen such gloating! "You'd think they just won a battle!" said Edyth, shouting to be heard over the din. She shook her head, laughing as William marked Iain's face with muddied hands, drawing lines of a warrior over his eye and cheek. William then made his way over to them, his boots heavy with muddy turf. His face was splattered with muck. Indeed, his entire person was black with mud, save for his chest and the front of his plaid-covered hose.

He bowed before them, his blue eyes alight with triumph. Cait handed him a handkerchief from her sleeve, amusement coloring her features. "Ye've done Ruthven proud," she said, though Edyth couldn't tell if she was mocking him or not.

"A kiss for the victor?" William asked, straightening up from his bow.

Cait looked over his shoulder at the other Ruthven players still congratulating each other. "Aye, and which shall I kiss first?"

William shook his head, just once, his eyes straying to Cait's full mouth. "Let their wives and mothers congratulate them." He stepped closer, so close that their entire bodies were near to touching, but he kept just enough distance as to keep from soiling her gown. Placing his hands behind his back, he leaned forward, his lips hovering over Cait's mouth as though waiting for her to close the distance. Her neck was long, her head tilted back. Her eyes stayed on her husband's, which were glinting with promise.

Cait's mouth twitched into a lazy, playful smile, a breath away from William. Edyth looked away, feeling as though she were intruding. Alec clearly felt similarly. He looked like a radish.

"I might, at that," said Cait, "if ye weren't the rankest mixture of vileness that has ever offended my nose."

"Come, Alec," said Edyth, tugging on his sleeve as William laughed outright. "I've someone I'd like to see." She hadn't asked further questions about Cait's marriage, but it seemed as though they were getting on well enough. They were flirting, at least. Well, she *thought* what they were doing was flirting. Insults didn't land the same way in England as they did here in Scotland. She'd ask about it later.

"Do you know if Beathan the carpenter has a stall selling his wares?" Despite Eachann's mother's insistence that Edyth was not wanted, she still wished to offer them her condolences for Eachann's passing. Ever since she's been dismissed from their home by the priest, something in her heart had felt disjointed.

Alec frowned in thought briefly. "I dinnae think they're participating this year."

Edyth nodded, not surprised. "You'll have to take me to them, then."

Alec, looking stricken, said, "Himself said as I should assure ye stay awa' from the village, as he distrusts the sheriff and his men."

Edyth waved a hand at the crowds of people, among which were a few of the sheriff's men, quietly surveying the goings on. "And yet here we are, already amongst them. My lord also said I should stay within the walls, yet he's lifted the gate and given me his most trusted squire for protection. I have every faith that you will keep me safe, Alec. Besides, I doubt the sheriff or his men will bother us in a house of mourning."

Looking uncomfortable, but unwilling to argue with her further, he nodded reluctantly, dogging her heels. Alec said nothing as they made their way through the throng of people eagerly awaiting the next group of competitors who would war over the rope.

As they made their way over the tufted field toward the village, they came upon another row of tents, filled with a variety of wares. One tent at the end of the line drew her eye, for she saw the kitchen maid, Ceana enter, carrying a tray of cups. As she ducked into the dim expanse of the tent, Edyth remembered their furtive conversation about the girl's interest in a certain boy. A boy Edyth just happened to have at her disposal.

"Let us stop before we go the village for a drink of cider or ale." Edyth bobbed her head in the direction of the last tent. Alec nodded, resigned. He was no doubt thinking of the extra chores and the sound tongue lashing he'd receive should Ewan find out where Edyth was taking them. She had no intention of Ewan finding out, however.

The wind was high and cut through Edyth's layers of clothing, making her glad for the warm plaid she'd thought to wrap around her shoulders before leaving the keep. A flag planted outside of the tent snapped like a whip in the wind as they entered. An outburst of raucous cheers met them in the shadowy confines of the shelter. It took a minute for Edyth's eyes to adjust to the dim, and when they did, she saw that three of the sheriff's men were gambling at a table, deep into their cups.

There were three other men that Edyth did not recognize seated with them who were celebrating their windfall. Perhaps they were Ruthven clan members come for the gathering or haps they were party to the Stewarts who had been invited. Either way, Edyth saw the trouble brewing before the clansmen did. One balding Scotsman pulled the substantial stack of coins and what looked like a dagger from the middle of the table toward him, gleefully unaware of the murderous look one of the sheriff's men was giving him.

"Mistress," said Ceana brightly, looking up briefly from the cups she was filling from a pitcher. The girl stood behind a table constructed from large barrels upended, with a wooden plank stretched across them. When Ceana spotted Edyth's companion, she seemed to forget what she was doing and spilled the ale she was pouring all over her tray.

"Saints above," she chided herself, sopping up the spill with her rag, her face pink.

"I didn't mean to startle you," said Edyth. "My friend and I are thirsty." Edyth stepped forward, Alec close behind, and in as offhand a way as she could, Edyth motioned to Ceana. "This is Ceana, one of the keep's invaluable servants. Have you had a chance to meet before?"

Alec's attention was divided between his mistress and the men at the table behind them. He nodded politely to Ceana. "I've seen her about."

"Ceana helped me with the hurt villagers some weeks past." The girl nodded, her eyes darting between them.

"Do ye have an interest in the healing arts, then?" asked Alec, taking the drink Ceana held out to him.

Ceana shrugged. "I might at that, if I only had to work with herbs and the like. I dinnae think I'd like tae stitch folk back together again."

"Are ye helping Idina and Donald then?" asked Edyth, remembering that the brewers had been removed from their home and were staying with family in the village. If she recalled aright, they were expecting a grandchild in the coming months.

"Aye, Idina asked me tae come for a wee bit today, while she keeps Deòiridh company. She hasn't been herself since her lad...." Ceana trailed off, looking uncomfortable.

"Since Eachann died," Edyth finished for her. "Yes, I daresay she wouldn't be feeling herself after such a loss. I'm going to pay her a visit myself today."

Ceana's mouth pressed into a line, maybe in disapproval, but she said nothing, of course. It would not be her place to speak against Edyth's wishes. Ceana looked to Alec fleetingly, then away, busying herself with organizing the cups. "Are ye participating in any o' the games, Sir Knight?

Alec cleared his throat and shook his head. "I'm no' a knight," he said quickly.

"Not quite yet," interjected Edyth. "Yes, I think he will compete." She looked Alec up and down. "His lord tells me that he's grown quite skilled with the blade."

Alec looked both embarrassed and gratified. "I'd love tae come cheer for ye," said Ceana shyly. But Alec did not respond. His attention, like Edyth's was pulled away by the conversation being held behind them.

"Looks like ye've got a bit o' bad luck, eh?" one of the clansmen gloated, eyeing his most recent procurement—a silver ring with a stone set in its center—with a keen eye before slipping it into this money bag. Edyth's fear grew. Her eyes roved over the patrons, many of whom looked just as nervous being in company with the gang of sheriff's men, but she did not see the sheriff himself.

The winning villager's companions were not so oblivious to the steely looks now boring into the balding man's shining pate. One friend laughed nervously, saying something in Gaelic to apparently alert him all to the growing danger.

"That's three in a row you lot 'ave won against us," growled one of the sheriff's gang, his dark brows furrowed in anger.

"Aye, that's right," said the balding man with bravado. "Some days is as good luck and some days as bad. Today's just no' yer day, aye?"

Alec leaned into Edyth from behind, hissing in her ear. "It's time for us tae go, milady." His hand gripped her elbow and tugged on her gently. She didn't need to be told twice. In the span of a breath, the table was overturned by one of the sheriff's men, spilling drinks all over the villagers and the ground. Shouts rang out after Edyth and Alec as he pulled her away from the ensuing fight. The sound of swords being drawn turned Edyth's blood to ice.

"Get Ceana!" urged Edyth, but when she looked over her shoulder, Ceana was there, with them. "Will they kill them?" huffed Edyth, grasping her skirts with her free hand. More people were fleeing the tent, crying out in surprise and fear.

"I cannae say, milady, but I'd rather have ye safe awa'. Himself willnae thank me if trouble should befall ye. Let this lot sort it out." Edyth noticed then that the disturbance had alerted some of the household guard. "There are three o' them," said Alec as they passed the two men she recognized from their duties in the keep and atop the walls. Alec's grip on Edyth's elbow was nearing the point of pain as he pulled her up the slope that led to the keep.

"Wait," gasped Edyth, fumbling over her own feet. "You're going too fast." Alec slowed slightly, his eyes roving over the crowd. At least a hundred people milled about, completely unaware of what was happening only a short distance away, cheering for the players, gossiping, or trading.

"We should tell someone. What if our men need more help," suggested Edyth.

Alec looked back over his shoulder to the tent now a good fifty paces away. The inside to the tent was dark, but Edyth caught shapes moving, swords swinging, but she could not hear any shouts aside from the cheering crowd.

Suddenly, the side of the tent wall bulged outward as if someone or something had been pushed up against the heavy material. A man fell through the opening in the tent, falling into the matted grass before stumbling to his feet. It was one of the sheriff's men, his arms full of what looked like a bundle of rags. He looked over his shoulder as he gained his feet, running around the corner toward the wood line.

Alec tensed to run but held himself still, his fists clenched. One of Ewan's guardsmen stumbled out of the tent, his helm askew. He righted it, looking frantically for the escapee.

"He doesnae ken where the scut got to. He's getting away," said Ceana.

Alec glanced at Edyth and Ceana, looking grim.

"Go," urged Edyth. "I'll stay with Ceana. We'll be safe."

"Aye, I'll see her safe tae the keep," Ceana agreed, grasping Edyth's hand. "Go after him."

Alec grimaced as if warring within himself then gruffly said, "I cannae, mistress. He'll have my bollocks if I leave ye."

"He won't," said Edyth, knowing "he" was Ewan. "Besides, did your laird not command you to do my bidding? Go. No harm will come to us, I assure you."

Alec's eyes were narrowed on the retreating form, now a good seventy yards away. Alec grumbled, bouncing slightly on the balls of his feet, looking like a caged dog. Edyth gave him a shove. "Go, Alec." He stumbled forward but caught himself, pushing and twisting through crowds of people in his haste without a backwards glance.

"It'll be a miracle if he catches 'im," muttered Ceana, her eyes watching Alec's dark head. Before long he was swallowed up in the crowd and Ceana, turning toward the keep, said, "Shall we go, then, mistress?"

But now that Edyth had no guard tethered to her, she had no intention of going back to the keep. This was, quite possibly, her only chance to pay her respects to Eachann's parents as she'd been wishing to. Here was her chance to change the way the villagers viewed her. Besides, her sympathy was the only thing she could give them, as they would accept naught else.

"No," said Edyth thoughtfully. "No, I think I'd like to take a walk."

"But—"

"Hush now," chided Edyth softly, giving the girl a confident smile. "It's been weeks since I haven't had a man dogging my heels. Besides, it's for a good cause. We'll be back before you know it."

Chapter Twenty-One

T he village square was usually a bustling and loud place and with so many visitors, Edyth had expected to find it just as packed as the gaming field. But as she and Ceana made their way down the winding road into the center of the village, an uneasiness crept up her spine. "Something's wrong," she mumbled to Ceana, who seemed to have caught the same, unseen danger.

Ceana's eyes darted around them, to the sparse woods between the villager's homes, to the long shadows cast by the afternoon sun. "Do ye think we should leave, mistress?" Ceana could not quite mask the hopeful suggestion in her voice, but Edyth would not likely have another opportunity to be free from the watchful eyes of her husband or his retainers.

No, Ewan would not be pleased with her wanderings, but he was busy with the Stewart chief, who seemed desperate to unite with the Ruthvens through marriage. Edyth's mind caught hold of their rather uneventful meeting last night and made a mental note to corner Iain later to ask what he thought of the mousy girl.

"No," mumbled Edyth, linking arms with the girl. "I might not get another chance to personally offer my condolences to Eachann's family." Besides, if there was something wrong, she would know of it.

As they made their way on to the main thoroughfare from the river bridge, Edyth stopped short, her skirts swinging softly around her ankles. Where she'd expected to see a bustling crowd, with rows of carts displaying goods for sale and trade, she saw, instead, a deserted square. Stalls were closed, draped with heavy cloths. She looked to the sky, wondering at the time, but there was still a few hours before the sun fully set. Still time enough for business.

"Haps everyone is up at the field?" suggested Ceana in a tight voice.

Edyth considered it, but no. There, in front of the fishmonger's stall, were lines of drying fish, caught from the river that morning. Their silver skins glinting dully in the afternoon light. A fire made from green branches coughed and billowed weakly around a rack of black bream and herring, tarnishing the shining scales into the dull color of earth.

"The fire has been abandoned."

"Let's do leave," urged Ceana, tugging softly on Edyth's elbow.

"Why are all the shutters drawn?" Edyth asked quietly, turning in a tight circle to take in the seemingly emptied square. "Not even the well has company."

Every other time Edyth had been in the village, in the center of the square, surrounded by crowded homes, businesses, and stalls, the watering well had been a bustle of activity. And at this time of day, when preparations were being made for evening meals and washings, there should have been a line of young people and women, waiting for their turn to draw the water. Edyth had even seen animals tied to the well's pully supports, but never had she witnessed such abandonment.

Ceana's hand tightened around Edyth's bicep. "Did ye hear that?" she hissed, her face drained of all color. It made her brown eyes look nearly black. Edyth listened hard. At first she heard nothing, and then she picked up on the soft, whimpering cries of a what she assumed was a child.

"There," gasped Ceana, pointing to the brewer's house. Or rather, the sheriff's house, as he'd taken it for himself and his men. Edyth squinted across the square, into the shadow cast by the towering trees and buildings and saw a person leaning heavily into one of the wooden supports holding up a small shelter, usually used for horses. It was unwalled, with four sturdy posts to hold up a slanted, thatched roof. But there were no horses tied there, waiting for their masters to leave the alehouse. Just a boy, from the looks of it.

Edyth wasted no time. "You there," she called, walking briskly toward him. "Where has everyone gone?"

But when she and Ceana reached him, Edyth forgot her questions. "Who has done this to you?" she demanded. The boy—seven or eight seasons, she would guess—turned his stricken face toward her, his eyes filling with fresh tears. "I...I didnae steal anythin'," he cried, his voice breaking on a sob. Edyth drew closer to the boy's hands, which were nailed to the post. His grubby fingers lay flat against the beam, the center of each hand pierced with one long, thick nail. Clotting blood coated his flesh, trickling in little, dark rivers between his fingers and down onto the thick beam.

"Who did this to you?" Edyth repeated, though she reckoned she already knew the answer.

His little body was trembling, from fatigue and shock, no doubt. His hands had been nailed up high, near his chest, so that he could not sit or kneel without causing himself extreme pain. "Ye mun leave, mistress," he said thickly. "They'll be back any moment. They said if they caught anyone helping me, they'd get worse."

Ignoring the boy's warning, she spun on her heel and walked to the door of the alehouse, not knowing what she would do or say once she confronted the sheriff. She only knew that she must condemn this ruthlessness. And who better, than she, the mistress of the keep? She pushed on the door but it was locked. Her fist pounded on the thick wooden slats, shouting, "How dare you harm a child! Open this door at once!"

"Please, mistress," sobbed the boy, "ye mun no' draw attention tae yerself."

Edyth bit back a curse, glaring at the door, before turning toward the square. There, across the open space, a pale, ghostly face glowed in a window before disappearing behind an oiled curtain. Edyth gritted her teeth. How was it that someone could watch such a thing happen and do nothing to stop it? Edyth might have felt the shock of such neglect, of such careless disregard for one of their own, but she could not. She'd lived it herself in England. Had escaped with little else save her own life. Instead, she could only feel a smoldering disgust.

Edyth tried to pry a nail from the boy's hand but it was stuck fast. "Ceana, go to the blacksmith's shop down the way and fetch me some prying tools. Hurry," she barked at the girl's hesitation.

Ceana nodded and rushed away looking terrified. "Where is your family?" asked Edyth, looking around for something for the boy to sit on.

"It's only me mam and me sister. Th—they took me mam intae the alehouse. She fought them fierce," he said with some pride. "Sc—scratched one o' the men good, she did, but they beat 'er and took her awa'. She's been quiet ever since." He cast a long, worried look at the locked door of the alehouse.

"How is it no one else has come to your aid?" she muttered.

"S—some did t—try, mistress, but they were driven back intae their houses."

Glancing at the window in which she'd spied the voyeur, her anger lessoned marginally. "Yes, well, I'm here now. I will try and help you." *And I won't run away when threatened, either.* Edyth spotted an empty crate at a nearby stall and brought it to him. It was too low for him to sit, but he could kneel upon it. She helped to steady him, her hand gripping his bony shoulder. "And your sister?" she asked.

He let out a shaky breath as his weight was taken off his feet. "I dinnae ken where she is. She ran away...most likely hiding. Thank ye, mistress; ye've done a great kindness, but ye mun leave now." His cheek was pressed against the rough wood, his eyes red rimmed and wide with fear. "They're searching the houses."

"For what?"

"For the stolen signet ring. One o' the men said they saw me with it, but I didnae have a ring. I cannae say what it even looks like. W—when they searched me and f—found that I didnae have it, they s—said I'd given it tae someone, hid it, or sold it. Th—then they nailed me h—hands tae get me tae c—confess, but—" Big, fat tears streaked down the boy's freckled, dirty face. He shook his head, his eyes wide and glistening with welled tears. "B—but I 'ave naught tae confess, mistress. I didnae take it."

"Hush now," said Edyth, stroking his feathery brown hair. "I believe you. Hush now." She recognized the powerful feeling surging through her, one she'd felt for the first time in her life only a short time ago when her mother and father had been ripped from her life: hate. Like fanned flames, the embers of her anger glowed to life, erupting to full blown abhorrence and she knew that if she had the strength or the chance, she would kill the wicked sheriff for this.

The bitter taste of iron filled her mouth and she realized that she was biting her lip so hard that she'd drawn blood. Edyth clenched her jaw and her hands into fists, peering down the road where the blacksmith's shop sat, dark and noiseless, silently urging Ceana to hurry.

There was a distant banging, like someone pounding on a door followed by indiscernible shouts. "I'm not afraid of them," Edyth muttered. It was a lie. In truth, she was terrified. Terrified of what would happen because of her stupidity, but she was just angry enough push her fear away.

What a fool she'd been! She shouldn't have left the keep alone as she had. She should have begged Iain, or Alec to come with her. She should have sought out Ewan instead of sneaking off. And now she was here, alone, and utterly useless to fight against such cruelty. But she didn't have to be alone.

Edyth looked over her shoulder, the way they'd come, toward the keep. She could run. She could go and find help, but she did not wish to leave the boy. "What's your name?" she asked, removing her plaid from her shoulders and draping it around his slender frame.

"Arthur," he said, his breath shuddering from so many spent tears.

"I'm Edyth." She tried and failed to conjure a sure smile but found she could not, so she simply said, "I won't leave you."

They sat in silence for what felt like a very long time, listening to the distant shouts from the field or from the villager's homes, before Edyth spotted Ceana coming down the lane, furtively looking over her shoulder. Distant shouts reached their ears and Ceana, frightened, rushed toward them, her eyes wide in her pale face.

"I saw some of the sheriff's men," said Ceana between gasps. "They tore open Deòiridh's mattresses. Feathers are everywhere. And they in mourning, too."

She frowned in a disapproving way that masked her fear. "What're they looking for, do ye think?"

She handed Edyth the pliers and she went to work, carefully grasping the end of the nail so as not to pinch the boy's skin. "They're looking for the sheriff's signet ring," Edyth answered, her voice wooden. "It denotes his privilege and power, so if someone took it, he loses his ability to send missives to de Warenne or to the King with any authority." She met Arthur's eyes, which were glazed and far away. It was plain that he was in complete shock. "This will likely hurt. Ready?"

The nail was so deeply embedded into the post that, even with all her effort, she could not get it to budge. Arthur's eyes were screwed up tightly, his lips a white, thin line. She wasn't strong enough. She tried the next nail, which had more of its head exposed. Tugging hard, she felt the nail shift. Arthur whimpered; his eyes screwed shut. His breath came in quick, hot bursts against her face. She pulled again with all her might, using her body weight to aid her, her knuckle bones white as she grasped the tool. The nail came free with a sudden jerk that had her stumbling backward.

Arthur immediately pulled his free left hand to his middle, cradling it against his midsection. He cried quietly to himself, his little shoulders shaking. "Once more," Edyth said needlessly.

Carefully placing the pliers on first nail, she used her body weight once more, pulling as hard as she could, but, again, it did not budge. "You try," said Edyth breathlessly, offering the pliers to Ceana.

Ceana nodded, white faced, but after a few moments of tugging and straining, gave up. "It's no use! It's in far too deep and I haven't the strength."

Edyth, anguished, bit her lip, and looked over her shoulder. Surely people would come and happen upon them. There were hundreds of people not too far away. And there were some villagers obviously still here, hiding in fear, but they could simply not wait for some hapless soul to leave the rare entertainment that was the festival and not only come their way, but be strong enough to help. *Or willing to*, she thought darkly.

Edyth looked to the shuttered windows and closed doors, letting her anger overtake her fear. She ran to the house that she knew was occupied and pounded upon the door. "Open at once! Help!" But one answered. Not even the curtains twitched. She pushed at the barrier, ready to force herself in and give the occupants a piece of her mind, but it was barred. "Cowards!" she shouted, kicking the door with her boot.

But Edyth did not give up. Running to the next house, she pounded her fist on the heavy door. "Come! Open your door. Have you no compassion?" She was just about to turn and go the next building when she heard the unmistakable sound of a plank being removed from a door. It opened only a crack, one narrowed, smoky eye peering through the small opening.

The person on the other side of the door hissed at her. "Haud yer wheesht, ye flap mouthed shew!" Edyth glared right back through the crack in the door.

"Hst," said the eye. "Do ye want tae bring the whoresons back? Ye flap yer gums any louder I fear ye'd wake the dead."

Edyth pointed toward the structure that held Arthur and pinned the old man with an accusatory glare. "How is it that you can hide away when one of your own is abused thusly? How can you shut your door and leave the lad to suffer so? Where is your honor?"

The old man had the good sense to look ashamed. His good eye darted to the ground, unwilling to meet Edyth's eye or, apparently, look upon Arthur, where he could be seen from his front stoop. The man mumbled something Edyth didn't catch, but she didn't care to ask him to repeat himself. "Do something of use and help unpin the lad. I am not strong enough." Edyth had her doubts that the old man had the strength for it either, now that she saw he was aged, but she was desperate enough to let him try.

"I cannae," said the man. He pushed against the door, trying to shut it in her face, but Edyth was able to stick her boot in the barrier just in time.

"You will," she demanded, pushing with her body against the door with all her body weight. The man didn't put up much of a fight, and when the door opened wider, revealing the man's body, she understood. She recognized him as the fishmonger. His gray hair was disheveled as though he'd just pulled himself from bed, his nose was bloodied, and the other eye that hadn't been peering through the door was purpled beyond recognition and swollen shut.

Not only that, but his torn sark could not hide the splotches of blood that crisscrossed his back and torso. In addition to a black eye, he'd been whipped, and soundly. He looked as though it was all he could do to stand, let alone help her with Arthur. Edyth felt her anger deflate as she gaped at his injuries. He still would not meet her eyes. His house was in disarray. Tables and chairs were overturned, baskets of dried beans, fish, and grain had been dumped in a pile on the planked floor.

"I did try tae help the lad," he said, his voice as rasp. "But this is what happens when ye meddle or interfere. The sheriff makes examples o' any who would speak against him or his men."

Edyth's mind whirled. Ewan had said nothing of such atrocities. Would he have kept this from her? She knew the answer immediately, knew as well as she knew her own mind, that Ewan did not know. He would not sit idly by and turn a blind eye to such brutality. She felt sick to the marrow. "How is it that your laird knows nothing of this?"

The old man shrugged one shoulder and winced. "The sheriff ne'r lifted a hand against us until Himself left for Caimbel lands tae see his sister wed. Until then, they only took our food...demanded our services with no payment. He...he threatens tae take out his vengeance for any complaint we might make on our daughters. Involving Himself would only hurt us. Ruin the wee lassies."

"I see," she said, and she did. She understood why mothers and fathers—why the village as a whole—would willingly give up of their sustenance and goods with nary a word of complaint in order to spare the sons and daughters of the clan from the sheriff's lechery. She looked out the door, to Ceana and Arthur. They were no doubt running out of time. The sheriff and whatever men he had with him in the village would be back before long and Arthur still not free. "I will help you with your wounds later, but I must help Arthur first."

The man waved her concern for him away. "Most of the village is up at the games," he said, shuffling toward a chair by the empty fire. He sat with shaky legs, falling into it when his legs could not hold him any longer. He hissed in pain as his back hit the chair. "If ye insist on freeing the lad, get ye tae Beathan's and Deòiridh's place. He and his wife are in mourning and havenae left their home in all the time since they buried their son."

The reminder of Eachann's death and his parents' grief felt like a weight in her belly, but she merely nodded and turned, pausing long enough at the door to ask over her shoulder, "Have any of the girls in the village been violated by the sheriff or his men?"

The fisherman's pained eyes met hers then as he shook his head. "Naught but threats, but we dinnae leave them alone tae let the bastarts try." With a firm nod, she left his doorstep and turned her feet toward Ceana and Arthur.

Ceana was still attempting to pry the nail from Arthur's hand when Edyth reached them. "Listen carefully to me," she said. "You must run as fast as you can and find a clansman. Find a guard...Iain, or Ewan if he is there...someone strong. Find a Ruthven or Stewart and tell them what has happened."

Ceana nodded and set the pliers down, glancing nervously at Arthur. "I will, mistress. I will."

Eachann's house wasn't far. Edyth knew the way well, but she was unwilling to leave Arthur alone. Besides, Ceana had said the sherriff's men were just there, destroying their mattress. Even if they had moved on by now, it was likely they would meet on the way. And they would no doubt take pains to torment her, especially once they learned of her attempts to help Arthur.

The poor lad's cheeks were tracked with drying tears, his eyes unable to hide his pain. Edyth picked up the pliers from the ground and tried her hand at the nail once more. It was no use. The nail would not budge and the hurt she was causing Arthur was not worth her poor efforts.

Edyth gave it up and instead stroked the hair from his brow. They said nothing, only sat in silence, waiting. Hoping. The seconds felt like minutes, dragging on and on. Every sound of bird in the bush or of a squirrel scampering along a limb made her heart stutter. She was going to get a crick in her neck for how often she turned her head to peer down the pathway leading to the keep.

Eventually, exuberant male voices could be heard coming down from the deeper part of the village. Her heart skipped a beat in anxious fear when she realized that the men were not villagers. Arthur's eyes, which had been closed in restless sleep, sprang open. His head swiveled, searching for the source of sound. Edyth squeezed his shoulder in comfort. She would not leave him.

"Did ye see the hag's face?" one voice sniggered. He adopted a high-pitched mocking tone. "No, no' my feather mattress!" He chuckled. "I'd bet there was naught but five cocks at most that died for that bed. Not worth getting beat o'er."

His companion agreed with a grunt. "These people dinnae have much, but I did find me a few new trinkets. I'll send this pretty little bit off tae Joanie the next time the courier heads tae de Warenne."

The men slowly came closer, their voices becoming more distinct. She saw their shadows on the ground, reaching toward the center of the path, but their bodies were still hidden behind a building.

The men paused, apparently to show off the stolen trinket. Edyth felt like her heart would beat out of her chest, but her feet remained as if it were she that were nailed there and not the boy. "Mmmph. Are those real pearls, do ye think, Richard?" He made a sound of approval in his throat. "Yer Joanie will make 'er sisters jealous with such a prize."

There was a sound of shuffling cloth before one of the men declared the need to relieve himself. What followed was the sound of something wet splattering on the hard ground while someone hummed a bawdy tune. "Hurry up, man, de Biggar will be about done with his rounds. He willnae be pleased do we no' get tae the last house."

"Aye, aye," grumbled the other man. And then the shadows moved, changing shape as the men turned the corner and came into full view of the square. They wore leather armor over their black tunics, making them appear as dark as their shadows. Like two demons fresh from the maw of hell. Arthur's breathing changed, growing faster, his eyes darting from the men to Edyth.

"Ye mun go," he urged quietly, fresh emotion coloring his words. "Hide."

Edyth squeezed his shoulder again. "I will not," she said. It was simple and perhaps not very comforting, seeing as how she was merely a woman. She could not fight these men and win. At least not with a sword. But if simply being there, refusing to leave, was all she could offer, then so be it. She thought, briefly, that she might gain some leverage with using her title, but dismissed it. These men did not honor her or her husband's authority. In fact, it might make things worse.

She squared her shoulders, waiting for the men to notice her. As they came down the lane, one turning toward a door and raising his gauntleted fist to pound upon it, Edyth waited with bated breath.

Bang, bang, bang! "Open up, by order of the Sheriff of Midlothian!" He waited for only a breath before pounding once more. "Get ye oot, or I'll go in after ye!" The door shuddered under the force of his fist. Edyth did not want to see what would happen should someone be home. But she needn't have worried, for in that instant, the man's companion, who was standing idly behind, turned his head in her direction.

Giving his friend a backhanded swat on the shoulder, he grunted something Edyth could not hear, but had no trouble in guessing. He'd seen her and was alerting his friend. As one, they both turned in her direction, forgetting the locked door, and stalked toward her.

"What 'ave we 'ere?" said the man on the left as they came to a stop a few feet away. He was tall and lanky with a pockmarked face and a crooked nose that told a story of at least one break. The man on the right was less memorable. He was of average height, with a full, round face that made him appear younger than he probably was, but the bulk and breadth of his shoulders told Edyth he was no green thing. He would be very good with a sword, she wagered.

Edyth took a steadying breath, curling her fingers into a fist. "Which is the coward that would harm this child?"

The tall, pockmarked man smiled in a nasty way that told Edyth he would enjoy whatever exchange was about to take place. "Coward, ye say?" He made a small sound of disappointment in his throat, casting a glance at his companion. "Do ye hear that, Richard. The chit doesnae care for the King's justice."

The shorter man rested his hand on the hilt of his sword, which hung at his waist. He shrugged dismissively but his eyes glinted dangerously. "This," he said, nodding to Arthur, who was shaking and cowering, "isnae justice. This was a mercy. He's still the use o' his hands, don't he?"

"Mercy?" scoffed Edyth, her eyebrows raised to nearly her hairline. "What crime was he to have committed, that would justify such cruelty?"

"That's none o' yer concern," sneered Pock Face.

"Who are ye, tae interfere in the sheriff's duty?"

Duty? Edyth's lip curled in disgust. "The sheriff's duty lies in nailing children to posts and stealing the villager's meager possessions?" She shook her head. "No, that is not duty, only brutality. You will remove the nail from his hand and let him go. Now."

Pock Face sucked at his teeth as if in thought before he shook his head once. "We dinnae take orders from the likes o' you, chit. What's he tae you, anyway? He yer servant or sommat?"

"What I'd like tae know," interrupted Richard thoughtfully, "is what she's willing tae do tae set 'im free." He looked Edyth up and down, eyeing her finery and her well cared for appearance. At least that's what she hoped he was assessing. A spike of fear drove through her heart and her resolve stuttered.

"Leave," pleaded Arthur, pained. Big, fat tears streaked down his face. "*Run*."

The two footmen glanced briefly at Arthur, unconcerned. They knew she would not run.

Edyth's hands were clammy with nerves, her knuckles aching from clenching her fists so tightly. She forced her hands open, her mind reeling. What could she say to deter them? Giving them her name now, as a final hope of reprieve, had the smallest of chances of freeing herself. And her name would not save Arthur.

What could she give them? She had no trinkets on her person. She had no money with her. Even if she did, she doubted they would let Arthur free once given a prize. They were tyrants. Brigands who gloried in causing fear. Edyth resisted the urge to glance over her shoulder, to the path toward the keep. Surely Ceana would have found someone by now. Surely they would be racing toward the village to aid the boy—and now her.

She swallowed and held her head high. "Yes, I will make a trade," she said, glad her voice did not waiver. "You set the boy free, and I will grant you your lives, as pitiful as they may be. Give him his freedom, and you win your own."

The sneering laughter was expected, but she hadn't been prepared for the arrival of the sheriff. Her eyes caught his movement, and those of his companions, as they entered the main street over the shoulders of the guardsmen. The wind caught the sheriff's blood-red cape, blowing it away from his muscular, stocky body. Edyth trembled with cold and with fear. There was no hope for her now. There were five of them to the one of her. All she had was the concealed dagger that Ewan had insisted she take wherever she go, but even with that, she had no hope of defending herself against such a force.

Her hand moved unerringly to the pocket of her skirt where she could feel the weighty object. She could feel it, even now in her mind, small and cold, and perfectly fit for her hand. She wondered if she could use it in truth. Could she make a man bleed or even take his life? She glanced at Arthur, at his trembling body and knew that she could.

But she clenched her fingers into a fist. If forced to fight one person, she might be able to defend herself or another well enough to damper their enthusiasm and flee, but five? There was no hope. She mentally set herself for pain, preparing for the familiar, dreaded sensation of a fist to her cheek. Of a hilt of a sword to her head. The fear of pain was just as bad as the damage itself, fanning the flames of her fear. She tried desperately to rein it in, to force it to the recesses of her mind, but it was like a wild, living thing.

Edyth's heart was beating wildly in her chest. Pock Face and Richard both looked like a cat given a bowl of cream as they, too, noticed the approach of the sheriff. Arthur was sobbing outright, reaching out his free, bloodied hand to grasp onto her skirts. He tugged, pulling her gaze. "M—mistress, please." But Edyth could not leave him. Even had she wanted to, her body would not have obeyed. *Ewan*. Surely he would find them. Find her. *Please*.

"The sheriff willnae care for yer threats," warned Pock Face, looking smug. "He's no' so forgiving as we are." They turned as the sheriff neared, standing stiffly in salute to his station, but he paid them no mind. His dark eyes glinted with promise, taking in, with one quick glance, what had transpired.

"You meddle in the affairs of the King." His voice was soft for such a large man.

Chapter Twenty-Two

E dyth jutted out her chin in a false show of bravado. "No worthy King would assault a child." While her voice was steady, her hands were another story altogether. She hid their trembling in the folds of her skirt, feeling the comforting press of her dagger against the back of her hand.

De Biggar's eyes fell to Richard. "Did you not warn her of what would happen should anyone meddle in my affairs?"

"Of course," said Richard with a stiff, slight bow. "But she doesnae seem to care for justice."

"Is that so?" The sheriff's gaze swiveled to her, raising a blonde eyebrow in mock surprise. He pursed fat lips, dry and cracking from the cold. "The King's justice is meted out through me," he said, closing the distance between them in two slow strides, "his loyal subject. I am given the task of ensuring his laws are obeyed and to punish those who would resist." She ignored the need to lean away from the man, and not only because she was afraid of him. He smelled of horses and bitter sweat. "I daresay it would be a fool who would resist the King's laws."

Edyth swallowed and carefully, slowly, moved her hand into the pocket of her skirt, her fingers finding and grasping onto the cool hilt of the dagger hidden within. It gave her a small comfort, despite her inexperience in wielding it. She could not win against him, but she did have the element of surprise. She might do some damage, however small.

But stabbing the sheriff would only ensure her own demise. She could not do it. At least not yet. Edyth swallowed, her grip tightening on the bone handle. "Then a fool I shall be," she said, her voice a rasp. The wind was picking up, teasing the small hairs the had escaped her plait.

De Biggar's mouth twitched. He seemed to enjoy her boldness. "My hand—my words—are one in the same as His Majesty's. To question my actions is to question the King. What is your name?" he asked quietly, genially. One might think he were asking after her health, if it weren't for the enlivened force of his stare. His eyes dipped lower, taking in her frame, assessing her in a way that brought a flush to her cheeks. It was *indecent*.

Edyth faltered internally. If she identified herself, the sheriff's retribution could be very severe indeed. The wife of the laird, the laird that had already angered the sheriff on more than one occasion, caught alone.... "I am a concerned citizen," she said.

His nostrils flared at her vague response, a smile playing at the corner of his full mouth. Edyth's mind searched for what Ewan had taught her. *Avoid being hit*, he'd said, but he'd said nothing about striking first. He'd said nothing about fighting more than one man. "Not any common churl, I'd wager," said de Biggar, his eyes flashing. "Shall we play a game?" He turned to his men, looking at them with raised brows before dropping his gaze onto the shaking, hunched form of Arthur, whose eyes were so red and swollen, she doubted he could even see. "Let's see how quickly her tongue loosens with the proper motivation."

He pulled the dirk from his belt and angled himself toward the boy, putting the sharp edge against the smallest finger of the hand tacked to the post. Arthur's response was immediate. His sobs increased until he was hacking and dry heaving. He pleaded between his sobs, begging them not to cut him.

De Biggar's eyes found Edyth's, a question there, as if he were asking would she take honey in her parritch? "Wait," she said, pulling her naked hand from her pocket. Without thinking, she curled her fingers around the iron blade the sheriff held, staying him. It was sharp and bit into her flesh, but she barely felt the sting. "Don't hurt him."

"Tell me your name."

Edyth took a shaky breath. "Let him go first."

The sheriff shook his head once. "That's not how we play this game. You don't get to make demands. And my patience is running thin."

Edyth only hesitated for the briefest of moments, looking toward the empty trail that lead to the keep, and despaired. Had Ceana been caught by more of the sheriff's men? Was no one coming? Arthur was leaning as far away from the sheriff as he possibly could, his eyes screwed shut in expectation of pain. "I—I am Lady Edyth Ruthven, daughter of Sir Ernald DeVries." Her voice did shake then, her words stuttering into the cooling evening.

De Biggar's smile, if you could call it that, showed far too many teeth. "*The witch*," he said with immense satisfaction. "I've been hoping we'd meet.

You have quite the reputation here, amongst your husband's people. Did you know?"

"Remove your knife, sir. I've kept my bargain, see that you keep yours."

The sheriff, to her surprise, agreed. She let her hand fall away, ignoring the pinching bite that marred her skin. The wound was small and not worth looking at just now. "With pleasure. I am a man of my word after all," he said, turning from Arthur to face her fully.

He cocked his head to the side, examining her once more, his eyes alight with curiosity and something she could not name, but it wasn't good. The wind blew an errant strand of hair across her face. De Biggar reached out a gloved hand to sweep it away, causing Edyth to flinch.

"Now, now," he cooed mockingly. "How is it that a woman of your talents would shrink from any man's touch? You, who are rumored to command hearts to break. You, who bewitched a man of power to forsake family for a taste of passion. You, who can escape the very clutches of God's own church? How is it," he asked, raising his hand once more to brush the hair from her forehead, "that such an enchantress could shrink in fear?"

Edyth willed herself to hold still, her hand slick with blood from her weeping cut. She swallowed heavily. De Biggar tucked the loose strand of hair behind her ear. "Surely someone who can cause wagons to collapse with a mere whisper and injure an innocent little boy is not afraid of *me*. Why did you do it?" he asked conspiratorially, leaning in as if waiting for her whispered secret. "Was it to steal the lad's blood? His bones?" His breath smelled of whiskey, hot on her cheek. Her face flushed in anger. So that was what was being said about her? "There are some who say you took his arm and fed it to him."

When Edyth did not answer, de Biggar's smile returned. He raised his dirk and laid the tip between her breasts. "Is that why you are so interested in this brat? What plans do ye have for him, hmm?"

Her heart would surely beat out of her chest. She willed her breathing to slow, for her mind to focus. "You know what I think?" he asked her, his breath warming her face. "I think that I've caught myself a great prize. It's my understanding that you recently were tried for heresy, yet here you remain." He looked her over, as if he could see under her clothes. "Unmarked and unblemished. Are not heretics purged of their wickedness through pain? And yet I can see no evidence of the Church's justice. Shall I take a closer look?"

Edyth's hand returned to her pocket, her fingers finding and grasping the handle of her knife as if it were a lifeline. She looked into his eyes. He was so close. She could feel the heat of him. He would not suspect the knife in his gut. The time was close. She would have to strike soon. Her aim would have to be true. And deadly. Perhaps she should shove it into the soft skin under his chin, where Ewan had shown her. Could she? She saw it in her mind, could feel the hot, reeking blood streaming over her hand.

But she would only have the time and strength for one. Once she struck de Biggar, the element of surprise would be lost, and the other men would be on her in an instant. The four other guards were rapt in their attention. She could feel their eyes, could feel their anticipation. No, they would not spare her should she strike the sheriff, but she would rather die here and now than let the sheriff disrobe and harm her.

A sound reached her ears then, like thunder, but it ran through her, trembling through the earth and into the soles of her boots. Horses. At least two, and they were coming fast. She felt weak with relief. *Someone was coming.* The sheriff's eyes snapped to a point over her shoulder. She heard the spray of rocks and turned in time to see the most welcome sight she'd ever seen. Ewan threw a leg over the neck of his horse and slid off, even before his steed had stopped moving.

He was dark with fury, his eyes glinting with barely suppressed rage. His wavy hair fell across his forehead, his teeth bared in a cruel grimace. Edyth barely had time to recognize the other person who'd come. It was the Stewart Chieftain. *How? How had they known?*

"Step away from my wife," growled Ewan, pulling his sword from its scabbard. "Or I'll empty yer entrails at yer feet."

The sheriff's sneer grew, but he lowered the knife from Edyth's chest. De Biggar dropped himself into a mocking bow, his arms thrown wide. "Laird Ruthven," he muttered. The man clearly hadn't suspected that Ewan would dare to touch him with four armed guards there to protect him, but he didn't know Ewan as Edyth did.

As Ewan's eye caught hold of the glinting dirk in the sheriff's outstretched hand, his controlled anger quickly changed into one of absolute fury. "You dare," he gasped, knocking the blade from the sheriff's hand with a flick of his wrist. Blood blossomed on de Biggar's thick wrist as he dropped the knife with a hiss of pain. Blood, nearly black in the low light, ran down his hand, dripping onto the hard-packed earth from wan fingers.

The four guards drew their swords but stopped when the tip of Ewan's blade found the sheriff's soft neck. "By all means," said Ewan, his hand steady, his eyes boring into the sheriff, "come closer."

De Biggar made a sound in the back of his throat that stayed his men. He straightened his body, Ewan's sword following as he moved, his hands held open in a show of apparent vulnerability. Edyth had no doubt that even without a weapon to hand, that the sheriff wasn't defenseless.

"Your wife is meddling in the King's justice," explained de Biggar. "It is within my right to punish anyone who interferes in the King's affairs."

Edyth had paid little attention to the Stewart chieftain that had come with Ewan, but she could feel him now, at her right side. Glancing, she saw that he too had his sword drawn. Could they fight five men and win?

"Hear me," snarled Ewan, "Ye touch my wife, and ye'll lose yer hands. Look upon her, and I'll take yer eyes. If ye so much as *breathe* in her direction, I'll bury my dirk in yer throat. Do we have an understanding?"

The sheriff, no doubt a gambling man, merely sneered. "As I've told you before, *Laird*, I am the governing force here. Your threats against me do little save impugn your loyalties. This viperous *thing* you call a wife is meddling. I suggest you take her to hand, lest she make life very uncomfortable for you very quickly."

Ewan bared his teeth. Edyth could see his urge to drive his sword through the sheriff's neck. Could see him contemplating the aftermath of such a choice. The corded muscles of his forearm bunched and twitched as he restrained himself.

"He's nailed the boy's hands to the post as retribution for a stolen trinket," explained Edyth hastily. "A trinket the boy never had." She laid a hand on Ewan's stony arm. His head turned slightly toward her, but he did not take his eyes from the sheriff. "They've beaten his mother and hidden her away in the alehouse. They've just returned from searching all the homes to fill their pockets."

"My signet ring is no mere trinket," snapped de Biggar.

"Aye, we've heard," intoned the Stewart icily. "The lad's sister delivered the news o' her family's treatment tae the men at the gate. Luckily, we were on our way down tae the fields and heard. We didnae ken aboot the looting o' the villagers' homes, though." *So that's how they knew*, thought Edyth. Arthur's missing sister had run for help.

Up until that point, neither Ewan nor the Stewart had spared the boy more than a passing glance, being occupied as they were with the present violent situation. "Free the boy, Alexander," commanded Ewan evenly with a quick jerk of his chin. His eyes bored into de Biggar, his cheeks flushed in anger. "Did ye find it? Find yer ring," he asked.

De Biggar shook his head once, definitively. "No, but we have only searched a handful of homes. Once the owners of those homes left unsearched return from the festival, I will be sure to find it. The guilty parties will be punished accordingly."

"You've already punished the lad, have ye no'?" asked Alexander softly, looking up from where he had been examining the nail in Arthur's hand. Edyth stood nearby, offering the retrieved pliers to him, which he had yet to take. "If he's no' the thief, then why pin him as ye have?"

The sheriff's eyes swiveled toward Alexander. "There is more than one guilty party here. Yes, the pickpocket has been punished, but what of the beneficiary? He gave it to someone. I would know who wanted it. I will have justice."

"Seeing as I'm the Laird, it's tae me that such matters fall. Aye? Ye will no' enter another home unless ye've been invited."

An amused look passed across de Biggar's face. He shook his head in a pitying way, as if he could not account for Ewan's complete lack of awareness of the situation.

"Empty yer purses. All of ye. I'll no' permit pilfering," demanded Ewan.

The sheriff, for his part, wasn't interested in Ewan's order. "Pilfering? That is a scurrilous charge, indeed. I am man of the law, sir. Remove your weapon from my person lest I have you arrested."

A muscle in Ewan's jaw twitched before he shook his head. "Nay. Ye willnae arrest me, no' unless ye wish tae cause an uprising. I dinnae think Longshanks will welcome the death o' one of his sheriffs, no matter how unpleasant he may be. For that is the way this will end, should you presist in defying me."

Ewan had struck a chord. De Biggar's look hardened, the smirk sliding into a grimace. "You have a high opinion of yourself if you think your insurrection will garner anything but further suffering to the people of Scotland. I would remind you that you and your neighbors have pledged fealty to England."

Arthur, now free, slumped to the ground, holding his hands. Edyth went to him immediately, hugging him tightly against her. She wasn't sure who was shaking harder, Arthur or herself. He clung to her, sobbing into her as she watched from the side. She thought it would be wise to leave, to slink away with Arthur where they would be safe, but her feet would not obey her.

Alexander pulled the dirk from his belt, holding it in his left hand opposite his short sword. "I kent ye tae be a pompous dobber, de Biggar, but I didnae ken ye tae be completely brainless. Yer actions will have deadly consequences."

The sheriff laughed humorlessly. "You dare threaten me?"

Ewan was as tightly coiled as a snake about to strike. "Two clan chieftains, two peers o' the realm, stand afore ye as witnesses tae crimes against my people. I alone have the authority tae meet out justice tae my people. You overstep, de Biggar."

Alexander spat very precisely at the sheriff's feet, who was mottled pink with rage, then said: "His Majesty might no' concern himself with stealing and raping during all-out war, but we're no' at war just the now. We've pledged our fealty and have, as such, brought peace to our lands. We will receive the respect that is due tae us. Noo, ye'll do as asked and empty yer pockets."

As if on cue, the sheriff's foot soldiers pulled their swords with a ringing of steel.

"Careful, Laird," warned the sheriff, the color high on his cheeks as his men drew closer behind him. "You may have pledged your fealty, but your true sympathies are showing. The King will hear of this rebellion."

Edyth felt sick. She was just about to step forward and do something, anything, to stop the eminent bloodshed, when the sound of running feet and raised voices caught her attention. Everyone braced themselves, turning to see who would emerge from across the bridge. In the low light, it was not immediately clear who was coming. If it was the sheriff's men, Edyth had no hope of preventing bloodshed.

But it wasn't the black and red uniform of the sheriff's men she saw, but the muted greens and golds of the plaids the Scotsmen wore. Alec and two others from the household guard joined them, followed by a loping, gasping Ceana. When she saw the sheriff and his men, she slowed to a stop, half hidden amongst the trees that grew at the side of the riverbank. Her face was as a pale oval in the growing dim, stricken with fear as she gasped for breath.

Alec and the other guards pulled their own weapons, evening the odds. Ewan said something in Gaelic that Edyth could not translate but at seeing the look on Alec's face, she wondered if it had been a rebuke.

"Turn oot yer purses," commanded Ewan once more. While his voice was even, there was promise in those words, a promise of power tightly reined.

The sheriff scoffed. "You would ruin the house of Ruthven over your precious pride."

Ewan seemed unconcerned. "I could kill you then open your purses. The choice is yours."

Sneering, his lip curling, de Biggar said, "Do it then, and damn yourself."

Edyth gritted her teeth. This was all her fault! If she hadn't come into the village, they would not be in such a delicate situation. But she found that she could not be sorry as Arthur sobbed and shook in her arms. If she hadn't come, the boy would still be nailed to the post and Ewan would still be ignorant of what was really happening right under his nose.

Ewan moved fast. With the smallest of movements, with a mere flick of his wrist, the purse hanging from the sheriff's belt fell to the ground with a dull thud. The air rang with the clashing of swords. Strong arms suddenly wrapped around her, pulling she and boy backward. A yelp of surprise lodged in her throat as she fumbled for her knife, one arm still around the boy's shoulders. She would fight tooth and nail, would protect Arthur with her own life if needed.

"Nay mistress," rasped a familiar voice. It was Alec, grabbing her wrist just as her knife came free of her pocket. "Dinnae fash; I'll get ye away."

"Wait," she gasped, her hand fisting into the shirt at his shoulder to stay him. "The boy's mother is in there. We must take her with us." Alec refused her plea before his eyes left her face to focus on a spot over her shoulder. The world turned over. Something fell against her, pushing her and the boy to the earth. She fell with a cry, trying to avoid hurting Arthur, who was entangled in her skirts. Two sets of legs danced around them, swords clashing overhead. Edyth grabbed onto some part of Arthur, she wasn't sure which, and pulled, rolling them out of the way.

She looked just in time to see Alec's sword swing toward the middle of his opponent. It was Pock Face, his crooked teeth bared in a cruel grimace. Pock Face jumped back just in time, barely missing being disemboweled. Alec followed the momentum of the swinging arc of his sword, turning bodily in a circle. With an almighty yell that raised the hairs on Edyth's arms, Alec swung forward, lunging, to slice his sword across Pock Face's chest.

Blood shot from the wound, spraying the ground and Alec's face and chest. Edyth's eyes caught hold of a jagged line of exposed bone, startlingly white against the field of black tunic and pink, weeping muscle. The man fell slowly, first to his knees, then onto his face, a strange, bubbling staccato of air escaping his chest cavity. Blood pooled at the corners of his mouth. He gasped once, twice, then the light left his eyes, the dull silver sheen, the same color of English skies tarnished into gray iron. Edyth stared at him, frozen. It was with some effort that she took her next breath.

"Wait," spat the sheriff, pulling Edyth's gaze from the enlarging pool of blood surrounding the dead man's body. De Bigger was on the ground, his weapon lost to him, the point of Ewan's short sword neatly nestled under the sheriff's chin. "I y—yield," he panted. Gone was his usual smug expression, replaced with reluctant concession and something else. Something like hatred.

Two others of the sheriff's men had lost their weapons as well. Edyth could see they had been wounded. Bloodied lips and noses, darkened patches of spilled blood on their tunics, but they did not appear grievously wounded to Edyth's eye. At least they were standing. There was a heap on the ground just beyond them where one of the foot soldiers lay quite still. They were held at sword point by Alexander and another of Ewan's guardsmen.

With bared teeth and barely suppressed emotion, Ewan looked down on his opponent, where a thin red line of dribbled blood marred his otherwise wan skin. "Ye've assaulted my people, stolen from them, and threatened my wife. It is within my right tae kill you."

The sheriff was breathing heavily through his nose, his chin tipped upward as if that could relieve the pressure Ewan was placing on his neck. "Apologize tae my wife," snarled Ewan. "Now."

De Biggar's wild eyes settled upon Edyth, then quickly away with a hiss of pain as Ewan pressed his sword harder into flesh. The trickle of blood flowered, then fell in a streak into the hollow in the sheriff's thick throat. "I didnae say tae look upon her," sneered Ewan. "I said *apologize*."

Edyth's eyes followed the bob of the sheriff's throat as he swallowed. He licked thick lips, his eyes darting from place to place, but never meeting anyone gaze. "I—I apologize," de Biggar said with reluctance, the words sounding as though they cost him something.

"For?" asked Ewan expectantly.

De Biggar's lips rolled together, the air whistling through his nostrils. He jutted his chin out, but his eyes did not rise to meet Ewan's when he said, "For causing f—fear. For—for looking upon you."

"Now, apologize tae the lad."

"You cannot expect me to apologize for—" began the sheriff, but at another press of the sword, the sheriff winced and conceded. "I'm s—sorry," he said on a breath.

Ewan removed his sword from the sheriff's throat, who sagged into himself. A hand went to his neck, fingering the cut that Ewan had caused.

"On your feet," demanded Ewan. The sheriff took his time doing so, sweat peppering his bald head as Ewan pointed the sword at his eye level.

"Alexander," said Ewan, motioning for his friend to search the purse he'd cut from the sheriff's belt. "Will ye kindly do the honors?"

"Aye, with pleasure." Next came the soft sounds of coins shuffling as Alexander sifted through the purse with a finger. He pulled out a rather beautiful pin of silver, inset with small blue stones that Edyth recognized as those that clansmen wore to keep their plaids fastened about them. Alex showed it to Ewan, who promptly frowned.

"That doesnae belong tae this sassenach, I'd wager." Alexander next drew out a small object, glinting gold, and held it between thumb and forefinger. "Weel, now. This is curious." It was a ring. Made for a man. He held it up, turning it toward the fading light. "Is this the lost signet ring, then?"

Ewan's eyes darkened. "Ye ne'er lost the ring. I should kill ye now, like the dog ye are."

Chapter Twenty-Three

"You kill me, any chance of peace for your people dies along with me," promised the sheriff.

Ewan looked as though he wanted to spit in the man's face. "Ye've provoked my people, threatened my wife, stolen and lied. Ye dinnae wish for peace. Ye want action. And action I will gladly give ye."

"The King's peace has been broken," said de Biggar hurriedly, his eyes wide with something akin to panic. "Your life will be forfeit if you take my own."

"Aye, the King's peace has been broken, but no' by me. All will ken what ye've done here, in *His Majesty's* name. What do ye think he will say, when he learns of your misdeeds, acted out in his name?"

De Biggar seemed to gather himself, his eyes darting to his men that still stood.

"If ye value yer life, Sheriff," said Ewan carefully, "ye'll shut yer gob. Ye'll be under my watch. If I hear o' ye laying a hand on any of member o' my clan, or those who are under my care and protection while on my lands, I *will* kill ye. Do ye hear?"

The sheriff took exception to this remark but wisely chose not to argue. Tugging on his doublet jerkily, his lip curled into a sneer. "Aye, I hear," he ground out finally.

"Noo lads," said Ewan, speaking to his men. "Let the soldiers go. I dinnae think they'll be causing any more trouble. The sheriff is going tae open up the alehouse and let my wife tend tae the lassie they've stolen."

"She is my prisoner," complained de Biggar. "She is under arrest for attacking one of my men." He pointed to the foot solider that had fallen to the ground. He was standing now, with the help of his fellow, a hand pressed to his head.

Edyth was gratified to see three long scratches down the length of his cheek, dark with dried blood.

Edyth backed further away as Ewan and de Biggar made their way to the alehouse door. The latter pulled a cord from around his neck, to which was attached a long, iron key. He unlocked the door with unsteady hands as Ewan loomed over him, sword still drawn.

There were muffled footfalls on the planks within the house. A candle was lit. Edyth watched as its light disappeared around a corner. After a short time, sobs could be heard. Edyth wished to go as well, but held steady at the look Alexander gave her. He went in himself, and they didn't have to wait long. Ewan and Alexander emerged from the dim recesses of the house with Arthur's mother, who was nestled carefully in Alexander's arms.

Arthur ran to her, crying all the harder. Edyth did not get to witness the happy reunion, however. Ewan was stalking toward her, a look of righteous judgement written on his face. He sheathed his sword and barked some orders to his men in Gaelic. All the while his eyes did not stray from her person. Edyth drew herself up, ready for a fight.

"Are ye hale then?" asked Ewan, not touching her. His gaze was stony, his voice holding no tenderness. She wanted him to sweep her into his arms. She wanted him to comfort her, but it was plain that he had none to give.

Was she injured? She felt numb. Her hand had been cut, she recalled, but the dull throbbing in her fingers seemed far away and was easily ignored. Something within her felt damaged, though she could not name the hurt. She shook her head, unable to speak. A lump had lodged there, formed at Ewan's chilly reception.

He loved her, she knew, but she also had no doubts about his anger. It was evident in the way he did not touch her save out of necessity, as he helped her onto his horse. It was evident in the way he sat rigidly behind her in the saddle. In the way that his silence filled all the desperate places in her mind.

His silence seemed greater still, when they left the village and crossed the great field where the games were played. They passed milling crowds of people, some stopping in their merrymaking long enough to wave or greet their Laird from afar. Cheers rang out as winners to some sport were announced. Fires winked into existence amongst the tents. It was a happy sight, one that should have, in some future time, been looked back upon with fondness.

A stone settled in Edyth belly and she felt sick as they passed through the gate and into the yard. A stable lad rushed forward to take the horse. Ewan did not speak even then, when he dismounted and reached up to pull her from the saddle.

"I'm sorry," she whispered, searching his face for any sign of forgiveness.

Ewan merely nodded, his jaw tightly clenched, and turned on his heel, disappearing into the shadows that clung to the garrison.

Feeling awash with guilt and anguished over Ewan's abrupt dismissal of her, she retreated into the keep to await the arrival of Arthur and his mother. The hall was littered with a smattering of people, drinking and eating. The buzz of pleasant conversation punctuated with the barking laugh of some happy diner only increased her feeling of unease, so at odds was the feeling in the room compared to her own misery.

She sat in a chair nearest the roaring fire, watching the flames with her arms around her middle, feeling cold. She didn't have to wait long. All too soon Ceana appeared at her side with two other guardsmen. Arthur, his mother—who she learned quickly was called Philippa—and his elder sister, Millicent were with them. Philippa for her part, was walking without aide, and aside from a bloodied, swollen lip and some bruises, seemed well enough.

"Let's come in here, shall we," said Edyth, trying valiantly to gather the pieces of her mind that were scattered and slippery. She motioned to the door on the far side of the hearth that led to a smaller, more private chamber. It was stuffed with comfortable furniture, fur rugs, tapestries, and end tables.

"I'll see tae the fire, mistress," mumbled one of the guardsmen. Edyth could not recall his name. Inan or Ivan...something of the sort. The coals were ashen, splintered sporadically with a pulsing orange in the cracks like lightning in a midnight sky. She nodded, feeling detached from herself in a strange way. She asked Ceana to go and fetch the herbs and wraps for Arthur's hands, as well as some food for the family, then motioned the family to sit. They did so, cuddled together in one of the larger chairs, unwilling to be apart.

"Are either of you hurt?" asked Edyth, looking between the two guardsmen.

"Naught tae trouble ye with, mistress," said one of the men, who was handing his companion a rush with which to light from the fire. "Nothing we havenae experienced afore. We'll bide. I'll just light the candles for ye and we'll take our leave."

"Where is Alec?" asked Edyth, frowning in thought as she watched him touch the flaming rush to a wick, brightening the room instantly. She saw his mouth tighten. his eyes pulling away from hers. When he answered, she knew he was being careful with his words. "I cannae rightly say, mistress."

"Himself said as he wished tae speak tae him," offered the other guardsman at the fire. "He'll no doubt be getting an earful about now, if no' a strap tae his backside." His words were uttered with the wry amusement that can only come from one who isn't troubled with such a punishment, but has experienced it before. Edyth thought he looked very young, with the unlined, pink features of youth.

"Johnne," said the other guard, a soft warning in his voice. "Are ye no' yet finished?"

Their banter fell away as a maid entered with a tray of food. She was followed closely behind by a lad carrying a bucket of water. "Ceana is coming, mistress. She's in the storeroom, gathering herbs as ye asked." The maid laid the tray down on the serving table as the lad filled the kettle hanging on an iron hook. He swung the iron holding the filled kettle over the fire then left with a brief nod.

"Will ye have a bite tae eat, mistress?" asked the maid, holding an empty plate.

Edyth refused, feeling queasy, and watched as Philippa took a hesitant bite of a bannock. She wondered if the woman had a tooth knocked loose. Millicent, a blonde slip of a girl, stared wide-eyed at her brother's hands, which were swollen and still weeping blood.

"Eat," Edyth encouraged Ceana. "I'll take good care of them. You were very brave," she added in an undertone. "You saved them." *And me.*

It was some time later, as she was finishing up with the bandages on Arthur's hands that Cait appeared, full of quiet command. Edyth's heart stuttered at seeing her friend. She wanted her comfort but held her tongue. It would not do to come apart here, in front of these strangers.

Edyth's hand shook as she cataloged the bruises along Philippa's cheek and jaw But other than a swollen and sore face, there wasn't much wrong with her. She hadn't lost any teeth, thankfully, but she did have bruised ribs where she'd been kicked. So far as she could tell, Arthur had seen the brunt of the sheriff's ire, though she had no doubt that had Philippa been left alone with the man or his foot soldiers, much more damage would have been inflicted on her. They had simply not had the time.

"You go," suggested Cait, seeing Edyth's shaking hands as she sponged Philippa's face. "I'll finish here and find them beds. I don't think they'll wish to sleep out of doors tonight." Edyth had learned that Philippa and her family had come from a smaller village a day's ride away. Her husband, a shepherd, was in the high country presently with their flock and their eldest son.

Edyth, feeling undone, agreed and made the trek to her and Ewan's shared bedchamber. She paused outside the door, but she heard no noise from within. She felt equal parts relieved and disappointed at finding the room empty.

She stoked the fire then cleaned her face and hands, trying to wash away the jittery feeling that had settled in her bones. It didn't help. She fidgeted and paced, a fist against her unsettled belly for what felt like a very long time. Was Ewan so angry that he could not bring himself to even speak to her? Was he avoiding her or was he still punishing Alec? Her guilt intensified as she thought of the squire. He was only following her orders. If anyone was to be punished, it should be her. The thought stilled her.

Quite suddenly, she remembered Ewan's clear promise, given so many months ago when the sheriff had first arrived. *Stay away from the village. Do no' disobey me, Edyth. I dinnae wish tae punish ye*. She groaned and folded into herself, her arms crossed against her middle. She did not want Alec punished, nor did she wish to be on the wrong side of Ewan's wrath. She could not believe that he would harm her, despite his words. He had warned her, though.

She swallowed, feeling hollow. Even knowing Ewan would be displeased and that a consequence would be meted out, she'd conveniently skirted around the fact in favor of the more pressing issue at hand. She'd chosen to ignore the fact that this moment would most assuredly come but it could be ignored no longer. And now, in light of everything that had happened, speaking to Eachann's parents didn't feel as pressing as it had mere hours before.

All in all, though, wasn't it better that they knew what the sheriff was doing? Yes, she'd been in considerable danger and terrified, but if it hadn't been for her, Arthur and his mother would still be in de Biggar's custody. She was certain that had Ewan learned of de Biggar's overreach after the fact—if at all with the way his people were keeping quiet in the name of protecting each other—the resolution would have had a very different outcome. He'd have had to contend with all of the sheriff's men at once, for instance, nor could he have so easily regained all that had been stolen from his people.

Edyth had just risen to retrieve her plaid when the door swung open, revealing an ashen faced Ewan. She stood still, as though frozen in time, her eyes locked onto her husband, the heavy material dangling from her hand. He stood there for a moment, staring at her, before he shut the door behind him.

He had changed out of his soiled clothing and had washed his face since she'd last seen him. He appeared to have cooled down considerably from their ride back to the keep. The sharp angles of his posture had softened into his usual self and he was looking at her. That was something at least. She replaced the arisaid, missing its absence as soon as it left her hand. She closed her fingers on air and prepared herself for the worst.

"I'll have sommat tae say tae ye," he said rather formally, indicating that he would like her to sit with a gesture. She did so, her back rigid as she sank onto the mattress.

Ewan took a deep breath and pulled up the stool near their bed. He did not touch her. He held his hands together, as though in prayer, carefully atop his lap. He sat silent, his long mouth held in a frown, his eyes clouded with thoughts. Finally, after what felt like an eternity, he spoke. "Why, Edie?" His voice was carefully emotionless, detached even. "Why would ye go intae the village when I expressly forbade it?"

She opened her mouth and closed it again to swallow. "I went to see Eachann's parents."

"Mmph," he said, color high in his cheeks. She could see his effort to remain calm wasn't coming easily. He pressed his lips together tightly, making the dimple in his left cheek wink into existence. "Aye. I see. And ye went, knowing well enough what sort o' man de Biggar is, but still ye went. Alone."

She hadn't gone completely alone, but chose not to mention it, as it would doubtless be as viewed as only another mark against her. She'd not only endangered herself, but poor Ceana. Edyth could only nod. Her fingernails bit into her palms, her breath coming shallow.

A muscle jumped in Ewan's jaw before he let out a careful breath. His steepled fingers rose to his chin, his dark eyes full of restrained emotion. Maybe he'd been hoping that, somehow, it had all been one giant mistake, one where his wife had not betrayed her word. She imagined he would have much rather heard that she'd been dragged there by the sheriff himself than to have willingly walked there.

"Do ye recall..." he started in a tight voice "Do ye recall me telling ye tae always stay with a guard when I wasnae able tae be with ye without the walls?"

"Yes. I went anyway." Her confession was clearly as painful to him as if she'd spat in his face. His eyes, which in the past had always held such tender feeling were changed. She reached for his hands, but he sat rigid and unmoving.

"And did I no' tell ye that I would punish ye, if ye disobeyed?"

Edyth's breath caught in her throat. She removed her hands from atop his, feeling both anguished at having caused him pain and frightened at what he might do to punish her. She had never seen him so angry. No, not angry, she amended. Hurt. He felt betrayed by her. And this was not the first time she had gone against his word. It was a first, however, that she would be punished for it.

Never in her life had she been struck by a man she loved. Her father had made her write endless lines or memorize scripts. He'd restricted her to the grounds, disallowed her favored activities. But never had he struck her. She deserved nothing less, but knowing that didn't make it any easier.

Her mother had been the one to dole out the rare physical punishment...a tawse to the back of the thighs, a slap on the hands with a rod. It had hurt of course, but she'd never cried. Her pride had not allowed her. But now, her heart was heavy with sorrow and the tears were far too close to the surface. He if did strike her, she would cry. And mightily so.

Ewan ran his hands through his hair, looking as miserable as she felt. He stood and walked to the fire, warming his hands. "The problem is that ye dinnae seem tae trust me." He turned to meet her eyes and her shame increased. "I dinnae wish tae bring up Dunbar again, but tonight makes twice that ye've put yerself at risk despite my requests no' to do so."

She nodded, sniffing. "I only wished to speak with Beathan and Deòiridh. I wanted to try and resolve this issue between us."

Ewan nodded, his lips pressed into a thin line. "Aye, I ken well enough why ye wished tae speak tae them, and I would have gladly taken ye myself, had ye only asked it o' me. If ye'd only waited until I was finished with my duties for the day."

She knotted her fingers in her lap, unable to say more lest she start to cry. He noticed.

Ewan sighed and came closer, his boots sounding rhythmically on the planks. Large, warm hands engulfed her own. "Edie," he said softly, a tenderness edging it's way into his voice, "Ye've got a good heart, but ye cannae fix their wound. They—they asked that ye stay away. I think ye should honor their wishes."

The room dissolved around her. The bed sank lower as he moved to sit beside her. "Ye cannae help them, nor can they soothe the hurt in yer heart. How could they, when their own hearts bleed for what they've lost? There is room for naught else save their own suffering."

Edyth knew what he said was true. What had she expected from Eachann's parents? She wanted her offer of comfort to be acknowledged and gratefully accepted. Somehow, her offer of sympathy and their acceptance of it would mean she was forgiven. Forgiven for what, she was not sure. She had done nothing wrong. Still, she craved acceptance. She yearned to belong.

"They will accept ye in time, Edie. As I've telt ye. But now isnae that time. They cannae do so, with their souls rent in twain."

Edyth nodded against his chest, breathing in the scent of him. Bergamot from the soap he'd used and something uniquely Ewan that roused and comforted her in the same moment. While his arms were a comfort to her, his words were like a knife to her heart. "The sheriff said the people of the village talk about me. They think that I made the wagon fall on Eachann with witchcraft, so that I might cause him pain and suffering. So I could take his body—his bones. What do you suppose I'm to do with an arm?" She pulled away to look into Ewan's face. "Why would they say such things? How can they believe that of me?"

Ewan sighed heavily and brushed hair from her face. "Aye, I've heard the rumors. The sheriff isnae the only reason I wished ye tae stay out o' the village."

The admission hurt. "You—you think your people would harm me?"

"Not with stones or blades. With words. I wished tae spare ye their gossip."

Edyth let out a shaky breath, feeling small and defeated. Her chest felt hollow. It hurt, as if a knot in her breast had been pulled tightly, straining the very beating of her heart and the breath in her lungs. She tried to fill them, her breath stuttering with so much emotion.

"What is to be my punishment," she asked hollowly. "I would have it over with."

Ewan's mouth twisted slightly. He shook his head and leaned forward to kiss her brow. He frowned slightly as he wiped the tracks of spilled tears from her cheeks. "I came here with the intent tae take my sword strap tae yer arse. Ye deserve nothing less for disobeying me. And fer ordering Alec tae leave ye. But," he said with a wry smile, "ye've marrit a coward." He kissed the corner of her mouth.

"You are no coward," whispered Edyth.

"Aye, I am. For yer pain is my own, Edie. I only need look upon ye and my heart softens." He laid a hand on her chest, over her heart. It seemed to answer his touch, quickening and growing stronger with each beat. "Ye've been hurt enough, *mo ghràdh*. I feel every hurt, every burden that lives in you, for its half my heart ye hold. How could I lift my hand against ye? It would tear at my own soul, and break my own heart. I cannae do it."

A sound much like a sob left her as she flung herself into Ewan's arms. His mouth found hers in a searing kiss. Arms enfolded her, hands stroked her back, her ribs, her neck, her face. His hands were in her hair, pulling her closer, lifting her chin. He clenched his fist in her hair at the base of her skull, eliciting a pleasant sensation that went all the way to her toes. "Dinnae weep, *m'eudail*," he whispered softly against her pulse point under her ear. "Give me yer hurts, Edie. Let me hold them now."

Her broken, undone heart seemed to come alive at his touch. "I love you," she said, wishing there were better words. They seemed woefully inadequate in comparison to the firestorm of emotion that had overcome her. With Ewan, it was never enough. She always wanted more.

Luckily, he was willing to give and then give some more.

***

Some time later, laying in the dark, Ewan stirred against her. She could not see his face, but she could feel his gaze.

"What is it?" she asked into the dark of the room. It felt as if they were in a confessional, private and secure.

He played with her hair and she knew he was searching for words, ordering his thoughts. "Why didnae ye come tae me, Edie, and ask me tae take ye myself into the village? Do ye no' trust me?"

Edyth shifted, straining her eyes in the dark to see his face. "Of course I trust you. It's me that...." Guilt threatened to blossom within her but she pushed it away, unwilling to sour the joy they'd found together. "That's twice now I've hurt you. Can you forgive me?

He took her hand and kissed it, the stubble of his beard scratching her skin pleasantly. "Forgiven. But why? Tell me why ye went alone after I asked ye not to, and ye knowing ye'd be punished."

She shrugged slightly. "It was important that you collected the rents and you were meeting with the Stewart chieftain, no doubt speaking of the potential union of the clans through Iain and Alice. I didn't want to interrupt you and..." she paused, taking a breath, "and I think part of me knew that you'd talk me out of going. Because, as you say, Beathan and Deòiridh don't wish to see me. It was a selfish wish, to be heard. To be accepted."

"I want ye tae trust me."

"I do. I do trust you."

Ewan was quiet for a few heart beats. "I appreciate that more than ye ken, Edie."

"What will happen now?" asked Edyth, "With the sheriff? Have I started a war?"

Ewan readjusted himself on the bed. "Weel, it's hard tae say. Only part o' the reason for Alexander coming was tae speak of a potential union. He's brought news that he didnae wish tae have written in a letter, lest it be discovered. There have been some uprisings in the south. The sheriff assigned tae the Stewart holdings has been called away tae help with a sacking of an English fort in Haddington."

Edyth's heart leapt to her throat. "What happened?"

"Not much is known yet about *who's* behind the revolt, but it's no' the first of its kind. So far there 'ave been three such attacks in the lowlands. Small bands o' men sneak in, under the cover of darkness, and kill the soldiers there, then burn the forts they've constructed tae the ground. With none caught, ye can imagine the mind o' the people. They are hungry tae fight."

"Do you think the Scots will unite in an uprising?"

Ewan shook his head. "Nay. At least no' openly, but they might no' punish those within their territories for doing such. They might even encourage it secretly. From the outside, the barons and earls seem as though they are loyal tae Edward, when in truth, they are undermining him where they might."

"Like your father," supplied Edyth. Malcolm Ruthven had done just that, by paying King Edward in silver, while also paying the French King with his son's blood on the battlefield against the English. Ewan had made it home alive and mostly whole, save for a nasty wound to his shoulder.

"Is that why you weren't worried about confronting the sheriff? You think King Edward will not wish to anger you?"

"Nay, I confronted him because he was *wrong*, Edie. But it's a good possibility that King Edward willnae condemn me for my actions against his sheriff." His words did not make Edyth feel any better. "Any man of honor can see that de Biggar's actions justify what happened this night."

"I thought that was the purpose of the sheriffs, to punish those who disturb the King's peace"

Ewan nodded. "Aye, tis. But as ye can see, de Biggar isnae playing by the rules. The King's peace punishes theft, among other things, yet that is just what de Biggar was caught doing. De Biggar kens this well enough but he cannae fight me openly. He only has a small force o' men with him."

"And we are many," supplied Edyth, understanding dawning.

"Aye. Edward will surely wish tae keep the chieftains happy now that he's gained their fealty and a semblance of peace rests o'er the land. De Biggar provoking my people by creating false crimes for an excuse tae cause fear," he shrugged here, "we can suppose Edward will no' sanction such actions.

"It's my belief that de Biggar will be called away soon, if he hasnae been ordered elsewhere already," he continued. "Rory tells me that he's been gathering supplies from the villagers as if they're going on a journey."

Edyth could only hope that was the case. "But Alec killed one of the men," said Edyth, her mind filling with the image of Pock Face's unseeing eyes. "And three others were injured. Surely the King will be displeased."

"Our actions against them were warranted," he said with confidence. "Dinnae forget we have witnesses against his ill deeds. The King cannae sanction de Biggar's mistreatment of my people without causing further rifts.

Edyth pictured in her mind, the leaking, earthen dam from her village of Carlisle that she'd seen when younger. She'd watched as men daubed mud over the weeping cracks to stem the flow. One hole would be patched only to have another leak appear. Controlling Scotland would be similar, she imagined. One skirmish here, another there. If the King were not careful, the dam that was holding Scotland back would burst.

"There's also the issue that there's no clear leader among us," said Ewan. "Many of those with the right to the throne are either locked in the Tower of London after the battle of Dunbar, or have sworn fealty to Edward." He was quiet for a time, lost in his own thoughts.

"What of that man your uncle wishes to help free from Chester? Would men follow him, do you think?"

"Aye," he said on a breath. "Aye, I think they might at that."

Chapter Twenty-Four

The herbs hanging from her mother's still room were pungent, flooding her mind with countless memories. Tufts of bound plants hung from the lattice overhead, casting wide shadows, inking and smudging the counter's contents with broad stokes. Bowls, jars, and linen sacks, carefully organized and labeled littered the surface. Edyth took a shuddering breath and turned in a tight circle. She knew this place, knew every line in the cracked tiles, every loop in the ragged rug she'd helped to make under her feet. The dried rushes in the rug poked at her bare feet. She flexed her toes, welcoming the familiar sensation.

This was a welcome dream, so different from those of recent days. Dreams such as these were not filled with dread and fear, but of longing and a desperate desire to hold the pieces firmly together, to savor what had been lost. These came seldom. Far too infrequently. She'd had only one other, when she'd needed it most, but she could think of no reason to be here in her childhood home now.

The thought of her mother brought her suddenly into existence. She could hear her humming, hear the soft suggestion of the pestle in the mortar, could smell the pungent aroma of hog's weed as her mother forced the oils from its leaves with fervent strokes. Edyth closed her eyes momentarily and listened to the humming, basked in the nameless tune that seemed to drape over her and sing in her very bones.

At last, Edyth turned, her heart in her throat, and could not stop the tears that came unbidden to her eyes. She was just as Edyth remembered: her long, dark auburn hair in a thick braid, head uncovered, elegant neck stretched over her work.

Marsilia was a handsome woman, and one that Edyth had not forgotten, but as always with absence and time, the edges of her mother's features had started to fade. She'd forgotten the freckles that kissed the shell of her mother's ear. Gone *from her immediate memory was the way her mother would shake and flex her overworked hands, only to immediately pick up her tools, unwilling to stop for more than a moment.*

"Fetch me the starwort, will you," asked Marsilia, as if death and time had not separated them these many months.

Edyth turned to an open crate that lived in the corner and found what she was looking for. She chose one of the larger roots still covered in a dusting of fine earth and placed it carefully upon the chopping board next to her mother, feeling as though her heart might burst. Her mother smiled in thanks, her bright blue eyes searching her face. Edyth, hungry to take her in, stared back. "I suppose you know why you're here," said her mother, tipping the gathered liquid from the mortar into a vial with a steady hand.

Edyth shook her head, silent, wishing to touch her mother, to have her arms enfold her once more. She ached with the memory of it, of how it would feel to have her mother's soft, reassuring touch upon her once again. Her mother picked up the root and began her work, scraping off the tough skin, exposing the yellowish heart of the medicine, glancing at her briefly. "You have questions. You brought me here with them, so ask."

"How can this be?" asked Edyth, her voice hushed. "You're dead."

Her mother gave her a sideways glance then sliced into the root with a neat 'snick'. "You've always dreamt, Edyth. Do you not recall the swineherd? That was the first portent of death you had. But not your last."

Edyth nodded, recalling the terrible dream of the fire, of the lost children, and the agony their father felt in the aftermath. And of another death she'd seen. Ewan's. "I didn't know it was a foreshadowing. I didn't know to warn them."

Marsilia gave her a sympathetic look. "Yes, I can see the memory still haunts you. It wasn't your fault, dearest. You must remember that."

"Why didn't you tell me what I was? What we are?"

Auburn brows rose in surprise. "And what are we, daughter?"

"Witches." The word fell between them, a vulgarity, considering how the name had killed her mother.

Her mother's look turned sour. She scoffed and set down the knife she was holding. Her fingers were stained green and blue from her endless tinkering with the herbs, of her ardent fiddling in growing things. She held her hand out in invitation and Edyth, breathless, hesitated only for a moment before she took it into her own.

Her mother's hands were warm and as solid as the ground beneath her feet. A desperate sound left Edyth's throat at the touch, her nose stinging with emotion. How was it possible? She wanted to throw herself into her mother's embrace, to feel all of her, to smell the forgotten scent that clung to her, but she held herself in check.

"What we are has no name," said her mother fervently. "We are only women, who dare to listen to the voice inside ourselves. To hear the calling given to us by our maker. Nothing more, nothing less." Edyth had a hundred questions, but her mother continued: "I have never dreamed, Edyth. My gifts have always been here, with the growing things. My mother's talents were the same and she taught me their uses, how to grow them, when to harvest them, and how to administer them. You though," she said, squeezing her fingers slightly, sending a jolt straight to her heart, "you've always been different. You can see into the dark, hidden places and, sometimes, the darkness speaks."

Edyth opened her mouth but her mother shook her head, forestalling her. "Hear me, daughter. Do not weep for wickedness." Edyth's brow wrinkled in confusion.

Her mother squeezed her fingers lightly, demanding her full attention. "Our time has come to an end," she said, softly, her eyes sweeping over Edyth's face as if to memorize it. She pulled Edyth to her, her arms encircling her shoulders and Edyth greedily accepted, taking in the feel and scent of her. She inhaled deeply, her eyes tightly closed. "I don't understand," said Edyth thickly.

But the edges of her mother were fading, the solidity of her frame lessening. Even the room beyond them dissolved into swirls of color. "No," whispered Edyth, knowing the dream was fading. "Don't go. I don't understand."

Her mother's voice sounded far away, as if carried away by an unfelt wind. "Do not weep."

Edyth's arms tightened, desperate, but only grasped air as her mother's form dissolved completely. She hadn't been given enough time.

She awoke abruptly to tears on her face and a weight on her heart so heavy it was difficult to draw breath. Ewan stirred next to her, pulling her close and tucking her into him.

"Wheest, *mo chridhe*. Tis only a dream."

She nodded, her body shaking, feeling lost and quite alone.

***

The following morning, Ewan was rather bemused to learn that the sheriff had gone before dawn. He couldn't really find it within himself to be angry that the man had taken half of their quarterly rents in the name of taxes. Granted, Ewan had only collected a fraction of what he was due—the rest hidden safely in the Stewart lands—but giving it up *had* rankled him. Now that he was gone, though, Ewan would need to speak with Alexander about delivery of the remainder of his rents.

The alehouse wasn't completely empty, though. Three of de Biggar's men had been left to watch over, and no doubt report, on the goings on whilst de Biggar was away. Two of the said sentinels watched silently from outside a tinker's tent as the crowd gathered in the field to watch a contest of swords.

"Where d'ye think the great smout ran off to?" asked Iain, not even trying to hide his distaste as they passed the foot soldiers. De Biggar's men gazed back coolly, their eyes shaded from the helmets they wore. Ewan didn't need to see their faces to know of their hatred, however. He could feel it quite keenly.

Edyth seemed to melt into Ewan's side, as though pressing herself closer to him could hide herself from their purview. He gave her hand a slight squeeze and whispered to her, "Do not let them see your fear, Edyth."

It angered him that his wife would have cause to shrink away from any man, let alone in a place she called home. It occurred to him belatedly that Perthshire was not the first place in which she found reason to fear a man. The thought set his teeth on edge.

Where the sheriff had gone, Ewan could only guess. Perhaps he'd gone the same way the Stewart's assigned sheriff had, and left to join ranks with the larger army to discourage any further uprisings in the south. Or perhaps he'd run off, tail placed firmly between his legs, to howl to de Warenne of the injustice of Ewan's intercession in the name of the King's peace. He couldn't know and he didn't wish to guess. Though, he had to admit to himself, he rather liked the idea of the man fleeing because of bruised pride.

He would be back, no doubt, and with reinforcements, seeing as one of his own was now buried in the ground. Ewan shook the thoughts away. He was looking forward to watching the contests this morning and did not wish to sully his mood further.

While he'd told Edyth he wasn't too concerned about the backlash of what had happened in the village, there was a small part of him that did worry. Should de Warenne side with de Biggar, Ewan would have to involve the King, which he really did not wish to do. "Might be a good time for some of the lads tae wander intae the village for some gambling. Haps they can get some information from them."

Iain nodded, pulling his eyes from a rather pretty brown-haired lass who was braiding leather at one of the many stalls set up along the thoroughfare. "Aye," he answered distractedly. "I'll set Rupert and Ulfkel on them. They're the best at cards and can hold their liquor better than most."

It took a long time to get to their destination with how many people stopped them, wishing to speak to him. He smiled and did his duty, but he was glad when they took their places on the raised stand that overlooked the practice yard. People were crammed into every available space, full of laughter and anticipation. Today would be the last of the games, and one which garnered the most respect. And the biggest prize. Cait and William were already seated, the latter looking as bright as a new penny. It did Ewan's heart good to see his sister looking at peace. He'd had no doubt that she would bend her will to marriage eventually, but he hadn't expected it to happen so quickly. He'd have to thank his uncle twice over for the suggestion of the Thane as a match for his Cait.

Alice was already seated next to her father, Alexander, a space kept open for Iain. Ewan wasn't sure yet about the match between the two. She was past the age for betrothal, at two and twenty, and she said so little that Iain had taken no real interest in the lass. Not that Ewan could blame him. Still, Alice came with a large dowry and a strong clan alliance.

He watched Iain surreptitiously as he took his seat next to her, lifting her hand to kiss it in greeting. She made no effort to smile, nor did her cheeks blush from the attention. She merely bobbed her head in courtesy and listened politely as Iain spoke to her. He rather disliked that Iain was pressed into such a match, seeing as how he, himself, had married for love, but they could not put off the alliance. The Stewarts were their friends and had sought for such a relationship for years. Iain was their last option.

The Stewarts would leave on the morrow, along with Cait and William. The latter being eager to depart before the weather turned sour farther north. Winter was soon upon them, the peaks of the mountains already dusted with snow. He would miss Cait, but he was glad to have her settled. It eased his mind to know that she would be far away from the troubles brewing at home. He couldn't put a name to the feeling he had, but he knew something was coming, Edyth's frequent visions notwithstanding.

Haps he should speak to William about bringing Edyth with them. He looked at his wife, who was watching the contestants warm themselves to the fighting, drawing swords against their squires in practice. She was rapt with attention. "Do ye wish tae compete then?" he asked.

She blinked and glanced his way with a small smile. "Would that I could. I am not strong enough to fight against the likes of these and sparring would grant me no honor, and they hold back."

"You are skilled with a sword," he granted. "Haps we will watch a contest between you and Cait. It's been some time since you sparred. Why did ye stop?"

Edyth's mouth fell open, her cheeks flushing pink. "You knew?" she gasped. "You knew and said nothing."

"Of course," he said good naturedly, shrugging. "There's little that escapes my notice, especially when it comes tae my wife."

"I thought you would be displeased."

"I willnae take exception tae ye learning tae better protect yerself."

"But...but I hid it from you. I kept it secret."

"Did ye? And here I thought ye were only sneaking off tae the orchard tae keep the servants from gossiping any more that they already were."

A horn sounded, signaling the start of the event. A raucous cheer rang through the yard as the first two contestants walked into the middle of the sparring space, clanking with each step as their armor shifted. This was a contest of long swords, which required a great deal of strength and skill, but Ewan knew the outcome of this fight already, being on such familiar terms with the contestants. Inan was skilled enough, but he was young and mostly untested. He would lose against the older, more seasoned of his warriors, who would not take risks or waste precious energy.

He felt Edyth's gaze and found her eyes. "I wouldnae wish tae change one thing about ye, Edie. No' a one. If ye wish tae spar, then do so, and let the tongues wag for all I care."

She lept forward, flinging her arms around his neck and kissed him soundly.

***

Cait's trunks were all packed and loaded onto the wagon in the yard. The sun was rising, tinting the world in the soft hues of a new day. Cait's hands were cold in her own and Edyth stared at them. Pink and chaffed with the winter weather, they were still beautiful.

"I've hidden within your things a special parting gift." Edyth kissed Cait's hands then pulled her into a hug. "Practice with it when you can. I will do the same." Cait pulled away slightly, a question in her watery eyes. Such tears were rare, and so all the more precious to Edyth. "A blade," said Edyth, "and I have its twin. They are sisters, just as we are."

Cait's arms tightened around Edyth. She could feel the quiet tremor that ran through her, at her desperate attempt to contain her feelings. "I will call it *caraid*," she said thickly, "*sister*, and think of you whenever I hold it."

Edyth nodded, too overcome to speak. Cait pulled away, wiping at her eyes and forcing a smile as she hugged Ewan, then Iain.

"*Soraidh*," she muttered, moving to William's side. *Farewell*. He helped her into the carriage and shut the door. Cait kissed her fingers one last time in parting as William motioned to the driver to pull out. William mounted his own steed and followed alongside, quiet and orderly. And just like that, Cait was gone. Her only friend in the world.

Chapter Twenty-Five

It had been two months since the sheriff had left, and although Edyth gloried in that fact, she missed Cait something fierce. The weather had turned colder and with it, the winds had stripped the trees of all their leaves. She'd kept busy, teaching the servants to read and write well enough to keep the inventory in the stores up to date as well as leave her any notes should they choose to do so.

Alban had warmed to her as well, much to her surprise. Well, perhaps *warmed* was the wrong word. He groused less, in any event. Last week he'd even set aside a slice of left over plum and honey cake for her, but when she'd thanked him, he'd only mumbled something about not wanting to give it to the pigs.

She'd merely smiled, her mouth full, and wondered at what had changed between them. Haps it was that the dowager was now gone and so he now viewed Edyth as the mistress of the keep. Haps it was that she had given up on controlling so much of the kitchen and left the majority of running it to him.

Whatever the reason, the change had lightened her heart. And with his grudging tolerance came the gradual acceptance of a few others as well. Even a handful of the villagers came to her now, asking for remedies to their ailments. She'd prepared a horseradish and garlic poultice to help with their chest complaints or bandaged wounds. With every complaint brought to her, she felt more and more hopeful that, soon, their acceptance of her would spread.

She was just finishing up with the latest batch of the aromatic poultice when Ewan entered the stillroom that she'd commandeered for her use in one of the rooms off of the kitchen.

"There ye are," he said in way of greeting and then immediately held his sleeve to his nose. "What is that godawful smell?"

"Medicine," she said, holding up the crock of prepared mush with a smile. He peeked into the bowl before she covered it, laughing at his wrinkled nose and watering eyes. "What's that?" she asked, noticing he held a letter in his other hand.

"This is what I came tae speak tae ye about. Do ye have a moment?"

She did. She wiped her hands on a rag and removed her apron. "Let's go where our eyes won't sting."

Ewan led the way, opening the door to the kale yard for her. The day was cold and blustery, but it had stopped sleeting. They walked to a space under the eave of the kitchen, where their shoes would remain dry. "It's from my Uncle Niael. Mam is well," he said, answering her unspoken question with a dismissive gesture. "There's a matter o' politics he wishes tae speak with me about, however. In person. He didnae explain in the letter, o' course, lest it be read, but he wishes tae meet with me at Inchmahome Priory Wednesday next."

Edyth blinked at him. "Do you know what it's about?"

Ewan ran a hand through his beard. It was still short and new, only a month old, but she liked it very much. Sometimes, when looking at him in profile, as she was now, she had a wild urge to run her hands over his cheeks and kiss his well-formed mouth. "Weel, I have my suspicions," he said, pulling her from her thoughts. "Do ye recall my telling ye aboot the Moray lad, held in Chester Castle? He was placed there after the battle at Dunbar."

She did. His uncle, the Caimbel, had reason to believe he was an important piece to the puzzle in the first steps toward Scottish independence. He wanted to help free the man. "Is it safe for you to go, do you think?"

Ewan shrugged. "It's as safe a time as we may get. De Biggar is still gone and with the troubles still brewing in the lowlands, he might be gone for some time. I willnae go, though, Edie, should ye no' wish it."

Edyth took a deep breath, her exhale clouding the air between them. She thought of her dream with her mother. Of the reminder that with such dreams came duty. She thought of her other dreams, full of pain and death. The way was unclear. She didn't understand yet, what she was meant to do or how. But, she conceded, how could she influence anyone without knowing what the Caimbel was planning? She bit her lip and nodded. She didn't want him to go, but she could feel that him doing so was important. She heaved a breath and said, "Yes, you should go. But you'll leave Iain?"

"Aye, and Rory. I'd feel better with them both here while I'm away. I'll take Fingal and Graham, as usual, and haps I'll bring Alec along too. It's no' too far away, just a day's ride. I dinnae expect to be gone more than a few days."

Edyth sighed, pulling the arisaid more tightly around her. "I will miss you while you're gone. Be careful, Ewan."

She could barely discern where his dimple was with his beard when he smiled down at her. He pulled her into his arms and was enveloped with his scent. It calmed her and stirred her blood at once. "I shall miss ye, *mo ghaol*. Noo, let's get inside."

***

The priory was well situated, nestled prettily on the banks of the Loch of Monteith and surrounded with a grove of leafless trees that seemed to wave in welcome. Ewan found his uncle in the severely pitched, thatched roof of the western cloister, where a lanky monk had directed him. The room was dim, what with the oiled hides covering the windows, keeping the weather out, but there was a fire and some candles, which offered a great comfort.

He pulled his plaid from his head, which he'd used to keep dry from the relentless sleet, and stomped warmth into his toes at the entrance. He was slightly surprised to see that not only was his uncle present, but Robert Dundas and Sir Gilbert Hay, his southern neighbors and political allies. He rolled his shoulder, feeling unaccountably nervous. Why he'd thought he would be meeting his uncle alone, he didn't know. There would be more players at hand than even present, he wagered.

Sir Gilbert Hay was as grim-faced as ever, his wan skin stark against his usual dark clothes. Robert Dundas, by contrast, was exactly the opposite. Round bellied and pink, he looked as though he were perpetually deep in his cups. Robert smiled at Ewan and he clapped him on the back in a good natured way. Niael was silent and still, his eyes roving over those assembled.

"Wonderful tae see ye, Ruthven. Wonderful," said Robert, swinging his arms as though he could not keep still. "Glad ye could make it. Congratulations are in order. I heard ye married some time back. An English lass, aye? Is that right?"

"It is. Lady Edyth DeVries lately of Carlisle."

Robert's bottom lip stuck out as he thought, his brows constricted. "De-Vries, ye say? I cannae say I recall the name, but I'm glad tae hear o' it all the same. Having an English wife might come in handy these days, aye?" He nudged Ewan with an elbow as one does to show they are teasing.

"The Comyn willnae be joining us, I take it," drawled Sir Gilbert, not interested in Robert's repartee. Hay had always unnerved Ewan. The man's eyes seemed to drink in all the light, hungry and intense.

"Aye, we're all 'ere," confirmed Niael, clearing his throat and stuffing his riding gloves into his belt. "We can commence with business. We're quite secure here, I can assure ye, gentleman. Quite alone. I would 'ave yer true thoughts on what I'm about tae divulge. Dinnae hold yer tongue, aye?"

"Aye, aye," said Robert, gesticulating genially. "Ye can trust us tae say what we feel, dinnae ye worry."

His uncle shook his head. "No' yet. No' without yer assurances. I must have ye swear that no' word of what is spoken here, will escape yer tongues, nor will ye write of what is discussed. If ye cannae swear it, then I'll ask ye tae leave. Now."

The air seemed to thicken with the burden of Niael's words, but they all agreed, the weight of their vows settling like a mantle onto their shoulders. Robert's tongue ceased its waging and all eyes fell to Niael. Ewan rolled his shoulder; it was aching again, as it so often did in dreich weather or in times of distress. In this case, he was feeling both quite keenly.

Ewan listened intently as his uncle explained what was afoot. Andrew Moray of Petty, who had great influence and power in the northern part of the country was locked away in the Tower of London. Escape from such a prison would be nigh on impossible. His son, however, of the same name, was not so unreachable. Ewan knew this from the previous discussion he'd had with his uncle. What had changed, however, was the plot.

"The time has come. We 'ave a plan tae free the lad, we only need the players. A servant within the castle Chester, where he's being held, is willing tae aid us. It willnae be easy, escapes ne'er are without risks, but with the servant's aid, Moray can get tae the outer wall and intae good hands. We must meet him without and hide him away. It must be soon. Within a fortnight."

The servant was to, according to his uncle, unlock Moray's chamber on a certain night, so that he could find his way to a large enough window to slither through in an adjacent room. Being held, as he was, in the upper levels of the fortress, a rope and a soldier's uniform would be provided in said room. He only had to change, tie off the rope, and slither down into the yard. He would then be met by another willing servant, who would lead him to the postern gate.

Once without the walls, the going would become less difficult, save for one problem: Moray must be hid for a time. "Once he is discovered missing, the English will assume he's making his way home, to Avoch." It made sense. Moray, most likely weakened from imprisonment would lack the ability to make it on his own up north, especially in the dead of winter. Without a horse and proper supplies, or a place to hide, he would be easily discovered on the moorlands and recaptured.

"So, as ye can see," said Niael, "the plan is in place. What is yer mind?" The men looked at each other in silence. A log settled in the fire, shedding sparks.

It was Sir Gilbert that broke the silence. "Supposing one could slip into the northwest of England undetected, where do ye propose Moray be hid?"

"The border is nae closed," remarked Niael coolly. "We among us have lands in England and have cause tae move freely to them as sworn loyal servants tae the King."

"None of us here have lands near Chester," said Ewan. "What business would we have in such a place?"

"Ye only need pose as merchants. Once ye have the lad, it's a quick ride north tae the River Mersey, where a birlinn will be waiting on ye. The passage up and around the wee islands will bring ye well intae the highlands and save ye weeks o' travel with cart and horse. Ye'll make land in Kilwinning, where ye'll be met with fresh horses and supplies. There's an abbey there that can serve as a refuge until ye're ready tae depart."

Robert rubbed his chin, doubt written in his eyes. "The waters in winter willnae make an easy passage. Even if we can get the lad safe there, it's a long way tae the north o' Scotland."

"The captain of the ship is a son of the Isles of Man. He says he can bring ye safe and no trouble. I have someone in mind tae hide the lad away," said Niael, his eyes darting to Ewan. "There is a man of power who would be willing to house him until such a time arrives that Moray feels ready to raise his standard. He has land and considerable influence over the burgesses himself, as do the Moray's of Petty. Together they could unite the people in the north."

An uneasy feeling unfurled in Ewan's wame. Was this "man of power" William? If so, had Niael suggested the union of their families just so he could ask such a favor of the man? Ewan's voice was as hard as iron when he asked, "Does this man ye've in mind happen tae be newly marrit tae yer niece?"

Niael inclined his head in a short bow. "The very same."

"No," growled Ewan, drawing sharp looks from all eyes. "How can ye even think 'o it, Uncle? Nay, I willnae put Cait at risk!"

"There is always risk, no matter where we live or what we believe," answered his uncle, his clever eyes boring into Ewan. "If we do not move forward, Cait is no safer than your own lady wife. Or your mother. This is the world in which we live, Ewan. We must be bold and take what chances we are given."

Ewan shook his head, thinking of how shortsighted he'd been. Of course he had trusted Niael's suggestion at the match, believing it was in Cait's best interest that their uncle was working. But Niael was just as so many other Scots, scheming and duplicitous, even when it came to his own family. *Just as my own father had been.* Still, Ewan could not tamp down his choler.

He'd told Niael that he'd wanted to marry Cait to remove her from the dangers that were building at home and further south and Niael had given him the name: William Cawdor of Nairn. The Thaneage was secure, given by King David. It had seemed so perfect. So protected and far away. But now...now his uncle would be putting her right in the sights of the King. If anyone ever found out about William's participation, Cait could be in considerable danger.

Anger spiked through him. He took a menacing step toward his uncle. "Ye've been planning this from the start, haven't ye, ye cagey bastard?"

"I did no such thing," said his uncle placidly, not at all alarmed by Ewan's outburst. "It was a good match for yer Cait."

"He's agreed tae this scheme?" demanded Ewan, his estimation of William falling low. "He is willing to put his wife at risk?"

"Wouldn't you?" asked his uncle, sardonic brow raised. "I recall a certain *glaikit eejit* who was willing tae risk his entire household at the pledging in Berwick...leaving the ceremony for all tae see." He shook his head. "Yes, Cawdor is willing tae take the risk, as are you. As am I."

"This is a risky move," remarked Sir Gilbert, his long, bony fingers steepled at his chin. "And no doubt fraught with potential and hidden dangers, but I can see the need for it."

Ewan barked out a mocking laugh, turning on his heel to look at Robert. "What have ye tae say in all this, Robert? Ye're awfully quiet."

Robert rubbed the back of his neck, shifting his weight to the balls of his feet then back to his heels. "I agree this is a bold affair, but one worth the risk. But I fear I cannot be the man you require," said Robert regretfully. "My lady wife is with child and is soon to deliver. It would be unwise for me to venture out when her time is so near. If we waited a few months, then I would be better able to leave her."

Niael shook his head. "It must happen now, before the winter worsens. Ideally, Moray would have the backing he needs by spring. If not Robert, then what of you, Sir Gilbert?"

"I am with ye," said Hay, "and am willing." He paused for a moment then, sucking, his teeth, said, "I can be your man. I will choose a few of my favored men and ride out in as soon as a week. That is, unless Ewan wishes tae take my place."

Ewan ran a hand through his hair, pulling at the curls. He clenched his teeth, feeling pained. He could leave Hay to do it and go back home to his wife, all the while agonizing over Cait's fate. He could. But if something happened—if Hay's men were not careful and the Cawdor's schemes were uncovered—William's current position would be lost. Cait would lose all.

Or he could do it himself, he being the only man among them that had reason to travel to Nairn. Ewan cursed, feeling the need to pace, to hit something. "Nay, Uncle," he ground out. "Ye ken it should be me. It's no' that I dinnae trust ye, Hay," Ewan added differentially. "I ken ye'd do the job and well, but I will have no peace within myself, should I no' be the man tae do it. My sister is lately married tae the Thane. I alone would have cause to travel to her."

His uncle's eyes swiveled between himself and Sir Gilbert. Hay nodded. "It's decided then," said Niael. "Let us speak nothing of what has been discussed. Should I need more from you, you will receive my message."

***

"There, there," said Edyth's matronly maid, patting her back in a motherly fashion. "Rinse yer mouth and lay yerself doon, mistress while I tidy up a bit. That's a good lass."

Edyth had come down with some illness and, as a result, had slept late; the sun was high and she had things to do, yet she couldn't quite convince herself to get out of bed. With Cait gone, and now Ewan on his quest to free the Moray, she'd been fighting a melancholy mood for the last few weeks. Waking with a sour stomach only seemed poetic.

"I'll be fine, Gelis," Edyth insisted. "No, don't take the chamber pot. I might have need of it again. I'll steep a bit of yarrow in my tea and feel better before the nooning meal."

"Ye should keep yerself oot o' the snow," advised the maid in her usual no nonsense tone. "And take a wee dram tae warm ye, aye? I'll just empty this right quick."

Edyth nodded. She'd tried to keep her mind occupied yesterday evening by digging horseradish, which was best harvested in the winter and very useful for cleansing the nose and chest of congestion, but the snow had turned into sleet, wetting her through. She didn't feel cold now, only exhausted, but haps Gelis was right.

Gelis left, arms full, and Edyth settled back into bed with a groan, thinking of Ewan. She worried for him, and for what he was risking, but did her best to keep busy. She'd written to Cait twice. The letters were neatly stacked, awaiting more news; she would add to them today, if she could think of something else to say that she hadn't already written.

A sound pulled her to her feet, one that pushed all thoughts from her mind. The kirk bell rang, its urgent peals signaling visitors, and none that were friendly. Her stomach roiled at her abrupt movements, but she was able to breathe through the worst of the sensations, clinging to the bed post. Once she felt she could move without losing what little was left in her stomach, she rushed to her window. She had just pulled back the heavy drapes and unlatched the shutters in time to realize that she would not be able to see the gate from this viewpoint.

She cursed under the breath and pulled her plaid around her shoulders. She didn't have time for hose and knew she would be very cold in the hallways, but she didn't want to waste a moment. She grabbed her slippers and shoved her cold feet into them, her heart hammering as quickly as the bells. The halls were mostly empty, but she did pass a few servants who were rushing, as she was, to the nearest viewpoint.

"What is it?" she asked one girl with a soot-covered apron and a billet of wood still in one hand.

"I cannae say, mistress," she confessed, her hazel eyes full of alarm, "but it's no' Himself come home, I can assure ye."

"No," agreed Edyth. She picked up speed and lost one of her slippers. She ignored it and turned the corner, pushing through a set of doors, and into a hall where she knew she would have a view of the bailey. Just as she pushed open the door, she met Gelis, looking pale and grim.

"Milady," said Gelis, breathless. "The sheriff has returned at last, and he's brought with him a host of men."

The breath caught in Edyth's throat, her heart seeming to stop altogether before hammering to life once more. She didn't know what to say, didn't know what to do. What *was* there to do? Ewan was gone, yes, but there was Iain and Rory. They had a garrison of over one hundred men at their disposal. Surely they were safe from any danger the sheriff might bring. Weren't they?

"Where is Iain?" asked Edyth. Her hands were clammy and her stomach threatened to heave once more, but she tightened her throat against it. *Not now.* She didn't have time for illness.

"He's on his way tae speak with the sheriff at the gates, milady. So much I saw afore I came tae see ye safe. Get ye back tae yer rooms, mistress. Himself wouldnae wish ye near the fellow, and 'im with evil in 'is heart."

Edyth moved past Gelis to one of the tall, arched windows that lit the corridor. She could only see part of the gate house and the garrison wall across the wet, mud-churned yard. It was full of soldiers, running to their places. "Is the gate shut?"

"Tis, mistress," said Gelis. "Himself demanded as such whilst he was awa', no matter that the sheriff was gone."

"Well, he's not gone. Not any longer," said Edyth. A chill ran through her and she pulled the plaid more tightly around her shoulders.

"Come awa', mistress. Go ye back tae yer rooms. Let me comb yer hair and get ye dressed, aye?" Gelis seemed relieved at Edyth's acquiescence, following her in her rolling, unsteady gait.

Well, at least now I'll have something more to write to Cait about.

***

It was a long time later that Edyth freed herself from her confinement. Hungry for both news and for food, she ignored Gelis' warning and left her rooms. Unfortunately, Alec was there, guarding her door, but she just as easily sidestepped him as she had her aged servant. His face, betraying his fear, loomed after her in the dim hallways. He hissed at her to stop, to turn back, then pleaded with her to obey, but she ignored him, knowing he would not dare to force her.

"What has happened?" she asked between his muttering, walking as fast as she could through the hallways and down the stairs.

"The sheriff came with nigh on fifty men," he said, his cheeks pink. "Please mistress, will ye no' listen? Will ye no' go back tae yer rooms?"

She had no intention of doing such a thing. "You can tell Iain I tricked you, hit you, poisoned you...whatever you need to, but I am not going to be holed up in my rooms if our people need me."

Alec huffed, looking affronted. "Hit me?" She seemed to have injured his pride in some way. Edyth brushed off his feelings and made her way down the hallway toward the great hall. There were several ways to enter the room, some from the buttery, which led to an exit for kitchen access, two from either side from the east and west wings of the keep, and one from the front entrance. Edyth paused outside of the east wing entrance, listening hard.

The wood of the door was thick and difficult to hear through, but she did hear the scraping of a few benches. No words. No buzz of conversation that could usually be heard as soldiers and clans member alike took their meal.

"I'll bring ye food," Alec urged. "Get ye back tae yer rooms and I'll bring ye anything ye'd like. Please," he begged.

"Nonesense," argued Edyth. "I'm hungry and the nooning meal is being served, is it not?" Without further discussion, she pushed open the door and entered the room. It was full of people. Very full. Every seat was occupied with at least score standing around the edges of the room.

She took a handful of steps then stopped short. Alec nearly bumped into her; he was following her so closely he resembled her shadow. The small hairs on her arms stood to attention and her head swiveled, looking for the cause. The clans people present were quiet, many not meeting her eyes, while others seemed to silently issue a warning. And then she understood.

The room was not only filled with the usual faces she dined with, but those of strangers. Many strangers. And there, upon the dais, sat de Biggar and another man, one she did not know. De Biggar seemed unchanged. The sneer had not left his face in any case. The other man was older, with gray at his temples and threaded throughout his beard. His clothes were very fine, despite their wrinkled and road-weary appearance. "Who is that man with the sheriff?" she whispered over her shoulder to Alec

"That's the Sixth Earl of Surrey, mistress, John de Warenne."

Her mouth turned into a frown, and she steeled herself, looking for and finding more faces she did not recognize. There had to be at least twenty of the sheriff's men here. She couldn't believe that Iain and Rory had let them within the walls. Something was very wrong indeed. "Where is Iain?"

"He's in the garrison dungeon, tending after Rory."

Alarm shot through her and she turned abruptly to stare at her husband's squire. What had they done to the man and why had no one bothered to come get her? She could have helped. But before she put voice to her thoughts, she already knew the answer. Iain would not have called for her because he would not have wanted her anywhere near the sheriff or his men. He'd ordered her cloistered away while he did what? Let the sheriff's men have free rein of their home?

"Rory will be fine," explained Alec with a whisper and bob of his head. "Naught tae concern yerself with." She bit back a curt refute and picked up her skirts, advancing toward the dais, where de Biggar and de Warenne sat in places of honor. She was trying and failing to rein in her temper. They had no right to be here.

When she neared the high table, the low conversation between de Biggar and de Warenne ceased. The sheriff smiled. He reminded her of a sneering fox, his teeth bared in what she assumed was meant to be a gloating smile. "What have you done with Rory?" she asked, trying to keep the anger from her voice. She fisted her hands at her sides to keep them from shaking.

"Mistress Ruthven," said de Biggar, in greeting. "Is that how you greet your betters? This is Sir John de Warenne, and you will show him the respect his station demands."

Edyth raised a brow, but gave a stiff curtsey all the same. De Warenne, for his part, seemed only curious and not offended. "Forgive me for not greeting you sooner, milord. I was otherwise engaged." *Holed away, wondering what the devil was going on, more like.* "Please, what has been done with my husband's captain? I would see to any hurts he might have...acquired."

De Warenne waved her words away, standing up to offer her his chair. "Do come sit. I'm surprised to find your husband not at home. His brother tells me he is away doing business, but I cannot account for any endeavor that would pull him from home so close to Yuletide."

Edyth bit back the curt reply that formed on her tongue and climbed the few steps and took the proffered seat, where she belatedly realized, would seat her between the two men. This was going to be most uncomfortable meal she'd ever had. Her eyes scanned the crowd of people, all of whom seemed very interested in what she was doing. Alec looked as if he didn't know what to do with himself and, after an awkward few seconds of standing at the foot of the dais, he finally moved to stand against the wall, his hand on the hilt of his sword.

"I'm gratified that you could join us, Mistress Ruthven," said de Warenne silkily. "I have asked your people to attend me so that I might make an announcement. Your husband's captain tried to hinder me in doing so, and therefore, had to be disciplined. Your, er, *relation*...what was his name? Ah, yes, *Iain*. I thought that he might try and stop me from doing my duty as well, but, thankfully, his better senses won the day. Do not alarm yourself, mistress," said de Warenne with some gravity, as if he regretted being the bearer of such painful news, "your husband's captain is in Iain's capable hands. You may tend to him after I'm finished here should you wish to do so."

Edyth tried very hard to control her features, but she could feel the heat in her cheeks as her anger turned to fear. She took a steading breath, looking at the crowd of people who looked just as frightened as she felt. She must be strong. She must be level-headed; be the leader her husband's people needed at this time. She turned toward de Warenne and, conjuring thoughts of her composed mother, said, "I see. I would hate to get in the way of your duties, sir, but I fear that any punishments come from Larid Ruthven, and in his absence, myself. Surely you can understand that such an obligation falls on the house of Ruthven, and not to an honored guest."

"The authority of a woman," scoffed de Biggar to her left.

"Come now, Baldwin," chided de Warenne, though he did not sound amused in the least. "We are in Scotland after all, and the heathens have their own way of doing things. Let us not cause any rancor between us. We are friends now, are we not?" He reached for a pitcher of cider and filled a cup, offering it to Edyth with a false smile.

De Bigger grunted and looked about the room. "Why have we not been served yet?" he demanded. "You," he said, pointing to a page boy standing near a side door. "Go and tell the maids we're ready for them. Go, and be quick about it."

The page looked to Edyth, his brown eyes full of fear. She smiled in what she hoped as a reassuring way, and off he went, his skinny legs carrying him through the doors that lead to the buttery. "The kitchen is no doubt waiting for word from Iain or from myself is all. They would not wish to serve the food without the master of the house."

"Speaking of," drawled de Warenne. "Where was it you said your husband is at the moment?"

Edyth took a sip of cider, forcing placidity. "I didn't say, but he is visiting his mother, who is ill. She wished to see him."

"I thought his mother lived here, in Perthshire," said de Warenne, picking up his own goblet.

Edyth explained that Roslyn stayed with her brother after Cait's marriage, but conveniently left out that she was now living with her brother, with no plans on returning any time soon. "She wished to spend time with her brother and his family."

If de Warenne was skeptical, he did not show it. He stood and motioned for quiet, though there was no discussion to be heard. The room was full of anxious silence, nervous glances, and bowed heads. He signaled to one of the guards standing behind their chairs and the man filled his hand with a neatly rolled scroll. The red wax seal had already been broken, but he pulled on the ribbon holding it closed and unfurled it, holding it open with long, straight arms.

Edyth saw the seal of King Edward on the bottom of the page and a scrawled, loopy signature. Her stomach dropped. "People of Perthshire," said de Warenne. "I have the great fortune to share happy news and glad tidings from His Majesty, the King of England. He has selected your shire as an optimal location for an English garrison, which, in time, will house three hundred of His loyal guardsmen and support personnel. Your village will be blessed with craftsmen such as carpenters, blacksmiths, stonemasons, and more, in addition to a chaplain. Your seat here within the shire will only grow and prosper in due time. In the interim, the sheriff, Baldwin de Biggar, has been given a large retinue of soldiers to begin the building process. They will share the Ruthven garrison until the King's fort can be built."

All eyes, some registering surprise, others fear, and some outright anger, swiveled to her ashen, tight-lipped face. De Warenne rerolled the scroll and picked up his goblet. "Let us drink together in celebration of the honor your King grants upon you."

No one moved immediately. Someone coughed. Edyth, hand shaking, stood and lifted her own goblet. "*Òl a-nis, sabaid nas fhaide air adhart,*" she said, stumbling with the correct inflection. *Drink now, fight later.*

A few people lifted their cups, waiting for others to join them, and once the room was standing, cups raised, they said "*air t'fhocal.*" *Upon your word.*

De Warenne glanced at de Biggar, speaking a silent language that made Edyth's worry increase tenfold. Did they know what she'd said? Surely not. She must do what she could to put them at ease. "Long live the King," she said brightly and gulped down her drink. All others followed suit, taking their seats as if in a stupor.

Chapter Twenty-Six

*C*hester Castle
   England

"Do ye see 'im?" asked Fingal, his voice rough from disuse. He squinted into the dark, his lined mouth puckered in a tight frown, pushing a limb out of his way. He'd just returned from checking in with Graham, who was hidden with the horses and a cart, closer to the road.

The wind was bitter, making the skeletal branches of the forest quiver just as his own body quaked with cold. Ewan pushed himself away from the boulder he was hiding behind with a shake of his head. They'd been watching, waiting, amid the heather and broom outside of Chester Castle since twilight. The moon and stars were hidden behind a veil of gray clouds, masking all light from the heavens. And while the dark was useful for escape, it made their job of spotting Moray all the more difficult.

Chester, like all castles, was well fortified and nigh on impossible to infiltrate. Luckily, they would not have need to scale the walls or contrive a way to sneak under the gates, but escapes involved great risk. If something happened and Moray had to change his plans, they would not know where to look for him.

As it was, they were waiting in the wooded glen some distance away from the postern gate, looking for any movement that might signal Moray's escape.

"I think my bollocks 'ave fallen off," grumbled Fingal, his voice like gravel. He stamped his feet softly in the dusting of snow covering their hiding spot at the edge of the forest.

Ewan shook his head. "They've only likely gone numb, as mine 'ave. Best check and make sure though, aye?"

Fingal sniffed, his mouth twitching with humor, but he did not smile.

"Any trouble with Graham?"

Fingal shook his head, squinting through the dark. "Nay trouble, save boredom. Wait—I think I see sommat. Is that—? Aye, there tis again. A wee shift in the shadow under the east tower."

Ewan squinted, his eyes searching the inky shadows where the gray stone tower met the broom. He held his breath, as if that would help him see better. Yes, after a few heartbeats, he saw it too. A ripple of movement in the dark. A black shape moving in stops and starts against a gloomy backdrop was making its way toward them.

Fingal brought his hands to his mouth and mimicked the forlorn hoot of an owl, which was their predetermined signal to Graham that something was afoot. No guards appeared on the walls. No bells tolled, indicating Moray's escape had been discovered. That was good.

As the shape neared, and Ewan could better see, it became clear that the person was injured. At first, what Ewan thought to be clever maneuvering so as to not be noticed from the castle walls, he now realized the person was falling to the earth not to hide, but because he lacked the strength or ability to run.

"He's hurt," muttered Ewan, his eyes darting to the walls of the keep and back down to the tripping shape still a hundred yards off. He grimaced, considering his options. He should go and help the man, but the risk…. Moray, or so he supposed the man to be, staggered like a drunken man then fell again after only a handful of steps. Ewan's concern turned to fear. They hadn't considered the prisoner being injured, and Ewan had brought no medicines. He made up his mind quickly and pulled his plaid more securely over his head. "Stay 'ere, aye? We dinnae need the both o' us tae be spotted by any man atop the walls."

Fingal grunted, his eyes fixed on the hulking black shape that was the castle, like a mountain sprouted in the midst of the great field. "I cannae say fer sure, laird, but if I cannae see *them*, they most likely willnae see *you*. Go canny though, aye?"

He hoped that was the case. Ewan crossed himself and said a silent prayer before leaving the relative safety of the tree line. The tightly nestled leaves of the heather gathered snow, making the mottled lights and darks of the landscape confuse his depth perception. Ewan went as swiftly as he dared, his hand going to his dirk out of habit. There was nothing he could do with a dirk against loosed arrows aside from cut them out once embedded within his flesh, but he still felt better unsticking it from its scabbard.

He pushed the thought of loosed arrows from his mind and closed the distance between himself and the person clumsily making their way across the field. Ewan chose a careful path from boulder to heather, stooping periodically to check that he was still undiscovered. Closer now, he could make out the small shape of guard, walking along the top of the wall. He waited, eyes squinted, as the shape passed a flaming torch, illuminating armor and helm, of bow slung over a bulky shoulder.

The guard passed without looking down into the field, but Ewan still held his breath, silently pleading for the man to lay still. He counted to thirty once the guard had gone and started forward again, stepping around heather, weaving between dark patches of wet earth that warned of bog, one eye on the wall.

He heard the wheeze of the man's breathing before he saw him, nothing more than a shadow, half concealed by brush and broom, laying facedown. Ewan knelt at the man's side, announcing his presence with a hiss. "Moray?" The man jerked from his stupor, rolling away with a wheeze and a suppressed cough. He was unshaven and thin, as a prisoner might be expected to be, but his sunken eyes and wan skin bespoke of illness. His chest was rising and falling in a rapid beat, his eyes wild.

"Moray?" Ewan tried again.

The man's breathing was ragged, his cheek bones sharp in the low light. "That depends on...who ye claim tae be," he rasped.

"Doesnae seem that yer in a position tae be choosey, aye? I'm Ewan Ruthven, nephew of Niael Caimbel."

"Aye, ye'll do," he said, grinning as if they had all the time in the world.

"Can ye stand?"

Moray nodded. "Got to. Cannae very well stay 'ere, can I?"

"The sooner we leave England, the better I'll feel," whispered Ewan, looking over his shoulder to the high fortress wall once more. He thought he saw the weak moon glinting off a helm but it could have been just a trick of the eyes. "Yer injured, then?'

Moray shook his head, closing his eyes, his breath coming in a cloud between them. "Ague. Been fevering for twa days. Nothing some warmth and decent food cannae fix. I'll bide."

"First we have tae make it off this moor." Ewan gritted his teeth, hoping there were no eyes on them. He wrapped his hand around Moray's forearm to pull him from the cold ground and was shocked with how hot his skin felt. Hot and thin. *Naught but a bag o' bones.*

He pulled Moray to a sitting position, thinking fast. If he slung Moray over his shoulder, they would surely be noticed. He couldn't drag him without causing him further harm and the going would be slow. He couldn't build a sled for him. There was nothing for it.

"Can ye crawl," asked Ewan, getting on his own hands and knees to lead the way. "Speak if ye need tae rest."

The frozen mud, covered in an inch of snow when it wasn't covered with heather, was hard on his hands and his knees, but at least they were moving. The going was slow. He paused often to wait for Moray, who was slowing by the minute. He had to stop to smother his coughs in his elbow, his entire body shaking. As they continued, the man's breathing became more ragged, his coughing more frequent the further they travelled.

"Get on my back," commanded Ewan quietly. "I'll carry ye for a ways." Moray, clumsy and weak, groped his way onto Ewan's back, wheezing in his ear. "Fist yer hands in my plaid."

Despite being a full grown man, Moray wasn't very heavy. Wasted from evidently poor conditions for the last eight months, he was no heavier than a red deer. Still, Ewan had never packed out a kill on his hands and knees. His fingers, toes and knees stung with cold, the small sticks and stones tore at his flesh but he ignored it. Soon, they would be numb and it wouldn't matter. The going was agonizingly slow and precarious with Moray teetering atop his back with each step, but at least they were moving.

It felt like it took a lifetime, with many stops and starts, but Ewan had never been happier to hear Fingal's voice commenting on the long wait. "Thought ye might've taken a wee kip oot in the heather. Glad ye could make it," he said wryly from above them.

Ewan was relieved to have Moray pulled from his back. He looked at his hands briefly, which were scraped raw and punctured in places from sticks and jagged stones. He cupped his hands and blew into them, his fingertips stinging painfully. He'd have to wrap them later, but he couldn't be bothered with it just now. He wasn't interested in spending another second out on the windswept moor. Ewan removed his plaid despite the cold and wrapped it around the Moray's shoulders, who was shaking like a leaf in the wind. They draped a listless Moray between them, slinging his arms over their shoulders and carefully picked their way through the dark forest.

With no light to go by, the going was infuriatingly slow, but by some miracle, they avoided tripping over roots and bramble alike. The wagon, packed tightly with their wares—mostly sacks of wool, sheepskins, spun thread, and a few small pieces of furniture belonging to Cait—was strategically prepared to hide a body within its depths. It came into view now, like some giant turtle squatting amid the alders and birch.

Fingal hooted low and Graham appeared from around the side of the wagon, his hand at the hilt of his sword. When he saw them, his shoulders relaxed into the casual lines that came with recognition. He immediately pulled back the draped canvas and removed a round topped chest from the end of the bed of the wagon, revealing an open space, just large enough for a man to lay. Stacked atop of this space were the over-stuffed sacks of wool they were supposedly peddling. From the outside, it looked to be a solid mass of tightly nested bags and boxes, when in fact, it was quite hollow.

Ewan had only just opened his mouth to explain that Moray was sick when a bell rang in the distance, as sharp as a shard of ice, splintering the winter quiet. Someone must have discovered that Moray was missing. The frantic knell continued, pushing them all into panicked action. Graham sprang forward, taking and shoving Moray bodily into the hidden space, who seemed too delirious to be alarmed. His dark head lolled sluggishly as Graham pushed him into the tight space, Moray trying without much success to crawl in of his own power. There were blankets there for him. They didn't have time to waste covering him properly against the cold just now.

The hiding place was closed off by the heavy chest with a harsh scrape of wood on wood. Graham busied himself tying the canvas tightly to the wagon bed while Ewan climbed into the coach box, urgently fumbling for the reins with frozen fingers. Fingal was astride his horse, its feet stamping nervously, blowing great plumes of fog from its nose.

"Make haste," urged Ewan needlessly as Graham climbed atop his own steed. "Go east and make a false trail. Draw them awa'. If ye can, meet us at the docks, otherwise, go canny intae Scotia. Dinnae concern yerself with meeting us. Get ye tae Caimbel lands or tae Perth."

The boat, as they all knew, would leave at dawn, which would be upon them within two short hours, by Ewan's guess. He clutched the reins, looking to make sure he held them as he could not fully feel them with the cold. Fingal grunted his farewell and kicked his horse into motion, heading down the road in the opposite direction Ewan would be heading.

"*Mar sin leat,*" muttered Graham. *Goodbye.* "See ye at the docks, God willing."

Ewan nodded and snapped the reins, jolting the wagon forward with a noise that set his teeth on edge. As they ambled down the limb-covered wagon road, Ewan could barely hear Fingal's *whoop* amid the tolling of the bells, drawing attention to himself.

The road was clear of debris, but full of dips and rises that forced him to slow. He could not risk breaking a wheel, even though the blood coursing through his veins urged him to drive the horses ever faster. The way to the docks was not difficult, nor was it far, but that didn't mean there wasn't danger.

When he came to a crossroad, where he would be forced to leave the relative safety of the forest, he said a silent prayer for good luck and gave the horses more rein. While this road was superior to the wagon trail he'd just left, he would be easily spotted from afar, and should he be spotted, he would have no excuse as to why a merchant was travelling in the dead of night.

It happened only a few miles outside of the forest. The horses' thundering hooves coming from behind him were at first difficult to make out over the rumbling of the wagon wheels. Be it either some sixth sense, his experience as a solider, or luck, he could feel them coming. His skin crawled with the weight of eyes upon him. With a glance over his shoulder, he saw there were three horsemen, their chainmail winking at him in the low light. Only three. He could take them if they did not shoot him full of arrows first.

He slowed the horses slightly, letting the distance between them shorten and tugged on his dirk and sword, unsticking them from their sheaths, which they were wont to do in such weather. They were gaining on him; he could hear the clinking of their mail above the hoofbeats now.

"Stop in the name of the King!" one of them shouted. Ewan glanced backward, effecting a look of surprise and slowed the beasts further. As the wagon came to a stop, the three men circled him, one to the rear, one on his left, and one man on his right. The one on the left dismounted and grabbed one of the horse's halters. "Drop the reins," he demanded.

He could not see much of their faces, what with the dark and their coned helms covering their brows and noses, but he knew them instantly for what they were. There was no doubting that they'd come from Chester Castle. These were seasoned men, weapons honed from years of training. They would not be bribed or easily deceived.

"What business do you have on this road at this hour?" asked the man to his right. He had a neatly trimmed beard and eyes that burned like coals under the shadow of his helm.

"I am but a merchant, taking my wares to the Kingsway Market," said Ewan, careful to hide his brogue. "I must get there early if I want the best market stalls."

Ewan did not need to see the man's face to recognize his skepticism. "Your goods will be searched," he said without preamble. Ewan nodded and made to step down from the board but the man on his right held up a hand. "You'll stay where you are." He jerked his chin toward the back of the wagon, signaling to the third man to begin unloading. Ewan sat, eyeing the soldier's weapons. The one holding the horse's bridle would be slower. He would likely not be able to reach the sword in time to prevent Ewan from planting his own sword through his companion. The man on the right would have to die first.

But if the man holding the horses bolted for his crossbow, which Ewan could see strapped to his saddle, he would likely be shot. There was nothing for it, though. He had no choice and his time was running thin. He could feel the jerk of the rope being pulled free of its tie, hear the rustle of canvas as it was folded back, away from the goods it covered.

Ewan flexed his still half-frozen fingers, bringing them to his mouth to blow heat into them. The man on the right eyed him warily, and Ewan sent him a nod and slight smile, effecting placid innocence. As soon as the man's eyes slid from Ewan's face to the back of the wagon, Ewan sprang into action. He lunged forward, pulling his short sword smoothly from its scabbard at the same instant, and lept from the wagon, plunging his sword forcefully into the space between chainmail and helm. Blood spurted, spraying Ewan's face, hot on his chilled skin.

The man was dead before he even hit the ground. Ewan stumbled, the momentum of his leap pulling him forward, but he caught himself and pivoted neatly on the balls of his feet, swinging his sword to meet his next opponent. A shout sounded and the horses, disliking the violence, sprang forward, jolting the wagon further down the road. The sound of steel being pulled from scabbards and a cry of alarm cut through the quiet.

Ewan pulled his dirk, hefting it in his left hand as he faced his next opponent. The younger man, the one who had been holding the horses ran to his own steed, pulling on the straps that held his bow. Ewan gritted his teeth against a curse, pulling his gaze back to the other man, who was in the middle of a swing of his sword. It came down in a great arch, powerful and full of righteous anger. It connected with Ewan's sword, which he had brought up only in the nick of time.

The judder of the contact sang in Ewan's bones, reverberating up the length of his arm and into his weakened shoulder. He ignored the pain and pushed against soldier's sword, shoving him will all his might. The man staggered backward and reset himself in seconds, coming at Ewan again with brute strength and a grace that was only won through experience. This would be no easy kill, Ewan realized, narrowly avoiding the blow with a parry.

Ewan struck first this time, wishing for his long sword, but he had not brought it. His short sword bounced off the man's armor, sparks flying, dazzling his eyes in the dim moonlight. As the man reset his stance, Ewan heard the resounding click of bolt cocked into crossbow and his fear grew. He did not wait, but dove to the side, rolling on the ground in a summersault just as a bolt was fired. He heard the whoosh of the arrow and the dull thud as the arrow embedded itself in the frozen ground.

He was on his feet in seconds, lifting his sword to block the incoming blow from the swordsman. No stranger to battle, Ewan's body and mind began the descent into the strange state it so often did during battles. The very air thinned as time slowed down, his senses sharpening with the intense focus of a destroyer. Muscle answered where memory lived, moving without hesitation.

A dull roar filled his ears. His breathing slowed and his sword became a mere extension of his arm, a deadly tool, featherlight and familiar. Light on his feet, Ewan easily sidestepped the blow meant to remove his head from his shoulders and came up behind his opponent, driving his dirk into the space between helm and chainmail, twisting the man's body to cover his own and take the next bolt.

The younger solider with the crossbow, most likely less experienced and desperate, had pulled the trigger despite his comrade being in the line of fire. He'd gambled and lost, the bolt punching through armor, through mail, to seat itself deep in the chest of his fellow guardsman.

Ewan let the man slump to the ground, his steely eyes narrowing on the young lad, whose eyes filled with fear. The look in his eyes warned Ewan that he was about to run, which Ewan could not afford. He could not allow the lad to escape and get back to Chester. Ewan sprang forward, his breath a rasp of cold fog that billowed before him, and charged the remaining soldier.

Ewan might have once gloried in the sheer terror that came over the soldier's visage, but now, away from battle in France all this time, it only sickened him. But he could not let the lad go. He had to be stopped, or himself and Moray were as good as dead.

Ewan was upon him just as the lad had scrambled atop his steed. He pulled him off with a quick jerk, the soldier's chainmail biting into his frozen fingers. The soldier fell in a heap upon the ground, his helm dropping to the frozen earth to expose a mop of straw-colored hair, shaved off his nape and up around his ears. The pink of his skin glowed in the moonlight.

The smell of piss filled the space between them as the lad wet himself, but, to his credit, he did not plead for himself. He only winced away from Ewan's raised sword, his eyes screwed shut. The lad could not be much older than Alec, his own squire. He felt himself falter. It was one thing to kill a man who was wielding a weapon against you, but quite another to take down a green lad with no hope of winning against a more experienced man.

Ewan grit his teeth against his own hesitance. *He must die.* His own life and that of Moray's depended on Ewan's sword. Here, now, Ewan must prove faithful to his uncle's plan. The soldier had tried to kill him, after all...had shot at him twice. But looking at him now, so afraid and reeking of his own terror, Ewan remembered his first time on the battlefield. He'd vomited all over himself, then cried himself to sleep much later, when he thought no one would see or hear.

Ewan swore under his breath. He could not do it. He could not kill the lad. The breath left him in a rush as he made his decision, bringing the pommel of his sword down on the lad's temple, dropping him as quickly and as silently as a stone.

He spent the next minutes dragging the fallen guards away from the road, laying them amid the heather a good distance away, where they would not be so easily spotted. He then tied the young soldier up and gagged him, leaving him at the edge of the forested glade. He led the horses into the glade as well, tying their reins to limbs so that they would not wander back to their stalls at the castle and inform their tenders that their masters had met trouble.

Once finished, Ewan retied the canvas on the back of the wagon and climbed atop the board, speaking softly to the horses, which were still nervous, but did not bolt. He snapped the reins lightly, wiping the blood from his face onto his shoulder with a shrug, a stone settling into his wame in the aftermath of what had just happened.

Death was never something he gloried in. He regretted the deaths of the soldiers at his hand, but knew he would regret his own death quite a bit more. He rolled his aching shoulder and cast his eyes on the horizon and beyond, where the sea awaited them.

Chapter Twenty-Seven

Brea, the cooper's wife was in labor—had been for quite some time—and was fast approaching the end. At least Edyth hoped she was. Brea's exhausted body slumped into a boneless repose upon the birthing stool between her pains, her elbows resting on the rails of the arm rest, her head bowed. Brea's breathy pants filled the small space until the next contraction came, the lines of her body pulled tight with pain, her jaw clenched. Edyth wiped her brow, slick with sweat, and crooned words she knew the woman did not hear.

A vein in the side of Brea's neck was fat and pulsing each time she bore down. Edyth smoothed the tendrils of hair away from her face, her own body feeling the ache of long labor in her feet and back. She stooped once more onto her hands and knees to look between Brea's milky legs.

"I see a head," she announced, wonder lacing her words. Edyth readjusted herself so that she could catch the babe, pulling the strip of linen from her shoulder with which to wrap the child. "You've done brawly. Almost done."

The head, which was covered with whorls of dark hair, retreated slightly as the contraction ended. Brea panted once more, resting in the short reprieve. Then, as the next contraction peaked, Brea pushed out the infant's shoulders with an almighty, animalistic grunt. Edyth pulled the mucous-covered baby into her arms, its slick body filling her hands. "It's a boy," Edyth declared, her water-filled eyes finding Brea's own tearful, exhausted gaze.

He was small and nearly purple, his body covered with streaks of his mother's blood, but beautiful in the way that only new life can be. Edyth swiped the little mouth clean with her finger and rubbed his body into life. He took a gasping breath and then cried, the sound as sweet as any bird song to her ears. Edyth wrapped him securely in the linen and placed him into Brea's outstretched arms as she and Idina waited for the afterbirth.

Brea's mother-in-law, Idina, was helping in a quiet, distanced sort of way, fetching cloths, warming water, and rubbing Brea's back when the worst of the pains racked the laboring woman. Edyth recalled her from the time she'd tended to the brewer woman's injuries caused by the sheriff's men so many months ago.

Idina hadn't spoken but a few words, which was no more than what she'd ever heard from the woman, but Edyth was grateful for her help and had said so. Edyth could not tell if Idina's dislike of her had changed, or if she was merely tolerating her for Brea's sake, but she found that, after so many hours in the cramped room with her, Idina was quite good at anticipating her needs.

Edyth had been present for births before, but never had she been the one to deliver a babe herself. She was filled with a deep contentment as she watched Brea and her son, staring into each other's faces, with grandmother looking on. But there was also another feeling: an ache that lived and breathed inside of her. One that she did not want and could not escape. It lurked in the quiet places of her mind and heart, emerging at times like these, when babies were brought into the world. Would that she could some day carry her own babe.

With the afterbirth delivered, and the cord tied and cut, Idina said, "Hold the bairn, mistress, sae I can settle the lass intae the bed." The woman placed the bundle into Edyth's outstretched arms in a practiced way. The boy's blue-gray eyes stared into Edyth's face, surprisingly clear and alert. He did not cry now, only took in this new world with placid interest that made Edyth marvel.

Looking at the braw, wee babe in her arms, feeling the small weight of him, of how his bottom fitted so perfectly into her palm, fanned the flame of the smoldering fire within her breast that had started so many months ago, burgeoning the yearning she'd fostered into a fierce desire. She clamped down on the feeling, stamping it out. It would do no good to dream and hope only to have such emotions dashed to pieces.

Edyth handed the babe into Brea's waiting arms, watching as her face, full of fulfilled happiness, glowed brightly. Edyth gathered the dirtied items littering the floor, her back aching. The father, who was waiting outside of the bedroom in the common area of their home would no doubt wish to see what his wife had brought into the world. She listened with half an ear while Idina announced to him that he now had a son.

Grasping the pail full of bloodied water in one hand and a basket of gathered soiled linens in the other, she slid through the bedroom door as the new father entered. Edyth was tired in a way she had not been in a very, very long time. It was a good tired, one borne of satisfaction. She would dump the dirtied water outside and refill the pail to let the rags soak, but she frowned as she looked about the small common space. The guard that had escorted her was missing.

Alefred had accompanied her here and had said he would wait in this room for her, but the chairs were vacant, the room silent save for the crackling fire. It had been hours. Perhaps he'd taken his leave to see to his needs or get a drink. Edyth frowned in thought but decided that she could risk leaving the house alone. Who would be out before dawn? She donned her cloak and opened the door, stepping into the flitting snow. Brea's home was on the outskirts of the village, close to a wellspring, lined with stones not but a short walk away, and though the way was dark, the trail was clearly seen.

Edyth passed darkened huts, the crunch of frozen slush breaking under her feet as she went. She did not hear the sound at first, near the well. She did not hear the mewling sob or the smack of skin connecting with skin over the creaking of the frozen rope above the well. It was only after she had refilled her pail and deposited the sullied rags into the freezing water, her fingers aching from the cold, that her ears caught the muffled cry on the brittle wind.

Edyth's spine straightened, her ears straining. Was that only the wind, whistling through the leafless trees? She scanned the empty street, the darkened houses. She cocked her head, searching for the source of the sound. Coming alone to the well seemed suddenly a very bad idea.

There, in an outbuilding, a smudge of gray-black nestled between two towering trees, a struggle was taking place. A sound like an animal thrashing about, of thumps and bumps as something hit a wall, filled the dark. Edyth swallowed heavily, setting down the pail that she had clasped in her right hand and took a cautious step forward. Was some animal caught in a trap? If so, whatever it was, it was big. Far bigger than a rat or even a cat. What could it be?

The muffled mewling came again and the fine hairs on Edyth's nape tingled to life. Something was wrong. She hesitated, afraid, but then moved closer, her hand sliding into her pocket to find the small dagger Ewan had gifted her. The shack was small, and built of wood, not stone. The gaps between the boards were narrow and dark, but now, standing only an arm's length from the door, there was no mistaking that the something within was no animal, but a beast. Of the human kind.

The sounds were unmistakable. She could hear the grunts, the gasps, the cries. She knew this struggle. The woman's muffled weeping filled her ears and brought her back to a distant glade on swift wings to a time when she, herself, had been overpowered. Rage filled her and she was moving without thought. She threw the door open on silent, leather hinges. The small room was dark and cluttered with lumber, tools, harnesses and a variety of things Edyth did not register, but there was no hiding what was so plainly occurring.

The hulking shape of a body, of a hand clasped firmly around a white throat, of skirts torn, of the smell of sweat and fear filled and overwhelmed Edyth's senses. Somehow the hand holding her dagger had come free of her pocket without her knowledge. Her body had obeyed some unthought command as the man turned his head toward the open door, the predawn light spilling through the threshold.

Baldwin de Biggar turned his head to Edyth, his eyes squinting against the dark silhouette that she presented in the doorway. "Get ye gone, lest you wish to be next," he snarled, his ruddy face marred with purple scratches. The woman under him whimpered, pushing him away weakly, her strength spent. A quick glance confirmed whom he had caught, whom he had overpowered and assaulted: a dairymaid called Ailith. A young widow, who had no man to protect her. She had no doubt risen to tend to her duties and had been waylaid. She'd been snatched up by the lurking monster that was de Biggar.

A breath *whooshed* from Edyth, her fingers tingling with a strange sort of energy. De Biggar's wide, heavy body had not moved from its place on the floor of the shed, from Ailith's small frame. The very world slowed. Edyth's mind caught hold of several important things all at once. The sheriff was without his leather armor. His back was exposed to her, his billowing shirt not able to hide the wide curve of springy ribs and the vulnerable flesh that waited just below.

She saw in her mind's eye Ewan's long finger stroking the same spot on her own back. Touching the soft flesh that covered her kidney, indicating where the tip of the blade should go. She could feel it even now, a whisper, an echo of his touch as her eyes settled on the same spot on de Biggar, waiting and defenseless.

She stalked forward, her shadow falling over them as de Biggar made to rise. His beefy hand slacked from Ailith's neck. Edyth saw the muscles of his shoulders bunch, saw his shoulder blades contract as he pushed himself upward.

Edyth's grip was strong, her fingers unyielding on the small blade, so perfectly suited for such a wound. He was on his knees now, turning, the target she had sought hidden from her as he faced her. "I said leave," he rasped, standing like a drunk man, his braes loose, laces dangling. He staggered into her, his breath reeking of whiskey, and pushed Edyth, hard.

Her breath left her as she staggered backward, her back hitting the door frame with a rattle that seemed to shake the entire building. She'd missed her chance. He was not much taller than she was; his eyes, so enraged and blind with anger, were level with her own. She saw as he registered her, identified Ailith's would-be savior, and his anger turned to malicious glee.

"*Witch*," he said on a breath, lilting slightly to one side as man on a wave-tossed ship, but his hand clamped down on her throat, strangling the cry that lived there. Edyth strained away from him, but his strength was far too great. "Glad you could join us. I was waiting fer you. Hours I spent out in the cold waiting for just this chance." He stifled a belch and leaned forward, his lips touching the shell of her ear. "I've never swived a witch before. What sort of power will I gain as a man who has taken what belongs to the devil?"

"Burn in hell," wheezed Edyth. She sucked in a breath, or tried to, and de Biggar laughed silkily. "Fly away then, or call up on your master to save you, for nothing less will protect you now." Her small *sgian dubh* was still in her hand, slick with sweat, the bone handle smooth and warm against her palm. She hid it in the folds of her skirt, her mind reaching for that day in the solar when Ewan had taught her how to wield it. But she had been stupid with desire and had wasted the opportunity. Where else was she to strike?

Ailith was moving, slow and pained. She rolled onto her side, her dark hair clinging to her tear-streaked face. Edyth could see her shaking, could read the pain that was etched in the lines of her body as she righted her skirts, covering her legs. De Biggar followed Edyth's eyes, and *tsked* softly, pulling Edyth by the neck further into the cramped room to place a booted foot into the center of Ailith's chest. "Do not even try to run, my dear. Do not scream, or I will hurt your mistress. That's a good girl," he said as Ailith closed her eyes and gave up fighting.

He leveled his dark eyes, black in the low light, onto Edyth. "You will comply, or I'll peel the skin from this lovely thing's body." His eyes, glazed and bright with conquest raked over Edyth. He lifted a heavy hand and pushed aside the folds of her thick, winter cloak, revealing her sweat-damp bodice. Her chest rose and fell rapidly as she fought the terror that threatened to consume her. *In the kidney, under the arm, in the throat, or in the groin*, she rehearsed.

De Biggar was large and thick. Wide. She did not think she could swing her arm around him with any accuracy to stab him in the kidney. Ewan had said her knife was too short to reach his lungs or heart from under his arm. It would have to be his groin or his throat, then. A savage desire to cut his manhood from him consumed her. He would deserve nothing less. But would such a wound kill him?

The hand on her neck pulled her face into his own, his hot, gaping mouth covering hers. His other hand found her breast and she squirmed, pushing away from him. He laughed against her mouth. "That's right. Fight." He pushed her until her back was once more flush against the door frame. Disgust filled her at the intimate touch. She gripped her knife all the harder, waiting for the chance.

The hand around her neck moved to grip the hair at the back of her head while the other hand moved down the left side of her body, to her hip. It did not linger long. All too soon, his hand stroked down her thigh, where he gripped her woolen skirts, pulling them up. He had to let go of her hair to employ both hands for the task, his dark eyes issuing a warning. Cold air snaked up her legs. She jerked as de Biggar's rough hands grazed her knee.

She waited a breath, then two, and when de Biggar sought out her mouth once more, his hands trailing to her thighs, she took her chance. With her heavy skirts now out of the way, she drove a knee as hard as she could into de Biggar's groin. The breath left him as he folded into himself, his hands covering his injury. He wheezed out a curse, his eyes watering as he fell to his knees.

She stood over him, the knife held aloft, but a sob from Ailith pulled her eyes away. In those brief seconds, de Biggar yanked Edyth from her feet. She tumbled in a heap and barely held fast to her knife. De Biggar crawled over her, murder in his eyes. As he reached his hands toward her throat, she brought her hand up between them, planting the knife in the soft folds of the Sheriff's neck under his chin.

Blood poured over her face, her neck, hot and pungent. A wet sound left him as she pulled the knife free, stabbing him again in the side of his neck. Again. Again. She was frantic. Her own sobs mingled with Ailith's as blood warmed her hands, streaming down her wrists to be soaked up by the sleeve of her cloak and of her bodice. Her face was hot and wet with her own tears and his life's blood. He fell atop her, with one last desperate gurgle, then lay quite still. She kicked and pushed, desperate to free herself.

A shadow fell over the threshold and she felt more than saw Ailith shrink in fear. Was it one of his men? With a strength borne of desperation, Edyth pushed and kicked her way out from under the man and stood, her knife held aloft in a shaking, blood drenched hand, ready to meet whatever danger was now present.

It was Idina. She had come looking for her. Steely, untrusting Idina had sought her out. Something within Edyth, a dam holding back all emotion, broke. She fell to her knees, the knife falling to the ground, falling into the bloody pool that still grew under the sheriff's body. Her breath left her on a sob.

Idina, small and shadowed, looked over her shoulder, at the purple horizon that was steadily spreading, coloring the clouds and touching the living things with its weak light. The world was cast into sharp relief, but left Idina's face black in the confines of the shed. Edyth could not see the woman's face, but she knew she was taking in the sherriff, the blood-soaked earth, and Edyth's bloodied hands. Would she call her a murderer? Would Idina call the guards?

After what felt like a long time, Idina's quiet voice beckoned Ailith forward: "Come tae me, lassie, he willnae be hurtin' ye again." Carefully maneuvering around the dead man, Idina wiped Ailith's face with her apron. "I'll see tae ye while the mistress' man deals with this rabble," she said in such a matter of fact tone, she might as well have been speaking about who would muck out a horse stall.

Ailith, coming to herself enough to nod, allowed the woman to lift her. "Dinnae ye fash, dearie. Come wi' me and we'll get ye cleaned up." The older woman wrapped a motherly arm around Ailith's shaking shoulders and said, quite calmly to Edyth, "Yer man is looking fer ye. He came in not long ago now. Ye'd best go tell 'im what's happened. Hurry now, afore village wakes and sees the state yer in."

Her man? Edyth's heart leapt at the words, thinking of Ewan. But that was impossible. He had been gone for nearly a month now. Had he somehow delivered Moray and made it back to her in such a short time?

Edyth, shaking with the fading rush of fear and struggle, felt as hollow and as fragile as a dried corn husk, but Idina's words spurred her, enlivened her. Having no desire to stay in the shed, she followed them out, trying and failing to control her quaking limbs, swallowing desperate sobs that clawed at her throat. Miraculously, Ewan was back and he was searching for her. He would know what to do. He would make everything right again.

The door to the shed shut with a soft thud in the quiet of the morning. The inky light was low still, but familiar sounds met their ears, carried on the wind. Such familiar sounds, of a new day dawning. A goat bleated, begging to be milked, a donkey brayed, a cock crowed.

It was all so familiar and homely. So at odds to the riot of feeling surging through her. Edyth didn't know what to do, how to feel. In a daze, she walked past the well, stooping to pick up the discarded pail and followed Idina and Ailith down the narrow path to Brea's house.

Alefred was racing toward them, his eyes registering Idina and Ailith then sweeping to Edyth. Horrified concern overtook him. She looked down at herself and shuddered, dropping the pail she'd been holding with a clang that sang through the trees. Water sloshed over her blood sodden cloak. Her soiled fingers tore at the clasp at the base of her throat, frantic to escape its weight. *Free.* She wanted to be free of the reek of it.

Her fingers could not open the clasp, numb and useless as they were. Alefred was at her side, grasping her hands. He was speaking to her. His mouth was moving, but it took a great effort to hear him. It was with some surprise that she heard herself crying as she asked, "Ewan? Where is Ewan?"

Alefred gave her a worried look, pulling her hands from the sodden fabric of her cloak. "Himself is no' yet home, mistress. Remember, he's gone tae visit his mother." The lie had been spread to explain his absence. She knew this, but she shook her head, willing it to be false. Edyth turned her head, searching despite Alefred's words. "No. He's back. Idina said he was searching for me."

"Nay, mistress. It's I who was lookin' for ye." The tears rolling down her cheeks were hot, leaving icy trails in their wake. It was quite plain that the blood was not her own, but still Alefred lifted one of her hands, searching for a wound. There was so much blood.... "Mistress! Who?" Alefred asked. His grip on her forearm was like an iron band. *"Who's blood is this?"*

Edyth's eyes looked through him, past him. Where was her husband? She needed him.

"*Who?*" he demanded again, his voice betraying alarm.

Idina, who had paused on the path, called over her shoulder softly, "The danger has passed. Get yer mistress inside. That's a good lad."

Alefred, to his credit, followed Idina's orders and gave up his questions, following in the old woman's wake.

Chapter Twenty-Eight

E wan had never been more glad to leave a place in his life. He'd abandoned his cart, extricated Moray, and boarded the ship as soon as he'd been able. He'd watched from afar as sailors reported to the ship, filled it with goods and tugged ropes into place all before the sun had risen.

The birlinn was swift and cut through the choppy waves of the Irish Sea. The water caught the weak sun, glinting like dull iron, the low clouds clinging to the mountains. Ewan squinted through the rain as they passed through the North Channel. The narrow passage where Ireland and Scotland reached, like lovers, for each other, was swept with such fierce winds that they captain had tied up the sails and reverted to oars only.

They were making good time despite the setback. What would have taken them a score of days on horseback over hostile lands and difficult terrain, had only taken them two days. And, as the captain had said, if the weather held, they would make land in the next six hours up the Firth of Clyde.

Moray, wrapped in Ewan's plaid was looking wrung out and green, huddled in the prow of the boat at his feet. Ewan glanced at him briefly, thinking the man just as ill, if not more so, since they'd boarded. Without medicines or herbs—nor hot meals—there was little Ewan could do to minister to the man. Getting him to land as fast as possible was the best he could do.

Graham was absent. The captain had waited as long as he'd dared, but Ewan had not spotted the blonde giant in the weak dawn light. He hadn't wished to wait around very long either, not wishing to give the English soldiers any time to catch them before they left.

As it was, it was only himself and Fingal on the ship, the latter making it in the nick of time. And while Ewan wasn't worried about Graham's ability to traverse the space between Chester and Caimbel lands, he was ever in the back of his mind. Had he been waylaid or captured? There was nothing he could do but worry at this point.

Fingal, for his part, seemed to enjoy the roiling waves and salt spray. Ewan had only seen the grizzled man smile a small handful of times before, but he was doing so now, his thin lips turned up slightly as the wind whipped his wet hair to and fro. "I think ye should have been a sailor," commented Ewan.

Fingal only shook his head. "Ye think I could man the oars? More like the oars would man me."

Ewan squinted through the rain. "Aye, I take yer point."

Moray spilled his guts into a bucket, losing what little he'd eaten. The poor wretch looked as green as a spring moor. "Not long now," said Ewan, patting the man on the shoulder. "Keep what ye can inside. I'd hate tae deliver a dead man."

***

Hours later, Ewan, Fingal and Moray sat in the rectory of Kilwinning Abbey, pouring hot tea laced with whiskey down the latter's throat near a fire. Their clothes were nearly dry by now, and a lay monk had been dispatched to deliver news to the Caimbel chieftain of their location and overall health. Horses had been promised, as Niael had stated, but Ewan doubted if Moray could ride very far.

Thankfully, monks had seen to the health of Moray, administering herbs and pottage as they'd seen fit. The heat and full belly had served them all well, especially Moray, who looked decidedly less green. Still, with the man's weakened state, Ewan had his doubts regarding the man's ability to take the trip over the mountain passes.

"The Caimbel has arranged for us tae meet the Thane Cawdor at a wee kirk on Loch Laggan. From there, he'll take charge o' ye, and we'll part ways," explained Ewan to Moray. "Can ye sit a horse, do ye think?"

"I can put my legs on either side of the beast," croaked Moray, "just point me in the right direction."

"Rest up, then. We leave at dawn."

***

True to his word, Andrew Moray was able to seat a horse. The sleeting rain had stopped in the night, which had allowed them to push through the tidal basin with relative ease come dawn, only having to stop once to give the horses a wee rest before they pushed on to the rolling hills of Renfrewshire. The looming mountain passes in the north grew ever nearer as they trudged through the frozen lowlands, white with snow and gray craggy rock. The real test of Moray's strength would lie there.

The horses had been provided by Niael, delivered and cared for by his faithful retainer, Delaney, who had been charged with seeing them through to Loch Laggan. Delaney, who had been waiting for them at the monastery, was perfectly stoic, bearing the brunt of the winter winds and icy conditions with a mild placidity that soothed beasts and men alike. He spoke to the beasts more than he did his human companions, whistling soft tunes that were caught in the wind and carried away.

They'd put in a good twenty miles that day before they could go no further due to the fading light. Thankfully, Delaney, who was a friend of the Lockharts of Barr, was able to secure lodging in a croft not far from the road. Their hosts had been kind enough to provide a place near their hearth for sleep as well as a share of their venison stew, which had done much in the way of thawing bodies and humors. Moray had been summarily ignored, having been draped with plaids to disguise him and the crofters warned of his catching illness.

The next few days were a blur of windswept moors, icy rain, and frozen appendages, but each time the sun set, they found themselves in a pile of straw, cold but dry. As they neared the highlands, however, their options grew fewer and farther between. As the altitude grew, crofts dwindled. The snow was deepening, clinging to the crags and accumulating in the low places between the Trossachs, the lochs choppy and churning as if hell burned below, sending the waters into a boil.

Moray had borne it all well until the fifth day. Wet from the day before and sleeping ill in a shallow cavity of a rock that night, he'd been difficult to rouse come dawn. Sluggish upon his horse, he bobbed and swayed with each movement, keeling from side to side as if drunk on wine. Ewan could tell, even without touching him, that the fever had worsened, despite the tonics the monks had pressed into his hands ere they left. Glassy eyed and drooping, he mumbled and shivered continuously.

"We mun find a dry place," said Ewan needlessly when they'd stopped around noon to warm themselves with whiskey on a treed ridge overlooking Loch Lomond. The rise and fall of at least a dozen more mountains greeted them, a grim sight indeed.

Fingal eyed Moray grimly, a twist to his mouth as he said, "Aye, and what is it ye propose? Sprout wings and fly off? We cannae move any faster."

He was right, of course. There was nothing they could do but push onward and pray God that they found a cave or a hunter's cabin along the way. Another night out in the elements would do them no good, Moray least of all.

***

Luck, it would seem, was on their side. As they made their way down the steep decline of a rather treacherous climb hours later, their snowy path showed sudden signs of life. Hoofprints of a horse that did not belong to them had walked this path not long ago, which meant the possibility of a warm fire and a roof over their heads increased dramatically.

With spirits buoyed, they hastened on, Ewan looking to the sky. It looked like snow was coming with dusk and he wanted to find the horseman who'd left these tracks before a storm covered them. Moray had been removed from his horse, instead sharing with Fingal, who was the lightest of them all, and would not burden the horse over much with two riders. They were wrapped tightly in plaids, Moray leaning heavily into Fingal's back.

"Can ye go a bit faster?" called Ewan over his shoulder to his bowman. "It looks like snow."

Fingal grunted in a way that Ewan took to be assent and urged his horse faster. The tracks, Ewan guessed, were hours old based on the dung they'd inspected that was periodically deposited along the trail. The path was leading down the mountain, toward an icy loch that blanketed the valley below.

"Smoke," called Delaney from the rear. Ewan turned, seeing the man pointing to some hidden place at the junction of two hillocks at the foot of the mountain. The trees hid any structure, but there was indeed smoke curling its way into the gray sky.

It did not take but an hour of riding before they found the source of the smoke. Indeed, the hoofprints led them straight to a hut, which was nestled neatly amongst the tall pines. It was small, but seemed to be mostly in good repair. It had a roof and four walls in any case, and he was not picky.

The horse that had led them here, or so which Ewan assumed, nosed eagerly near the base of a tree in its paddock. It lifted its head as they approached, its doleful eyes observing them benignly. "Hello the house," called Ewan, dismounting.

The door opened after a short pause, revealing a fur-clad woman, a dead animal gripped in her fist. She stepped out, dropping the animal—a rabbit, by the looks of it—onto a table set beside the door.

Ewan approached her but stopped when she lifted a dirk. "My son and I dinnae mind guests, so long as they're invited."

He pointed toward Fingal and Moray. "We have a sick man among us. We mean ye nay harm. We only wish tae rest free from the weather."

The woman, looking wary, who Ewan realized was not so young as he had first assumed, eyed Moray and Fingal with suspicion. "What's wrong with 'im?"

"Ague," rasped Fingal, nodding to Ewan for help. Ewan went to him and caught hold of Moray as he slid from the horse. He coughed mightily, his body shaking and stumbling. "He needs warmth and tae get oot of these wet clothes."

The woman's mouth twisted as she watched Moray stumble, only staying upright by the strength of Ewan's arm. She huffed and muttered to herself, then, with a jerky movement of her hand, beckoned them forward, looking as if she were already regretting her choice.

She stopped short of the door, turning to look each man over in an assessing way. "Is there one among ye can dress a rabbit and no' butcher the skin?"

"Aye," said Ewan with a nod. He couldn't speak for Delaney, but he could for himself and for Fingal.

She jutted her chin to the waiting carcass pointedly as she opened the door. "Best get to it, then."

Fingal grunted and pulled his dirk, nodding to the woman before she entered into the dim of the cabin. The room was bare, save only a few necessary pieces of furnishings: a bed, a table, and a hearth with a mud-daubed chimney in good repair. Sprigs of herbs hung from the ceiling, lending a homey smell to the place. It made Ewan think of Edyth and his heart stuttered. He hadn't thought he'd miss her as keenly as he did. He'd thought of her with nearly every step of the journey.

He could see her hands, stained with the juices of some plant or another, of the slope of her neck, of the feel of her in his hands, of her laugh and the turn of her lips as she smiled. As the weighty tug in his chest grew near to pain at the thought of her, he forced them away, returning to the little hut at the feet of the mountain.

"Set him down and help me pour this broth doon 'im, aye?" said the old woman, taking off her fur mittens in a businesslike manner. "And if ye've got whiskey, get that too."

Chapter Twenty-Nine

Alefred, looking like he would like nothing less than to stick his sword through something, dispensed with decorum and peppered Edyth with questions in the little common room of Brea's home. Edyth was seated near the fire, but could not feel its warmth. She couldn't stop shaking, could not get warm.

"Are ye hurt, mistress? Can I get ye sommat? Here, take a wee nip o' this. Not too much, now." He pounded her on the back as she sputtered. "Whose blood is this, mistress. Haste, please, lest justice be prevented."

Idina was not present just then, having taken Ailith into the small bedroom where Brea, her newborn son and husband were located. The latter entered after only a short time, the elation of his son being born replaced with grim resolve. His gray eyes fell on Edyth, taking in her trembling, soiled body, at the hair that stuck to her neck, held fast by coagulated blood.

"Enough questions," he rasped, his gaze swiveling to a concerned Alefred. "Leave her Ladyship tae the care of women. We've got work tae do." He stalked to the door and pulled on his boots with swift jerks, then reached for his plaid, hanging limply on a peg.

Alefred stood, looking between them. "What's happened, John?"

"Her Ladyship has done a great service," said John pointedly. "We will finish the task, but we mun hurry."

Edyth took no notice of their leaving, the hollow feeling growing from her heart and spreading to her limbs. *Where was Ewan?* The part of her brain still capable of rational thought recalled that he was far away and unreachable at present. What had she done? What would happen now that she had killed the sheriff? *Killed him*...stuck the blade into his throat. She could hear the gurgle of his breathing at his desperate attempts for air and shuddered violently. She had damned them all to the King's wrath. Surely he would not suffer them to live peaceably now. He would lay waste to Perthshire, to clan Ruthven. To her entire world.

Hands touched her shoulder, making her jump. Idina was speaking low to her, as one might a spooked horse, her wrinkled face slack and carefully blank. "Come and we'll get ye oot o' these clothes."

Edyth let the woman undress her, glad to have the sticky weight peeled from her person, welcomed the cold that bathed her skin. Idina bade her stand in a bathing tub near the fire as she doused a rag with water from the kettle and scrubbed the crusting blood from her limbs, her chest, her neck. Rivulets of sullied water ran down her body to gather in the pool at her feet. Her toes looked pink under the growing puddle. With each sweep of the rag, swirls of red curled around her calves like smoke.

They did not speak for some time. They did not need to. Idina's hands were strong and sure as she rinsed Edyth's body, then washed her hair. Clothes were produced, none which Edyth paid the slightest bit of attention to; her hair was combed, and her soiled belongings burned in the fire. Edyth watched the cloying smoke rise up the chimney as Idina knelt in front of her. Finally, Edyth asked where Ailith was and if she was alright, her throat tight and her voice hoarse.

"Brea is seeing tae Ailith. Dinnae ye fash. The lassie will be well with time, as will you."

Edyth looked over the older woman, at her plaited, silver streaked, dark hair, at her strong jaw and serious brow. "Why are you helping me?" asked Edyth hollowly. "You hate me because I'm a witch."

Idina paused in her ministrations, looking up from where she was tying the ribbons of the stockings above Edyth's knee. She leveled Edyth with a steely eye and said quite simply, "Aye, but yer *our* witch."

It was not long after that Idina left, instructing Brea to bar the door after her, to tend to Ailith's milking. "We dinnae want the coos and goats tae suffer needlessly, nor tae draw attention tae ourselves."

Edyth did not know how long she sat there, next to Ailith near the fire, vacant of expression save for a grimace of pain when she moved or a wince as unbidden thoughts wormed their way into her brain. Food was brought to them, which sat untouched. The babe cried, rousing Edyth long enough to surface from the recesses of her circling thoughts to check on Ailith, whose left eye was swollen shut.

"We'll say you were kicked by a cow," muttered Edyth, breaking the long silence. She reached out a finger and touched the injury softly. "And that's why

Idina had to finish your milking." Ailith nodded, wordless, and they lapsed back into silence again.

Some time later, Idina returned, taking Ailith away, speaking to her in low tones about seeing to her child, who was next door, breaking her fast at Deòiridh and Beathan's croft. Edyth could not sort through her feelings, so tumultuous and agonizing, but she wanted to move. She could not stay here in the small house, with the walls too close and the baby continuously greeting. The neighbors kept coming, knocking to no doubt offer their well wishes for the new addition. They did not answer.

Edyth could still smell the sheriff's blood despite it being washed away, could feel it coating her skin. She rubbed at her neck, her chest, her hands, and she rose from her seat to pace. She walked to the door, but coward that she was, she could not open it. She stalked away, then back, muttering to herself. She should go to the keep. People would wonder where she was. Would they suspect her, once the sheriff turned up missing? Would they know?

Idina had called her *our witch*…had claimed her as one of their own. Did that mean that, if some people did suspect Edyth of the crime, they would keep her secret? The sheriff was not well liked. Indeed, he was hated. But if giving a name to the sheriff's murderer would win peace from the King, would they give her up? Yes. Of course they would. She wouldn't blame them if it came down to it. She would confess outright if it would save Perthshire from utter destruction. The King's men would come and take her away to be punished, for justice's sake, and he would leave Perthshire alone. She would gladly go to her punishment if it meant keeping peace in Perthshire.

A knock sounded on the door, startling Edyth. Her body reacted, her hand going instinctively for her dagger that was not there, but it was only John and Alefred returned. It was still early in the day. The light from the doorway told Edyth that not but an hour or two had passed since they'd left. How could they have buried him so quickly?

"It is done," said John, his voice soft in the quiet of the room. His hand, outstretched, held her cleaned dagger. With trembling fingers, she returned the familiar gift to her pocket.

"So quickly?" she asked with a croak. "Where have you buried him?"

"We did not bury him," said John. His eyes swept to the back of the room, to the door that hid his wife and babe. "We left him for the rats."

"A fitting end," said Alefred with a sniff. "The rats will hide what injuries he sustained by your hand," he explained further at Edyth's look.

"W—where?"

"Do not tell her," said John, taking off his plaid. "It will be better if she finds out when the rest of Perthshire does."

***

Three days. It only took three days before Baldwin de Biggar was discovered. A flock of corbies signaled where his body lay. A guardsman found him without the walls, near the rarely used postern gate behind the garrison. Curious, the man had investigated, had found his bloated body, gnawed and pecked so severely that the sheriff was identified only by his belongings.

Apoplexy, some said. A sudden death and unpreventable. A failed heart...just as unpreventable. Others suspected poison, but never did they wonder about a knife to the throat.

Chapter Thirty

They made it to the wee kirk at Loch Laggan in a total of eight days, three longer than they had anticipated it taking them. The weather, deep snow in the passes, and Moray's illness had slowed them considerably, but never had Ewan been more relieved to see William Cawdor of Nairn.

Moray, still weak and fevering off and on, was not dead, at least. Ewan could only feel relief as he passed the man off to his brother-in-law. Ewan did not stay long, leaving Moray and Delaney in the Thane's hands.

For his part, Ewan only stayed the one night, giving his horse rest as well as allowing for him to restock his provisions. He could only think of home. And of Edyth. He wished to see her, to reassure himself that all was well with her, for a feeling had crept upon him in the long days and nights of quiet travel with naught but his thoughts to distract him from the miserable cold.

He felt that something was wrong, though he could not think of what. Iain was there. As was Rory and a full garrison of retainers. He could think of no harm that might come to her with the sheriff gone. *If* the sheriff was still gone. *If*. Such a dreadful word.

With that thought, a fire had kindled within him, pushing him forward, onward, burning all the brighter the more he thought of the sheriff's potential return. He'd left well before dawn, waking a disgruntled Fingal from a sound sleep, and pushed as fast as he'd dared. The road home would not be nearly as arduous, as they would have no need to slog through the high places. Two days at best, three at worst, and he could see for himself.

He urged his horse faster, Fingal trailing behind. *Home.* In all his time away as a lad or while soldiering in France, the word had never sounded so sweet on his tongue. He'd missed Yuletide, missed the festivities and joyous atmosphere, but no celebration would ever shine as brightly as a smile on his Edie's lips. He could not wait to sweep her into his arms and kiss her.

They did not stop for food, nor for rest until nightfall, but pushed through the cold wind all the day, thankful that the snow held off. They made good time, and so it was with great anticipation as the long hours and miles passed, when he and Fingal crested the last hill that overlooked the winding river, that they finally slowed. The frozen ground crunched under their horse's hooves, the yellowed grasses swaying in the wind poking up through the crusty snow as the sprawling village came into view.

The sun was low, nearing dusk, but no lack of sun could ever disguise the scar so clearly visible from the hillock on which they stood. A swath of trees had been cut from the western forest, a hole in the canvas that made up the picturesque scene. Logs had been stacked, rocks gathered and piled in a heap where could be seen, not far away, the start of a foundation.

"What the de'il?" muttered Fingal, shock evident in his voice. "What's Iain done?"

Ewan's heart began to beat a quick tattoo against his ribs, the nagging sense of something being amiss growing to new heights. "Iain wouldnae do such a thing." His brother would never sanction a build without his own express command.

"There," said Fingal, pointing to men emerging from the forest edge. They were far away enough not to be able to identify them.

Ewan spurred his beleaguered horse forward once more, slowing only when crossing the stone bridge that spanned the river lest there be ice. The laborers were carrying a saw between them, hefted atop their shoulders. It bounced in step with them. He and Fingal turned down the path toward them, their breath coming just as fast as the beasts under them.

As they neared, Ewan's alarm grew. He did not recognize these men. He did not know them. He looked beyond, to the forest, but saw no one else as yet. The men, seeing them coming—and perhaps sensing the emotion welling from Ewan—faltered as he pulled his horse to a stop and dismounted. They nearly dropped their saw as he stalked toward them, faces gone white.

Ewan was a large man, and formidable even when calm. Roused to anger, and all soft lines and strains of gentleness melted away, left only the honed weapon that he was to view. "By whose authority do ye dare tae trespass here?" he demanded. "Speak!"

The first man sputtered and backed away. "Please sir," said the man in the rear. He swallowed heavily, pointing toward the keep. "We was just following orders, we were. We was brought here from Middlesbrough, tae work as laborers for the King's garrison."

Ewan took a menacing step forward. "What do ye mean, King's garrison?" he asked with a voice like thunder.

"The King 'as proclaimed that one be built 'ere, sir. 'Ere upon these lands, tae house three 'undred 'o 'is men at arms."

The world seemed to fall away from Ewan's feet. His eyes swept the gouged forest, the field littered with the evidence of what the man claimed. He wanted to scream, to plunge his sword into something, but his hands only grasped air as his mind reeled. It couldn't be true, and yet.... "Wh-who brought this news?" he asked, already knowing. His stomach turned sour.

"Why, twas the Warden o' the Kingdom, Sir de Warenne, come with the sheriff just afore Yuletide with the news. And we come not long after."

He left the men immediately, the warm glow of anticipation that had urged him on shriveling away into dust. The sheriff had returned and had brought with him such carefully honed revenge that there would be no way to avoid it. Ewan would kill the sheriff, that much was certain. He would kill him for this, consequences be damned. What worse fate could there be, when hell was at your very doorstep?

A bell tolled at their arrival, signaling to the household that he'd come home at last. As he and Fingal neared the stable, members of the household exited, gathering in the cold muck of the yard. Members of his guard trotted from the garrison, eager to greet them. Ewan saw no smiling faces as his eyes scanned the crowd, searching for his wife. For his brother. For his captain.

He saw Iain first, pushing through the throng of soldiers in the yard. His stubbled face was creased with the troubles he'd borne while Ewan had been away. He came to him in a rush, clasping arms, one hand on his bearded face. "Brother," said Iain, looking relieved to see him. "You are well, I see."

Ewan had no time for such salutations. He squeezed his brother's shoulder and said in an undertone. "Where is the sheriff?"

Iain shook his head, communicating him with only a look that now was not the time to discuss such things. "Dinnae trouble yerself o'er him, *mo bhràthair*. Let us go inside and celebrate your safe return."

Ewan, taking the cue, stalked after his brother, waving and greeting people that he did not fully see in the moment. Just as he entered the keep, pausing to remove his gauntlets and hand them off to the waiting servant, he saw her. She was rushing toward him, his name on her lips. Her pale skin was like a beacon in the dim light of the entrance hall, shining as brightly as the moon in the night sky. Her body fell into his, her arms wrapped around his middle. She was safe. She was whole.

"How is it possible that ye grow ever more beautiful as the days pass?" he said into her hair, squeezing her as though she might flit away into mist should he ease his hold.

She did not speak, but he could feel her trembling. Stroking her hair, he pulled back to look upon her once more. She'd been sleeping ill. He could tell by the purpled smudges under her eyes, in the tired turn of her mouth. More dreams? Or the invasion of the sheriff and de Warenne? He would have time to ask her later.

"This is the face I saw each night as I closed my eyes," he whispered. "And these are the lips for which I rushed so eagerly home." He bent his head and kissed her then, feeling the wetness of her tears on his face. He pulled away and caught a tear with the pad of his thumb. "I am come home at last, Edie. Rest yer mind."

***

They retreated to the private room behind the great hall with a quiet request of food and drink to be brought. Iain was there, as well as Fingal and a brutalized Rory. He'd been severely beaten and, what's more, his right hand was heavily bandaged. *Burned*, Iain had told him, grim faced and full of righteous anger. As it was now, Rory's sword hand was useless, his blistered fingers curled inward and immobile. *For raising his weapon against de Warenne*, Iain had explained at Ewan's questions. He would likely never wield a sword again. Edyth had done all she could to aid him, but only with time would they know what abilities would return to his hand.

De Warenne was currently absent, thankfully, gone off on some other errand of the King, but leaving nigh on forty men behind to tend to the task at hand: building the King's garrison.

Once the fire had been stoked and drinks poured, the tale was laid bare for Ewan. The sheriff and de Warenne had come just before Yule, disrupting any festivities they'd planned, and had fully wedged themselves into their lives and home. The sheriff had turned up dead not long ago, a surprise and a nuisance to de Warenne no doubt, who would now have to appoint another.

There was much discussion of his death and speculation on what had happened, but in the end, all they knew for certain was that de Biggar had been found without the walls, near the southern gate behind their garrison. Ewan was only sorry that he hadn't killed the tyrant himself and said so before informing them of what had happened to him since they had last seen each other.

It was with an aching tiredness that Ewan finally made his way to bed. Edyth bade the servants carrying in buckets of hot water for his bath to leave. She helped him undress, quiet as a mouse, and gathered the soap and rag, waiting for him to step into the wooden tub. It was a tight fit, but he managed to get in, his knees up to his chest. The hot water soothed his aching hips from so many hours in the saddle so well that he could not help the groan that escaped him.

Now that they were alone, he wasted no time in asking Edyth what else had happened that had been left out in the briefing below stairs. She shrugged, dipping the rag into the water at his feet and rubbing the wodge of soap upon the material. "I can see that sommat is heavy on yer mind, Edie. Have ye had more dreams, then?"

She met his gaze, her lips pressed tightly together, and nodded. "Do you remember when I dreamt of my mother?" she asked quietly. "At the time, I didn't understand what it was she was telling me." She licked her lips, the water from the rag dripping down her hands and wrists to dribble across his shins. "She—she referenced the swineherd's family that lived in Carlisle. They lived in a hovel with a litter of children they couldn't feed nor clothe." She shook her head, dismissing her words as unimportant. "I...I dreamt of a fire. The first dream I ever had related to death. I didn't know—couldn't know—that it would come to fruition."

Here she made a helpless gesture with her hands and, seeming to recall that she was holding a washing rag, applied it to one of Ewan's knees, swiping it down his shin. "The dreams disturbed me, but not nearly as much as finding the destruction after the fact. I carried the weight of their deaths for years."

Ewan made a sympathetic sound in his throat. "Which is why ye were sae intent on seeing me safe at Dunbar."

She nodded absently and dipped the rag into the water once again, moving to his other knee. "But I was able to forget after a time. Not forget what had happened, mind, but forget what it might mean. I never dreamt of such a thing again. That is, until I met you."

Ewan waited for her to continue, watching her hands wash away the recent week's grime. After a time, she continued. "In my dream, my mother said that I should not weep for wickedness. I didn't know what she meant then, but I think I do now." She made a motion with her hands, indicating that he should lift a foot. He did, settling it onto the edge of the tub, where she could wash his feet clean with swift, gentle strokes.

"But I cannot help but weep." She took a shuddering breath, emotion evident in her voice. "The sheriff...he...he died at my hand. I d—drove the blade of the dirk you gave me in—into his n—neck until...until he died."

The blood drained from Ewan's face. He gripped the sides of the tub with his fingers so tightly several of the joints popped. He forced air into his lungs and swallowed the curse words he wanted to utter, hating himself for leaving her. "Tell me all, Edie. Who else knows?"

She insisted on washing his body as she spoke, her voice hitching with emotion now and again. It wasn't until she spoke of the coagulated blood being washed from her skin in the middle of Brea's and John's croft that she waivered. "I—I can still feel it." Tears tracked down her face, her freckles stark against wan skin. "It clings to me even now." She was looking at him in desperation, silently pleading for help, her clean, wet hands, pink from the hot, soapy water held out to him in supplication. "No matter how well I scrub them, the feeling does not leave me."

Ewan, his heart breaking, reached for her trembling hands. He took the rag from her and turned the palm of one to face him. Dipping the rag into the soapy water, he ran the cloth over her skin, stroking down to her first finger. "Yer hands are clean," he said on a breath, bending to press a kiss in the center of her palm.

The rag stroked the next finger. "Ye did right." With each swipe of the rag, he spoke peace to her, punctuating each of his sentences with a kiss to the ends of her fingers. When he had cleaned each of her hands, he looked into her face, which was streaked with tears. "If it hadn't been by your hand, it would have been by my own. *Ye did right, Edie.* Mind yer mam's words, *mo ghràdh.* Dinnae weep fer removing his wickedness from the world."

A sob burst from Edyth and he stood, gathering her into his arms, soaking her clothes. She didn't protest his wet embrace, but fell into him, her weeping muffed against his bare chest. He stroked her hair, kissing the crown of her head. "My brave lass. I do love ye so."

She held tightly to him, sobbing. "I w—wished for you. I wanted you to come to me, to take away the pain of it, but y—you were so far away. Every day I waited, hoping, but you...but you couldn't. Y—you couldn't come to me."

A vise gripped his heart. "I *am* sorry, Edie." He kissed her tears away. In trying to ensure his sister's safety, he had caused his wife great pain. "I'm here now, *bu ghràidh.* I came as quickly as I could." His hands roved over her back, up the expanse of ribs and shoulder blade to delve into her hair.

"I am sorry for it, Edie," he said once more, his voice betraying the emotion he felt. "My heart aches knowing the pains ye've had tae bear, for I ken well what it is tae kill a man. I would take the guilt o' it from ye if I could." He lifted her chin and looked into her water-filled eyes. "My brave Edie. Ye cannae see yer own strength, but I see it. Ye didnae need me, lass. Ye alone saved our people from a tyrant and I thank ye for it."

She sniffed mightily and, pulling away from him, gathered one of his hands and placed it low upon her belly. "Another thought haunts me. What if.... After what I've done—after what I've become...." She trailed off, her eyes on their hands, resting against her. "H—how can these violent hands, stained as they are, nurture a child?"

Ewan stiffened slightly at her words. His heart seemed to stop altogether before pounding into a rapid rhythm once again, his breath stolen. He swallowed, a desperate hope filling in the spaces between the sharp edges of his heart. He searched Edyth's eyes. *Could it be true? A child?* He placed his forehead to her own, whispering, "Are ye certain?"

Edyth nodded and gripped his hand all the more tightly. "I am now. I have not bled in all the time since you first left to see your uncle."

He lifted her chin with his free hand. "Hear me," he said softly, "there can be no better mother for a child in all the world, for ye're fierce and brave, and ye love with yer whole heart. Ye'll protect this child, just as I would, with yer own life."

He stepped carefully out of the tub and carried her to the bed, where he wrapped them both in a quilt and held her as she softly wept. He did not know what he could do or say, only knowing that he must hold her now, and wait. She did not speak, only held tightly to him as he stroked the long lines of her body.

His murmured words against her ear ceased as her breathing slowed. Ewan felt overwhelmed with emotion. Pride for his wife, anger for what had been thrust upon her, quiet joy for the child growing under his hand, and a burning hunger to shape his child's future.

As Edyth slept, he made plans. He would wait. He would bide his time, and when the Moray raised his standard, and moved against England, he would be with him. He would strike the usurping sassenachs from his lands and live free.

The End

Acknowledgments

Thank you, as always, to my loving and supportive family, who voluntarily take time from their busy lives to read and listen, and to cheer for me. Valarie Dixon, thank you for letting me come stay with you and get some writing in away from the troubles of life. Thank you to Valarie and to Melanie Patterson for your thoughts and for lending an ear when I'm overwhelmed.

Thank you to my mother, for her relentless efforts in inviting others to read and enjoy my work. I'm sure people will soon start to scatter when they see you coming, lest they have to hear about another of my books. Your willingness to read whatever I put in front of you is so very appreciated. I must also thank my father for his encouragement from a young and tender age to dream big. I love you both.

Thank you to my husband. Thank you for your frank opinions and willingness to listen when I've written myself into a corner. You have shouldered a greater portion of parenting since I've set off on this course and I appreciate you immensely. I'm so glad you're mine.

Thank you to my muse, Kristal Winsor, who always picks up the phone, even after all this time. I would not be four books deep into this great adventure if it weren't for your willingness to listen to me think out loud. I love you, Dear Friend. I could not ask for better.

Thank you to Michelle Beach, my friend and beta reader extraordinaire. You have read my stories so many times and given me much needed feedback. Thank you. I must also thank my editor, Kelly Horn, whose talent and love for story craft is apparent. I appreciate you more than words can adequately express.

Last, but certainly not least, I would be remiss if I did not thank my readers. Your support of <u>The White Witch's Daughter</u> and <u>The Fate of Our Sorrows</u> left me speechless at times. *Thank you.*

About Author

Jalyn C. Wade is an American author who currently lives in northern Virginia with her husband and three sons. Married to a military man, she has had the great opportunity to move often and fall in love with people of all walks of life. Her works merge multiple genres, featuring elements of historical fiction, romance, fantasy, and adventure. She has been a public educator—specifically a teacher of the Deaf and Hard of Hearing—for most of her career but has dabbled in creative writing her entire life. Outside of writing, Jalyn also enjoys gardening, painting, and spending quality time with her family.

If you enjoyed reading A Conjuring of Valor please consider leaving a review.

If you'd like to receive updates on upcoming works, you can join her newsletter here or by visiting her website: jcwade-originals.mailchimpsites.com

Also By

Other books by J.C. Wade include:

The Fate of Our Sorrows: a prequel novella

The White Witch's Daughter

There is no such thing as a secret kept, so long as the bearers live and breathe.

—England 1296—

Losing her mother to the witch's noose—and her father to those who placed her there—Lady Edyth DeVries flees for her life into the wilds of Scotland. With all her hopes pinned upon reuniting with the only family left to her, Edyth is tormented as a keeper of a dangerous secret—one that she is only just beginning to unravel. As King Edward I of England dismantles loyalties and spills innocent blood, Edyth traverses the deadly landscape with little hope of success. On all sides bitter conflict looms yet help comes from an unlikely source. But can Edyth trust Ewan, the heroic, young Scots knight with her secret -or with her heart?